TIME RELEASE

TIME RELEASE

Martin J. Smith

JOVE BOOKS, NEW YORK

TIME RELEASE

A Jove Book / published by arrangement with the author

PRINTING HISTORY
Jove edition / March 1997

The Putnam Berkley World Wide Web site address is
http://www.berkley.com/berkley

ISBN: 0-515-12028-6

A JOVE BOOK®
Jove Books are published by The Berkley Publishing Group, 200 Madison Avenue, New York, New York 10016.
JOVE and the "J" design
are trademarks belonging to Jove Publications, Inc.

PRINTED IN THE UNITED STATES OF AMERICA

10 9 8 7 6 5 4 3 2 1

To the parents who gave me the tools,
not the material

Acknowledgments

Many people helped me research and write this book.

Chemist James Ellern of the University of Southern California helped make sure the cyanide poisoning scenario in the story would be plausible, but also helped me create a circumstance that probably could never be duplicated in real life. No one, I suspect, will ever die by consuming any form of cyanide dissolved in yogurt, frozen confections, breakfast cereal or injected into citrus fruit, for a variety of reasons. And drug-industry innovations since the 1982 Tylenol killings have made capsules and packaging virtually tamper-proof. In some cases I sacrificed accuracy to create a story that likely will remain fiction.

For their insights into the workings of memory and human psychology, I thank pediatric psychiatrist Amy Mandel of the Children's Hospital of Orange County, California, and Ruth Eva Shaffer of Pepperdine University, as well as psychologists Michael and Mindy Sefton and Ann Greeley.

Former FBI agent John W. Warren helped me understand the scary topic of product tampering.

Barbara Mitchell of the Orange County Sheriff-Coroner's Office and F. James Gregris, former deputy coroner of Allegheny County, Pennsylvania, were extremely helpful in explaining autopsy procedures and the conduct of a publicly funded morgue. Pittsburgh Detective Rich Meister shared his insights, and Lynne Cox taught me about the mental challenges and physiological responses of a cold-water distance swimmer.

Marjorie Luesebrink of Irvine Valley College convinced me I could write fiction at a time when, in retrospect, it's clear that I could not. Members of my two writing groups helped maintain that illusion until this book finally took shape. The contributions of Susan Ginsburg, my agent, are incalculable and very much appreciated, as are those of my editor at Berkley, Hillary Cige.

Finally, nothing would be possible for me without the sustaining love and support of my wife, Judith Johnson Smith, whose quiet courage inspires me; and our children, Alayne and Parker, who are, quite frankly, perfect.

—M.J.S.

1

The tape recorder stopped, its final click as startling as a gunshot. The first two times he'd played it, Downing hit the stop button as soon as the speakers fell into that eerie electronic hum. This last time, after five minutes of recorded death, he'd let it run two more minutes to the end to make sure there was nothing else.

He checked the hallway outside his office, making sure no one had heard the killer's taunt—a crazy, irrational fear, he knew, because the door was shut and it was late. But he checked anyway.

With a pencil, he turned the envelope over, postmark side up. That's when he knew for sure, knew Corbett was playing his mind games again. Mailed from the post office three blocks from Downing's house. Corbett was twisted, but very careful. The envelope and the cassette box would offer no other clues, Downing was sure, but he pulled an evidence bag from his jacket pocket and dropped them both in, then dropped the bag into his bottom drawer.

It had been ten years. Why now? Downing pressed the rewind button again and watched the sliver of black ribbon spin back onto the left-hand spool. This time, he set the timer on his wristwatch.

Play.

". . . a Channel 7 exclusive, and we'll play that tape for

you now," it began. "We should note that it is graphic and disturbing, so viewer discretion is advised."

A low hiss: the electronic crackle and hum of a 9-1-1 tape recorded from a television speaker. Then:

"Greene County Fire. Is this an emergency?"

"Yeah, uh, it's my mom." Young kid, early teens, voice cracking. "She was just putting the groceries away and, oh God, she's really having trouble breathing. I'm the only one home."

It was a Wednesday, late afternoon, early November, the temperature dropping fast. Downing knew that much from other news reports and the week-old *Waynesburg Courier* clipping that was folded into the envelope with the cassette. He imagined the rest: A bored dispatcher, a woman, expecting another space-heater fire out there among western Pennsylvania's shivering rural poor. She'd have swept the mouthpiece of her headset down to her lips and jabbed the pickup button on the Automated Location Identifier, and the caller's phone number and address would have flashed onto her video screen.

Downing checked the newspaper story. 29 Ruff Creek Lane, Waynesburg.

"What's your name?"

"JoAnn Cuddy."

"That's your mom's name, right? What's your name?"

"Mark."

Downing closed his eyes. The dispatcher would have typed in the name and poked another console button, channeling that information through the county's Computer-Aided Dispatch System. An electronic form would have blinked onto her screen, listing the nearest major cross streets to 29 Ruff Creek Lane and a code signifying which local ambulance company covers that area.

"Okay, Mark. Can your mom talk?"

"No. No. I don't think so. She's really—"

"How old's your mom?"

"Thirty-eight. No, thirty-nine."

"Is she conscious?"

"Yeah, but, oh God. Can you send somebody really quick?"

She should have typed "conscious" into the form and transmitted it to—Downing opened his eyes and checked the newspaper story—Weaver Ambulance and Rescue in Waynesburg.

"They're on their way. So your mom's still breathing then?"

"Trying."

Something glass shattered in the background, followed by the crunch of splitting wood and the heavy, sickening thump of flesh on floor. The phone banged again and again, hollow and sharp, like it was hitting a wall.

"Sir? Are you there? Sir?" Downing checked his watch. The digital timer raced through ten, fifteen, twenty seconds.

"She fell, then she threw up." Kid's voice panicky now.

"Is she still conscious?"

"Don't think so."

"What did she throw up?"

"Just some yogurt. She was eating it a couple minutes ago when she started, like, choking."

The dispatcher probably went for her allergic reactions key-question cards. The prearrival instructions are printed on the back of them. Downing winced at the thought. So logical, but so useless.

"If she's unconscious and still vomiting, I want you to turn her onto her side and make sure her airway is clear so she doesn't choke. Can you do that?"

"Just a minute." Panicked whimpers as the kid worked. Downing checked his watch again. Sounds of desperation filled his head.

"Okay. She's on her side, but she's hardly breathing. Oh God. Jesus! How long until they get here?"

"Stay with me now. Your mom have allergies? She wearing any sort of medical-alert bracelet?"

"This is really bad. No. No. She wasn't allergic to anything, I don't think." Kid sobbing now.

"How's her skin feel? Is it pale, cool, moist?"

"Hang on." Downing flinched at the dropped handset's hollow report. "Skin's cold, and really, really white."

"Okay, listen. She's going into shock. I want you to put her feet and legs up on something. If she's on the floor, grab a kitchen chair and put her legs up on it. Got that?"

Silence, then the rhythmic cadence of convulsion, as unmistakable as the sound of lovers. Downing put his head down on the desk. *So goddamned useless.*

"Sir? Are you there?"

"She's having a seizure or something. She's—where the fuck are they?"

"Listen. This is important. Your mom is having convulsions. You need to move everything away from her, anything she could hurt herself on."

"She's—"

"Pots, pans, kitchen utensils, furniture. Make sure it's all out of her reach. If she's wearing a collar, loosen it if you can. And don't try to restrain her. She'll be all right."

"Now?"

"Now. And don't put anything in her mouth, especially your fingers."

Downing's head filled with more sounds—chairs tipping, a table being shoved aside.

"Oh God, she's dying!" Kid screaming now. "What's wrong with her?"

"Stay calm. She needs you. Is your mom pregnant?"

"No. No. What else should I be doing?"

Downing could almost see her struggle. The body overwhelmed, the eyes uncomprehending, reaching, clutching, dying.

"She stopped shaking, but I don't think she's breathing. Not breathing at all. Mom. Mom! What should I do?"

Downing could hear the dispatcher fumbling through her key-question cards. One choice left: CPR. But there was a commotion as she started her instructions.

"In here!" the caller shouted to the arriving paramedics, and the line went dead.

Downing poked a button on his wristwatch. The timer stopped with a tinny beep. Did anyone hear? He checked the hallway again, then peeked around the corner into the squad room. Silverwood looked up from his typewriter.

"Jesus, Grady. You look like hell."

Downing nodded, forced a smile. "Long day."

"Go home."

Downing went back to his desk, sweating, dizzy, wiping his hands on the leg of his pants. *Why now?* A deep breath. Then another.

He pulled a clean notepad from a drawer and wrote a large number 7 at the top, then circled it. He wrote the name JoAnn Cuddy on the top line and underlined it twice. Beside it, he added the date of her death as described in the *Courier* clipping, realizing what it meant as soon as he lifted the pen and looked at the numbers: God damn. Ten years to the day.

"Vt. consumed yogurt approx. 7 mins. prior to resp. arrest," he scribbled, his hand suddenly gone weak. "Rec. excerpted 911 tape by mail. (Anon.) Recorded from TV-7."

He wiped his hands again so they wouldn't smear the ink then checked his watch. The numbers were frozen where he stopped them, and he copied them onto the notepad. Five minutes, nineteen seconds. So fast. So damned fast. They all were.

2

The commuter mug tipped halfway through a screeching, yellow-light turn. Its lid held just long enough to mute Jim Christensen's panic, then gave way. Hearty Kona Blend pooled between his legs in the Explorer's leather seat, long past hot but uncomfortable nonetheless. He steered with one knee into the morning glare along Fifth Avenue and reached behind him for something to absorb the disaster.

He found something papery, pulled it forward for a look. One of Annie's art projects—a blue construction paper deal with a feather, two strips of felt, and elbow macaroni pasted on. Nah. He tried again, this time snagging a pair of Melissa's band uniform pants. At least they'd wash.

He lifted himself from the seat and sat back down on the navy-blue wad. A dark crescent bridged his crotch, extending halfway down each thigh of his heavy cotton khakis. An unsettling dampness crept slowly up his ass toward his waistband, softening the starch-stiff tail of his blue oxford shirt and the back of his heavy tweed overcoat. The dashboard's digital clock read 8:43. His first morning client was the Oppositional Defiant sophomore with the worried faculty advisor, due at 9:15. No time to drive back home to Highland Park. And not much desire. He'd been back once already to retrieve Annie's forgotten dance clothes and, as always, was unnerved by the silence of the empty house. No, he'd tough it out until noon, when he could stop by the dry cleaners and pick up an order he was sure included at least one pair of suitable pants.

The empty parking spot in front of the Soldiers & Sailors Memorial was his first break in an already foreboding Monday. It was right across Fifth from the William Pitt Union, giving him a mercifully short, if bowlegged, walk through the late-fall chill to the third-floor offices of the University Counseling and Student Development Services office. He buttoned the coat to hide the disaster in front and folded a *New York Times*, casually, he thought, across the spreading aft stain.

Nothing seemed amiss when he caught his reflection in the lobby door. His clothes hung just so since, at forty-two, he still had the same trim physique he'd had as a college distance runner. The gray-flecked hair was reasonably in place, swept back off his forehead and down to his collar. Rimless spectacles sat high on a too-long nose, balanced by his neatly trimmed beard. All in all, the door's pale mirror reflected the image of the dedicated educator, psychologist, and behavioral researcher that his colleagues thought him to be. He peeled off the Power Rangers sticker Annie had affixed to his lapel after breakfast and strode toward the elevator.

Lil McGill shook her head as he opened his coat in front of her reception desk. She was thirty-six, acted fifty, and aggressively mothered him and the eight other counselors who volunteered at the center two afternoons a week. She opened the doors at seven, closed them at five, and as far as he knew vanished into some parallel universe where everyone is nice and concern is always genuine.

Christensen checked himself fully for the first time, arms extended, head bent low. "How do I look?"

"Like an incontinent bird. What's the story this morning?"

"Usual Monday madness."

"Forgot Annie's dance clothes, I bet. Then you probably

drove like a nut to get her to preschool and Melissa to first period at eight-thirty."

Christensen plucked two pink message slips from his mail slot on Lil's desk. "And we made it. But I dumped the commuter mug on Fifth, four blocks from here. Lid came right off."

Lil checked her logbook. "You're clear until nine-fifteen, you know."

"I'll survive." He executed an awkward pirouette. "How's my back?"

She grimaced. "Affected."

Christensen sighed and stiff-legged down the cheerful hall toward the unadorned office he used to counsel Pitt students for two hours every Monday and Thursday. He passed the student waiting area, where Lil kept survival pamphlets on everything from bulimia to intimacy in neat little stacks, alphabetized. His eyes lingered briefly on the "Loss of a Loved One" pile as he fished into his wet pocket for the office key.

The door opened several inches as he slid the key into the lock, so he pushed grimly into the tiny room, eyes still surveying the coffee damage.

"Morning, Chickie."

Christensen startled, then felt a cold shiver of recognition creep up the back of his neck. Grady Downing was tilted back in the desk chair, wing tips propped on the sterile institutional desk in the murky light of the shuttered window. Sometimes the guy reminded him less of a cop than a stalker. How the hell did he get in? Christensen opened his mouth, but all that came out was, "Jesus."

"Nope, just me," Downing said.

The psychologist caught his breath. His hand trembled as he reached for the light switch. The office, normally scented by the night janitor's lemon-oil cleaner, stunk of tobacco and something intestinal. A thin haze filled the room. Half a dozen cigarette butts lay crushed on the upturned plastic lid of the homicide detective's foam coffee cup.

Downing shrugged, stroking his brushy mustache. "No ashtrays."

Christensen liked Downing. Owed him his life, in a way. But Downing handled conversation with all the finesse of a street mugging.

"Lil didn't tell me you were in here."

Downing squinted as the overheads blinked on, then fixed his eyes on the befouled pants. "Scared the piss out of you, eh? Who's Lil? You finally dating again?"

Christensen couldn't imagine how Downing had slipped unseen past the receptionist. He must have been here since before Lil unlocked the outer door at eight, but how? "Been waiting long?"

"Few minutes. Got a sec to talk?"

Christensen hung his coat beside Downing's filthy London Fog on the wooden rack in the corner, then crossed behind the detective to the window. He cranked it open several times, hoping a draft would pull the smoke and stink from the room.

"You're not sucking me into another investigation, Grady. Not after Tataglia."

"Tataglia was a fluke."

"No, Grady, Tataglia was a hostage situation. You strolled me up the front walk like an Amway salesman just about the time Bruno's medication wore off." Christensen felt a tingle in his right shoulder where a ricocheting spray of shotgun pellets had drawn blood less than a year earlier.

"I said I was sorry."

"Before Tataglia it was Petrovich."

"That was two and a half years ago."

" 'They got nothing,' you said. 'Nada! *Nichts!*' Damned right. You guys put me on the stand so they could pick at my credentials for two days."

"You testified against Petrovich because you knew that sorry sack of shit was bullshitting on the memory lapses. And you knew the jury wouldn't convict without testimony from the most credible memory expert in the state."

"You sweet-talker."

"Whatever. That was your conscience doing the right thing. Besides, I don't prosecute. So don't pin that on me."

"Two goddamned days I spent testifying in the Petrovich trial. Two of Molly's last days."

Their eyes locked. Her name struck a chord that left both of them silent, staring. Downing spoke before their memories unspooled too far.

"So, Jim, you been okay? You and the girls?"

Christensen relaxed. Once they got past the initial spike on the stress meter, they always fell into something less hostile, like any friendship spawned by tragedy. It was hard to keep the pushy homicide cop separate from the man whose compassion had kept Christensen out of prison.

"We're fine, Grady. Thanks for asking."

"Really fine?"

Christensen felt himself flush. "We've got our bad days. Melissa's still not comfortable with what I did. Kids get on her at school, and tenth graders can be brutal. And Annie, she just misses her mom. Sleeps with one of Molly's silk nightgowns every night. But fine, mostly."

Downing kicked his feet down and stood up, folding that morning's *Press* and tucking it under his left arm. He adjusted the window blind, letting the morning light slice through the still-dim office, then stared quietly out the window. Beyond him, across Bigelow Boulevard, the Gothic mass of Pitt's Cathedral of Learning rose forty-two stories into the granite-gray sky. The detective didn't seem to be looking at it so much as through it. When he finally spoke, he kept his back turned.

"Remember the Primenyl case?"

Christensen looked up from the briefcase he'd begun unloading onto the desk. "Might as well ask someone from Dallas if November 22, 1963, rings a bell."

The detective turned, more reaction than gesture, and seemed to force a smile. "Got a favor to ask."

Christensen sat down in the hard plastic chair usually reserved for troubled students. "Now there's a shocker," he said, smiling. But Downing had turned away again.

"How much do you remember? About Primenyl?"

How long ago was it? When was Molly's accident? It was

eight years before that. "Didn't I just see a newspaper story
about the tenth anniversary a couple weeks ago?"

Downing nodded.

"Who could forget? Six people dead. City half out of its
mind over product tampering. No arrests. No suspects."

The detective waited a long time, squinting into the
daylight. Tension drifted back into the room like a fog. "One
suspect," he said.

"I don't follow. You mean the guy that worked for the
drug company, right? The one that killed himself?"

Downing shook his head from side to side.

"Then you mean you've got a psychological profile of the
killer," Christensen said.

"No, I mean we know who he is."

Weighing the implications took Christensen no time at
all. In late 1986, someone had slipped powdered potassium
cyanide into capsules inside supposedly tamper-proof packages of the painkiller. That person had watched without
apparent conscience or remorse the horrific deaths that
followed, then for years hovered like a reaper over the city,
watching, maybe waiting to kill again, a presence as
undeniable in Pittsburgh's collective psyche as any Carnegie or Mellon or Heinz, yet without a name. Christensen
knew better than to ask who.

"When's all this going to break, Grady? Haven't read
anything about it."

Downing ran a finger along the edge of the desk, then
seemed to trace something on the desktop. He looked up.
"You won't. Unless things change."

Christensen sat forward, knowing Downing would interpret the movement as a sign of his interest. But he couldn't
help himself.

"Look, I'm not gonna dance around this," Downing said.
"You know how much an arrest in this case would mean.
For everybody in this city. Truth is, we knew who did it
within a week of the first death. And we've got circumstantial evidence out the gazoo. A lot more than that, but it's not
enough to file. We've got a DA that won't take anything to

the grand jury unless it's a slam dunk, especially when it's high-profile."

Agitation strained the detective's voice, an edge Christensen had never noticed before. Even Downing's forced smile was gone, replaced by the hard mask of a man struggling with something unseen.

Christensen felt suddenly vulnerable. "Wait a minute. Why are you telling me this?"

"Because I need some advice about repressed memories," Downing said.

"That I can give. But what does it have to do with Primenyl?"

Downing smiled broadly, walked around the desk, and sat on its edge. "Thought you'd never ask."

The detective pulled a pack of Winstons from inside his nightmarish hound's-tooth sports jacket, offering a flash of leather shoulder holster as he did. The reflected flame of his butane lighter danced in the Plexiglas "Thanks for Not Smoking" sign on the office wall.

"Our guy had a wife and kid—two kids, at the time. Oldest boy was fifteen, youngest was twelve. They all lived in this big old house in Irondale a couple blocks from the Pharmco where the first capsules were found."

"Molly used to shop there. The one on Chislett."

Downing nodded. "Old man's a classic case—alcoholic, abusive, a gutless little nobody trying to make his mark. Pharmacist by trade, which explains a lot. Anyway, we're pretty sure Mom and the boys knew what the old man was doing, pretty sure they saw some things, you know?"

Christensen exaggerated a roll of his eyes. "And you think they're repressing the memories."

"Just the youngest boy."

Christensen couldn't stop an involuntary laugh. Downing had been watching the news. "The California case, right? Daughter remembers Daddy bashing her little pal twenty years after the fact and goes to the cops."

"Jury believed her," Downing said.

"Overturned on appeal."

"What are you saying, Jim? People don't repress things?"

"They do. All the time. But you're talking about something way beyond that. It's one thing to get somebody who's been traumatized to confront memories like that. A painful, dangerous thing. It's another thing to try to mine those memories and then twist them into a criminal prosecution."

Downing held up both hands, palms out. "Don't get ahead of me here. I'm just trying to get an expert read on the kid."

"I know you better than that."

"Just talk to the kid, Jim. He's twenty-two now, been through every social service agency in the county. There's a file a foot thick on him, and at least two of his counselors saw red flags. If there was ever a candidate, it's him. Just feel him out, let me know if it's a possibility. Unless his old man makes a mistake, he may be our only shot."

Christensen's mind was racing. "It's the media. That's the problem. Give them something sensational like the California trial and they swarm like bees. Ritual abuse! Satanic ceremonies! Reporters are so busy looking for the next big outrage that they never look at what's really happening. The big story never gets told as long as there's a goddamn trial lawyer willing to hold a press conference on the courthouse steps or a quack therapist who'll let some poor bastard 'remember' sacrificing babies and eating their spleens."

"Ever consider decaf?"

Christensen took a deep breath. Repressed memories. "In seventeen years of private practice, I've seen maybe a dozen legitimate cases stemming from posttraumatic stress. In the few years since publicity started on the California trial, probably half of my clients decided they must be repressing something."

The detective stared.

"Look, Grady, I'm not saying your kid isn't legit. But just because one sharp prosecutor built a case around repressed memories doesn't mean they're the key to every unsolved crime in the country. In my experience, severe posttraumatic stress, the kind that forces the bad stuff into the darkest corners of somebody's mind, isn't all that common."

Downing turned away, stooped down, and examined the blue spine of the *Diagnostic and Statistical Manual of*

Mental Disorders that Christensen kept on a low shelf by the door. "*Nothing* about Primenyl was all that common."

The detective stood. His face was softer, almost pleading. "Think about it, Jim. Just talk to the kid. If you say it's not there, I'll drop it."

The Primenyl case. Hell of a Monday.

"What's the kid's name?"

Downing smiled like a man holding a fistful of kings. "Corbett. Michael Corbett. Everybody calls him Sonny."

"I don't like this, Grady. But I'll think about it."

Downing pulled the morning *Press* from under his arm, casually unfolded it, then laid it on the desk so Christensen could read the banner headline across the top of the front page: "Coroner confirms cyanide in Greene County tampering death." It triggered something visceral in him, a prickly wave of dread.

Downing looked back over his shoulder as he opened the door. "Not to hurry your decision, Chickie, but we think he's killing again."

3

Christensen followed the sports jacket from a distance, certain that no one else on campus was wearing one like it. He hurried across the Cathedral of Learning lawn, down the service stairs, and into the tiny loading dock between the Cathedral and the Stephen Foster Memorial, where a beige Ford was parked between a mail truck and a vending company van.

Downing was leaning against the Ford's fender, his overcoat folded over his crossed arms as if he was waiting for someone, smoke curling from a new cigarette between the fingers of one hand. He smiled. "Gonna freeze without your coat."

"The only cars made this ugly are unmarked cop cars, Grady. Everybody's onto that. You guys should wise up."

"Want a ride?"

"Let's take a walk. I postponed my nine-fifteen until eleven," Christensen said, shaking his head. "At least you could act surprised that I followed you out."

Downing opened the car door and crawled across the front seat, pulling a thick file folder and a rumpled black-and-gold Steelers jacket with him as he backed out. The jacket snagged briefly on the black barrel of a shotgun mounted beneath the dashboard.

"People with consciences are so fucking predictable," Downing said. "Wear this."

The sleeves were short, since the detective was at least half a foot smaller, but it was roomy in the shoulders. Christensen wondered how Downing, who at sixty-two so casually abused the notion of fitness, was able to maintain such a broad and powerful upper torso which could fill the jacket as well as some Steelers linemen might have. He pulled the massive thing on, grateful for its warmth.

"I made a lot of promises to myself and God after Molly's accident," Christensen said.

"Thought you gave up on God as things got worse."

They'd talked a lot in the interrogation room that day. "At least I'm trying to keep the promises I made to myself, and not to forget what I learned." Trust your moral compass. Damn the consequences. He'd ended Molly's life, such as it was at that point, for all the right reasons.

They walked south along Forbes Avenue, feeling the wind's bite, moving silently among the students headed to morning classes. Christensen loved the manic pace of youth, fed off its energy. He loved the urban campus, too, especially the gritty history that spoke from its still-sooty buildings and immense granite memorials. They passed the Forbes Quadrangle, where Forbes Field once stood. Decades gone, but the university, bless it, still maintained a commemorative section of the brick center-field wall, a street named for Roberto Clemente, and the glorious, spike-scarred home plate. It was entombed under glass in the floor of the Quadrangle building lobby.

"Hungry?"

He looked back at Downing, who was stopped in the surreal light of a flashing Iron City Beer sign in the window of Primanti Brothers.

"There's a coffee place on the next block. Great latte," he pleaded as Downing disappeared inside. He followed into a warm wave of aroma, frying fish and onion.

"Two fried eggs and baloney on Italian," Downing said to the counterman.

"Home fries on top?"

"Lots of ketchup." Downing turned to Christensen. "Want something?"

Christensen made a face.

"Sorry, professor. No croissant."

They stepped out again into the chill, stepping around a woman knotting her head scarf in the doorway.

"All right, Grady. What's this about?"

Downing took a bite and shifted the file folder from one arm to the other, balancing the sandwich.

"Things are curiouser and curiouser down in Greene County," he said in a spray of greasy mulch, swabbing ketchup from his mustache with a hound's-tooth sleeve. "Definite product tampering. Cyanide again. Tox report confirmed it yesterday, but we've pretty much known all along. That's why the regional recall on the yogurt."

Christensen flashed back to his frantic refrigerator search five days earlier. "I heard about it, but all I really know is the recall. I went berserk. My kids eat it by the gallon."

"Standard precautionary stuff for manufacturers," Downing said. "Good PR, but even the local cops knew within an hour we were dealing with tampering, not contamination. Found a pinhole in the foil lid where the syringe went in. Think about it. Yogurt's a semiliquid. What does somebody do just before they eat that crap?"

"Stir it up."

"So there's nothing off-color, no reason to suspect. Probably tasted like hell, but the first spoonful might have been enough."

Christensen tried to imagine the scene. "Random?"

"Just some kid's mom putting away groceries. You tell me: Sound like the work of anyone in particular?"

"What about a copycat?"

"Come on, Jim. Ten years to the day after the first Primenyl killing?"

Christensen blew into his hands, then shoved them deep into the jacket pockets. His pants were still damp. "It usually happens in cycles, you know."

Downing stopped walking, giving him his full attention.

"I'm talking in real general terms here, okay? Think of

the mind as a gyroscope. It stays pretty balanced for long periods of time. But from time to time it gets unbalanced, for whatever reason. And when that happens, the mind does what it needs to do to right itself."

Downing turned suddenly, to the right and up the hill on Atwood Street. Christensen felt a twinge as the tower of Mount Mercy Hospital came into view. He scanned the building face, eyes fixing against his will on the left corner of the seventh floor. Intensive care. He realized Downing was ten steps ahead, waiting.

"'Right itself'?" Downing asked as Christensen caught up.

"For me, that might mean going out for a long run when things get bad. I did that a lot, you know, after Molly's accident and everything else. You do things like that, too, I'm sure. It's how we stay sane. And whether we realize it or not, most of us get unbalanced in predictable cycles."

"But ten years?"

"Not typically. But if we're talking about the Primenyl killer, we're not dealing with a typical mind. So yeah, ten years between the really severe imbalances is possible."

Downing shook his head. "Hell of a way to keep your balance."

"Considering the symmetry, though, my guess is you're dealing with something else here. The newspaper stories about the anniversary could have been enough to set him off again. If your theory is right, they may have reminded him how much he missed the attention."

Downing walked north again on Fifth Avenue. Christensen tried his best to ignore the massive medical center to his left. Why did Downing have to turn on Atwood? And why was he stopping again, right across the goddamn street? The blood in his ears rose in tempo with each step. Was it his heartbeat, or the echoes of the frantic night nurse who'd pounded and cursed and wept outside the barred ICU door until the firemen finally broke through? They'd found him hugging Molly's limp body to his chest, her respirator disconnected, and watched him grieve until police arrived.

"Symmetry aside, Grady, there's no shortage of people

walking the knife edge these days. Random killings are a strong salve for someone feeling powerless. There must be some other reason you think there's a link between this one and Primenyl."

A Port Authority bus roared past, trailing a virulent cloud of warm air. Downing stared it into the distance.

"Our guy lives just a few miles outside Waynesburg, little place called Outcrop. Just a bunch of shacks, really, kind of place somebody might go to disappear. Been there since right after the 1986 killings. Probably drives the same roads our latest victim did, banks at the same bank, shops in the same stores."

"And the local cops put all that together?"

Downing laughed. "The local cops questioned her husband for five days."

"So why are you involved, then?"

Downing's smile disappeared. Whatever he said was lost to the dull roar of passing traffic. Christensen cupped a hand to his ear.

"I said I'm not involved, officially. At least not yet. But I'm trying to get back into it."

"Back into it?"

They moved slowly away from Mount Mercy and the memories there, crossing one street, then two, before the detective spoke again.

"I was part of the original Primenyl investigation in 1986, but I never got to see it through." He held up a hand, its thumb and index fingers an inch apart. "We were this fucking close, Jim, this close, but never got enough for an arrest."

Christensen studied Downing's face, saying nothing, letting the weight of the moment pull the detective deeper into his story.

"Okay. The short version," Downing said finally. "Name's Ron Corbett. Like I said before, real family man. Abused the wife. Abused the kids so bad the older boy, Sonny's brother, bit the pipe when he was fifteen."

"Suicide?"

Downing nodded. "After the poisonings started, Corbett

took off. A week after that David, the brother, takes the .38-caliber cure. Two weeks after that, Mom breaks down and winds up in Borman."

"The state hospital."

"Bingo. Sonny ends up in foster care with nobody to pick him up. For years."

"So Dad's a son of a bitch, Grady. The world's full of them."

"A *pharmacist* son of a bitch," Downing said. "Knows about shelving methods, packaging, everything. There's some other stuff, too; trust me on that. But somebody in that house knew what Corbett was doing, maybe everybody. Add it up."

Christensen tried hard not to react, figuring the more Downing talked, the closer he'd get to the truth. But there was an obvious question: "You're sure it wasn't one of the others?"

"Like who? The mom? If you'd ever met her, you'd understand. A couple teenage boys? Not likely. It was too calculated."

The detective rubbed a hand across his face. Christensen noticed the wedding band and tried to remember Downing's wife's name.

"I'm retiring in five months, Jim."

"About time. You've been eligible for, what? Five, six years?"

"I didn't want to leave it unfinished. I don't. Can't. You have mill-hunks in your family?"

Grady Downing, King of the Non Sequitur. After fourteen years in Pittsburgh, Christensen was getting good at spotting the descendants of Eastern Europeans who settled here to work in the steel mills. Hiring was based on the crassest of stereotypes: Poles and Slovaks for lifting, Jews for accounting, the Irish and blacks for shovel work. He'd actually seen a yellowed copy of a foreman's hire sheet that spelled it all out. Downing seemed like the son of a lifter.

"I didn't grow up here, Grady. You?"

"Three generations. And I remember my dad—he's dead now, probably mid-forties then—talking about the stage in life where you have to start letting go of your dreams. He'd started out in the rolling mill, strictly heavy-lifting stuff. After thirty-five years he clawed his way into some mid-level management job. First one in the family out of the mills. White shirt. Wing tips. The whole bit. But at some point, he said he knew he'd never be president of U.S. Steel, or USX or whatever the hell they call it now. Just wasn't the hand he was dealt, and there was nothing he could do about it."

"That's pretty typical of men that age," Christensen said. "My age."

Downing shook his head. "But this isn't some midlife crisis, sport. Christ, I wish it was as simple as my dad said, of letting go of a dream. Shit. I stopped imagining myself as chief of detectives years ago. This is different. It's got me by the short hairs and won't let go."

"You want to resolve it before you retire," Christensen said, waiting for some sign of insecurity.

"I have to."

"So, what then?"

"So I want to convince . . . I've got a meeting in a couple days with my lieutenant, maybe with the chief himself. Like I said, Corbett's no stranger. We're all on the same wavelength on this. But we've pumped everything else dry, so I want to take a new tack. Get 'em thinking about the Greene County case, and when I've got 'em listening, I'll tell them about Sonny. They all followed those repressed-memory cases pretty close, too."

Like every other cop with a wish list and an unsolved murder. "And?"

"Maybe they'll cut me loose for a while to check this stuff out. I'm figuring I could nose around in Greene County while you got to know the kid. I'd really like your take on him."

Neither spoke as they passed the twenty-story cylindrical dormitory towers labeled A, B, and C by the Pitt administration, and dubbed Ajax, Babo, and Comet by the students who lived there. They walked silently past the university bookstore and back into the parking lot of the William Pitt Union. Christensen opened the lobby door for Downing, then held it open for a woman walking about ten steps behind them. She nodded her thanks but stopped along the curb.

The psychologist pushed the elevator button and glanced at his wristwatch. Ten-twenty.

"All right, Grady. If this kid did see something that traumatic, that's the sort of thing that *could* force memories into the subconscious. But that stuff doesn't just sit there. It comes out in strange ways, even physical symptoms."

Downing went wide-eyed. "Like numbness or something?"

"Any of a thousand ways. Why?"

"Sonny Corbett's got this thing with his hands. They go numb on him, and nobody can figure out why."

Christensen waved off the words. "Look, let's make a deal. You investigate crime scenes and arrest bad guys, I'll handle the mental health issues, okay?"

"Temper, Chickie, temper."

"This just isn't as simple as you make it sound, Grady. Sure the possibility exists. But hell, you mention repressed memories in a roomful of psychologists these days and you'll have a riot. And if I had to pick sides—"

"You think it's horseshit?"

"Didn't say that. But there's a weird hysteria out there right now. I mean, something's wrong when half the population of the United States remembers sacrificing babies by firelight."

The elevator door opened with a soft rush of air. Christensen boarded first.

"I'll buy that," Downing said. "But what about the cases where it's real? Does anybody listen now when somebody cries wolf?"

Christensen ran a finger along the groove where the elevator doors met. "Guilt won't work on me, Grady."

"Sure it will."

The doors opened and Christensen stepped out. He turned and blocked Downing's exit, holding the elevator open with an extended arm. "I'll talk to him. Once. Just to gauge his suggestibility. But repression as you're imagining it is very rare. And even if there's something to it, trying to recover the memories would pose incredible risks to this kid. Handle it wrong, you nudge him into psychosis. Understand what I'm telling you?"

"Spell it out," Downing said. "Don't want any hard feelings from this."

"If there's any reason for me to talk to this kid more than once, he becomes my client. Our conversations are private. And I won't endanger someone under my care."

"Deal. But you'd tell me anything relevant to the Primenyl case, right?"

"That's up to the client."

The detective touched his arm with surprising gentleness. "You'll talk to him, though?"

"Have him call."

The detective stiff-armed the elevator door as it tried to rumble shut, then stepped out. He hefted the file folder, thick as a phone book, from the crook of his arm and offered it with both hands.

"I'll talk to Sonny tomorrow," Downing said. "Thought you might want a little background."

Christensen eyed the file. "Such as?"

"Sonny's juvenile court records."

Christensen looked around, relieved that no one was passing by. "You're not supposed to have those, Grady. They're private."

Downing shrugged. "It's just copies."

"That's not the point."

"You want it or not?"

Christensen reached for the file. Its weight surprised him. Downing followed him to Lil's desk.

"Anybody call, Lil?"

The receptionist gave Downing the stink-eye. She wouldn't easily forgive him slipping in unnoticed this morning. Christensen marveled at how Downing could bring out the worst in the best people. "No," she said. "But Brenna's here. She was in Squirrel Hill for a deposition and said she's taking the afternoon off. She's offering to cook for you and the girls tonight, so I didn't toss her out. Those are her groceries."

Two plastic bags from Frieda's Deli in Squirrel Hill sat in one of the waiting-room chairs. Two students sat opposite the bags, fidgeting with brochures. One gave Christensen an uncertain smile.

He felt a tug on his sleeve, sharper this time. Oh right, the Steelers jacket. Christensen pulled it off and Downing took it, but the detective's face was frozen in an unmistakable leer as he absently wadded the jacket into a ball.

"Brenna?"

Christensen ignored the bait. "So you'll have Sonny call me tomorrow?"

Brenna Kennedy poked her blond-red head out Christensen's office doorway, just down the hall. She saw him smile a lover's smile, then disappeared again. She emerged in full stride with her overcoat in one hand and a briefcase in the other. Everything about her projected power except her face, which betrayed a deep well of compassion—a devastating combination for a defense attorney who sincerely felt every client's pain.

Brenna's smile, that wonderfully imperfect smile, wavered the moment she recognized Downing. Nothing personal, Christensen knew. Just her gut reaction to cops in general. She coasted to a stop a chaste distance from both men, then seemed to force the corners of her mouth back up again.

"Detective Downing. How long has it been?" Brenna shook Downing's extended hand without enthusiasm.

"Two years, I'd say." Downing made no effort to disguise his wink. "Working a little overtime, counselor?"

4

The old green marshmallow of a chair wasn't meant for this. With its overstuffed upholstery, the BarcaLounger was the perfect Sunday afternoon receptacle for a high-density Steelers fan. But as Brenna moved above him, knees braced on the worn padded arms, Christensen thought maybe his dad's old throne was just now enjoying its best years.

In the darkness, he could feel her long, fine hair more than he could see it. It tickled his face, neck, and chest as she touched her forehead to his, then kissed his eyelids. Except for the chair's rhythmic creaking, they were quiet, not for lack of passion, but because a child monitor on the windowsill transmitted every cough and rustle from Annie's bedroom, where his five-year-old and Brenna's four-year-old son, Taylor, were sleeping. The kids in the adjoining main house couldn't hear *them*, he reminded himself, but still. Plus, noisy passion didn't seem proper here, in Molly's writing room. Her photo enlarger was still in one corner.

Christensen buried the thought. Brenna deserved his full attention, without the irrational guilt he felt about this place, this woman. As their movements quickened, he forced himself to think of less erotic things—the tried-and-true stalling tactic of men given to early release. His mind fixed improbably on the BarcaLounger's history. His parents had exiled the once-proud centerpiece of their den to the basement as the 1970s fascination with avocado shades began to dim. He and Molly gave it a reprieve when they got married, offering it a prominent place in the living room of their graduate-school apartment. Two houses and two kids later, it finally ended up in the garage loft he built for her overlooking the house he now shared with their two daughters.

Brenna arched her back, shuddered, and lurched forward, biting his upper lip. He pulled her to him, lost in the moment. They moved together on warm leatherette, Brenna cradling his head to her breasts as he guided her hips through their fevered, clutching climax. It would have been memorable even if the recliner hadn't tipped backward and spilled them both onto the carpet beside his desk.

They knotted again, laughing, and held each other for what seemed like days, listening to the cold rain.

"Impressive," she said. Her voice was like spilled honey after they made love. "I do believe you're getting the hang of this."

He sighed. "Maybe we should stick to the futon."

"Boh-ring."

He felt that way with her sometimes, worried that his fondness for routine wasn't adventurous enough. This was a woman who once dove off the New River Gorge Bridge, then complained that her bungee cord had been too tight. He admired her appetite for thrills, but it was a little intimidating.

"So that's all he wanted then? To see how you and the girls were doing?"

Christensen opened his eyes, pulled from the edge of sleep.

"Hmm?"

"Downing."

Oh, right. The conversation they'd postponed forty minutes earlier when, with Annie and Taylor finally asleep, they'd retreated to the loft. "Sort of. He needs a favor."

Brenna sat up, shifting her weight to one arm and with the other pulling the hair away from her face. In daylight, it was

the color of a new penny, and just as bright. She wore it
down, even in court, resisting the notion that female
attorneys should be relatively sexless. He liked that, for a lot
of reasons. The moon winked improbably from behind the
rain clouds and filtered through the window, defining her
body with the palest of lines. Oh the secrets a Jil Sander suit
can keep.

"You don't owe him anything, you know." The sudden
edge in her voice surprised him.

"So you've said."

"How big a favor?"

Christensen sat up. "Not big. He wants me to evaluate a
kid, about twenty-two, I think. Downing thinks he may have
witnessed something in a case he worked about ten years
ago. He jumped with both feet onto this repressed-memories
bandwagon, just like every other cop who's running out of
options." He reached over to tuck a strand of hair behind her
ear, but Brenna pushed his hand away.

"So that would have been about 1986?"

Christensen couldn't figure the attitude, but he sensed
trouble. "About then, yeah, '86. Something like that."

Brenna stretched, a sharp movement, not leisurely.

"Grady Downing only worked one major case in 1986.
Every cop and lawyer in town knows that."

"Meaning?"

"Meaning Primenyl." She stood and walked to the
window. "Or didn't he mention that?"

Christensen felt uncomfortable for the first time since his
conversation with the detective. Brenna knew local law
enforcement as well as any cop. Attorneys who knew her
well told him she practically lived in the courthouse during
her years as a public defender, taking more than her share of
cases to get the widest possible range of experience. It
ruined her marriage, but she'd probably cross-examined
every cop in the department at least once, making unlikely
friends of most. They all shared departmental gossip with
her, a function, he was sure, of the vague promise they
imagined in her jade-green eyes.

"I'm not on the stand here, Brenna. He just needs an evaluation done."

She watched raindrops wriggle down one of the window-panes. "And you need a history lesson. How much do you know about the Primenyl investigation?"

Christensen walked over to her, tried to hold her. But she moved away with a disciplined kiss.

"There was a task force or something. Downing was on it. I remember talking to him about it after Molly died, but just in passing."

"He wasn't *on* it. He led it for the first few months, until they yanked him off."

Something unspoken was driving the conversation. He knew of only one time that Brenna and Downing had been potential adversaries, two years earlier when Christensen had ended what Molly's doctors described as a "persistent and irreversible vegetative state." She'd died twelve minutes after he removed her respiration tube. But that uncomplicated act of love took place in the city's largest Catholic hospital, and Christensen's decision quickly became, to his horror, a morality play that divided the city. In the hours after Molly died, he stood alone on one side, joined eventually by Brenna, acting as his attorney. On the other side stood J. D. Dagnolo, the headline-whore of a district attorney who was shopping for a high-profile trial to impress the county's heavily Catholic electorate.

Downing, the investigator, had been caught squarely in the middle. In the end, he was the only thing that stood between Christensen and the public spectacle of a murder trial. He'd gathered the evidence, listened to Brenna's argument that the law leaves room for mercy, and then simply told Dagnolo the case would be a damned messy one to take to the grand jury. Without the detective's enthusiastic backing, Dagnolo looked for someone else to flay.

"Brenna, can I stop you here a minute? I feel like I wandered into the middle of an old feud or something. I know Downing's not the most attractive personality, but the three of us do have a history."

She followed a raindrop down the windowpane with her

finger. "Your pal Downing has had an interesting career in homicide, you know."

"Well, I guess so. Especially if he's been tracking the Primenyl killer all these years."

She turned suddenly. "That's what he told you?"

"Brenna, help me out here. What am I supposed to know but obviously don't?"

At Molly's desk, Brenna shrugged into her coffee-stained oxford shirt and started to button it. When she finished, she rolled the cuffs one, two, three times until her hands finally peeked out of the sleeves.

"Primenyl was a badly compromised investigation," she said, sipping from the same glass of chardonnay she had nursed through dinner. "All kinds of problems. Downing was one of the best product-tampering investigators in the country. That's why he got to lead the task force even though the feds were involved. But something went way wrong for him on Primenyl."

Christensen pulled his faded Pitt sweatshirt over his head.

"He made some big mistakes early on, senseless mistakes," she said. "Word is the investigation never recovered."

"Follow. What kind of mistakes?"

"Two things, but I don't remember all the specifics. First there was that business about the lot numbers. The killer apparently bought a bunch of bottles from the same shipment, probably off the same store shelf, then took them home, loaded them with bad capsules, and delivered them to a half a dozen other stores. If Downing had spotted the matching lot numbers on the first few tainted bottles, they might have identified Primenyl as the poison source three days earlier. Product-tampering 101, but Downing overlooked it."

Christensen recalled a vivid image from the recent newspaper stories about the enduring mystery of Primenyl.

"Did you read the big tenth anniversary piece the *Press* ran on Primenyl a couple weeks back?" he asked. "It said it was like a neurologist looking at a brain scan and missing a tumor the size of a baseball. That was Downing?"

Brenna nodded. "Downing and company did identify Primenyl as the source, but only after the coroner kept finding undigested capsules—"

"They got the bottles off store shelves in record time or something, didn't they?"

"Once they figured it out," she said. "But that didn't make up for the time they wasted. Or help the four people who died during the delay."

"Whoa."

"Downing booted the big one, plain and simple," she said. "No one ever really figured out why."

"Any theories?"

Brenna shook her head. "It was a monster case— emotional, lots of pressure. Who knows? Maybe rage overtook reason."

How much did she really know? Time for a quiz. "They ever get close to a suspect?"

"I've only heard it thirdhand." She finished the last of her wine.

"Heard what?"

"They built a strong circumstantial case within a week of the first death, but Downing made some rookie error on the search warrant. They found some pretty incriminating stuff during the search, but Dagnolo wouldn't touch it. Fruit of the poisoned tree and all that. Can you imagine the publicity if the Primenyl charges got kicked on a technicality?"

She sifted the clothes pile on his desk and picked out her panties. "The one case they couldn't afford to screw up," she said. "Biggest damn case they ever handled."

Now Christensen was at the window, peering across the backyard and down the driveway to the street. He glanced at his watch as he clasped it around his wrist. Melissa was due home from her date ten minutes ago.

"So, what did they find?"

"A typewritten list."

"Of victims?"

"Worse," she said. "State-licensed cyanide distributors. But it wasn't perfect. The guy apparently had someone else place the capsules for him, because he never turned up on any of the security camera tapes at the stores. There's reasonable doubt right there."

There's no reason Downing should have told him the story, Christensen thought. And he probably has his version, too.

"I don't get it," he said. "If Downing blew it the first time, why would they let him reactivate the investigation now?"

Brenna stopped dressing. "Who said that?"

"Downing seems pretty sure the Greene County case is related."

She shook her head. "Even so, I can't imagine Downing's going to be involved."

Christensen stepped into his jeans. They slid to his waist without a struggle. "He's about to retire, you know," he said.

"So?"

"So maybe he wants another shot. If you're right about all this, it'd probably be his last chance for some kind of professional redemption."

Long silence.

"Are you going to talk to him?" Brenna said.

"Downing?"

"The kid."

"Haven't decided," Christensen lied. "You know how I feel about what's been happening. Repression's in vogue. Has been since the early eighties. Look at the Menendez trial. There's always a defense lawyer pushing from behind."

He felt her glare even in the darkness.

"Present company excepted, of course. But I mean, look at the McMartin case. Repressed memories became a joke. Kids are so suggestible."

"And this is different?"

"This kid's got nothing to gain, Bren. He's not in trouble. He's probably trying to get on with his life. If he did repress something, recovering the memories would be the most painful thing he'd ever do."

"And Downing thinks you can just coax him into therapy?"

"He just wants my opinion on whether he's capable of repression, that's all. He was twelve when it happened. I don't know anything else about him, but I do know the mind's pretty fragile at that age. Besides, what if this is the key to the Primenyl case? How can I walk away without at least trying it?"

He didn't see her approach until her arms were around his waist.

"I'm sorry." She laid her head on his chest and they both looked out the window. "But be careful with this, and not just because the wacko's still out there. Downing's another reason to steer clear." She nodded toward the child monitor. "Think long and hard before you get involved."

On the street outside, an unfamiliar light-colored car coasted to a stop in front of the driveway. It was pale, almost white, he decided before the headlights blinked off.

"Melissa's home," he said.

"I still think she's too young to be dating," Brenna said.

Me too, he thought. "I'm walking such a fine line with her on the independence thing. I just want her to know I trust her. Mind if we head in?"

They finished dressing in silence, turned off the monitor, bundled themselves into sweaters and raincoats, and crept in the back door, pretending they'd come in the back gate from a walk. Maybe Melissa wouldn't notice their dry hair and lack of umbrella.

The house was quiet. "Melissa?"

Christensen checked her second-floor bedroom. "Melissa?"

Brenna had Taylor wrapped like a pierogi in his blanket, ready to leave, when he got back downstairs. He nodded toward the street and checked his watch again. "First date must be going well," he said. "They've been out there for ten minutes."

"How does Dad feel about that?" Brenna said.

"I say time's up."

Christensen snapped on the porch light and opened the door, but the spot in front of his driveway was empty. The wet street reflected the street lamps and a bright quarter-moon in the slowly clearing sky. He checked his watch again.

Brenna wrestled Taylor onto her shoulder. "When are you supposed to talk to the boy?"

"Downing said he'd have him call."

She kissed him and turned away. Without another word, she carried her son out the door and down the steps to the driveway. Before her car was out of sight, a white Mustang rolled into the driveway, preceded by the low throb of overcranked bass speakers.

5

The concrete felt like cold steel on Sonny's bare feet, and the wind bit into his skin. He kneaded the yellow silicone swimming cap between his fingers as he paced the rim of Point State Park. Brown water swirled just below, taunting him.

He hated the cap, hated that he needed it to preserve body heat during his two latest training swims. But whatever core fuel kept him alive during these early fall workouts wasn't enough. Not lately.

He'd shaken off the grim news on the Coast Guard information hot line an hour earlier. All three of Pittsburgh's rivers were trashed after last night's rain. The basin was like a giant storm sewer on days like this. Whatever wasn't nailed down during the region's vicious late fall storms washed down the hills and into the Allegheny and Monongahela Rivers, which met and formed the Ohio at the spot where he stood. The Point.

Sonny curled his bare toes over the rim and watched. Sewage was the least of it. Seat cushions. Thorny planks. An empty rabbit hutch. About fifty yards to his left, a full-size camp cooler in full sail. He'd stroked through worse. Just deal with it, he thought, dipping a foot into the water.

"Okay," he said. "Okay."

Fifty-five degrees, the Coast Guard said. Four degrees
colder than yesterday. The air temperature was 56, but
winter was coming. In a couple months, if the snow belt
slipped forty miles south of normal, as it did every few
years, he'd be able to walk from bank to bank. Then where
could he train?

"I seen this on TV," came a woman's voice from behind.
"Whachacallem. Polar Bear Club or something"

People usually ignored him during his spring and summer
swims. But as September dragged into October, he'd noticed a change. Each swim brought the quiet rustle of down
jackets as Point State Park visitors coasted to a stop directly
behind him. By the first of November, they were less
curious than concerned. Just last week, a woman grabbed
his arm and urged him to reconsider.

"Ain't no polar bear." Man's voice, same Pittsburgh
accent. Had to be the husband. "Those fat old shitbags come
dahn do their swim on New Year's Day. Swim, hell. They
jump in until the TV cameras go off, then haul out to the
bars. Check ahht the shoulders. This guy's a swimmer."

Sonny tucked the cap under one arm and ran his thumbs
around the drawstring of his Speedo, eventually laying the
tops of his hands against his bare back. He knew the risks of
hypothermia better than most, knew he was even more
vulnerable because of the unexpected squiggle of arrhyth-
mia his doctor noticed on a heart monitor last year. But for
two years, he'd conditioned himself to maintain a perfect
balance between body heat generated and body heat lost.
Not many people could survive prolonged exposure in water
this cold. But at seventy-five strokes a minute, he felt sure
he could maintain a stable core temperature even in water as
cold as 45 degrees. And he could always stroke faster if he
felt himself failing.

Besides, no swimmer had tried a winter crossing of Lake
Erie. Why not him? Who else had worked so hard to adapt
the human body to cold water? But he was a long way from
where he needed to be for a late February attempt. Only
long training swims on days like this could push him
beyond the known barriers. If a swimming cap could help

him survive ninety minutes in the river on a day like this, he'd wear it. At least until his body caught up with his mind.

He snapped it into place over his long brown hair, letting the short ponytail dangle down the center of his back. With his right hand, he massaged the tight muscle between his left shoulder and his neck. When it swelled with blood, he did the same on the opposite side. He windmilled his arms to pop the joints and remembered something his older brother used to do when they were kids. David was double-jointed in the shoulders—what a swimmer he'd have been—and early on discovered he could pretzel one arm behind his head. Once, he ran into the house screaming, planning to tell their parents he'd been hit by a trolley. David laughed too soon, before he fooled anybody. But it was one of the few times Sonny remembered his parents laughing out loud at the same time.

A shiver. Sonny pulled his goggles on and looked around, first at the dozen or so people gathered behind him, then at the water running fast and high. He dipped his foot again, felt another chill. Just relax, he told himself. Roll the shoulders awake. Shake it out. Focus.

"Keep this up, Chickie, your balls'll look like BBs."

That voice, like screeching brakes. Still, Sonny laughed. "Detective Downing," he said without turning around. Sonny raised the goggles and faced Downing. Had he been there a second ago? No, he would have recognized that sports jacket, even with the goggles. Where'd he come from?

"Saw that piece-of-shit Toyota of yours in the Point parking lot, so I booked down to say hi. What do you pay those extortionists for a couple hours' parking? You could park all day at the stadium for two bucks."

He didn't see Downing often, which was fine. But as unnerving as the detective could be, he also was nicer than most other adults Sonny knew. No one had tried as hard to help him in the last ten years, at least no one who wasn't getting paid by the county to do it.

"Thanks for the tip."

"You ever talk to that kid at CMU I told you about? The

one selling the '83 Aries? The little Einstein didn't know squat about quality, selling a classic K-car for a song. Where else you gonna get that kind of style for under five hundred dollars? I'd of bought it myself, but I really wanted to see you in something American."

"No, the Toyota's still—"

"You never called him, did you? You little shit. Can't beat a K-car. Pitt still treating you okay? I might be able to help you find something else if that's not working out."

Sonny shivered, suddenly aware of the cold. "Still in the chem department, stocking the labs and stuff. It's good, four to midnight. My choice. Gives me time to train during daylight. Listen, if I don't get my blood pumping pretty soon—"

"I know, I know. Serious about the BBs, though. Cold water makes you suck 'em up into your body. Water like this, they may never come back down. That'll kill you long before that heart murmur or whatever. More painful, too."

Sonny laughed again. He liked Downing.

"Not that I'm concerned, you understand," the detective said. "Just with my luck, I'll be the one sent down to fish you out of this river someday. And I'm not partial to floaters. Nothing personal."

The detective reached into his pocket, pulled out a business card. He started to hand it over but stopped, apparently realizing Sonny had nowhere to put it.

"Why don't I just slide this under your windshield wiper?" he said.

"What is it?"

"Guy I'd like you to call. Psychologist."

Sonny studied him carefully. "No thanks."

"This one's different. Specializes in kids like you from broken homes. Told him about what happened to you, warned him you'd probably gag if you talked to another therapist. But after I told him about your hands, he insisted I have you call."

Shivering hard and steady now. If he didn't get in the water soon, start generating some body heat, there'd be real problems.

"Sorry, but I need to start swimming," Sonny said. "What did he say about my hands?"

Downing stepped forward with the card. He snapped it between his fingers and held it up so Sonny could read the name: James K. Christensen. Then he tucked it back in his pocket. "You swim. And be careful. Rivers are full of garbage. Under your windshield wiper, okay?"

What about my hands? Sonny wondered. He pulled the goggles on again, and just that quick he was back in the moment. Deaf to the traffic on the yellow-gold bridges at the Point. Numb to everything but the task: to dive through the pain that would slide the length of his body like a cold metal ring, and then stroke into the swirling brown Ohio. The rest would follow, but that first step was the toughest.

The current carried him quickly into the center of the muddy river. He swam faster than the water, maybe eighty strokes a minute, trying to clear the river's main channel before boat traffic resumed. At the bottom of his stroke, about three feet below the surface, 48-degree water numbed his fingertips. Each stroke sent waves of chilled satin over his shoulders and down his spine. During his first minutes in water this cold, he often imagined himself retreating down his throat and into his belly. It was safe there, with the warming blood flowing around him as his heart rate climbed.

Sonny once thought he'd invented the snug-in-the-guts fantasy, but Cox told him other open-water swimmers he trained talked about it, too. It's physiological, he'd said. Small capillaries near the skin's surface constrict in extreme cold, shunting blood into the body's core where it can warm the vital organs. It's the body's best survival mechanism and makes the bloodless skin feel, with a little imagination, like a protective shell.

Sonny reached the shallows along the river's north rim before he stopped. Behind him, the city's redeveloped skyline rose like a dream, the crystal tower of PPG Place at its center, flanked by half a dozen new skyscrapers, some even taller, that went up as the steel industry went down. Distance washed away the city's warts—the crumbling

roads and bridges, the averted eyes of displaced steelwork-
ers, the human garbage displaced by redevelopment along
Liberty Avenue. From downriver the city looked clean,
untroubled, and Sonny liked that.

He checked his watch. Using his marathoner's no-legs
stroke, it would take him a little less than thirty minutes to
reach the McKees Rocks Bridge, twice as long to get back
upriver to the Point. He started, paced by the same inner
drum that brought him to the water these days against Cox's
advice.

To relieve the tedium, he reviewed his trainer's early
warnings about cold-water distance swimming in these
waters. Tugboats and barges were the least of it. Bacteria.
Exhaustion. Dehydration. Disorientation. Hallucinations.
Hypothermia. Death. "You want to be a swimmer? Learn to
dive when a gun sounds and swim as fast as you can," Cox
had said when Sonny introduced himself two years earlier.
"But you don't need a coach if you want to swim that kind
of open-water distance. You need a fucking shrink."

True, Sonny thought. At least some sports offered a shot
at glory or money, or both. Distance swimming offered
neither. And explaining it to others only complicated things.
Assuming he could pull himself back onto the Point's rim
and struggle to the Ayatollah Corolla, he could look forward
to thirty minutes of violent shivering inside the sun-warmed
car. If there was sun. That would go on until his body
temperature stabilized. Eventually, he would wiggle the
loose wire underneath the dash and drive to his apartment.
If he was lucky, sleep would pull him beneath the surface of
a life that sometimes seemed as vast and cold and empty as
Lake Erie.

Someday, he figured, he'd understand it all. For now, he
just wanted to keep pushing himself. Colder. Longer.

About a mile downriver, his hands began to tingle. Not
from exposure. That was a different feeling altogether. This
was the phantom-prickle sensation that worried his doctor,
like his hands suddenly fell asleep. He stroked on, boosting
his pace to eighty strokes a minute, then eighty-five, but he
could feel himself slowing down. He screamed at the river

bottom, the word *shiiit* bubbling up around his ears, then angled toward the bank just beyond the Kaufmann's warehouse. He thrashed into the shallows, both hands dead at the ends of his wrists.

Up the muddy bank, onto the curb of the giant warehouse parking lot. Asphalt to the horizon. No towel. No shoes. No warm-up suit. Just his marble-bag bathing suit and a twenty-minute jog between him and a car that might or might not start. He was halfway there, shivering like a junkie, when he remembered the goggles and cap. He tried to rake them off his head, feeling totally spastic, but the fingers just weren't working.

6

Christensen had reviewed hundreds of files from the Department of Children's Services, but none as thick as this. It dominated the center of his home-office desk, a presence, like an unwelcome guest. Downing was right about one thing: Sonny Corbett had a history.

He opened it to the summary page and again scanned the long list of dates running down the left side, each one representing the arrival of a child welfare investigator on the Corbett family doorstep. He checked the birth dates listed in the upper right corner, then noted the date of the first entry—June 1974. A caseworker's notes read: "Domestic. Both children temp. removed as precaution. Placement: Morningside Shelter. Duration: Six days."

Sonny had been four months old; his brother, David, just past three years. A short childhood for both.

Reproductive organs should be licensed, Christensen thought, like concealed weapons, only stricter. Assholes carry handguns all the time but only a few actually hurt anybody. When assholes have kids, though, they inflict themselves not only on their children, but on generations they'll never live to see. "I had no idea you were Aryan," Molly had said the night he mentioned his licensing idea after a particularly bad day, but she'd never spent much time with the children of monsters, never heard a nine-year-old recount a rape, never watched a child numbly describe a parent's unstoppable rage.

The sound of machine-gun fire and the amplified screams of its victims filtered in from the adjoining den, along with Annie's unrestrained laughter.

"Annie! What are you watching?" He raised his voice loud enough to be heard, but controlled, calm. "Melissa! Anybody?"

No response, save for a sudden increase in volume. Melissa had the remote control. He took a deep breath. Then another. One more before he opened the door into inevitable confrontation.

"Hey, guys. School night. Let's wrap it up."

Sylvester Stallone appeared on the screen, camouflaged, rippling, lethal. He hoisted a gun the size of a Cadillac bumper and put down another charging cadre of screeching VC.

"Almost over," Melissa said.

"Dad, watch this." Annie sat upright and pointed one of her five-year-old fingers at the screen, across which had bloomed a gory fireball. Bodies everywhere. Close-up of Stallone's sneering grin.

"You've seen this before?"

Melissa shrugged with the studied indifference of a fifteen-year-old. "Third time. It's war movie month on HBO."

Christensen heard himself sigh. He usually held back, but not tonight. Damn her right to teenage self-determination. She was baiting him.

"Turn it off."

Melissa glared from beneath a loose curtain of black hair, her mother's hair. "It's almost over."

"Good night," he said. He crossed the room and jabbed the TV's power button with more force than necessary.

Annie bolted to her feet, hands on her tiny hips. Her shoulders were squared. The blond pigtails that Melissa braided for her that morning were mostly unraveled, Heidi with an attitude. "That's not appropriate, Dad."

Melissa rolled her eyes, collected her ice cream bowl, and

padded off toward the kitchen. Christensen stepped to the couch and hugged Annie to his chest.

"You're upset, and I understand that. But we've talked about how some movies just aren't suitable for kids your age."

"Rambo's like the Power Rangers, only grown up."

"Sorry. Brush your teeth?"

Annie tightened her thin lips over two gleaming rows of baby teeth, going bug-eyed to enhance the presentation. The telephone rang once, twice as he inspected her mouth.

"Beautiful. Got Silkie?"

She held up the remains of Molly's favorite nightgown.

"Guess who-oo?" Melissa said as she walked the cordless phone in from the kitchen. She handed it off and headed up the stairs without making eye contact.

"Hi," he said. "Can you hang a minute? I'm putting Annie to bed."

"Call me back," Brenna said.

"No, wait. Please. Ten seconds."

Christensen hugged Annie and began their ritual song, loosening her surviving braids as he sang. "Night night. Sleep tight. Please don't let the bedbugs bite."

"If they do, hit 'em with a shoe," Annie replied, echoing the unfortunate refrain taught her by a former nanny, "till they're black and blue."

Something crossed behind his eyes like a raptor's shadow, something he'd just read on a decade-old record in Sonny Corbett's file. An injury report. He pulled his daughter to him and hugged her again until she wriggled away.

"'Night," he called as she followed her older sister up the creaky wooden stairs. "Ask Melissa to brush your hair out, okay? And tomorrow's Share Day, so don't forget to pick out something before you go to bed."

He didn't speak again until his daughters were out of sight, and even then in a whisper until he realized how ridiculous that seemed.

"Rough night," he said.

"So I gathered," Brenna said. Hearing her voice made him lonely.

"Cramming for the Cheverton trial?"

"Nope. I needed a break. Got Taylor to sleep by nine, took a long bath, and brought a glass of wine to bed."

Loneliness transformed briefly into lust, then receded as he checked his watch. Lust was out of the question. But he let his mind linger on the thought of her between the sheets, scented by bath oil and smoothed by lotion, her white cotton nightshirt clinging to the gentle curve of her still-damp breasts.

He picked up Annie's Garfield slippers and put them on the end of the banister. "Spent the night working on my 'Daddy Dearest' routine."

"We all play hardball sometimes, Jim. Don't be too tough on yourself."

"I got tied up reading a file tonight, and didn't realize until too late that they were watching some bloodfeast on TV. Annie too. Now I'm a dictator for making them shut it off."

"It's your job," she said. "What file?"

Sometimes she was more prosecutor than defense attorney. "Don't start," he said. "You know what file."

"The one you're not supposed to have?"

Long silence. "Look, it's late," he said. "Why don't we try this again tomorrow."

"Oh, lighten up."

"Sorry. This whole thing has me a little on edge."

"The Primenyl case did that to people, I hear. How is Detective Downing, anyway?"

Christensen ignored the jab. Some sort of grunge nihil-rock suddenly issued from the stereo in Melissa's upstairs bedroom, at a volume clearly intended to provoke. He backed into his office and closed the door.

"I think his instincts are damned good," he said, thinking: That should shift the conversation a bit. "I can't imagine a better crucible for memory repression than 154 Jancey Street."

"Where?"

"Casa Corbett. The Irondale house the family lived in for a while."

"In 1986?"

"For two years before the killings and for a few weeks afterward. As twisted as the family was before then, that's where it all seemed to disintegrate. For everybody in the house except Sonny."

"So?"

"So what's wrong with this picture? You've got three people in the family who crash and burn, psychologically speaking, but the fourth, the youngest, walks away without a scratch?"

"It happens," she said. "There was that study on resilient personalities. People with totally screwed-up backgrounds who survive and succeed. Maybe Sonny's that type."

Christensen shook his head. "Irrelevant, counselor. There's a big difference between resilience and repression. A resilient person acknowledges the past, deals with it, and moves on. Someone who's repressing never gets past step one. And I think there may be a lot Sonny never even confronted. Hold on, I want to read you something."

Christensen circled his desk and opened the file again, flipping to a 1988 foster care placement report. He picked up his desk telephone from its cradle and hung up the cordless, trying at least to eliminate the cordless's annoying static from the rest of the aural assault.

"Sonny was in and out of half a dozen foster homes, right? And each time he was placed, they sat him down with a therapist. Once in late 1986. Twice in 1987. Sonny never talked about his family in those three sessions, and apparently no one pushed him to do so. But in February 1988—this is two years after his mother went to Borman, his father abandoned him, and his big brother committed suicide—Chaytor Perriman had a session with him. His notes are in the file. Interesting stuff."

"Chaytor's a good guy," Brenna said. "Not that I want to encourage you in any way."

"It says, and I'm reading from Chaytor's notes: 'Sonny initiated an extended discussion about his brother. Described in some detail the car accident in which his brother died and his recent progress coming to terms with brother's death.' "

Christensen counted four beats before Brenna spoke. "Wait," she said. "You said it was suicide."

Gotcha. "It was. They shared a bedroom. Sonny found the body."

"Chaytor noted all that?"

"He did. Plus, there's a coroner's report in the file. In his summary, Chaytor wrote something pretty intriguing: 'Sonny's recollections about his family seem scoured of the instability reflected in police reports and court records.' "

" 'Scoured'?" Brenna said.

Christensen took a deep breath. He wanted Brenna to feel at least some of the chill that passed through him when he first read the therapist's report. "Sonny doesn't talk about his brother at all for two years, then when he does, he puts the death into a fantasy scenario so he can deal with it. Very telling."

"A form of repression." She said it without emotion. "Anything else?"

"Something very weird. Got no idea what to make of it. The file's full of old police reports, mostly domestic calls to the Jancey Street home in '84, '85, '86. A few incident reports about the brother, just vandalism and stuff. Not the most stable kid, apparently. But there's one about Sonny, from 1989."

Brenna sipped her wine again. "So he was, what? Fifteen? Sixteen?"

"Something happened at his mother's apartment. She was out of Borman, living on her own, and caseworkers dropped Sonny off every couple weeks for a visit, just a couple hours at a time. But there was an incident, and it's not clear."

"Something Sonny did?"

"That's what the report said. His mom apparently watched a neighbor's kid in the afternoons to earn a little money. Well, when the caseworker comes back to pick up Sonny, there's a patrol car outside. Neighbors heard this commotion. Turns out Sonny was playing with the neighbor kid, two years old, I think, when the kid almost drowned in the apartment's bathtub."

He waited. Finally, Brenna asked: "Why would Sonny have him in a tub?"

"No idea. Both of them were soaking wet. The kid wasn't hurt, more scared than anything, but Sonny never said a word to the police about it. His mom apparently was in another room at the time, so she wasn't much help either."

"So?"

"I don't know. Really, I don't. Peculiar, though, don't you think?"

The music upstairs stopped as suddenly as it had started. He knew it would if Melissa didn't get an immediate reaction, but it left him waiting through a long, uncomfortable silence for Brenna to continue. His eyes strayed to the right corner of his desk, to the wood-framed portrait of Molly and the girls, taken for him just two weeks before the accident. It arrived with the photographer's invoice on the day of Molly's funeral.

"So when will you see Sonny?"

Her voice made him jump, but he wasn't sure why. "Tomorrow. Downing talked to him yesterday, said Sonny could call any day to set up a get-to-know-you session. Mostly I want to test his suggestibility. There are a couple ways to do that."

He stopped. The tonelessness of her voice made him recall the chilly discussion they'd had on the day Downing first approached him about the case.

"Look, Brenna, are you okay with this? I'm not committed to anything. And I wouldn't do it if there was any risk."

"Reality isn't really your thing, is it?" she said. He was at least grateful for the sudden life in her voice. "I know you better than that. You wouldn't walk away now even if I *could* convince you Downing's a flake."

He laughed. "But really, aren't you curious now?"

She didn't answer. "Just be careful, all right? Don't let Downing drag you into the quicksand."

Except for the ticking of the ancient radiators, the house was quiet after they hung up. It was the same healing tranquillity he sought at the end of every hectic day, and he leaned back in his desk chair to enjoy it. But when his eyes fell again on Sonny's file, the familiar silence suddenly made him edgy. He snapped off his lamp and left the room, closing the door behind him.

7

Cold rain soaked Downing's face, like he'd opened his door halfway through a car wash. He struggled from behind the Ford's steering wheel and stepped into the early evening gloom. A cutting wind swept the left side of his raincoat behind him like a cape and bent the stem of the red rose in his hand. He tucked the broken flower inside his sports coat, right next to the Glock nine, then cinched the raincoat's belt.

St. Michael's Cemetery was old Pittsburgh, the Pittsburgh he knew best. Carved into Mount Washington high above the South Side, it could have been a three-acre model for the city itself. Poles and Slovaks over here, Italians over there, just past the Irish and the Greeks. Like the city, the European working stock remained segregated into tidy little ghettos, even in death. The Jews and blacks were with their own, of course, somewhere else.

Not that it was a bad place. Of the city's million or so cemeteries, St. Michael's, with its big-screen view of the Downtown skyline, was one of the best kept. Even now, with the brutal late November rain and the trees nearly bare, it had the feel of a high-end headstone showroom. Even so, Downing hated graveyards. Strictly a professional opinion: The colder the body, the less use a homicide cop has for it.

Carole was Italian, one of a couple Marinos among the

Borellis and Cippolas and Tambellinis spread across a slope on the east side. Time blurs everything, even this, he thought. Could he find her again? He did, and stooped in the dim reflection of his headlights to brush leaves from the flat granite marker.

Carole Marino Carver. She'd kept her married name for the options it gave her in a town obsessed with ethnicity. But with her waist-length hair the color of Kona coffee, not to mention Italo-short fuses on her temper and her passion, Carole didn't fool anybody.

"How you been, baby?" Downing said.

He closed his eyes. He'd stopped praying ten years ago, but he always tried to remember the dead as they were premortem. And what came to mind first were Carole's panted whispers as she moved beneath him that last time, arching her back and stretching her arms through the spindles of her cherry-wood headboard. Only woman he ever knew who did that, and she'd done it even when they were in college.

Then he thought of the first time they met. He was eighteen, maybe nineteen, at a party. Bunch of kids just drinking and trying to get laid. She came in, and he heard himself sigh when he saw her. More of a moan. The air just left his chest, involuntarily. She told him she'd had nearly the same reaction. Within a week they started a relationship that lasted four years, off and on, until they graduated. Four years of blowout fights followed by the kind of sex he'd fantasized about ever since. Fight, fuck. Fight, fuck. When they got tired of the roller coaster, they'd talked themselves into separate lives, knowing it was the best thing. He remembered what she said on her way out the door: "We're two live wires, Grady. We both need grounds."

He saw her under the Kaufmann's clock one morning thirty-four years later, standing there like she was waiting for him. They had lunch and laughed about the disaster that might have been their marriage, agreeing that both had found their grounds: Trix for him, CPA Gerald Carver for her, at least for the ten years their marriage lasted. Then they rocked Hilton room 663 all afternoon, breaking only to nibble fruit and sip cold duck from a room-service tray.

Downing tried to enjoy the memory, but a videotape began replaying in his head. It showed them sitting in his car, talking, kissing, vulnerable to the stalker behind the viewfinder. Then, like static interference, something else crackled into his mind. A high-pitched whine, like a dentist's drill, only coarser. The Stryker bone saw. And an image: a scalpel tracing a Y incision from the clavicle to the mons veneris. And another: that outrageous hair dangling to the floor, trampled and crusted with blood.

Downing willed the thoughts away.

"Told you I'd be back when I had some news," he said.

A trickle of rain scored his spine, channeled along the deep gorge that divided his back into two muscular halves. Shivering, he felt his stomach tighten, reminding him of the slight cop gut he'd been able to avoid until the past few years. Rain made his right shoulder ache where a bullet entered years ago, but he'd learned to live with the occasional twinge.

Downing stood up, pulled his raincoat collar tight around his thick neck, and licked the raindrops from his mustache.

"Still don't know why, or what sets him off," he said. "But Corbett's killing again."

He'd got the word from some young Waynesburg detective who called to pick his brain two days after the latest killing. They had a product-tampering case, he'd said, a poisoning, as if Downing didn't read the papers. "You're the guy that did the Primenyl case, right?" the cop asked. Downing had winced at the word, then set aside the Texas Ruby Red grapefruit he'd been peeling. The cop told a story Downing had heard six times already, but with a twist.

"Still holding the yogurt container when the paramedics found her on the kitchen floor," the kid cop said. "We won't have final results for a few days, but tox is pretty sure it's potassium cyanide."

"Probably not." Downing remembered his crash course in chemistry in 1986. "Probably not sodium cyanide, either. Too unstable. The powders start reacting with carbon dioxide and moisture as soon as they're exposed to air. After more than a day or so in a container like that it wouldn't be potent enough to be fatal."

Then he'd remembered another option: hydrogen cyanide, the liquid form. It's unstable, too, he'd thought; hell, it boils at 80 degrees Fahrenheit. But then, wouldn't yogurt be the perfect delivery vehicle for it? From your grocer's refrigerator to yours. The stuff tastes like hell, but who thinks about that first spoonful? And one would probably be enough.

"Get word out fast," Downing told him. "Get any brand with the same packaging off the shelves of the local stores. You check the lot number on the container?" The kid cop said he'd done that first thing, adding, "We learn from mistakes."

Downing pulled his collar tighter. *Fuck you*, was what he'd wanted to say. Have the spine to say what you're thinking: After the Primenyl screwup, everybody knows the drill. Say it, you son of a bitch. But no. He'd taken a deep breath and swallowed the words, then asked: "What's the chance it was a family thing?"

"We're talking to the husband, but they're the Waltons, man. And her boy—maybe twelve; he was there when it happened—he says she ate it right out of the grocery bag."

Downing hadn't listened as the cop described what happened next. He already knew. Racing pulse within seconds. A few pathetic minutes of gasping as the poison constricts the chest. Face pale as the body forces blood to the organs in a hopeless attempt to save itself. Falling blood pressure. Convulsions. Violent skittering of the limbs. Death. Downing saw everything long before the 9-1-1 recording hit the news, including the shit stains on her kitchen floor.

He'd wheeled his desk chair to the computer terminal as the deputy talked. "Where'd you say this happened?"

"Waynesburg. Near the college," the deputy said.

Downing stopped, his hands frozen above the keyboard. "Name some of the other little burgs around there."

"Old mining towns, mostly," the deputy said. "Enterprise. Gypsy. Outcrop."

Downing traced the grave marker's chiseled "1986" with his toe. Despite the rain and the hour, others were around. A car passed slowly along the cemetery road, washing him briefly in high beams. He looked away, just in case he knew them.

"You believe it, baby? Outcrop. Just one guy in the whole goddamned computer living near Waynesburg. Been there since right after the '86 killings. Knew it was Corbett even before he sent me the tape, even before I checked the database."

The database. What started with his own scribbled notes about a random series of deaths that year became the most intensive manhunt in Pennsylvania history. He shuffled the numbers again: twenty-five thousand pages of finished reports by a hundred fifty federal, state, and local investigators stored in twelve different file cabinets. A computerized catalog of the sixty thousand names gathered between the end of 1986 and late 1988, when the Primenyl task force was disbanded. From the beginning, Ron Corbett's name stood apart.

"It's the opening I need," Downing said. "Don't really want to jump back into this thing. Nearly killed me last time. But I got to, baby, because he won't stop at one. Got to for you. For the other five—now the other six, I guess. For me, too. So I'll get him this time, one way or the other."

Soon he'd make his pitch, lay out the theory he'd been researching for more than a year, persuade his new boss to give him a second chance. He needed one thing to prosecute the bastard—a witness. And if Christensen didn't seem enthusiastic about working with Sonny, he at least seemed willing to help.

A thorn caught on Downing's wedding ring as he tugged the rose from inside his raincoat. He pulled it loose, relieved that the bud was intact and starting to open. He held it into the faint light and pouring rain and again tried to conjure pleasant memories of the woman beneath his feet, and of the last time he saw her alive. But the rose was the color of old blood, and the memory it triggered took his breath away.

He shuddered, closed his left fist around the flower, and turned his back. When he opened his hand, he was nearly at the car and panting. Had he been running? He dropped the crushed petals into a muddy pool, folded himself into the driver's seat, and eased the Ford toward the graveyard gate and down into the city.

Steam rose from Downing's pants as they dried on the heat vent beneath his office window. Through the mist, he could see the tugboat lights as they shoved silent barges along the inky Monongahela River three stories below. Across the Mon sat Station Square, once the gritty rail crossroads for the city's iron and steel exports, now a postindustrial shopping mall, fresh-scrubbed and trimmed in neon.

Half the guys in this bunker would kill for his window, he thought. After twenty-eight years with the department, the last nineteen in homicide, he'd finally got the lead investigator's office and the window in 1985, the year before the Primenyl killings. Lost the title two years later, an awkward rump-fuck of a demotion that nobody really talked about. But nobody ever asked for the office back, and Downing never brought it up.

The only problem with the view was just upriver, about a mile north of the Public Safety Building—the old Duquesne brewery. He'd played in its shadow as a kid, back when it was working three shifts to slake the quitting-time thirst of Big Steel. Big Steel was dead now and the leprous brick building was lifeless except for the clock face that covered a quarter-acre of the front wall. Its giant hands swept away the hours, mocking him, erasing the five months he had left until mandatory retirement.

Quarter to eleven. Jesus.

Downing snapped on his desk lamp, recoiling from the harsh, sudden light. He knocked over his open jar of freeze-dried coffee as he checked his watch.

"Damn."

What must he look like to the night-shifters passing along

the corridor? Rumpled. Puffy. Squinting like a mole through his bifocals. Bare legs propped on the windowsill. He turned out the lamp, smoothed his still-thick brown hair, and wriggled into his pants, which were damp below the point where his raincoat left off. He swept a mound of grapefruit peels into the wastebasket, then turned the lamp on again and snatched the phone from its cradle.

Trix wasn't answering, but he knew the game. On the fourth ring, he started to stroke the bronze elephant next to his Rolodex. The punch line of a private joke was taped to its side—M40. *National Geographic* once did a story about an old, dying elephant that in field research jargon was identified only as Male 40, or M40. The researchers tracked M40's last tortured walk to a clearing, where during the elephant's final agonized hours they witnessed behavior that scientists had never before seen. As M40 lay there, helpless and unable to stand, the younger males who'd followed him began, one by one, to mount him in a spirited show of dominance.

He'd laughed when Silverwood posted the story on the department bulletin board and scribbled, "Make reservations now for Grady Downing's retirement party!" He'd even laughed when somebody left the little brass M40 on his desk two days later. But nobody ever took credit, which he thought gave the whole thing a darker, meaner edge. Truth be told, it cut close to the bone.

His wife answered after the tenth ring, like she always did from bed on the nights he forgot to call.

"Very nice, Grady." He knew the rasp in her voice.

"You asleep already? It's . . ." He checked his watch again, as though she could see the gesture. "Jesus, Trix, I'm sorry. Just got—"

"Forget it."

How many nights had they had this conversation? How many times had she tamped her anger and disappointment down with that simple response and rolled over again into fitful sleep? How long until she went berserk some night and carved his heart out while he dozed on the couch?

"He's killing again." He paused, waiting for a prompt.

None came. He knew she'd need no explanation or context, so he just continued. "About an hour from here, in Greene County. Near Outcrop."

"I wondered. Not Primenyl again?"

"No, but cyanide."

Silence. Ten seconds. Twenty. He'd meant to tell her in person; now he knew he should have.

"What are you thinking?" The tremble in her voice told him this was going to be tough.

Deep breath. "Still waiting for more details. But if it looks like Corbett was involved, I'm going to DeLillo with my repressed-memories idea. Or maybe I'll just take it straight to Kiger."

"The chief? DeLillo will love that."

"Going over his head would be tricky, but I may have to. Kiger wasn't here in '86, so I've got no baggage with him."

No reaction. And he needed to talk. Proceed with caution.

"Got five months left, Trix. And I think Kiger'll go for it, especially if I can convince him Corbett's involved in this one. But I'll argue to reopen even if he's not convinced. We know a lot more about how memory works than we did in '86. Corbett's wife is still around. So's Sonny, his youngest kid. Trix, they must have known what went on in that house. Maybe if I can get them thinking about it again, it'll nudge them enough. I'm sure the memories are in there. Getting them out is the tricky part."

"Grady—"

"It was like somebody dropped a bomb on that family, Trix. The killings start, and within a couple weeks three of the four family members are a few shrimp short of a cocktail? You tell me what the fuck they saw Corbett doing."

The line hummed, electronic silence.

"How's it going to end?" she said, her voice flat but not emotionless. It made him uncomfortable, mostly because he wasn't sure what she meant. "After it's over, are you ready to deal with it either way? Win or lose?"

"Trix—"

"I mean, if you reopen this case, Grady, it could happen

to you all over again. And I'm not sure I can help you through it this time. I never understood why you got so involved, because it never happened before or since. But I see it happening again. The way you talked just now. It takes you over. I know part of you died with those people, but you did your job. You just can't make witnesses out of clay. You can't pull evidence out of your hat. And you can't wall me out again."

Finally: "I'm scared, Grady."

Scary damn business. "He's not finished, Trix. Everything I've read predicted he'd kill again. Now he has. And there's no reason to think he'll stop now."

"You don't know that. You've made an awfully big assumption here. I don't understand you sometimes."

Downing picked up the elephant and considered heaving it through the glass of his office door. She could never understand, because she would never know about Carole.

"There's still time," he said. "I want to use it all."

"Have you mentioned it to anyone yet?"

"Christensen. Just to run the repressed-memories theory past him, see if he'd talk to Sonny."

"And?"

"He reads the papers, too. Totally agreed with me. Said this sounds at least as strong as the stuff in California last year. And after the Primenyl killings, he said he'd heard Mom and the kid had their emergency lights flashing."

Trix sighed. "What time you coming home? I haven't fed your dinner to Rodney. Yet."

Dinner. Right. Downing swiveled in his chair and propped a foot on the window ledge. In the distance, the brewery clock showed no mercy. He smiled anyway.

"I'll leave now. Don't give it to the dog. Nothing worse than a basset hound with calluses on his belly. Notice how he's starting to drag?"

He expected a laugh. They'd always shared that much, anyway. But Trix didn't laugh. He turned back toward his desk and propped his elbows on the contents of a coroner's file labeled "Corbett, David." An image of every parent's nightmare stared up at him: a black-and-white photograph of a troubled fifteen-year-old hunched grotesquely in a sturdy wing chair, left dome of his skull gone, the gun balanced improbably on his right shoulder. Another print of the same frame was in the file he gave Christensen.

The edge was back in her voice when she said good night. Downing closed his eyes. "Trix?"

"What?"

"Come on. It'll be fine."

"Sure," she said. "You've got that dead man's brake, remember? Stops you right before the cliff. That's what you always say. But God, Grady, can you be sure it still works?" She hung up, and he listened to the phone's disconnect pulse as long as he could stand it.

8

Christensen compared the unfamiliar number flashing on his beeper with the one Downing had given him. They matched. Sonny Corbett was trying to reach him.

He'd waited three days for the call, wondering when—if—Sonny would take the first step. The long run he took after dinner had helped clear his head, and by the time he panted up the front steps and struggled out of his sweats, he was sure Sonny wouldn't call. Ever. Forty minutes later, his beeper went off. Monday night, 9:46 P.M., according to the digital clock on the stove. Why now?

Just to be sure, he set aside Annie's beloved plastic palomino, Pugs, whose broken foreleg now was a gooey web of poorly applied household cement, and picked up a pen. He scribbled the flashing number on the back of a Lucky Charms box and checked it again. Then he picked up the phone, and was startled to hear Melissa's voice, which stopped in mid-sentence.

"I'm *talking*," she said from an upstairs extension.

"I thought you were in bed, Lissa. Sorry." He started to hang up, then reconsidered. Something about the attitude. "Somebody's trying to reach me, so I'm going to need the phone for a few minutes. Sorry to interrupt, but it's important. Let me know when you're off."

While he waited, drumming his fingers on the kitchen

table, Christensen reviewed how he wanted to begin his relationship with Sonny. Under no circumstances would he ever directly suggest that the numbness in Sonny's hands might be the result of repressed memories or posttraumatic stress. He knew better than to pursue that conversation, even though recent studies were profound. One in particular, a study of Cambodian refugees living in Long Beach, California, suggested a direct link between posttraumatic stress and hysterical blindness among older women who'd watched the Khmer Rouge butcher their husbands or children. After seeing the unthinkable, their eyes had simply stopped seeing.

But Christensen couldn't suggest anything that would lead Sonny in any particular direction. To initiate a discussion about Sonny's childhood traumas could skew Sonny's recollections, and the last thing Christensen needed was to be accused of luring Sonny into repression therapy. That was happening too often, with reckless therapists allowing false memories to take root and grow. Which is bad enough in the privacy of the therapist's office, but even worse when the cops use those memories as the basis of a criminal prosecution.

Upstairs, a door slammed with rattling force. Melissa was off the phone.

"Thank you," he called.

He did intend to plant *one* seed with Sonny, though. To gauge the young man's suggestibility, he intended to work into their initial conversation a detailed description of a memorable moment from Sonny's life. It would be emotional, vivid—and entirely fictional. Then he'd wait. If that false memory turned up in a subsequent conversation with Sonny, and if Sonny treated it as a real memory, Christensen intended to go no further. He would tell Downing that Sonny's recovered memories would be too unreliable for meaningful therapy and, he assumed, utterly vulnerable to cross-examination, if it ever came to that. At that point, he would end his role in Downing's investigation with a clear conscience.

Christensen cleared his throat and dialed. The phone rang

only once. "Hello, my name is Jim Christensen and I'm returning—"

"Yeah, hi." A young man's voice, gentle, a little unsure. "Is this Sonny Corbett?"

"You called back right away," he said. "I didn't think you would."

Christensen tried to conjure an image from the sound of the voice. He saw a young Art Garfunkel. "Actually, I've been expecting your call since I talked to Grady Downing earlier this week. He told me about the numbness in your hands. I hear you're a swimmer, and numbness has to be pretty awkward. Grady thought maybe I could help."

"It's weird is what it is," the voice said. "Been to two or three doctors, plus my trainer. None of them can figure it out, because after a while the numbness just goes away until the next time. I told my trainer I was thinking about calling you. He said, 'What the hell. We've tried everything *but* a shrink.'"

Christensen laughed. "The last hope of lost causes. I'll take it as a compliment. You must swim competitively, then?"

"Not on a team or anything."

Christensen tried to make sense of that, then decided to push on. "So what's it feel like?"

"You ever sleep on your hands?" Sonny said after a long pause.

"Like when one just goes dead in the middle of the night and you have to move it around with the other one until it finally starts to tingle again?"

"Like that," Sonny said. "Except it can happen anytime, and sometimes it stays like that for hours."

"Does it ever happen when you're swimming?"

"Mostly. I swim a lot."

Christensen considered the predicament of a swimmer with useless hands. "But you're able to get to the side of the pool okay?"

"I can get out of the water, if that's what you mean."

"Have you ever pegged it to anything physical—carpal tunnel syndrome, maybe some other repetitive stress injury?"

"That's what the doctors thought. First thing they checked, but that's not it."

"You've tried physical therapy?" Christensen asked.

"Helps control the numbness, but doesn't prevent it."

Christensen suggested a few more possible physical causes, but none seemed likely. And Sonny was familiar with them all, making him think Sonny's doctors had traveled this road before.

"Tell you what," Christensen said. "Can you stop by my office in the next few days—nothing formal. We'll just talk, see if we can start figuring this thing out."

They set a time for Thursday, apparently one of Sonny's rare free weeknights. Christensen told him how to find his private office on one of Oakland's ambiguous side streets.

"You must know Grady Downing pretty well," Christensen said, feigning an afterthought.

"I guess. Why?"

"Just my impression. He and I were talking about your hands and he seemed to know so much about you."

"Like what?" Sonny said.

"Nothing in particular. I forget how we even got on it now. But he told me about the time you got lost in Three Rivers Stadium during a Pirate game."

Sonny said nothing.

"When you were about seven or so? You got separated from your parents for about an hour?"

"I don't remember," Sonny said.

Christensen tried to seem casual about forcing the conversation. "I don't even know why Grady mentioned it. He said you told him about how you heard your name echo across the field and saw it on the center-field scoreboard. About how the stadium security guard had to pry your fingers from the upper-deck railing so he could take you to the lost-child area. That must have been the connection— we'd been talking about your hands."

No response.

It wasn't graceful, but at least the seed was planted. "So anyway," Christensen said, "six P.M. Thursday?"

9

Christensen stood up reflexively as the door to his private counseling office swung open, wondering too late if he should have been more casual.

"Sonny?"

The young man offered a noncommittal smile. He was tall, much taller than Christensen had imagined, with the unmistakable shoulders of an athlete. His oversized white oxford shirt funneled down into the unstrained waistband of perfectly faded Levi's. Frayed hole in the right knee. Docksiders, no socks. This was not the fragile boy Christensen had assembled from their phone conversation and the puzzle pieces in the juvenile records. This was someone who reminded Christensen of himself at that age—confident, almost cocky, as lean and tight as piano wire.

His cheeks were bright pink, probably from the late fall winds. The color contrasted sharply with the dark crescents beneath his eyes. He looked like every frat boy on campus after cramming for spring finals, right down to the bare ankles.

"I'm Jim Christensen, Sonny. Glad you could come. Did you leave your coat out in the reception area? I have a rack in here."

Sonny looked confused. "I didn't bring one," he said finally.

Christensen remembered fighting the late November gale between his car and the office door an hour earlier. The temperature may have been in the 40s, but the wind felt like flying glass. He looked again at Sonny's bare ankles. "I'm glad you could make it," he said.

Christensen walked over to the wing chairs beside his desk and took the one nearest the window, then gestured to the other. Sonny moved toward it, but stopped. For a moment, his confidence seemed to vanish.

"I don't have much money," he said.

Christensen smiled, again offering the chair. "I won't tell if you won't."

Sonny still hesitated.

Christensen thought a moment, then asked, "You take any classes at the university?"

The young man shook his head. "Just work there."

"Really? You're staff, then. Students and staff have access to the University Counseling Center over in the student union. I volunteer there two days a week. Let's just pretend we're there and call it even. Deal?"

Sonny sat down, moving again with a relaxed power Christensen found unsettling. Nothing in Sonny's life should have added up this way. During the fifteen minutes they'd spent on the phone arranging this meeting, Christensen's presumptions about Sonny Corbett remained intact. The rhythms of Sonny's voice were slow and quiet, almost annoyingly so, like a dripping faucet. Christensen imagined him as withdrawn, distracted, and damaged by a childhood of apparently constant turmoil. But in person Sonny seemed a full-on alpha male, all calm power and controlled confidence.

"What do you think it is?" Sonny said, almost without inflection. Then he added, "My hands."

"How do they feel now?" Christensen leaned back in his chair, hoping a relaxed body posture would encourage a more meandering conversation.

"Fine. Just happens once in a while."

"Usually when you swim, you said." Christensen laced his fingers together and clasped them behind his head. He tended to overuse his hands when nervous.

Sonny looked away, then picked up the inflatable Wham-It from the coffee table that lay between them. It was an eighteen-inch version of the large stand-up punching bags that Christensen had enjoyed pummeling as a kid. Someone had taken that concept, reduced it to desktop size, and successfully marketed it as an executive stress-relief toy. Christensen kept the Wham-It within easy reach of all his private counseling patients as a focus for their anxieties. Everyone picked it up sooner or later.

Sonny gave the Wham-It a slow once-over before putting it back on the table. "Usually," he said.

A gust of wind rattled the wide office window, drawing their attention. The sky was the color of a bruise, promising more rain. The only thing worse than Pittsburgh now, in early winter, was Pittsburgh during winter's last gasps. Both offered the same ground-zero landscape apparent through the window, but at least now the streets weren't coated with the brackish sludge of melting snow.

"Human beings are pretty complex creatures," Christensen said. "I don't know how familiar you are with it, but a lot of studies have been done on the interrelationship of the body and mind. But I'm guessing you know that, or you wouldn't be here."

Sonny said nothing, clearly at full attention.

"Say you break your nose," Christensen said. "Not only is the pain intense, but you're also dealing with a lot of issues that have nothing to do with physical healing. Self-image. Confidence. Mental injuries, if you will. I'm not saying that's the case with your hands, but one theory goes that if a physical injury can affect your mind, why can't a mental injury affect your body?"

"Psychosomatic," Sonny said.

"No fair reading ahead."

Sonny leaned forward and absently flicked the Wham-It with his finger. It fell backward onto the tabletop, then slowly rose again. "Sounds pretty bogus."

"Some people think it's bogus, some don't," Christensen said. "Smart people sometimes disagree. But the human brain has a pretty remarkable defense system. It's nothing but a big filing cabinet, and sometimes it files the things that hurt or frighten us way in the back so we don't have to deal with them as often, or ever."

"Like the baseball game thing?" Sonny asked.

Bingo.

"Like the baseball game thing. You remembered it then?" Christensen tried not to seem pleased. He had expected Sonny to absorb and repackage the story as a memory, but not this quickly. "The other day you sounded like it didn't ring a bell."

Sonny shook his head. "Still doesn't," he said. "We weren't much for family outings. I'd remember if we ever went to a Pirate game."

Christensen picked up the Wham-It, then put it back down. "Not at all?"

"Sorry. Maybe Detective Downing was thinking of somebody else."

Christensen stood and walked to the window, stalling, wondering what to do next. Sonny had passed his first test. If he continued to resist suggestion, his memories probably would be credible. And God knows a young man capable of denying his brother's suicide was capable of wholesale memory repression. What if Downing's last-ditch scenario was right? If the young man before him was the missing piece to the city's biggest crime puzzle, how could he turn away?

"I'd like to start meeting here twice a week, Sonny," Christensen heard himself say. He turned and leaned back against the window. "How free are your evenings?"

"I told you, I work nights except Thursdays," Sonny said.

"Any day-shift openings?"

"I like working nights," Sonny said. "I'm the only one in the whole chem department, and it leaves my days free to train."

"But that doesn't solve the numbness problem with your hands," Christensen said. "No promises, mind you, but maybe we can find a way to stop that. That's got to affect your swimming."

Sonny said nothing for a few long moments. Finally, he stood. "I'd have to think about it."

"Tell you what," Christensen said. "You off any days during the week?"

"Thursdays, like I said."

"Then let's get together next Thursday evening to talk, about six again. We'll just take it one day at a time. And if you don't get anything out of it, we'll stop. That seem fair?"

Sonny started for the office door, then paused only long enough to say, "I'll let you know."

10

Five-thirty and nearly dark. Headlights from oncoming cars along Fifth Avenue played across the stray water drops on the Explorer's windshield. Cleared by the wipers, they pooled at the edges and began their windblown wiggle. Annie, his five-year-old poet, called them dancing water worms.

"What?" Melissa snarled, lifting the earphone from her Discman. Her head kept pace with the music's insistent cadence.

"Nothing," Christensen said, flustered. He'd nearly forgotten she was in the car. "Didn't realize I was talking out loud."

His older daughter rolled her eyes, then shut him out again. She clamped the headphones back on and tapped out a beat on her knees with the fat drumsticks she'd brought from band practice. He wished he knew more about her musical tastes. The CD case read "Nine Inch Nails," but the band name meant nothing to him.

He touched his daughter's shoulder, and she lifted the earpiece again. "I need to stop at the Giant Eagle to get stuff for dinner," he said. "It'll just take a few minutes, and we've got time. As long as we pick up Annie from Mrs. Taubman's by six."

"Whatever."

"We also need to talk about something," he said, trying to seem upbeat.

Melissa stabbed the Discman's stop button with her middle finger, then pulled the headphones off, clearly unhappy with the prospect of having to conduct a conversation. She stared straight ahead. "What?"

"Something came up at work that may keep me pretty busy for a while. One night a week for now, a couple evenings a week if it works out. So we're going to have to figure a way to get Annie home from day care, you home from school on band practice days, and then how to get your dinners on the nights when I can't be there."

"I'll just stay at Jerilyn's after practice," she said. "I can eat there, too. Her mom's cool."

"No, see, that doesn't solve the problem. Someone needs to walk Annie home from day care and get her fed. And I'm going to need your help on that."

Melissa finally turned toward him, if only to glare. "You need me to do it, in other words."

"Afraid so."

"That means I have to ride the bus with all the dorks."

"It's only Thursdays, for now. And if it's on a band practice day, you can always get a ride home with somebody. So it shouldn't be that bad."

Christensen splashed the Explorer through a flooded gutter and into the supermarket parking lot. Though he'd maintained an even calm in his voice, he realized his stress level had risen when a speed bump rocked them back in their seats. He slowed to a more reasonable parking-lot speed.

"It's not something I can help. And I'm not sure how long it'll last."

She turned away again and stared out the windshield. "You just want me to watch Annie so you can go out with Brenna," she said. "Why don't you just keep doing it in Mom's loft so I don't get screwed, too."

Christensen wheeled into a parking space, tires squealing, and crushed a shopping cart against the concrete base of a light pole. He backed off two feet, but said nothing. He thought he saw his daughter smiling as he shoved the gearshift into park and yanked the emergency brake. She knew exactly where his buttons were, and exactly how hard to push them. He turned the engine off and sat, knowing he'd explode if he tried to talk.

He reached for Melissa's arm as she lifted the earphones to her head. She looked down at his shaking hand, then directly at him. Her smirk disappeared, and he saw real fear in her eyes. Maybe she knew she'd gone too far. He took a deep breath. Another. And another, until he felt back in control.

"I'd like an apology," he said.

"Sorry." She shrugged. "You really wasted that cart."

"No, a real apology. You don't need to assault me like that. And this has nothing to do with Brenna. There's a special client I need to see, someone the police asked me to work with. Evenings are the best time for him."

She pulled her arm away. "I'm sorry, okay?"

With the wipers stilled, the wet windshield began to twinkle with reflected lights, reds and whites, from cars moving around the lot. Christensen unbuckled his seat belt. Maybe now was the time to talk about their real problem.

"I miss your mom," he said.

Melissa sniffed indifferently and unbuckled her own seat belt. He wanted to talk, to confront the thing that for two years had stood between them like a wall. But he felt the opportunity disappearing as she pulled her arm away and reached for the door latch.

"I did what Mom wanted, what she needed me to do at that point. And you're still punishing me for it."

"Yeah, well," Melissa said. "You made your choice."

The car door slammed, and he watched her jump puddles until she stood in the fluorescent frame of the grocery store door waiting, oddly, for him to catch up. His hands still shook, less from rage now than from an overwhelming sense of frustration. He was losing his oldest daughter because, in her mind, he had killed her mother. Forget the mercy of that decision. Forget the shades of gray that even the district attorney had been forced to acknowledge. Forget his own emotional devastation in the wake of Molly's death. He had killed her mother. And he was now involved with the woman who'd entered their lives on the very day that Molly died. So, in purely clinical terms, Christensen understood his daughter's reaction: Her mother was gone, and her father was trying too soon to fill the hole in their lives. But understanding it didn't make the gulf between them any less terrifying.

He stepped down into a puddle, slammed the door, and checked the Explorer's unscathed front bumper. The shopping cart hadn't fared as well. It was standing but unstable, its wheelbase radically compressed. He tipped it over and leaned it against the base of the light pole.

"Need a fresh cart?" Melissa asked as he approached. Her smile seemed less hostile than mischievous, so he smiled back.

"I really crushed it."

"No heroic measures," she said, then turned and pushed through the automatic doors into the store.

The aisles were empty, surprisingly so for this time of day. Christensen had never got the hang of the sort of leisurely weekend shopping that Molly used to do. She'd spend hours among Strip District produce vendors every Saturday morning, looking for deals, buying in bulk, enjoying the sensory experience of the city's chaotic warehouse marketplace. He, by contrast, was always fighting predinner crowds at the supermarket, scavenging for that evening's meal.

Melissa stopped at the dairy case. She loaded a half-gallon of 1 percent milk and a brick of cheddar cheese, then started pulling yogurt containers from an upper shelf. Christensen absently chose one from the cart and looked it over. The brand name, Yo-ssert, triggered something visceral.

"Wasn't this stuff recalled?" he said.

Melissa stopped, but offered only a blank stare until interrupted by a short young man who was stocking the shelves.

"New shipment," he said, carving open another Yo-ssert

carton and stowing his retractable knife in a back pocket of his jeans. "Check the date. We took all the others off the shelf a few weeks ago."

Melissa resumed her selections, unconcerned, clearly partial toward blueberry. Christensen set the container down, then picked it back up. He rolled it in his hand, initially to check the expiration date. But he found himself trying to imagine it as an instrument of death. What had Downing said about the Greene County case? The killer injected cyanide through the lid? He turned the container right side up and examined its colored foil top. A puncture in the black lines of the printed Yo-ssert corporate logo would be invisible to all but the most discerning eye.

The chill Christensen felt didn't come from the refrigerated display case. It was a Bambi-in-the-meadow feeling, a sudden and palpable sense of danger that surged through him like an electric current. He looked around, wondering if someone was watching, but he was alone in the dairy aisle. Melissa had moved on to baked goods.

As he walked, the yogurt still in his hand, he scanned the shelves, seeing the market in a way that was less familiar than frightening. He'd never thought much about product packaging, assuming manufacturers made everything tamper-proof after the Tylenol poisonings in, what, 1982? But what was tamper-proof? That cardboard half-gallon of milk seemed pretty vulnerable. All those tucks and folds where someone could hide a needle prick. How would milk react to the poison? Why did only the expensive brand of cottage cheese include a tamper-proof plastic seal around the container's rim? What color was liquefied cyanide? Clear? If cottage cheese already was curdled, would a fatal dose of clear poison make any difference in the way it looked? What about sour cream?

He was holding a carton of eggs, wondering what kind of damage a syringe might do to an eggshell, when Melissa asked, "Raisin bread okay?"

Jesus. His heart was pounding.

"Fine," he said.

She dropped it into the cart. "I think we have a coupon,"

she said. "We already have a dozen eggs at home, don't we?"

In the condiments and sauces aisle, Christensen's mind shifted to vacuum-sealed pop-up lids. Great theory, but during a predinner rush, who'd really notice if their Ragú jar had already been opened? And would some hungry bachelor really let it stop him from dumping the thick red sauce into a pan after a long day at work? What did cyanide taste like? Would it be noticeable in a heaping spoonful of, say, Grey Poupon? If someone got it into a jar of pickles, would a single pickle absorb enough for a lethal dose?

By the time he reached the end of the aisle, his eyes were those of a killer in search of opportunity. Reaching into another refrigerated display, he opened a tub of margarine and closed it again. No safety seal. And no one saw him. How long would it take? He did the same with a container of off-brand salsa. The pudding snacks Annie loved had foil lids just like the ones on Yo-ssert containers. If someone wanted to inject something into a packaged hot dog, how hard would it be?

The meat case stretched across the back of the store. Chicken breasts, pot roasts, hams, sausage. A micron of plastic wrap was all that stood between them and someone with a syringe. To his left, a freezer case. Ice cream! He imagined a calculating killer prying the lid from one of the round containers of vanilla, sprinkling in white powder like some demented Jack Frost, and calmly putting the lid back on. It wouldn't be any more complicated than opening a carton to check for cracked eggs.

Melissa had disappeared. He checked the next aisle. Lightbulbs, diapers, and baby food. No sign of her, but he thought back to the harried days when the girls were younger, to countless scenes of him and Molly pushing mush into one tiny mouth or the other. Would either of them have noticed during the feeding frenzy if a jar of strained carrots didn't open with a reassuring *shhhtk*? Or if a cardboard apple juice box had a tiny hole near the top of one side?

He passed a young man, probably a student, and he

thought again of Sonny Corbett, of Sonny's father, of 1986. Suddenly there weren't academic questions about product packaging. These were questions that begged for reassuring answers, considering what the young man in his office the day before may actually have seen; considering the psychopath, whoever he was, that still walked free. How deeply could he allow himself, and his children, to be pulled into Grady Downing's Primenyl investigation?

The grim possibilities drew him down aisle 4, even though Melissa wasn't there. Bottled water in plastic jugs. Cooking oils in plastic bottles. He picked a kids' fruit snack from the shelf, wondering how its "squishy center" might be manipulated. Ten feet farther, he stopped again. The tiny jars of antichoke hearts, asparagus, and other marinated vegetables did not have pop-up safety lids, even the name brands. He unscrewed the lid from a classic glass ketchup bottle and peered in, finding nothing between him and the contents. Up and down the aisles, Christensen imagined the worst.

Melissa was in produce, bagging oranges. Fruit and vegetables were stacked in neat and colorful piles all around him. He usually lingered here, savoring the fresh smells, but his mind was racing. Packaged products were one thing, he thought, but my God, how easy would it be to poison an orange? Or a tomato? How difficult to get cyanide into a watermelon or cantaloupe? How much poison could a single grape hold? Enough to take a life?

"Do you need more oranges?" Melissa asked as he approached.

He answered without context or explanation, a reflex he couldn't control. "Too risky here. And no grapefruit, either."

Melissa seemed confused.

"I'll get a case in the Strip," he added, trying to recover.

Melissa rolled her eyes, then picked up three large oranges, placed them into a plastic produce bag with a dramatic flourish, and twirled the bag shut. She tied its neck into a tight knot, dropped it into the cart, and stalked off toward checkout. Christensen followed, mentioning to an assistant manager he saw along the way that he'd be glad to replace the cart that lay mangled outside. The manager told him not to worry, but Christensen's mind already was on other things.

The phone rang a dozen times before someone answered, "Homicide."

"Grady Downing, please."

Christensen drained the last of his coffee. Without Annie, dinner would have been a slow-motion conversational disaster. She kept him laughing, explaining that the photographs she'd carefully clipped from a magazine at Mrs. Taubman's that afternoon were from a publication featuring "mostly girls, makeup, and sparkly things." *Cosmo,* he guessed from the cleavage, although Mrs. Taubman hardly fit the magazine's demographics. Annie presented the clippings of lipsticks, anorexic models, and garish jewelry with a reverence he found odd, especially in a child also enthralled by Rambo.

Melissa, on the other hand, ate in silence, resuming her brooding even though he apologized for his odd behavior in the produce section. Paranoia had got the best of him in the store, but even now he couldn't shake it completely. Maybe Downing could help.

"Investigations."

"Grady? Jim Christensen. You're in? Aren't you guys always out stomping around crime scenes, chasing perps, that sort of thing?"

"Yeah, well. Slow week. Sonny ever call you?"

"Met with him yesterday, believe it or not. Interesting kid," Christensen said, then waited.

"So?" Downing asked.

"Very casual. Didn't talk about anything significant. But I'm going to try to get him to meet again next week. If it goes well, I hope we'll start getting together a couple times a week. I'm trying to work my schedule around it."

He waited for some reaction from Downing, but heard none. "You're right," he continued, "the hand thing is pretty odd. So maybe I can help. We'll just see where it goes from there."

The detective sighed. "So you don't think I'm totally off-base?"

"Do I see any big red flags? No. But I read his file and felt him out a bit. There are indicators I'd like to explore. I just want to make sure we give him every chance to deal with things, if that's what he needs."

"Never mind what everybody says," Downing said, "I knew you weren't such an asshole."

"Thanks so much," Christensen said. "But I've got to be honest. I'm not willing to take the kind of risks I've taken with you in the past. If one of your suspects goes after me now, I leave two orphans. What if Tataglia had had better aim last year? The girls would have lost me just a year after losing Molly."

"Totally different situation," Downing said.

"Bullshit, Grady. There's a particularly vicious mass murderer out there somewhere. If you're right, he's still operating. And he's smart. His victims die without ever knowing what hit them. I went nuts in the grocery store tonight thinking of all the ways he could get me or the kids if he decided to try. If you weren't a cop, would you want to be involved?"

Downing seemed to consider the question. "Do you think you weigh more or less after you fart?" he said finally. "Think about it before you answer."

"I'm serious."

"I think more, since methane is lighter than air. Makes your body like a hot-air balloon, you know. Once you let 'er rip, I think you'd weigh more."

"Goddamnit, Grady. Are you listening?"

"Whoa, whoa, whoa, Chickie, lighten up," he said. "But you're right. I suppose there's some exposure on your part, talking to his kid and all."

"Exposure?"

"You know. Risk. But not much."

"Explain."

"I've seen the report the FBI profilers down at Quantico did on the Primenyl killer," Downing said. "Dead ringer for Corbett, by the way. More important, it says randomness is his thing. That's the thrill. So it'd be completely out of character for him to fuck with people like us. He's not motivated by revenge or because he's afraid of getting caught. He's got some other agenda. So I really don't think it's an issue."

"Not an issue," Christensen repeated. It wasn't the reassurance he'd hoped for, but Downing was probably right.

"Don't just blow me off, Grady."

"Got to, sport. Gotta run. Some crackhead down in the Hill just blew a big hole in his dealer. Sent him and two handfuls of cash through a second-floor window onto Wylie Avenue. Quite a party when he landed. Somebody's gotta clean up the trash."

Drug killings in the Hill District. Rookie stuff. "Who'd *you* piss off?" Christensen said. During the long silence, he remembered Brenna's story about Downing's fall from grace during Primenyl. He suddenly regretted the words, knew they must have cut deep.

"You'll keep me posted on Sonny, then?" Downing said.

"Sure, Grady," Christensen said. "Listen, I didn't mean—" But Downing had already hung up.

11

The Maverick coasted down the Interstate 79 exit ramp, stopping finally in the loose gravel beside a peeling chamber of commerce sign: "Work where you must, but live and shop in Ridgeville!" The driver studied it a moment, snorting when he was done.

"Sure you want out here?"

Sonny fumbled for the door handle, which came off in his hand as the door sprung open. He handed it to the driver, hoisted his daypack onto one shoulder, and scratched the head of the panting hound in the backseat. Then he pointed to the southbound entrance ramp just across the road. "Appreciate the ride. You can get back on right there."

He watched until the car wheezed up the ramp, trailing vapor in the 40-degree air, and was gone. No, he didn't want out here. Hitching rides was bad enough, but this place flat-out scared him. Ridgeville was dominated by Webber Industries, the town's biggest employer, operating out of an industrial terror of a plant just across the interstate. All rusting metal vats and screeching noise and random puffs of chemical-smelling vapor. He recognized the company's Pegasus logo from the Pitt chem lab stockroom, and for the first time it occurred to him that his mother had lived much of her life in the shadow of the country's most frequently indicted industrial chemical producer.

To Sonny's left sat one of Ridgeville's other booming enterprises, a drive-thru beer distributorship. The owner of Boboli's Beer Haus never met an ID card he didn't like. Sonny stopped to marvel again at the ballsiness of it all—a line of beater cars lined up from the loading dock into the street, a cocky teenager behind the wheel of each one. On Saturday mornings like this, the line never seemed to shrink.

The path to his mother's apartment ran along Hartwell Creek, a twenty-yard-wide gash of rust-colored water that ran right past the Webber plant and never froze, no matter how cold the weather got. Sonny noticed, but it didn't seem to bother anyone else. The plant was all the town had left after I-79 started carrying most of the traffic past, rather than through, Ridgeville. But Sonny saw the creek water with the eyes of an open-water swimmer, and swimmers had a phrase for water like that: death soup.

In the distance, maybe half a mile beyond Webber, the front face of Borman State Hospital rose like a redbrick tombstone. The lawn was well-barbered in summer—with dazed patients always shuffling along behind lawn mowers— but the grass had turned crisp and brown with the early frost. What in August usually looked like a stately old plantation seemed, under the threatening sky, like the Hollywood version of a mental hospital, which it pretty much was.

He'd visited his mother there once during her six-month stay, but only once. A social worker brought him out on a Sunday a month or so after his dad left, a couple weeks after David's funeral. He remembered because it was the day he realized, as they drove out through Borman's wrought-iron gate and away from a woman who didn't seem to recognize him, that he was alone. He'd never felt the same about Ridgeville again.

Until then, his impression of his mother's hometown was shaped by her stories of growing up there, rosy small-town memories she told often and fondly when he was a kid. The Borman hospital in those stories was just a place she played, the biggest yard in town, a place with a secret tire swing and a creek and a rope just long enough to reach deep water. That Borman, the one his mother talked about, sounded like a kids' paradise. The Borman just ahead, the one she wouldn't talk about anymore, had bars on the windows and smelled like piss and disinfectant. Sonny remembered that much from one visit eight years ago, that and the vivid sounds of corralled madness.

The path veered left, then plunged into a thicket of dead blackberry bushes and scrub oak. Branches scratched his bare arms, but he didn't try to clear the way. Best to push on, do his duty, then hitch back across town before the whole day was shot. He came out in a clearing just twenty yards from the entrance to Lakeview Pointe Estates, apartments with no lake view, pointe, or estates. Sonny took a deep breath, then walked up the crumbling driveway, stepping carefully to keep the pea-gravel out of his shoes.

The curtains of his mother's second-floor apartment were drawn. Maybe he'd misunderstood. Or maybe she was out of medicine again and depressed. As he knocked, he noticed that her car wasn't in its usual spot. Where could she have gone? The drapes suddenly parted and his mother squinted out, offering a smile and a timid wave. Sonny waited while she undid the door's various dead bolts and chain locks.

"Saturday already?" she said. She pulled a strand of gray-streaked brown hair from in front of her face and tucked it behind her ear. "Oh, Sonny. I haven't cleaned. I haven't cooked."

"Mom, it's okay."

She waved him off, then started pacing, arms folded, hands cupping her opposite elbows. She was wearing a long flannel nightgown underneath a knee-length Penguins jersey, topped by the peacoat he bought her for $12 at a Goodwill store in East Liberty. "I didn't get any groceries. I haven't been hungry," she said. "So I don't have anything for you to eat. I'm just so tired all the time. God, it's good to see you. Look at me. I'm such a mess. My teeth aren't brushed. They're so yellow. I don't know why. I brush and brush but nothing helps."

She always seemed small when she was depressed. Her narrow shoulders rolled forward, her head dipped, her voice became little more than a stage whisper. Her eyes drifted, caught on things that didn't matter, then drifted again. He thought she was pretty, even on bad days like this. When he was a kid, she wore her long hair in a tight bun anchored by a single crossways chopstick—something he'd always found exotic and wonderful. Now her hair was dirty and unbrushed, and she seldom saw the point in getting dressed. He knew enough about mental illness to understand, but affection isn't easy after being stranded for five years in foster care. Duty was the only thing that brought him here on Saturday mornings.

Sonny gently moved her aside so he could get into the apartment. It was like walking into a desert, dry and hot. "Where's your car, Mom?"

She shrugged, then started to dead-bolt the door. The room smelled like the stale air inside a basketball, but with a trace of tobacco. The Road Runner and Wile E. Coyote carried on their endless chase on the tiny TV in the living room. Sonny turned down the volume and adjusted the antenna. He passed his hand over the electric heat register under the apartment's single front window. It was blowing hard. The thermostat needle was pegged at 85.

"Did you loan your car to Mr. Balkin again?"

"Can I get you some Gatorade? I still have Gatorade. I like the strawberry kind."

Sonny put his hand on her shoulder, but she wouldn't look at him. "Mom, does Mr. Balkin have your car again?"

"He's a nice man. You know him, don't you? Lives over in C? Longish hair? Very nice, really. Helps me out with things. He changed one of those fluorescent bulbs in the kitchen the other day just because I asked him."

Real nice man, Sonny thought. Borrowed her car for an afternoon last month and kept it two weeks. Brought it back, no apologies, with an empty tank and a crushed left taillight. He didn't admit it happened during one of his low-grade parking-lot drug deals until Sonny threatened to call the cops, and only then did he peel off five twenties to pay for it. Sonny used the money for her groceries and put that month's disability check into her bank account.

Seeing her treated like a doormat still bothered him, but

it had been that way as long as Sonny could remember. She seemed to bring out the worst in people who prey on the weak, people like his dad. At the end, he was such a bastard. Sonny flashed on a scene: A Sunday afternoon. Summer. The Jancey Street house. He and his brother sitting, bruised and crying, in the window seat of an upstairs bedroom. All they'd done was ask him for another dog, but he'd been drinking and it set him off. When he was done with them he turned, as usual, on their mother. From above, they watched the torture carry into the front yard. His father's twisted laugh. The neighbors' dumbstruck faces. Their mother on all fours, still in her nightgown, barking each time his bare foot landed on her rump.

Sonny checked the refrigerator. She still had two bottles of insulin left, but she hadn't been to the grocery store since he'd gone the Saturday before. At least she'd eaten most of what he bought. She was down to ketchup, pickles, bread, and Gatorade, which for some reason she considered essential.

"Mr. Balkin's taking advantage of you, Mom. He knows you won't do anything about the car until I come to get it back. Tell him no next time, okay?"

She smoothed her hair again. "He says he needs it for his business. I just use it to run around in. Pick up little things, run to the pharmacy, that kind of stuff. So I don't mind, really. It doesn't matter."

Sonny scanned the kitchen cupboard where she kept her medicine. The lithium bottle was empty. Her needlepoint frame and a mound of fabric sat on the counter just below. Ivy leaves in two shades of green thread were taking shape on yet another dish towel. He already had a dozen.

"You need to eat, Mom," he said. "And I need the car to get to the store and back. If I have to walk, I can only carry a couple bags."

She unfolded her arms and fingered the blue buttons on the peacoat. Then she folded them and started pacing again. "I go to the store if I need something. I do. Just jump in the car and go—"

Sonny cut her off. "You need your pills and your insulin,

Mom. The refrigerator's almost empty. You keep giving away your car to that prick across the way. We've talked about all this before."

She turned her back. "Strawberry Gatorade's the best, don't you think? I took a bottle to Dr. Root. He likes it too."

Sonny leaned forward, resting his elbows on the Formica countertop. No point in talking about it again.

"How is Dr. Root?" he asked.

His mother smiled. When she did, the outside corners of her eyes dipped, giving her face a sad, fallen look. "I think he's crazy," she said.

"Then you're even."

She looked hurt. Her eyes fixed for a second on his, long enough to register damage, then they were off again.

"It was a joke, Mom. Come on." Sonny struggled to recover. "Hey, I'm seeing a shrink, too."

Her pacing slowed, then stopped. She fingered the hem of the Penguins jersey, then stopped that, too. Suddenly, his mother was motionless. It was like watching a mime's version of a toy robot with dying batteries.

"Why?" she said, her attention suddenly diverted by the bread crumbs on the countertop. She'd probably eaten nothing but toast for a few days. She brushed the crumbs into the oversized sink, which was full of unwashed, unmatched plates, bowls, and cups, and turned on the water. When it ran hot, she squeezed some blue Dawn in a slow figure eight over the pile.

"Your mother is so disgusting," she said. "So you're seeing someone?"

"No big deal," he said. "My hands still bother me sometimes. Nobody else has figured it out, so why not? That's all."

"I know a lot of doctors," she said.

"He's not at Borman, Mom. He's down at Pitt. And he's just a counselor or a psychologist or something."

Her gaze held his until he looked away. He opened the refrigerator and peered in. He wasn't thirsty, but he rinsed a plastic cup in the hot-water stream and filled it with reddish Gatorade, then set the half-empty bottle on the counter.

"What's his name?" she asked.

"Christensen. Jim, I think. Know him?"

She shook her head, face blank. "What do you talk about?"

"Nothing much so far," he said. "Swimming. Growing up. He talks a lot about his kids. It's real casual."

She shoved her hands into the peacoat pockets. He couldn't remember seeing her so still.

"There's good doctors and bad doctors," she said, her laugh strong and steady. "We've probably seen them all."

Sonny smiled. She didn't joke often, even before things got bad. But she had a point. During her time at Borman and the years of therapy since, she'd probably talked to dozens. And it seemed like the county hauled him into the Children's Services office once a month during his years in foster care to talk to one psychologist or another.

"Yeah, between you, me, and David——," he said, then stopped. He hadn't thought much about his older brother lately, and it made him sad. He turned his back to his mother and refilled his cup.

"David was weak," she said. She was tugging a pack of Camels from the peacoat pocket when Sonny turned around. The cup slipped from his hand to the floor, exploding in a strawberry-red gusher that soaked his feet and sprayed the kitchen cabinets.

"Shit," he said, scrambling for the dishrag hanging from the faucet.

His mother leaned back against the counter, watching him wipe up the puddles. "Make sure you get it good," she said. "I won't have ants."

He rinsed the rag twice to clean up the sticky mess. As he finished, he heard the crinkle of the cigarette pack. He looked up just as she pulled one out and retrieved a disposable lighter from the other coat pocket. Sonny flinched at the smell of smoke. His chest tightened.

"Could you not do that?" he said. He was breathing hard, still on his hands and knees. His mother just smiled. He stood up. His throat burned. He felt dizzy. The cigarette glowed brighter as she inhaled deep and slow.

Fuck this. He had to get out, out into the cold air, away from her. Get your own car back. Get your own medicine and groceries. When were you ever there for me? But even as he took the stairs two at a time to the ground floor and ran back toward the interstate, he knew he'd be back next Saturday. It wasn't until he stuck out his thumb on the I-79 entrance ramp that he realized the red-stained rag was still in his hand.

12

Downing pushed through the front door of the Waynesburg PD and lit a cigarette, blowing his first drag like an exclamation point into the overcast early afternoon murk. Fucking amateurs. They'd done some decent work with the physical evidence, but they couldn't see the big picture. Couldn't see the connections. Didn't understand a mind like Ron Corbett's.

How old was that investigator, Ramsey, anyway? Maybe thirty, tops. Probably still chugging beers at his fraternity and skipping crime-scene-procedures classes in 1986. The latest killing was a baffling mystery to him; to Downing, it was a familiar story. After their morning-long conversation, Downing was not only sure Corbett had poisoned the woman, but that the bastard was getting smarter about it.

He wedged himself into the Ford's driver seat and pulled the small spiral notebook from the inside pocket of his jacket. Flipping to the section he'd headlined "Insertion Method," he studied his notes while he peeled another grapefruit. How simple. Elegant, really. Insert the needle in a dark part of the printed foil yogurt lid, inject liquid hydrogen cyanide, seal the hole with an invisible dab of clear polyurethane, return it to the store.

By contrast, penetrating the triple-sealed Primenyl bottles in 1986 had been major surgery. But even then, Corbett was smart. He'd made a basic assumption about protective product packaging—that people check what they're supposed to check. A pre-1986 Primenyl bottle held upright in the hand seemed secure enough, the bottle's mouth double-sealed in foil and protective plastic, then sealed again inside a glued display box.

So Corbett worked backwards, razoring open the glued *bottom* flap of the boxes to remove the plastic bottles. So much for seal one. Then he took an X-Acto knife and cut dime-sized holes in the bottle bottoms. After inserting a loaded capsule, he superglued the plastic piece back to the bottle, then simply sanded the incision smooth. Who'd ever suspect as long as the seals at the bottle's mouth weren't broken? Then it was just a matter of putting the bottle back into the box, regluing the bottom flap, and putting his little time bomb back on a store shelf.

Once Downing and the other investigators had understood what was happening, Corbett's technique was as obvious as a red flag. But it was effective. Not a single victim suspected.

Downing remembered all the hype about "tamper-proof" packaging after Tylenol in 1982. When Primenyl happened four years later, the drug companies threw up their hands and quietly started using the term "tamper-resistant." What else could they do?

Downing rummaged through his glove compartment for the Greene County map. Even on that, Corbett's community of choice was a speck at the end of an unpaved road. And since Downing hadn't been to Outcrop in at least a year, he wasn't exactly sure where to turn to get up into the hills. There were definite risks in nosing around on his own. If the locals found out, they'd accuse him of big-footing their doomed little investigation. If DeLillo found out, Downing figured he'd be retiring sooner rather than later. Fuck it. It's my day off, he thought. He crushed his smoke in the ashtray and started the car.

Waynesburg was like a lot of other small college towns in Pennsylvania—a pretty campus surrounded by fast-food joints surrounded by crappy off-campus apartments and run-down rental houses owned by townies who'd moved out. Here and there were the imposing fraternity houses, which on the outside looked like colonial mansions. Inside, usually, they looked like the path of a tornado.

The road that took him off the pavement was in much worse shape than last time, little more than a rutted goat path that had been the access road to a strip mine worked out years ago. He'd been here a few times, just to keep tabs on Corbett, but he didn't remember much detail beyond a general impression of the place as a grim pocket of rural poverty. Corbett's state disability income—a stress claim, probably bogus—no doubt made him the richest guy in town. The Ford bumped along, its ball joints creaking and moaning like a haunted-house sound track.

A quarter-mile in, he passed a rusted trailer on the right. In a small front window plastered with UMW stickers, the paper-thin curtains suddenly parted, then closed again. What looked like an outhouse stood about ten yards beyond the trailer, as did a small mound of coal and a satellite dish. The Home Shopping Club comes to Appalachia.

The road dropped sharply, then rose. Downing steered across a one-lane wooden bridge above a small frozen creek, then into a stretch where he was surrounded on both sides by snow-covered pines. It was almost pretty, but it didn't last. The road opened into what looked like a bomb crater the size of a city block—the mine—then veered right and ran along the mine's perimeter for another quarter-mile.

Downing stopped the car. About a hundred yards away, a dozen houses stood in two tidy rows along each side of the road, an outhouse behind each. Smoke rose from a metal vent pipe in every roof, and plastic garbage bags were taped as insulation in most of the windows. He backed up past the T-intersection he'd just passed and into an open area hidden from the houses by a small mountain of gray slag.

He knew which house was Corbett's. He'd spent a summer night crouched in a dense grove of pines just behind it, watching through an open bedroom window as Corbett and a guy he recognized as Corbett's next-door neighbor took turns with the neighbor's peroxide-nightmare of a wife. When he wasn't part of the humpfest, Corbett kept busy videotaping the action and draining most of a bottle of Jim Beam. Real high-society stuff, but something kept Downing there longer than he really needed to stay.

He took off his shoes and pulled on his snow boots. A trail that started just behind him circled wide of the houses and ended near the clump of trees. Even during the day he could probably get within twenty yards of Corbett's house without being noticed. He just wanted to see how the old boy was doing, see what car he was driving these days, see if he'd made any new friends or picked up any new hobbies. He definitely didn't want to get in Corbett's face, not like in 1986. He'd paid too high a price for that luxury. This time he planned to work the perimeter quietly until it was time to pull the trigger, so to speak. He'd even let the locals take credit.

The trail was where he remembered it, and Downing climbed up a steep bank and followed the frozen path. The cold air should have been refreshing, but the sulfur smell of burning coal stung his nose. If living near an abandoned strip mine had any benefits, cheap heat had to be one. There was usually enough coal left open and uncollected to keep a few small furnaces burning for years.

Downing stumbled on an exposed root as he entered the clump of pines just behind Corbett's house, and was startled how loud his whispered *Fuck!* seemed in the surrounding silence. He'd have to be more careful. He wasn't worried about being seen—thank God for evergreens—but hadn't considered the possibility of being heard. He leaned around the sturdiest trunk, looking for some sign of life.

The house hadn't seen paint in decades. What remained of the last coat was chipped and chalky, its original color uncertain. The entire structure leaned at the same angle as the outhouse, like they'd been precision-engineered to look like hell. But someone was in there. Smoke trickled from the roof vent. The snow between the back door and the coal pile was worn into an icy path. A fresh carcass hung by its neck from a rusted metal pole beside the coal pile—a small deer, skinned and gutted. The snow underneath it was pink, but the deer had been cleaned somewhere else. Its eyes were half closed, not wide with terror, like it had been expecting death. The protruding tongue was the only feature that ruined a look of utter calm.

Around the left side of the house, Downing could see the rear quarter of a pale yellow car parked around front. Not the same '79 Mercury that Corbett was driving the last time he was here, but he was sure Corbett hadn't moved. He still got his mail at the same post-office box in Ruff Creek.

Downing shivered. He wasn't dressed for this. He pulled his overcoat closed, buttoned it all the way to the top, and cinched the belt. In the bottom of the pockets, he found a forgotten pair of worn leather gloves. They weren't lined, but they'd do. This would have to be quick. He'd love to watch Corbett come and go, but that wasn't going to happen, at least not today. If he could just verify Corbett was still here, he'd be satisfied.

After ten minutes of nothing, he made his way toward the house, hiding first behind the shithouse, then the coal mound, his heavy breathing the only sound. The back windows were too high, and he didn't see anything to stand on. Plus, the windows were covered in black plastic. That was good, in a way. While he couldn't see in, at least Corbett couldn't see out.

The back-door window still had glass. If he could get up the three concrete steps unnoticed, he could at least get a quick look inside. He waited another couple minutes.

Bent over, staying low, he moved quickly from the coal pile to the back-door steps. All three were covered by compressed layers of snow. They looked icy, so Downing skipped the bottom two and stepped with some effort onto the top step. The ice creaked, loud, as his weight settled. Shit. How loud?

Downing leaned against the house, still bent at the waist, keeping his head well below the window. He was breathing hard, and told himself that he was too old for this stuff. The only sound inside was the television, a game show. Probably toward the front of the house, since the bedroom and the

kitchen were toward the back. He lifted his head and peeked
through a corner of the back-door window.

The kitchen was neat, filled with garage-sale castoffs.
The refrigerator had seen better days, and the oven door of
the battered electric range was wide open, probably on for
heat. The one chair at the small table meant Corbett
probably still lived alone. Steam rose from the percolator
coffeepot on top of the stove. Through the doorway into the
front room, Downing saw an overstuffed chair and a
footstool facing the television, which he could see was fed
by a rooftop antenna. The chair was empty.

Not good. Corbett was up and around. Probably in the
bedroom, maybe asleep, but how many other rooms could
there be in a mine-company shack like this? If Corbett was
sleeping, Downing figured, he could back down the steps
and retrace his track to the trees without being noticed. If he
wasn't asleep, goddamnit, where was he? Two doors, front
and back. He was vulnerable even if Corbett went out the
front.

"The fuck you doing?"

Downing froze with the click and slide of a pump-action
shotgun from the right corner of the house. That voice,
unnaturally deep, a cross between a hoarse baritone and a
heavy-equipment breakdown. The man sounded like an
idling Harley. Downing stood up but didn't turn around as
he raised his hands above his head. He'd stand a pretty good
chance, the Glock against a shotgun at close range. But it
didn't matter. His pistol was buttoned up tight inside his
overcoat.

"Hey, asshole, look at me."

Downing turned slowly. Corbett was sighting down the
barrel of a 12-gauge Winchester, about twenty feet away. He
wasn't aging well. Probably forty pounds heavier than he
was in 1986. A week-old beard, flecked with gray, started at
his trachea and covered his neck, chin, and face, nearly up
to his eyes. Same Nixonian hairline, and one of the worst
haircuts Downing had ever seen on a grown-up. A half-
finished cigarette dangled from his lips, waggling as he
talked and leaving a tracer trail of smoke in front of his face.

Big smile. "Say, aren't you Ron Corbett, the famous ex-pharmacist?"

Corbett stopped squinting, took a hard look, then put Downing back in his sights. "I could drop your body into one of the pits around here and nobody'd ever know," he said. "One of the nicer things about rural living. Tight little community like this, nobody trusts a stranger. You kill one for looking in your window, everybody understands."

"Ron. I'm hurt. I'm no stranger. Besides, half the cops in Pittsburgh know where I was headed today."

No reaction. Corbett took his finger off the trigger long enough to flick the smoldering butt of his cigarette at Downing. "I know who you are, asshole. Figured you'd be around again, but figured you'd at least be smart enough to bring a search warrant this time."

Downing imagined Corbett's knobby head exploding. Why had he buttoned his goddamned coat?

"I usually call first, just as a courtesy," Downing said. "But I was in the neighborhood and all. Old friends shouldn't need an invitation."

Corbett jerked the shotgun to one side, and the snow at the base of the steps exploded in a roar that echoed into the hills. Downing's left leg collapsed, like someone had knocked it out from under him with a baseball bat. He caught himself on the doorjamb before he fell, wondering how bad. He was still standing. Probably just a spray of pellets bouncing off the concrete. Corbett pumped another shell into the shotgun's chamber, aimed the barrel back at Downing's head.

Downing checked his leg, his fingers digging into the door frame. A dozen tiny holes in the rubber of his left boot. Felt like a deep bruise from the knee down. A man poked his head out the back door of the house behind Corbett. The guy with the willing wife.

"Need any help over there, Ray?"

"Got me a salesman," Corbett said. "You got any use for him?"

The man laughed. "Be needing some fertilizer come

spring," he said, then went back inside. Downing's leg was on fire, but he steeled himself. No fear. No fear.

"Ray?" Downing said. "Now what kind of upstanding citizen goes by a different name when he moves to a new neighborhood? Not trying to hide anything, are you, Ron?"

"Got more secrets than you'll ever know, asswipe, but you got nothing on me. Never did." Corbett shuddered, drew his shoulders tighter. All he had on was a sweatshirt and jeans. "You just like busting my balls."

Blood was seeping into Downing's sock. It wasn't bad, just a trickle. He could probably dig the pellets out himself.

"Oh, but we do have a problem, Ron," he said. "Just wanted to warn you, you know, as a public service. There's some bad yogurt going around. Nasty stuff. Just check those expiration dates carefully next time you're in the dairy aisle."

Corbett lowered the gun, but only a couple inches. For the first time, he opened both eyes. "Been almost six weeks since," he said. "Take you this long to find me?"

"Something I don't understand, Ron," Downing said. "Where *are* you getting the poison? Help me out here. There's three ways I can think of. But since you're not an authorized business, and you're not a college or university, I figure you're just stealing it from somewhere. Am I close?"

Corbett raised the gun again. "What size hole you think I could make in you from here?"

"And this one wasn't your style, either, Chickie."

"Because I didn't do nothing," he croaked. "Never did. You got no goddamned right." Corbett was trembling, probably more from rage than the cold. People make mistakes when they're mad, Downing thought. How far could he push?

"You're just not that smart," Downing said. "This one was slick, boy. Not like in '86. No messy powders. No clumsy capsules. Just got the liquid stuff and squirted it right through the top."

"You're so fucking ignorant," Corbett said. "You got no idea."

"Made '86 look downright inefficient. I'm no expert, Ron, but the yogurt thing seemed like a lot less work. And all that effort to get the capsules back into the bottles!"

"Fuck you."

"Practice makes perfect, I suppose."

"Fuck your mother," Corbett roared. "You think somebody who filled prescriptions for a living would waste their time carving up the bottoms of sealed bottles? There's lots easier ways."

Their eyes met and held. Downing couldn't suppress a smile. "Guess you're right, Ron. Maybe I've been too hasty." He lowered his right arm and extended his hand to Corbett. "Best friends?"

Corbett waved him away with the shotgun. "Get the hell off my property."

The euphoria carried Downing back to his car and down the goat path to blacktop. He stopped at the first pay phone he saw, outside a convenience store, and called his boss despite his second thoughts. He had to tell somebody.

"DeLillo around?" he asked. He was wearing one shoe; the left foot was too swollen. The sock that covered it left damp red tracks, and his pants leg was sticking to his calf.

"May I say who's calling?" The new receptionist, the councilman's niece with the tits.

"It's Grady Downing. Just put him on, would you?"

"Oh, hi! Thought you were off today."

"I am," he said. "Get DeLillo."

Papers rustling. "Your wife called looking for you. And the morgue. Doctor, um, Pungpreecha-whatever-it-is said you'd know what it was about."

"DeLillo, please. Now. Thanks."

"Hoo-boy. Must be important. This job is so cool, like *NYPD Blue*."

"Would you put goddamned DeLillo on the phone?"

He waited, ignoring the throbbing in his leg. The pellets had gone deep. He'd just have a nasty bruise once he dug them out.

"What do you want, Grady?" His ever-cheerful boss.

"Loose shoes, tight pussy, a warm place to shit. What more can a man ask, really?"

"Don't screw around. I'm in a meeting."

Downing cleared his throat, trying not to sound excited. "Just had some luck with Ron Corbett. Wanted to run it past you."

"Ron Corbett?"

"I told you yesterday I was coming down to see what the Waynesburg cops had on that product tampering a few weeks back. You said it was fine."

"I said what you do on your own time is your business, Grady, but what the fuck are you talking to Corbett for? You're supposed to steer way clear of him."

"Pure luck. Ran into him in Waynesburg."

"Like hell."

"Really. You want to hear this or not?"

"I don't know," DeLillo said. "Do I?"

Downing waited, let the anticipation build. "He knows how the loaded capsules got into the bottles in 1986. He knows about the holes in the bottoms."

"So?"

"So, since there was a total product recall, we never released that detail. It never got into the papers. How would he know?"

Downing waited, imagining that little bombshell rolling around in DeLillo's oversized head. An immense woman waddled from her car toward the convenience-store door, eyeing Downing's leg. He gave her his best smile.

"I'm not sure I like this," DeLillo said.

"What's not to like? It's an opening."

"For shit, an opening. You got this conversation on videotape, did you?"

"I told you I saw him in downtown Waynesburg," Downing said. "It's not like it was in an interrogation room."

"Tape recorder running? Witnesses?"

"No, goddamnit. It was a fucking street conversation. Why are you chopping me here?"

"Because you've got no business talking to Ronfucking

Corbett, that's why. I ought to take this to Kiger and get your ass fired, is what I ought to do."

He could hear DeLillo opening drawers, shuffling papers, agitated. "I don't get it," Downing said. "I bring you some pretty hairy information about the biggest unsolved case in the country and all you do is squeeze my goddamned balls?"

"First off, you got nothing," DeLillo said. "And God only knows how you got it. If the sheriff's people have anything that seems relevant, tell me and I'll pass it along to Pawlowski to check out. But otherwise stay out of this thing, you understand? You had your shot on this one."

The line went dead. Downing smashed the phone onto its cradle, then kicked a newspaper box so hard its door fell open. Searing pain. Wrong leg. A circle of damp red tracks around the pay phone as he walked it off. That son of a bitch. Pawlowski. Christ. Guy hadn't lifted a finger on Primenyl in two years.

Downing checked to see who was watching, grabbed the afternoon edition of the *Courier* from the box, and limped back to his car, ignoring the stare of the fat woman lumbering out of the store with a Slurpee. He scanned the headlines before starting the car, his eyes settling finally on the one above a story on the lower right corner of the front page: "Collapse of Boy, 11, Baffles Police."

KUHNTOWN—A Union Elementary fourth-grader collapsed this morning while eating a frozen confection as he walked to school, then later lapsed into a coma.

Kuhntown police described the incident as "suspicious" but offered no further comment about what may have caused Kevin Usher, 11, to suddenly fall ill.

Police say the boy was walking to school with his older sister, Staci, and eating a Popsicle-type snack shortly before 8 A.M. when he complained of a severe headache and dizziness. He appeared confused, his sister told police, then fell to the ground and began convulsing.

Downing closed his eyes, squeezed them shut with all his might to blind himself to the image already forming in his mind. But it came anyway: Carole face up beside her car, gazing through clouded eyes at the overhanging trees and the stars beyond and on into the black night above where she fell. He opened his eyes and read on:

Nearby residents heard Staci Usher's screams and called for an ambulance. Paramedics arrived within minutes and rushed her brother to Washington Medical Center, where he remains comatose.

Local police cordoned off the area and an investigator from the Waynesburg Police Department arrived shortly after 10:30 A.M. to collect evidence at the scene. The investigation is continuing.

Downing checked his county map. Something didn't make sense. Waynesburg was at least twenty miles from Kuhntown. He could see the local cops treating it like a crime scene until they knew more, but why would they call in an investigator from Waynesburg, and so soon? He already knew the answer. He pulled the notebook from his jacket pocket and checked a number, then fished into his pants pocket for another quarter as he hobbled back to the pay phone.

"Detective Ramsey, please," he said to the dispatcher.

"He's unavailable right now. Can I take a message?"

"Tell him it's Grady Downing, Pittsburgh PD, calling to follow up on our meeting this morning. I'll wait."

"But he's—"

"Just tell him."

Downing tested his leg. It was getting stiff. Ramsey picked up, humorless as ever.

"You had a busy morning after I left," Downing said.

The young detective volunteered nothing. "You heard about the incident in Kuhntown, then?"

"Read about it." Downing waited until he could wait no more. "So, you gonna tell me, or what?"

"Tell you what?"

"Come on, Chickie. The paper said they taped the scene and called you. They found something."

Downing waited again. "We're not sure if it's significant," Ramsey said finally. "And there's no reason now to think it is. We'll have a statement tomorrow morn—"

"Look, sport, you're not talking to John Q. here. I know you don't *have* to tell me what you found, but I'd like to think we can trust each other."

"Sorry. It's just—"

"Look, the paper said the kid was eating a Popsicle or something. What's up with that?"

"I can't, you know, details like that—"

"That's all I want to know. Really." Downing waited some more. "I've been in your shoes, you know. Maybe I can help."

Ramsey finally sighed. "You have kids?"

"One," Downing said. "Grown. I know what you mean, though. Cases like this hit awful close."

"Then you know how they do stuff, goofy things you just can't figure."

"Like?"

Downing heard riffling paper, the sound of someone flipping the pages of a spiral notebook. "Seven-thirty in the morning, right? Kid's headed to school, and it's what, thirty-five degrees outside? Cold as a well-digger's ass. And before heading out the door, his mom says he stops by the freezer and takes out a Squeezie Pop for the walk to school."

"One of those things on a stick?" Downing leaned his head against the pay phone as he waited through the long silence.

"That's the thing," Ramsey said. "It's different than a Popsicle, one of those push-up things in the cellophane sleeve."

Downing flashed back to lazy summer days spent squeezing frozen tubes of neon sugar water into his mouth. He remembered his daughter's joy whenever she saw a box of those flaccid, liquid-filled sleeves in Trix's grocery bag, how she hustled them into the freezer, waited for them to get solid enough to eat. An instant later, grim possibilities crowded the memories from his mind.

13

Winter was a wonder. On mornings like this, with the first feathery dusting of flakes piled a half-inch deep on his front steps, it made Pittsburgh downright beautiful. As Christensen stood shivering, still in his bathrobe, broom in hand, he allowed himself a moment of appreciation before sweeping it away.

His morning *Press* was still dry in its plastic wrap. A rare treat. It usually was soaked through and unreadable. A plastic bag dangling from the front doorknob diverted his attention from the headlines. It was printed with the *Press* logo and had a jumble of sample products inside. All along both sides of the street, identical bags hung from every front door. He brought it inside and laid it with the papers on the kitchen table, then returned to the bottom of the stairs.

"Let's go, ladies!" he shouted. "Last call for breakfast! It's show time!"

The second-floor bathroom door slammed, its report echoing through the quiet house. At least Melissa was up.

"Annie!" he shouted again. She'd been sitting in bed when he last saw her, groggy but awake, clutching Silkie with both hands and wondering aloud, "If a dinosaur and a giant fought, who would win?" "Get dressed so I can do your hair, okay?"

He heard her feet hit the floor, smiled, then returned to the kitchen to assess the options. The Honeycomb box was almost empty, enough for one helping for Annie. He'd long ago given up trying to enforce Molly's no-sugary-cereals rule. The only other cereal in the cupboard was his Fruit & Fibre, which Melissa detested. He thought he might assuage her with raisin toast, but a quick bread-box check ended that hope. Only the heels were left, and she hated heels. What else? *What else?* She was coming down the stairs.

"I thought I'd make some orange Danish," he said as she collapsed into a kitchen chair. "It'll take a little longer, but we're on time this morning for once. What do you say?"

"Cereal's fine," she said.

He lifted the Honeycomb box from the counter and gave it a shake.

"Oh," she said. "Great."

"Sorry."

"Raisin toast is fine."

"Sorry."

She surveyed the kitchen with a predator's eyes, which settled on the sample product bag. "I'm not hungry," she said, then stood up. "What's this?"

Christensen poured coffee, noticing too late that he'd grabbed the hand-painted "World's Best Mom" mug from the cupboard. His daughter noticed it too and looked away.

"Some promotional thing that came with the paper," he said, holding the cup out for an arm's-length inspection. "I remember the day you brought this home. I've seen coronations with less ceremony."

"Third grade," she said. A slight smile. "Mother's Day."

Neither spoke for a long time. Melissa's lips tightened and she started to get up, but he wanted desperately to keep talking.

"I think Mom used it every morning since," he said.

"Not lately."

Christensen set the mug on the tile countertop and crossed his arms. Enough. This had to be settled. "We need to talk, Melissa. There's too much we've left unsaid. I don't want to lose you, too."

She dumped the plastic bag onto the table and rummaged

through the product samples. A one-load box of laundry detergent, a small tube of toothpaste, a sample box of Frosted Wheat Squares cereal, dental floss, miniature glass bottles of shampoo and mouthwash. " 'Lose' is such a passive word," she said.

"Meaning?"

She ignored him, studying the sample cereal box. She tossed it aside and picked the shampoo and mouthwash from the pile. "Nothing."

"Meaning we didn't just 'lose' mom, right?" He knew he sounded defensive, but he couldn't stop himself. "Is that what you're saying?"

Melissa held his glare while bending slowly toward an electrical socket in the kitchen wall. He felt himself flinch as she pretended to pull a plug. His chest tightened and his eyes stung with sudden tears, which he wiped without embarrassment on the sleeve of his robe. He didn't try to hide the damage in his voice, either.

"That's so unfair."

"Life's not fair sometimes," she said. "That's what you said after the accident."

"People can be fair, though. People have brains. People are capable of logic and rational thought. And mercy and forgiveness."

Her face transformed into a cruel mask of wide-eyed insincerity. "Why would I need to forgive you? You said you only did what was right. I read it in the papers. I heard you say it on TV. Everybody saw you hug Brenna outside the jail when they let you go."

He felt sick. How might her reaction to Molly's death have differed without the storm of publicity and his high-profile arrest? It hadn't mattered to her cruelest schoolmates that he was released after two days, or that Brenna was the main reason he wasn't tried on a murder charge. He steadied himself on the edge of the counter.

"I hope—," he started to say, then stopped, trembling. "Just hope you never have to make a decision like I did."

Melissa looked away. "I'm taking a shower," she said,

nearly knocking over her little sister as she bolted up the stairs.

Annie sat down in her chair and laid the rumpled Silkie beside her cereal bowl. He couldn't remember ever craving a dose of unconditional love more than he did at that moment.

"A dinosaur, I think," she said.

He was still shaking from Melissa's assault, but he tried to smile as he poured her Honeycombs. Upstairs, the bathroom door slammed again.

"Not the giant?"

She shook her head decisively. "Dinosaurs have big teeth; giants just have clubs."

"Good point. When do I get my morning hug?"

Annie stretched her arms wide. He held her until she shoved him away and demanded milk for her cereal. "And pour it on this side," she ordered.

The pipes running behind the kitchen wall groaned as Melissa started her shower. Molly was the one who'd truly loved this old house; he'd simply learned to live with its idiosyncrasies.

"I wonder, though," he said, "do you think fighting is the best way for the giant and the dinosaur to solve their problems?"

Annie rolled her eyes.

The bathroom door opened as violently as it had closed, and the wooden stairs creaked. Melissa appeared at the kitchen door, hair soaking wet, her blue terry-cloth bathrobe gathered loosely at her waist. She was holding her left hand palm up, and Christensen could see from across the room that something was wrong. The skin was bright red at the center, and her fingers were curled in obvious pain.

"Dad?" she said, crossing the room to him. "It burns."

Purely by instinct, he turned the sink faucet on full cold and guided her hand beneath it. Her whole body shuddered as he held it there. The skin already was starting to blister.

"Was it the radiator in the bathroom? That thing gets hot as a griddle," he said. "Sometimes I hate this house."

Melissa shook her head, blinking back tears. "The shampoo," she said. "It started as soon as I poured some into my hand."

Christensen turned toward the kitchen table. Annie was using the tiny sample tube of toothpaste like a rocket, blasting off from the tablecloth.

"Don't touch that!" he said.

Annie dropped the tube, startled by the volume and urgency of his voice. The toothpaste splashed down in her cereal bowl. He struggled for composure as they all stared at the sample products scattered across the tabletop.

"Get away from the table, honey," he said. "There may be something wrong with that stuff. Keep your hand under the water, Melissa."

She was crying now, losing control, staring at the angry skin beneath the cascading water. Jesus. He snatched the handset from the wall phone and punched in 9-1-1. Annie backed away from the table and stood against the far wall, looking lost, Silkie in hand.

"It'll be okay," he said.

Two rings. Three rings.

"We'll be fine," he said. "It'll be okay. We'll be fine."

The operator answered. "Allegheny County Fire. Is this an emergency?"

Up and down his street, Christensen's neighbors continued their vigil. Standing on their lawns and sitting on porch steps despite the cold, watching a scene Christensen still couldn't comprehend.

The paramedics had come, treated Melissa's hand, and left an hour ago. But still there was a lot to see. Two black-and-whites were parked out front. An ambulance idled in front of old Mrs. Donati's house three doors down, the attendants having disappeared inside twenty minutes earlier. Two blocks down, a discreet coroner's van was parked outside a house on the north side of the street. Investigators were still going door-to-door, collecting the sample bags, looking for anyone who might have seen who left them.

"Ever kill anybody?"

Annie's voice, distinct from the low murmur of the investigating officers, diverted him from the window. She was standing beside a uniformed cop in the living room, hands in the pockets of her overalls, eyes at holster level and very, very wide. The cop seemed annoyed. He looked to Christensen for direction.

"Annie, why don't we get you to Mrs. Taubman's?" he said, moving her gently toward her backpack at the base of the stairs. "I'm staying home with Melissa, but there's no reason you should. I bet Corey and the other kids are wondering where you are."

"I'm staying," she said. "This is so cool."

Even the cop laughed.

"Come on, I'll walk you over," Christensen said. He called up the stairs. "Melissa? You need me for the next few minutes? Melissa?"

He took the steps three at a time. She was curled into her beanbag chair, headphones on, studying the white gauze on her left hand.

"Lissa?" he said.

She looked up, then away, then back at him as she peeled the headphones from her ears. She must have been reading his face.

"I'm fine," she said. "I'm missing a World Cultures test today."

He leaned against the doorjamb. "So this isn't all bad, then?"

Ordinarily, Christensen would have interpreted her shrug as hostile indifference. But this time his attempt at humor seemed to connect. She was smiling.

"Putting it under cold water was the right thing to do. That's what the paramedic guy said." She stopped just short of a thank-you. Christensen knew that's what it was, though.

"It just looked like a burn from the minute I saw it, and that's the best thing for burns," he said. "Okay if I walk Annie over to day care? You need anything?"

"Don't get all spastic. I'm fine."

The phone rang as he and Annie were halfway out the

front door. He started back in to answer it, and was surprised when the plainclothes investigator answered it first.

"What have you got?" the man said. His face betrayed nothing. "That helps," he said, hanging up.

"What helps?" Christensen asked.

The investigator wheeled and stared, seemingly annoyed at Christensen's presence in his own home. He had a broad, open Slavic face, and when he turned Christensen saw a flash of leather and metal beneath his overcoat. The man considered him for a moment before replying.

"Things sure have changed since I was a paperboy," he said. "Used to be you just stuffed and folded the papers and threw them on the doorstep. Now they've got these poor kids doing inserts and promotions and that kind of crap. Hope the pay is better than when I was a kid."

"That was the *Press*?" Christensen asked. "What did they say?"

"Not the *Press*, exactly. I know some of the Teamsters down there on the loading docks."

"And?" Christensen knew the cop wasn't going to tell him anything if he didn't keep asking.

The cop nodded toward the kitchen table, where the sample products delivered that morning were gathered neatly into a see-through evidence bag. "I called to find out how promotions like that are handled. Where this stuff comes from, who bags it, who delivers it, everybody who has any contact with it along the way."

He seemed to weigh his next thought more carefully.

"Last time the *Press* did one of these was four months ago, in July."

"I don't get it," Christensen said.

The man nodded again toward the evidence bag. "Somebody else delivered that."

Nothing made sense. "To the whole city? Why?"

The man cleared his throat. "That's the other thing," he said. "There's no real pattern so far. Just single streets in a few different neighborhoods, here and there. Bethel Park. Cranberry Township. Penn Hills. All over."

Christensen excused himself and went to the front door,

which was still wide open. To his left, three doors down,
paramedics were wheeling Mrs. Donati down her front
walk, a thick white bandage taped across her eyes. Her
ancient husband trailed the gurney; he was fully dressed
except he was still wearing bedroom slippers. A knot of
neighbors gathered outside the house where the coroner's
van was parked.

Annie was lying flat on her back in the yard, spread-
eagle, no jacket, making a snow angel. The hell with day
care, he thought. No way he was letting either girl out of his
sight. At least not today.

14

The marching band below was loosely configured. A rocket maybe? A ketchup bottle? Christensen couldn't tell, even from the top row of bleachers. He recognized the "Hakuna Matata" song from their *Lion King* video, but it offered no clue.

Melissa was sitting halfway down, at the fifty-yard line, a solitary form in the otherwise empty stands. In her heavy down parka, and with no hint of scale, she might just as well have been one of the ponytailed football players. But he knew it was her. He saw the white bandage on her left hand when she waved to the drum major.

She moved to her right, as if making room for him to sit. "Hi," she said over the din. "You're way early." She moved again when he sat too close.

"I know," he said. "Drum section sounds really weak without you."

A shrill whistle brought the music to a disorderly stop. From atop an aluminum stepladder, the balding band director screeched realignment directions through his bullhorn to a gaggle of trumpet players. "First time in the W.P.I.A.L. playoffs this decade, people!" he said. "We want it right!" It still looked like a ketchup bottle, only now with a bubble on one side.

Christensen cleared his throat.

"The crime lab finally finished the tests. I just talked to Detective Downing."

"And?"

"We've got a few answers, anyway." Damned scary answers, despite Downing's reassurances. His daughter stared straight ahead.

"It was some kind of acid, like car-battery acid," he said. "I should have known something was wrong because it was in a glass bottle. Nobody puts shampoo in glass bottles anymore."

Melissa pulled the bandaged hand from her parka pocket and studied it. In the week since the injury, most of the dead skin had flaked and peeled away. Her palm was still red and tender, but healing nicely. Christensen imagined again how much worse it could have been. What if she'd poured it directly onto her head like old Mrs. Donati and thirteen other people who got samples?

"The two people that died?" she asked.

He put his arm around her, surprised that she let him. "The cereal."

"And nobody saw who delivered it?"

"The Mymans got home at midnight and didn't see bags on any of the doors. But the bags were there at four when Mr. Capelli got up to let their dog out. So whoever left them came pretty early."

The director excused the band. Most of the players headed for the heated gymnasium at the far end of the field, amid the bleating of stray brass notes and random paradiddles. A young man carrying a set of three tom-toms started up the stadium steps toward them, but retreated when he saw Christensen with his daughter.

"Anybody I should know?" His question was more reflex than inquiry.

Melissa just smiled. "How many bags were there?"

"A couple dozen in each neighborhood, usually every house on a single street. That's why I didn't think anything of it. Everybody on our street had one, so I just assumed it was some big marketing gimmick."

Christensen cleared his throat again. "There's something else," he said, "but it has to stay between us, okay?"

He tried to stay calm and reassuring, but his voice sounded emotionless and flat.

"I got involved in something at work in the last few weeks that I think may have been a big mistake, and I want to tell you about it. I don't know that it had anything to do with what happened to you. It probably didn't, not directly anyway. But I want you to understand what's been going on, and why I'm going to put a stop to it."

For once he had her full attention, but there was no victory in it for him. And why was everything he said coming out like the drone of an outboard motor?

"Years ago, in 1986, there was something called the Primenyl poisoning case. Somebody killed six people by putting poison into these headache capsules and then putting them back on store shelves. Do you remember any of this?"

"Sort of."

"Nobody was ever arrested, but the police think they know who it is. And a few weeks ago they asked me to help out in the case."

"I thought you weren't going to do that anymore after that guy shot at you," she said. She was right. Did she worry about him, or did she just enjoy catching him in a contradiction?

"Let's just say I got talked into it," he said. "They really thought I could help, and it was hard to say no because . . . just because of the kind of case it was. Is. See, there was another product-tampering case about a month ago, and they think maybe it was the same guy. It's kind of complicated, but they thought somebody with my background could help."

Melissa reached into her backpack and pulled out a cherry Chap Stick.

"They needed a psychologist?" she said, tracing the balm over her lips.

"Someone who knows a lot about how memory works," he said. "So I wanted to help if I could. But now, with all this, I wonder if it was a mistake, my getting involved. So, I'm sorry."

His daughter stopped mid-pout, the Chap Stick still poised. "For what?" she said.

He could see her mind kick into instant replay, trying to make sense of his story and to figure out why he was telling it now. "Wait. You're saying this same guy put the acid in the shampoo?"

"I don't know. But—"

"And sent it to us?"

He shook his head. "Not specifically, no, but there weren't really that many of those sample bags. It's just got me spooked is all."

She pulled her injured hand from her parka and examined it again.

"What if it's not just a coincidence?" he said. "You know I'd never do anything to put you or your sister in any danger. I told the police that right off, and I believed them when they said we'd have no problems. But even the thought—" He hugged her tighter. "It's just not worth it, Lissa. They can handle it without me."

Melissa put the Chap Stick back into her pack and zipped it shut, taking care so he couldn't see the pack's contents.

"I don't understand what help you could be," she said.

He hadn't intended to share details, but he didn't see how he could avoid it now.

"The killer has a son, a little older than you," he said. "Police think he may have seen something back in 1986. But they also think he may not remember seeing it. With something awful like that, sometimes those memories can get tucked so far in the back of the mind that they're pretty much forgotten. So they wanted me to talk to him to see if I could help him remember anything."

"That's what you've been staying late for on Thursdays," she said.

"Right."

"And that's what you were talking to Brenna about the other night when I came in the room and you all of a sudden told her you'd have to call her back."

"Probably."

"And how many people do they think this guy killed?"

"Six in 1986. One down in Greene County a few weeks ago, and maybe another one down there a few days ago that left a kid in a coma. Now these two. What's that, nine dead so far?" He sighed. "There was a lot of Primenyl stuff in the news around the tenth anniversary of the '86 killings. That may have set him off again."

Melissa stood up, slung her backpack over her right shoulder, and started up the stadium steps toward the parking lot. As she walked, she pulled something from her coat pocket. He recognized it by the colored foil wrapper as the jam-filled Nutri-Grain breakfast bar he'd put in her lunch. How carefully had he checked it?

She stopped about ten feet away and turned back toward him, then held up her bandaged left hand until he looked away. She waited until he looked her in the eye. "And you'd just quit with this guy still out there?"

15

"Agentleman named Sonny Corbett is here, Jim. He says he's early for an appointment, but I don't see his name in the book."

Christensen stared at the intercom, then checked his watch. 5:20. Sonny wasn't due for another forty minutes. He was always prompt, but never early, in the five weeks since they'd started their Thursday sessions. Christensen had kept the after-hours meetings private, so his secretary and Sonny had never before crossed paths.

Christensen shuffled the stack of pink phone messages in his hands. Downing was driving him nuts.

"I was expecting him, but not until six. It's okay. Just tell him I'll be a few minutes. No need for you to wait around."

Christensen arranged the messages chronologically. Downing had called at least once a day for the past week, sometimes in the morning, sometimes in the afternoon. He'd called him here at his private office, at the Pitt counseling office, at home. He'd been so persistent, Christensen started having Melissa screen his calls. Not only did he have nothing to report about Sonny's progress, but he was troubled by the escalating urgency of Downing's messages. The most recent one, left just an hour earlier, was the most troubling of all.

Christensen read it again: "Det. Downing. Please call. Re: Sodium amobarbital."

Where was Downing getting his information? Sodium amobarbital wasn't much known outside a small circle of therapists and researchers who considered the drug a chemical shortcut to repressed memories. A shortcut with dangerous and incalculable side effects, as far as Christensen was concerned. That Downing would research it and mention it as a possibility for Sonny's therapy mirrored the helpless panic Christensen sensed in nearly everyone he knew. The pattern of deaths was emerging, and like in 1986, it wasn't a pattern at all. But to that familiar randomness had been added a chilling new dimension: the killer's mastery of inventive, almost casual, terror. He'd tapped into the very lifeline that sustains a consumer society, and he was poisoning it at will.

Still, Sodium amobarbital simply wasn't an option, and not just because Christensen wasn't licensed to conduct drug therapy. From what he'd read, the drug was especially risky for someone like Sonny, whose medical records noted an irregular heartbeat.

Christensen set the message slips aside, careful to place them well out of sight. He'd intended to call Downing, if only to ask him to back off. But that could wait. He crossed the room and opened the door into the waiting room. His secretary was already gone. Sonny looked up from his magazine, his eyes somewhere in the shadow of his baseball cap's bill.

"I'm early," he said. "Sorry."

"It's fine. I'm clear until six anyway. I was just catching up on some stuff and—"

Sonny brushed past him and into his office, taking his usual chair in the sitting area without taking off the cap. He sat forward, head up, forearms on his knees, a posture very different from the casual, almost indifferent, way Christensen was used to seeing him. Something was on his mind.

"Everything okay?"

"Not sure," Sonny said.

Sonny's body language suggested a level of agitation that Christensen hadn't seen in him before, and his face was drained of the confidence that had so struck the psychologist

during their initial meeting. Christensen picked up a notepad from his desk and sat down in the wing chair.

"Nice hat," he said, smiling.

Sonny took it off. The comment seemed to divert him, as
Christensen hoped it would.

"My dad's," Sonny said. "He was this big stud player.
Third base." Sonny examined the cap's interlocking C and
A emblem, which Christensen recognized as the trademark
of major-league baseball's California Angels.

"Clairmont Affiliated," Sonny said. "Lettered all four
years."

Christensen stole another glance at the emblem. "The
college in West Virginia?"

Sonny nodded. "Got invited to try out with the Pirates'
Columbus farm team his senior year, but he broke his leg.
That was that."

Christensen wrote "Clairmont Affiliated?" on his notepad. "It happens," he said. "So what's on your mind?"

Sonny looked around, saying nothing. Slowly, apparently
without realizing it, he started rocking back and forth, his
tempo picking up as the awkward silence continued. "Had
this dream," he said finally. "Had it a couple times in the last
two weeks. Switching to a daytime work schedule screws up
my sleeping pattern, so maybe that's why."

A thousand questions ran through Christensen's mind.
"Want to talk about it?"

"I'm here, aren't I?" Sonny snapped.

"I'm glad you came," he said, absorbing Sonny's glare
like a body punch. "I'd like to hear about it."

Sonny waited. The rocking started again. "It's about
water. I'm on my back, but my head's underwater. And it's
a really weird feeling. It's like I know something's wrong,
but I'm, like, helpless."

Christensen tried to imagine Sonny in full backstroke, but
with his head beneath the surface. "I don't think anybody
could swim like that for very long. Could they? I mean, it
seems like an awkward position."

"That's the thing," Sonny said. "It's not like I'm swimming. I'm just a kid, maybe twelve or thirteen. I didn't start

swimming until later. I'm just on my back and there's this
light above me, kind of a square light, and it's not like I'm
floating. More like I'm lying on something hard, and I'm on
my back, and I can't breathe. And I'm really cold. And I try
to pull my head up out of the water but I can't."

He stopped rocking and sat forward. Christensen watched
the rise and fall of Sonny's chest and wrote "Respiration up"
on his notepad, careful to maintain eye contact.

"You can't pull your head out of the water?" he asked.

Sonny nodded.

"Then what?"

"I wake up," Sonny said. "It's pretty ugly. Usually I don't
get back to sleep."

He was breathing even harder now, and his face had
changed. Christensen wasn't just seeing shaken confidence;
Sonny was scared.

"I don't get it," he said. "Why can't you pull your head
up?"

Sonny closed his eyes. "I try, but I can't."

"Why not?"

"I don't know."

"Is anyone with you?"

Sonny looked away. "I don't know. My brother's there.
He helps me."

"What kind of place are you in?"

"I don't know. Dark."

"But with a square light above you? Are you inside or
outside?"

Sonny closed his eyes again, apparently trying to make
sense of what was replaying in his head. "It doesn't seem
like outside."

"How'd you get there?"

"I don't know," Sonny said. "Down some steps maybe?
It's a dream. Not everything makes sense."

Christensen laid the notepad on the table. "I wonder why
this dream upsets you, though."

"I'm drowning."

"But you're a strong swimmer."

"I'm not swimming, I told you. It wouldn't be like that if I was swimming."

The phone chirped once. Christensen ignored it. The answering machine in the outer office picked up after the second ring.

"Why do you think your brother is there?" Christensen said.

Sonny shifted in his chair, rocking, crossing and recrossing his legs. "I don't know."

"But he helps you?"

"Yeah, I think."

"Do you dream about him much, Sonny? Since he died, I mean."

"Sometimes."

Christensen waited. Sonny crossed his legs again.

"There's one other thing in the dream. Maybe it's later, or a different dream. I'm in this room, and there's a dog. On this sort of checkerboard floor."

"And then what?"

"That's all."

Christensen thought of the packet of coroner's photographs in Sonny's juvenile records file. What had led Sonny to David's body in the upstairs bedroom the day David shot himself were the bloody paw prints that one of the boys' frantic dogs left on the kitchen floor. The packet contained several shots of the grisly path across a distinctive checkered linoleum-tile floor, as well as a photograph of the dog.

"Is David there?"

"No. Somebody else."

"Besides the dog? Who?"

"I don't know."

"Are you sure?"

"I said I don't know." With the back of his hand, Sonny swatted the inflatable Wham-It off the coffee table that sat between them, then stood up. "Can I get a drink of water?"

Sonny had led them to a door, but didn't want to open it. Christensen pointed to the compact refrigerator across the room. "In the fridge. Help yourself."

Sonny twisted the cap from a bottle of Evian. "Sorry," he said as he sat down. "Unreal, isn't it?"

"Is it?" Christensen said.

"Meaning?"

Time to take a chance. Christensen retrieved his own bottle of water. He wasn't thirsty, but he needed time to frame his thoughts. Nudge him, but ever so gently.

"It sounded pretty real to me, at least parts of it."

"Like the dog," Sonny said. "I guess that was Izzy."

"Izzy?"

"Izzy Vicious. One of our dogs. We had two until Trooper ran away."

"That must have been hard on you."

"We used to travel a lot. Three, four weeks at a time. So neighbors would keep both of them for us. And one time Trooper just took off. Never found him."

Christensen wasn't interested in the dog. "Those are long trips. Where'd you go?"

Sonny's eyes roamed the floor. "All over. Europe. North Africa once. Spent my tenth birthday in Algiers. Anyway, Trooper ran off right before I went into foster care. And when I did, I had to give Izzy away."

Christensen wrote "Birthday, Algiers?" on the notepad, then spoke slowly, trying to add weight to his words. "Sometimes things that upset us never really go away. Maybe that's why Izzy's in the dream."

"The house seemed like this place we used to live in Irondale, on Jancey Street. But I can't make any sense of it."

Christensen opened his water. "Dreams are funny things," he said. "Why do you think that one bothered you so much?"

"It's just so weird."

"But you never had that dream before, right?" Christensen let the question hang.

"Not that I can remember," Sonny said.

"Why do you think you had it now?"

Sonny shrugged.

"I ask because we've been talking a lot these last few weeks about when you were a kid. And now here you are having dreams about when you were a kid, with your dogs and maybe your old house and everything. Maybe talking about that period of your life planted the seeds that grew into dreams. That happens. Or maybe something else is going on there."

"Like what?"

"Ever hear the song 'Dream Weaver'?" Christensen said. Sonny's face was blank.

"Before your time. Never mind. Anyway, dreams really are woven from a lot of things. Fantasies. Fears. Bits of memory. Things that happened to us that day or things that happened years ago. When we sleep, our brains mix all that together and come up with a story. The hard part is figuring out which parts of the story are fantasies and which ones are fears, or memories, or experiences. It's tricky business."

Sonny walked to the window and stared into the darkness. An inch of fresh snow lay on the sill, and the bitter cold outside had left frost on the inside corners of the single-pane window. It reminded Christensen that Christmas was less than a week off, and of how little time he'd had to shop for the girls.

"Trooper didn't really run away," Sonny said.

"The dog?"

Sonny laid one of his palms on the window, then the other. He pressed his cheek against the pane. For half a minute, maybe more, Christensen watched Sonny frozen in tableau, as if seeking the cold. When he finally pulled away, his palm prints were melted into the window frost and his cheek was bright red.

"I want to talk again tomorrow," he said.

"Tomorrow?" Christensen returned to his desk and checked his calendar. "Friday night is bad for me. High school football, and my older daughter plays in the band. Could you come during the day?"

Sonny shook his head. "I swim in the morning and work noon to eight now," he said. "It's okay. I understand."

"How about if we get together two nights next week instead of one?" Christensen said. "I can plan around that for as long as you want. How about if we meet at six next Tuesday along with our regular Thursday meeting?"

"I just—"

"Sonny, it's fine."

"But you have family. And the holidays and all."

Christensen pretended to scribble on his calendar, but wrote "Sensitivity to my family commitments" on his notepad. "They'll understand," he said.

From his office window a few minutes later, Christensen watched Sonny's solitary form cross a snow-covered parking lot lit only by neon signs and the garish twinkle of Christmas lights from nearby stores. The single trail of footprints across the virgin snow disappeared down one of Oakland's countless side streets, and only then did Christensen wonder if Sonny was spending the holidays alone.

He poked the answering machine's playback button as he shrugged into his coat. "If you're there, Jim, pick up," the message began. "We got a positive for hydrogen cyanide on the Squeezie Pop, but sucking it frozen just delivers a sublethal dose. Not one of Corbett's better ideas. The sugar on the cereal was probably cyanide powder blown in through the bottom of the box and a hole in the wax-paper liner. Add enough and shake it up good: boom, boom—the morgue gets two more. Final tox is due back on all those other free samples in a couple days . . ."

Downing's tiny voice, full of muted panic, sounded like a trapped bumblebee as Christensen locked the office door.

16

What a depressing goddamned shithole. Downing had been in some pretty grim places in twenty-eight years of police work, but Ridgeville was one seriously decaying little burg. He turned left into the gravel drive of Lakeview Pointe Estates and hoped the Ford's snow tires would get him up the steep rise.

He had no idea what to expect. Sandra Corbett lost it after her husband split in 1986, that much he knew. She already was losing it when he first interviewed her at their house during the initial investigation. Once he read the incident reports from all the domestic calls to the house, he knew why. Then, a couple months later when he tried to talk to her at Borman, she was worthless. What an unforgettable fucking scene. She smoked as they talked. Actually, she smoked while he talked, since she spent the whole time staring like a zombie at Borman's sticky gray floor. Downing watched the cigarette burn slowly toward the soft flesh between her index and middle fingers, and then keep burning until it broke the blisters from her last cigarette. Then it went out. She never even flinched.

Never said a word, either. But besides Sonny, she was the only other person still alive who was in the Jancey Street house in 1986, the only other person who might have seen Ron Corbett pull it off. It was worth a shot. He heard she'd

come around in the last couple years, even loosened up
enough to hang occasionally at Tramp's, Ridgeville's only
real meet-and-mate bar. He hadn't talked to the regulars
there to see if she'd ever talked about Ron. Maybe he
should. But he took her going out again as a sign that she'd
finally figured out what a shitbag her husband was. Maybe
she'd talk now.

Before he knocked, he took in the view from the
second-floor balcony. Lakeview Pointe Estates. Christ. He
held his shield up to the window when the curtains parted a
crack, then counted at least three pieces of heavy hardware
as she unfastened the dead bolts.

"Mrs. Corbett?"

She opened the door until the chain lock caught, then
peeked out. This was not a healthy person. She was as pretty
as he remembered, slender even in that getup, but obviously
not all there. He'd caught her by surprise on a Saturday
morning, but who wears a heavy peacoat and a wool-knit
watch cap indoors?

"I remember you," she said, looking away.

"Detective Downing of the Pittsburgh Police Department,
Mrs. Corbett." He poked one of his business cards through
the opening, and she took it. "May I come in?"

"I can't . . . no. It's not a good day. What's your name
again?" She wouldn't look him in the eye.

"Grady Downing, Mrs. Corbett. We met back in 1986,
and we talked once in 1987 when you were in the hospital
over there."

She unfastened the chain and disappeared into the apartment. Downing gently pushed through and into a wall of
warm air. Where'd she go? He followed the Looney Tunes
theme song into another room, where she was sitting on a
folding metal chair in front of a small TV. This didn't look
promising. Even if she told him the whole story, he tried to
imagine her in front of a grand jury or on a courtroom
witness stand. He couldn't. If she was as nuts as she seemed,
no prosecutor would dare.

"I don't much like cats," she said, gesturing toward the
small screen. Tweety was setting a trap using a vacuum

cleaner and a rope. "That Sylvester, he's always trying to eat him."

Downing groped for a suitable response. Or did it matter? "I'm not a cat person either," he said. "Always had dogs."

She turned and faced him for the first time. "We had dogs once," she said. "What kind?"

"Beg pardon?"

"Your dog. What kind?"

"Basset hound. A sad thing with a swayback and epilepsy and kidney problems. Only three years old and he's already half blind. But a pleasant sort if you can stand the smell."

"What's his name?" she said.

"Rodney King."

"I've heard of him," she said. She stood up and walked toward the kitchen. Downing followed, watching as she bent toward a low shelf of the refrigerator. Bonkers or not, peacoat or not, she had a great butt.

"You want an apple? I have some apples," she said. "If I don't eat on time I get the diabetes."

"No, but thanks."

"Good oranges, too. Can I get you one?"

"No thanks."

Her eyes wandered for a moment and settled, apparently, on the kitchen sink faucet. "Grapefruit?"

"No," he said, then reconsidered. "What kind?"

"The red kind," she said. "They're so good this year."

A woman after his heart. Texas Ruby Reds.

"Best year I can remember," he said. "Sweet as sugar, but no thanks. Just had one in the car on the way over. I probably eat a half-dozen a day when the winter crop comes in. I'd like to ask you a few questions, Mrs. Corbett, if you don't mind."

She closed the refrigerator and rinsed an apple in the sink, which looked like it held every dish in the place, all dirty.

Downing cleared his throat. "I was wondering if you keep in touch with Mr. Corbett."

She set the apple on the counter and opened a nearly empty silverware drawer. The knife she chose was better suited for an infantry charge, a black-handled job with a

blade a foot long and a point like a bayonet. Downing
tensed, pure instinct, but then relaxed as she quartered the
apple and dropped the knife into the sink. It clattered onto
the crusty dishes. She found her only clean saucer in a
cupboard crowded with medicine bottles, then arranged the
apple slices on it with elaborate care, like the pattern was
her way of communicating with her home planet.

"My husband ran off," she said. "Dr. Root says he was
sick. I don't think he was sick. He didn't look sick. But Dr.
Root says he shouldn't have hurt me and the boys. Sometimes I miss him, though. Sometimes he was nice. Funny,
you know? You like Gatorade? I have Gatorade. Both kinds,
the red and green. I like the red."

She carried the plate to the small kitchen table, sat down,
and started to eat with an exaggerated politeness Downing
found odd, especially since she was eating the core, seeds
and all.

"He never calls?" he said. "You haven't kept in touch at
all?"

She chewed slowly, deliberately, then swallowed. "He
ran off," she said.

Not far, Downing thought; Outcrop couldn't be more than
thirty miles from here. But she probably wasn't lying.
Sonny told him once that he'd got a birthday card from his
dad when he was about fourteen, but that was it. Ron
Corbett wasn't the sentimental type.

"Mrs. Corbett, I know this is a personal question, but
we're still interested in why your husband left so suddenly
way back when."

Downing watched her nibble off the end of an apple
quarter, oblivious to the stem. She chewed the woody thing
for a long time. He couldn't be sure she was crying, but her
eyes got wet and even more vacant.

"Mrs. Corbett?"

"He just ran off," she said. "He didn't like us. The boys
either. Too bad, too. He was a funny man."

Funny? Downing tried to fit the word to the croaking
scumbag with the shotgun.

"Know what?" she said. "He had a nickname for everybody on our street. The Inspector. Odd Todd. Miss Clairol. There was this nun from the church he called Sister Teresa Lambada. Oh, he made us laugh sometimes."

"I had no idea," Downing said.

"That was fun, laughing."

Downing watched her work on the apple stem for a long time. "Mrs. Corbett, do you remember if anything happened that day, or that week, when he left? Was there something you or the boys said that set him off, or did he say anything when he left?"

"The dog died," she said.

"That day?"

"No. My husband left a few weeks after. But he didn't like Trooper much anyway, so that's not why. I remember the boys were so sad. They cried. About Trooper, I mean. Not about their dad. Maybe they were sad about him leaving, too."

Her gaze drifted back across the room to the refrigerator door handle. "You know Sonny, don't you?"

"Yes, ma'am."

"I know you do. He comes here sometimes."

"A very nice young man."

She looked away again. "I had two boys. David died."

"I know he did. I'm sorry."

"You have boys?"

"One girl, but she's off on her own now. Grow up fast, don't they?"

"Some don't grow up at all," she said. She bit into another apple quarter and chewed until it was gone. Downing felt like a shit.

"Mrs. Corbett, we're still looking into a series of killings that happened back in 1986, right around the time your husband left. Do you remember when we talked about that before?"

"Terrible thing," she said. "All those people."

"Do you remember how it happened? With the poison in the headache capsules?"

"We were so scared."

"Everybody was. It was a scary time because product

tampering is so hard to control. Now there's a couple of cases down in Greene County that are a lot like it, and that's got everybody scared again. Because we never caught anybody."

She shook her head. "Terrible."

"Thing is, Mrs. Corbett, the latest killing was in Waynesburg, just a few miles down the road from where your husband's been living since 1986. And the first time around, if you'll recall, the poison was sold at stores that were all within a couple miles of your house down on Jancey Street."

He waited for a reaction. Nothing.

"There's been other incidents, too. I'm sure you heard somebody put poison in some sample packages. Killed two people and burned a bunch of others. We don't know if it's the same person, but you can imagine how anxious we are to find out who's doing this stuff."

"Why would somebody do that?" she asked.

"Exactly, Mrs. Corbett. Any ideas?"

"We don't watch much news here." She smiled. "You want this last slice of apple?"

"No, but thanks."

"I don't think I want this last piece. This wasn't a very good apple."

This was going nowhere. "Mrs. Corbett, do you have any reason to believe your husband was involved in any of these incidents, either in 1986 or recently?"

She traced the edge of her plate with the apple slice. "I think I'll fix a grapefruit. You want a grapefruit? The man at the store told me they're from Texas. I've never been to Texas. You ever been to Texas?"

Downing reached across the table and lightly touched her hand. "Mrs. Corbett, I asked you a question about your husband. Do you have any reason to think he put the poison in those headache capsules ten years ago, or in any of the other stuff in the past few weeks?"

She pulled her hand away and shoved it into the peacoat pocket. "Why would he do that?" she said.

"That's what we're wondering, too. Did he ever say anything to you that made you think he was involved? Or did you ever see him do anything? Because if he was loading capsules in 1986, he probably would have done it at the house."

"He's a pharmacist."

"We know that, ma'am. But it's not something he would have done at work where somebody might see. And we found some things at your house that made us wonder if—"

"He sent money for a while," she said.

Ron Corbett had fallen off the state unemployment dole after a year, then tried twice to claim disability. Turned down once, according to state records, but the second time was a charm. From what Downing could tell, Corbett hadn't worked since 1986. Real father-of-the-year type.

"He stopped sending it after Peebo Balkin nearly drowned," she said.

"Peebo who?"

At the sink again, she wedged the saucer among the other plates, then swept into the other room without another word. When he heard the creak of her wooden chair, Downing moved to the cupboard for a peek. An old investigator's habit, but one he'd found worthwhile over the years—the contents of a medicine cabinet read to him like a personality profile. Hers was mostly over-the-counter stuff: cold remedies, vitamins, laxatives. The prescription stuff was predictable, especially the full bottle of lithium. If she was like this medicated, he wondered, how much more crackers would she be without it? A few expired bottles of antibiotics. A roll of Tes-Tape for checking sugar in the urine, a glucometer for testing blood sugar, a jar of hard candy for quick sugar fixes, a bottle of rubbing alcohol—a diabetic's tools for living. The chair creaked again. He closed the cupboard quietly and followed into the other room.

She was back at the TV. No sense wasting more time. Unless she had home movies of Ron loading the capsules, nothing here would be of any use.

"I'm going now, Mrs. Corbett. Thanks for taking the time."

She pointed at the tiny TV. "Look! That little tornado,

he's really that Tasmanian Devil guy." She seemed transfixed.

"One of the great ones," he said. "Take care, Mrs. Corbett."

She didn't move, hands in the pockets of her heavy coat,
watch cap pulled down tight over her ears, eyes glued to
images of cartoon mayhem. He left her there, wondering if
she had always been that pathetic or if life with Ron had just
taken a toll. He pulled the front door shut behind him.

The snow from the midweek storm was nearly gone. All
that was left were little drifts in the building's shadow and
under the cars that hadn't been moved. The road back into
town would be clear, maybe even dry. But while he was
inside, the clear sky had turned gray and the temperature
had dropped. He buttoned his coat as he moved down the
steps. Spring was a hundred years away.

17

Somewhere past the two secretaries, down the carpeted hall, and behind the sturdy walnut door, the chief of police for the city of Pittsburgh was roaring, a bellowing sound Downing hadn't heard in the three months since Kiger took over. The secretaries looked at each other, and he knew they couldn't stand their new boss.

"He'll just be a few more minutes, Grady," the older one said. He could never remember her name. "Coffee?"

"Sure. Great. Freeze-dried?"

"Nope. Fresh pot," she said, getting up.

"Oh. No thanks," Downing said. She stared. He shrugged. "I like freeze-dried."

Another roar. Laughter? Shouting? Downing had no idea why he'd been summoned. He wished he had a better handle on the man he was about to see. Patrick B. Kiger came to the city from Memphis, where as chief he was known as a savvy cop within the department, and as a brutish Neanderthal with the press. What killed him there, Downing heard, was his appetite for publicity and his sarcastic overuse of the word "alleged" during bust announcements. "Mr. Bowling became our prime suspect because he allegedly can be seen on a videotape bringing the alleged fire extinguisher down onto the skull of the alleged victim, Mr. Phong . . ."

The sort of stuff cops loved, the sort of stuff that

made newspaper editors and ACLU lawyers swallow their tongues.

Kiger's looks didn't help. At 5-foot-8 and pushing 200, he was a gritty hamburger of a man with a Beelzebub beard that followed his jawline to his chin, where it arced into an evil goatee. A smile led to a squint, which led to the general impression that Pittsburgh's new police chief was capable of eating his young.

With the unexpected rise in Pittsburgh's gang and drug hostilities, Kiger seemed the perfect choice. His first week on the job, he had laid out his style during roll-call meetings at each precinct: You got a problem, come to me. Be prepared to lose every argument, but I'll listen and look you in the eye before I throw your sorry butt out of my office. Forget that community-based policing crap that's turning good cops all over the country into school crossing guards and parking-squabble umpires. My cops are good guys with guns. Convictions count, arrests don't. You want my attention? Work your ass off, plain and simple. Don't fuck up.

Downing wiped his palms on his pants, shifting Ron Corbett's file from one knee to the other.

The door suddenly swung out like there'd been an explosion. Kiger plowed through, full speed, followed by J. D. Dagnolo, the district attorney. Papers clenched between his teeth, Dagnolo was wrestling his open briefcase as he walked.

He was probably the most powerful man in the city. Knew so much about so many people that a lot of cops called him J. Edgar instead of J. D. But never to his face. Scrambling in Kiger's wake, he seemed more like the spineless toady he was. Kiger peeled off into the copy room halfway down the hall without a word. Dagnolo pulled the papers out of his mouth. "So long, chief!" he said, the words bouncing off Kiger's back. Downing tried hard not to snicker as the DA passed, then nodded and said, "J. D."

"Grady." Dagnolo kept walking, past the secretaries, through the glass doors, toward the elevators.

First words in years. What did Dagnolo say the last time they'd talked? "You just fucked up the biggest homicide case in the city's history, Grady. Where you going now? Disneyland?" Took three uniforms to pull him off the son of a bitch, or so Downing heard later.

"Get that a-hole's fax from Washington, Jude?" Kiger drawled from the copy room. His Tennessee accent oozed through the office.

"On your desk."

Jude. That's the name. Jude the Prude.

"You expect me to find it there?" Kiger said, rounding the corner from the copy room. As the chief lumbered toward him, Downing realized Kiger was much shorter than he remembered. But wide. All solid shoulders and belly, a beer keg with legs. And probably under more pressure.

Downing stood. "Got a message you wanted to see me, chief," he said, extending a hand. Kiger's grip was noncommittal.

"Who are you again?"

"Grady Downing," the Prude said before he could answer. "Homicide. The letter from Musca, Hickton?"

A flicker of recognition. "Right," Kiger said. "Primenyl." What letter?

Kiger's office was about as organized as a tossed salad. Books stacked on chairs. Family pictures still in boxes. The only thing on his desk not issued by the city supply clerk was a round, brown needlepoint pillow. The word "Bullshit" was stitched on it in white thread, block letters.

"Mail call," the chief said, collapsing into his leather desk chair. He handed a photocopy across the desk, then picked up the pillow, cocked it behind his head, and waited.

Downing took one of the straight-back wooden chairs on the other side of the desk and opened the envelope. He unfolded it and read the letterhead: Musca, Hickton & Cook. The letter was signed by an attorney, Cheryl M. Musca, addressed to Patrick B. Kiger, Pittsburgh's Chief of Police. It began: "We are the law firm retained by the Commonwealth of Pennsylvania to represent the interests of outpatients currently under the care of Borman State Hospital. This letter carries our concern about the recent interrogation of

Sandra Preston Corbett, a patient of Dr. Douglas L. Root, by
your detective, Grady Downing."

Downing looked up.

"Read the whole thing," Kiger said.

He scanned the two-page letter. Downing had entered her
home without an invitation. His intrusion caused her great
personal distress. He was insensitive to Mrs. Corbett's
condition and ignorant of the preferred techniques for
dealing with individuals who suffer depression and dissociation. A photocopy of a newspaper clipping was stapled
to the letter's last page, and Downing felt his gut clench
when he recognized the headline. It was part of the *Press*'s
recent Primenyl retrospective, and it quoted unnamed department sources and FBI officials who blamed the investigation's failure on "sloppy police work" and "inexplicable
errors of judgment" by investigators. The story also noted,
without comment, that "veteran detective Grady T. Downing was in charge of the original investigation."

"Before we get to that," Kiger said, "you mind telling me
why it was too inconvenient for you to let me know you
were reopening the biggest fucking homicide case ever?"

Downing felt sick. "It's preliminary work. I mentioned it
to DeLillo, and he didn't have a problem with it."

The pillow hit Downing in the forehead, crushing the
wave of hair he'd combed into place ten minutes before.
Kiger leaned forward. His forearms looked like legs of
lamb.

"Bullshit?" Downing said. He shoved his hair back with
his hand.

"You told Lieutenant DeLillo you were checking to see if
the Greene County case was relevant. You didn't tell him
you'd be reinterviewing possible witnesses to the 1986
killings. I like your initiative. Your methods suck."

Downing kept quiet. There was an agenda here. Kiger
pushed away from his desk and retrieved the pillow from
the floor. He carefully picked off a dustball and returned to
his chair, again cocking the pillow behind his head.

"Mind filling me in?" Kiger said.

"From the beginning?"

The chief shook his head. "I read the goddamned file. Tell me what's not in there."

Downing took a deep breath. "Apparent homicide in Greene County a few weeks back. Female, thirty-nine. Looks like product tampering. Lab reports indicate hydrogen cyanide, the liquid form. The methods were different, but it was all there. Same attention to detail. Same weird silence afterward. No notes. No barroom bragging. Just did the deed and gone. Same with the more recent cases."

"I watch the news," Kiger said. "Tell me what I don't know."

Downing tried not to squirm. "With the yogurt and the Squeezie Pop, local cops found sealed pinholes, probably from a syringe. We're not sure yet on the free-sample stuff."

"What makes you think it's related to Primenyl? That investigation went belly-up five years ago."

Did Kiger notice him cringe?

"The Greene County cases happened in a rural area, maybe ten thousand people in a twenty-mile radius. One of them's a guy named Corbett. Ron Corbett. Name ring a bell?"

Kiger leaned forward, tight grin, a remember-what-I'm-about-to-tell-you look. "I've read the file." The chief picked up a thin, plastic-bound report that had been at a far corner of his desk. Downing recognized the cover as standard FBI, suspected what it was. This was no spur-of-the-moment meeting. This guy was loaded for bear.

"Wait a minute, detective," Kiger said, flipping it open. "Corbett's not the name the feds fingered in . . . What was it?" He checked the report's date. "In 1988. Some guy named Griffin the drug company fired about the time the killing started. Confessed to the whole thing in a suicide note in early '88, then bit the pipe, right?"

Downing tried to wring the anger from his voice before he replied. "Got nine more written confessions in my Primenyl files, sir, but I'm not much for fairy tales."

"So you're not buying it?"

"It's a crock. The bureau spent close to two million bucks on Primenyl, swept in here like God's own avengers and got nothing. Griffin gave them the perfect out, and I think they took it. He had motive. He confessed. He's black. And, best of all, he's dead. Made a perfect little bookend, didn't he?"

"Black?"

"That was just gravy. On top of everything else, the bureau found a bad guy who played into local prejudices. You'll understand that better after you've been here longer."

That sounded just condescending enough to have blown it, Downing thought. But when Kiger spoke again, he said, "Tell me about Corbett."

This was a test, Downing figured. New or not, Kiger had to know about Corbett. For a while in 1986, the bastard couldn't peek out of his front door without every newspaper photographer and TV crew on the East Coast peeing their pants. Kiger wants my take, he thought, wants to know if he can trust my analysis. Spare the venom. Just the facts. Don't raise old questions.

"Pharmacist. Very familiar with lot numbers and shelving habits. Lived close to most of the stores where bad capsules were sold. Some record of domestic violence, indications he was abused as a juvenile. FBI profilers at Quantico say he fits a profile—something called a 'nonspecific multiple murderer.'"

"Goddamned profiles," Kiger said. "I probably fit it, too. Anything else?"

"He was uncooperative, not hostile but closemouthed, when we talked to him in '86. But he made pretty clear he knew more than he was saying. Guilty man's bluff, I figured."

Kiger studied him a moment. "That's it?"

Downing looked down at the file. "No. But that's all we can use. Corbett was"—he cleared his throat—"problematic."

The pillow hit Downing square in the forehead.

"Sure you told me everything?" Kiger said.

"Everything you asked."

Kiger shrugged and picked up the pillow again. "Good answer," he said, collapsing back into his chair. "We'll save the hard questions for next time."

"I'll answer now."

Kiger ignored him. "First, this ain't my call. You got a division head, right? DeLillo knows where he needs you. But if I was him, I'd tell you to steer clear of the '86 witnesses for now. Ride herd on the boys down in Greene County, check in with whoever's working the local case, and we'll take another look down the road. Right now what you've got is damned thin. We shouldn't jump on Corbett just because a couple victims live in his neighborhood. The free-sample stuff was all over the map. Besides, the crack trade being what it is, we got plenty here to keep us busy."

The words hit hard. Maybe there *is* no proof that Ron Corbett is killing his fellow citizens again, sir, or in 1986 for that matter. But you play this game long enough and you learn to trust whatever it is that raises the hair on your arms, learn to recognize when you're probably damned close to the truth. And the truth about Primenyl, sir, is that the killer is still out there, waiting and planning the next one, king of the goddamned western Pennsylvania hills.

Downing swallowed. "Maybe it's Corbett again, maybe it's not. Hard to say based on what we know so far. But there may be another reason—a stronger reason—to reopen the old investigation and go after Corbett again."

"Sure you didn't get your fill of this case last time?" Kiger asked.

Their eyes locked. Downing had wondered if he was being baited. Now he was sure. Kiger hadn't just read the Primenyl case file. He'd read his personnel file, too. Shit. Time to shoot the wad. He eyed the pillow as he stepped off the ledge.

"Last time, sir, I didn't believe we had a credible witness. Now I think we might. But it'll take some work."

Downing looked up, expecting another needlepoint fastball. Kiger hadn't moved.

"I'm listening," he said.

Slow down. Tell him about Ron Corbett, about *all* of the evidence: the list of cyanide distributors, that Corbett knows how the capsules got into the sealed bottles. Tell him about Sonny and repressed memories, about the California case that gave him hope. Make him understand. Downing breathed deep and started to talk.

When he was finished, the chief laid the pillow down on the desk, stood up, and walked around Downing and out of sight. Downing heard the rustle of cloth on the coat rack in the corner by the door; then, sooner than he would have thought possible, he felt the chief's coffee-sour breath on his ear.

"We never had this conversation," Kiger hissed. The door opened, then shut, and Downing was alone. The letter in his hand was shaking like a leaf.

18

"Which Beatle was the coach? The dead guy?"

Annie sat on the kitchen counter, shoulder-dancing to "A Hard Day's Night," watching him chop vegetables for a salad. Christensen wasn't particularly good at answering his five-year-old's unanswerable questions. She framed the world in ways he couldn't begin to comprehend, and her literal interpretations and skewed logic sometimes left him sputtering and helpless.

"The coach? I'm not sure what you mean, honey," he said. He tossed a handful of cut carrots onto the shredded pile of romaine, then unwrapped a new container of blue cheese, carefully checking the wax coating for flaws.

"The coach," she said, snatching a lettuce leaf and offering it to her box turtle, Thinky, who was riding the crook of her arm like a football. "Which Beatle was the coach?"

Where to start? "You mean like Mr. Villeran, your soccer coach?"

"Was it the dead guy? Is that why they aren't a team any more?"

Ah, a clue. He remembered a scene from their morning commute. "Paperback Writer" had been on the Explorer's tape deck; Melissa was deep into her headphones, into her own rhythms, in the backseat. The Beatles were like a team, he'd told Annie. The best team ever. But after a while they decided they couldn't play nicely together and decided to break up.

Deciphering this latest question, though, was no help with an answer. Best to get out as quickly as he could.

"Yes," he said. "John Lennon was the coach."

She hopped down, apparently satisfied, and disappeared with Thinky into the living room. She'd have an equally baffling follow-up question, but right now he was too busy checking the safety seal on a jar of Niçoise olives to clarify the Beatles' coaching situation.

"Think about this," Brenna said, reading the back of the *Sgt. Pepper's* CD as she entered the kitchen. Beatles music was one of several passions they shared. "Lennon and McCartney probably wrote 'She's Leaving Home' in 1966. They were, what, twenty-three, twenty-four years old at the time?"

"You were that wise at twenty-three, right?" He held the olive jar up to his ear and twisted the cap, reassured by the pop of the vacuum seal.

She pulled a silver clasp from behind her head. A cascade of blond-red hair spilled onto the padded shoulders of her pale green power suit. She'd been in trial all week, defending another of the indefensible, and seemed grateful to have someone cooking for her and Taylor. She seemed just as grateful to have something to think about besides the confession-prone Mr. Cheverton and the carnage he created one ordinary afternoon last year in a suburban postal station.

"Let's see, I was twenty-three in 1976," she said. After a moment's thought: "Don't ask." She unbuttoned her jacket and slid it down her arms. Her white silk blouse offered the most alluring hint of lacy brassiere beneath. The woman knew her lingerie. He imagined her repeating the same motion as a tactical move in front of a jury. Or would she? She might sway some men, but she'd risk irritating the women.

"Do you think these artichoke hearts are okay?" he said. "There's no safety seal."

Brenna shot him a look. "There's a difference between caution and paranoia."

"Sorry." He opened the jar when she turned away and passed it beneath his nose. Seemed okay, but what would a doctored jar of marinated artichoke hearts smell like, anyway? He ignored his sudden sense of helplessness and arrayed three of the oily hearts on the cutting board.

Someone rapped hard on the front door, ignoring the doorbell and both brass knockers. He heard Annie and Taylor scramble madly to answer it as he checked his watch. Who'd stop by unannounced at seven-thirty on a week-night?

"Chickie!" the visitor said. Christensen picked up a dish towel and walked into the front hall, where Downing was bending low to shake Annie's tiny hand.

"He's a cop," she was explaining to Brenna's four-year-old, who seemed impressed. "Show us your gun before my dad comes."

"Grady?" Christensen said. "What's up?"

"Oops." Annie stepped aside. "Come on, Taylor. Let's play Ninjas."

Downing watched them pound up the stairs. "You got trouble in her, I'm telling ya," he said. "Keep the tranquil-izer darts handy. Got a minute?"

Brenna poked her head around the corner, offered a cool greeting, and disappeared back into the living room. Still drying his hands, Christensen led Downing into his office and closed the door.

"You never write, you never call," Downing said as he scanned titles on the bookshelves. "Darling, don't tell me you've fallen for someone else."

"I don't have anything to talk to you about, Grady. Remember our deal? Unless Sonny starts bringing up things that seem relevant, what we talk about stays private."

The detective held up his hands, palms out. "Don't get all bunched up. Just curious. It's been six weeks now. You've got nothing so far?"

Christensen sat down behind his desk. "I'm not an investigator. I'm a psychologist."

Downing immediately perched on the edge of the desk, one leg anchored to the floor and the other dangling, looming over him. It felt menacing in a way Christensen couldn't quite define. "How's Melissa?" the detective asked.

"Fine. The hand's mostly healed up. It bothered me more than her, I think."

"Why?" Downing seemed sincerely curious.

"Why?" he said. "You coax me into helping you on a product-tampering case where the killer's still loose, then suddenly we end up with acid in our shampoo. And you really wonder why I'm bothered?"

"Whoa," Downing said. "Bit of a stretch, don't you think?"

Christensen stood up. Fuck these games.

"No, Grady, it's not." He held up his right hand, his thumb and index finger a centimeter apart. "I was this close to calling you after it happened and telling you to find somebody else. I don't know if there's a connection. Maybe it was just a weird coincidence that our house happened to be on the hit list. But if there's even the slightest chance, I want out. I won't put my kids in that position."

"Sonny never talks to his father," Downing said.

"You don't know that."

"Come on, Jim. We've got Ron Corbett under constant surveillance. If he was skulking around your neighborhood in the middle of the night, we'd know. Whenever he shits, the chief gets a memo."

Christensen stared, reluctant to concede the point. He was pissed and wanted Downing to know it. He angled the photograph of Molly and the kids on his desk so Downing could see, then retreated to the window across the room. The gesture made no apparent impression.

"You get my message about that drug?" Downing said. "Sodium whachamajig?"

"Amobarbital. Not an option."

"No? I heard it speeds things up."

"Sometimes. Sometimes it nudges some people into psychosis, too. Sometimes it kills them. It's experimental and dangerous and I won't recommend it."

"Sure be nice to pick up the pace. Something's come up."

Downing's face carried no further information. The comment hung between them, sodden, full of implication. Christensen's first instinct was to end the conversation there, to leave the room and ask Downing to leave his house, to sever his relationship with Sonny Corbett, to return his study of human memory to the safe, abstract world of volunteer subjects and controlled tests. His second instinct was to punch Downing in the mouth. Instead, he found himself losing to the irresistible force of curiosity.

"Go ahead, tell me," he said.

Downing circled the desk and sat in Christensen's chair. He was still wearing his trenchcoat, and wet tracks followed him across the carpet. He hadn't bothered to wipe his feet when he came in.

"I interviewed Sonny's mom a few days ago," he said. "Figured it was worth a shot, what with her being in the house at the time, too. But she's way too far gone in the head to be much use."

"You weren't counting on her anyway, right?"

"Like I said, it was worth a shot. But now I've got a problem."

Christensen sat down in the chair, facing Downing across the desk. His desk. How did Downing always manage to end up behind *his* desk?

"She's got this shrink out at Borman, name's Root. Douglas Root. Know him?"

Christensen shrugged.

"Well, this Root guy calls me practically the minute I get back to my office after talking to her, and he wants to know what the hell I'm doing harassing his patient. I handled it like a pro, very polite, but he doesn't let up."

"Harassing?"

"I talked to her. That's all, swear to God. Swapped a few pleasantries. Talked a little about Sonny. Just felt her out about Ron to see if she kept in touch or if she remembered anything from 1986."

"And?"

"Brain mush," Downing said. "Watches cartoons all day.

So I thanked her and left, and the next thing I know her
shrink's in my face talking about harassment and how I
could have fucked up years of therapy. Between you, me,
and the fence post, if she's better now, she must have been
a total drooler before."

Mr. Sensitive.

"Sonny talked about his mom a little last week," Christensen said. "Sounds like a classic case. History of docu-
mented abuse going back at least to her father. I'm guessing
the Bible wasn't the only thing he thumped. Incest a definite
possibility. So, big surprise, Sandra grows up to marry an
abusive husband. Therapy can help, but some wounds don't
heal."

Downing stopped, sniffed the air. "Dinner smells great,"
he said. "What are you having?"

Brenna must have taken the lasagna tray out of the oven
and started serving the kids. Christensen ignored the question, then checked his watch as obviously as he could.

"Anyway, this Root starts getting a little heavy with me,"
Downing said. "I had no right to take advantage of her, that
kind of stuff. So I kind of blew him off. That's my problem.
His lawyers wrote this letter."

Downing reached into his coat for something in an inside
pocket, then handed a piece of paper across the desk. The
letter unfolded easily. Its pages had been stapled, but the
staple was gone. The letterhead read: Musca, Hickton &
Cook.

Christensen looked it over carefully. From the closing
paragraphs and vague reference to an enclosed newspaper
clipping, he sensed a carefully worded but unmistakable
threat. Leave Mrs. Corbett alone, it said, in order to avoid
the "potential embarrassment" of a civil suit that would
expose the department's "continued but misguided faith in
Det. Downing."

"This went to the police chief?"

"CC'ed to my department head. Can you believe that?
The guano really hit the fan."

"Why? They knew you were going to talk to her, right?"

Downing suddenly seemed to notice the picture of Molly

and the girls. "Certain people did, sure. But like I told you when we first talked, there were problems with the original investigation. Somebody had to wear the goat head, and that was me. You've got to understand something about a police department. It's like a shark tank. Word gets out I'm back on Primenyl, there's a feeding frenzy. So I've been trying to keep it low-profile."

Christensen didn't like the Polaroid impression of Downing that was forming in his mind. The man now sitting casually behind his desk had set Christensen and Sonny off on a very risky journey. At the same time, he apparently was treading into some murky areas of department policy. Downing's renewed interest in the Primenyl case was making waves, but not the kind Christensen had expected.

"Grady, I've got to be honest. I'm starting to get really uneasy about this."

Downing waved him off. "I got it all smoothed over already. I called this Root guy back and made nice. Apologized for blowing him off. He's really just worried about his patient, and I can respect that, even if his lawyers are thugs. I just explained what happened, that it was a chat, not an interrogation. And I told him I wouldn't talk to her again. She's of no use to me."

"What about this other stuff?"

"What other stuff?"

"The department knows what you're up to, right?"

"Oh, yeah. Everybody who needs to know is on board."

"And they know I'm involved?"

Downing looked him straight in the eye. "Absolutely. What pisses me off is my bosses cut me some slack so I could work this case again. Something like this could make them change their minds. Pfft. I'm back working junkie snuffs until I retire in a couple months and Primenyl never gets out of the files again. It's always easier to do nothing than take a chance."

The detective sniffed again. "Man, what *is* that?"

"Lasagna."

"She cooks, too?"

"Frozen. Just pop it in the oven. I'm raising two kids on frozen food."

Downing's laugh was sharp and forced, then his face went serious. "Look, won't you tell me anything about what Sonny's talking about? I need to know where we stand. I'm running out of time. Don't be coy."

"Grady . . ."

"Be your best friend."

Christensen sighed. "Friends like you I don't need."

Downing waited. And waited.

"It stays between us, right?" Christensen said.

"Absolutely." The detective leaned back in the desk chair, still waiting.

"Okay. Basically, we've come up with nothing you can use."

Downing forced a smile. "For that I promised my lifelong friendship? Come on."

Was it fair to toy with this man, who was so obviously emotionally invested in the case? Probably not. "Here's the Cliff Notes version, all right? Sonny's made some progress. He's convinced the numbness in his hands could be psychosomatic, and he came to that conclusion without much help from me. He just couldn't find any other plausible explanation for it. I'm not sure he sees the numbness as a symptom of posttraumatic stress, and he's definitely not thinking of it in terms of repressed memories. He *is* talking more about his past, though, and some things are bubbling up as dreams that may or may not be memories. But nothing in any way related to Primenyl."

Downing clasped his hands behind his head and put one foot up on the desk. "What makes you think they could be memories?"

A checkerboard tile floor swam into Christensen's mind, and a dog named Izzy Vicious. "He dreams in pretty good detail. Physical detail. And some things he's said seem consistent with what I can get out of the files."

"That's good, then." Downing sat forward, returning his foot to the floor and resting his elbows on the desk.

Christensen weighed his words carefully before continuing. "But there's something you should know. Some things he's described are dead-on, making me think they're memories. But some things he's talked about are pretty clearly fantasies and buried fears. I'm no prosecutor, but I'd think long and hard about relying on a supposed witness to something when the memories are as polluted as Sonny's."

Downing shook his head. "What's that mean, polluted?"

"As we've talked, he's started using more and more detail about growing up. But some of the things he's 'remembered' are just dead wrong. It's not like he's whitewashing anything, although that's apparently what he's done for years. This is more like he's making things up out of whole cloth. And you have to wonder where that's coming from."

"Lying?" Downing said.

"Hard to say."

"A fer instance?"

"I can't be specific, Grady. Really."

"But what makes you think he's making stuff up?"

Christensen winked. "Just damned good detective work."

Downing brought his hands together and folded them on the desk. His knuckles immediately went white. "Goddamn you, Jim. Don't leave me hanging. Tell me what you're talking about."

Christensen *was* being coy. But at least he was getting honest emotion out of Downing rather than his usual bullshit.

"Couple examples," he began. "Sonny talked the other day about his dad and baseball. What a great college player his dad was. Played third base, I think he said. The Pirates scouted him, according to Sonny. He was invited to try out with their Columbus farm team. All very vivid and detailed memories of Dad as Honus Wagner."

"So what's the problem?"

"It's all fantasy. He said his dad went to Clairmont Affiliated—it's a small pharmacy school down in West Virginia. And he did. I checked. But it never had athletic programs, baseball or otherwise."

"Maybe he's confused. Maybe it was high school."

"Doubt it. There's been other stuff like that. You should hear him talk about the traveling they did. He detoured onto that a couple of weeks ago, and he's brought it up a couple times since. Makes it sound like they were Swiss aristocrats. Four months in North Africa. A year on an island in the South Pacific. A six-month caravan across Alaska. Of course, none of that jibes with his school records. He's had pretty good attendance for someone who did so much globe-trotting."

Downing looked away.

"Grady, he's 'remembered' schools he never attended, places he never lived, relatives that don't exist. He's talked about an Aunt Rachel. Only problem is she doesn't exist, on either side of the family. I even checked his foster families. Nothing."

"So where does that stuff come from?" Downing said.

"Who knows? The name Rachel turns up once in his file, a neighbor lady two doors down who reported one of the domestics when the family lived in Highland Park, before they moved to Jancey Street. Maybe she baby-sat him. Maybe she gave out great treats at Halloween or did something else to scratch her name in his mind. But do you see what I mean by polluted? I couldn't ever testify to the accurate memories without talking about the fantasies."

Downing's gaze remained fixed somewhere between the window and the bookshelf. The only thing there was a wall socket. "So you're saying Sonny's not going to be much help."

"Grady, even if he remembered stacked cases of cyanide in the cellar, or Mr. Science working with Primenyl capsules at the kitchen table, is a jury going to believe him when I tell the whole story?"

Downing stood up and started to button his coat. "Gotta run," he said. "Thanks for your time. Hope I didn't ruin dinner."

The detective left so quickly all Christensen could do was close doors behind him. His tracks went down the front steps and disappeared into the dark. Somewhere down the block, a car door slammed, an engine revved, and the potent sound of Downing's Ford slowly withered to nothing. The silence he left behind was unnerving.

19

Trix had the place looking great. The bare branches of the maple tree out front were strung with tiny white lights, and she'd managed to get a seven-foot noble fir into a corner of the living room. Practically New Year's and it was still up. Downing could see it through the window, strung with the same white lights, as he crunched up the front walk and onto the porch. She'd lit a fire in the fireplace across the room and was sitting with her back to him, holding Rodney across her lap. Nothing like the smell of wood smoke on a winter day. How long had it been since they'd lit a fire?

He hung his coat on the front-hall rack, threw his sports jacket across the banister, and slid out of his wet shoes.

"I'm late," he said, walking toward the flames. "As usual."

She looked up. Mascara had run down both cheeks, and her eyes were rimmed in red. She started to talk but nothing came out. She'd really stoked the fire. The heat was intense.

"Look, I'm sorry. Had to stop by Jim Christensen's for a few minutes."

Then he noticed the dog. Rodney's eyes were open, but not moving. His mouth was open, too, locked in a way that made him look like he was gagging. Trix was rocking him gently on her lap, but he seemed too rigid. Junkie, gang victim, dog—didn't matter. Downing knew the look.

"Jesus, Trix. What happened?"

A cherry log popped and hissed. They both jumped. His wife said nothing, rocking the dead dog and crying softly. Downing bent down and stroked Rodney's head. Didn't look like he'd been hit by a car. No blood anywhere. Except for the open-eyed grimace, he could have been sleeping.

"He was lying in the backyard when I got home from work," she said. "He's frozen, Grady."

Suddenly, the fire made more sense. His wife was thawing their dog. A Currier and Ives scene, a Rod Serling production. Downing's reflexes took over.

"What time did you get home?"

Trix checked her watch. "About six-thirty. Forty minutes ago."

"Where in the backyard?"

"Along the fence, back in the corner."

Frozen, so he'd probably been there since at least mid-afternoon. Still daylight then. The back fence is chain-link and open to the alley. He struggled for comforting words, much like he did at crime scenes. "He's not even four years old, for Chrissakes. He cost three hundred dollars. What the hell?"

Trix gave him the glare. He knew that look, too.

"Yeah, boy, they don't make 'em like they used to," she said.

"That's not what I meant, Trix." He stood up. "I'll be right back."

He flipped on the spotlight and pushed through the back door. Christ, it was cold. No wind, though. He walked carefully along the stone steps toward the fence, letting his eyes adjust to the light. He remembered the advice of George Kovacic, his first partner in homicide. God's in the details, George used to say. God's in the details.

About four inches of snow remained from the latest storm. It was three days old and crusted on top, thanks to an afternoon of unexpected and brilliant sun. Nothing odd about Rodney's tracks. Most were around the mouth of his doghouse, where he stayed most of the day when it was cold. Downing had rigged a crude heater by mounting a 200-watt lightbulb high on the doghouse wall, then putting an empty one-gallon paint can over it. The cord ran, undisturbed, to a wall socket on the back porch. Since Rodney's stomach dragged in the snow anytime more than a couple inches accumulated, the only time he left his doghouse on days like this was to pee on the crab apple tree or crap in the garden right next to it. The snow in those areas was stained and packed by his passage.

Downing stooped and looked into the doghouse. A ring of light escaped beneath the paint can, so the heater was still working. From the doghouse's mouth, though, one set of tracks stood apart from the path to the crab apple tree. They branched off at a 45-degree angle directly from the dog-house to the back fence, a deliberate departure, like some-one in the alley had called him to come. And Rodney, friend to all, would have done just that, especially if they had food.

Downing stepped over the tracks and followed them to the chain-link. He looked both ways down the alley, but saw no obvious tracks near the fence. This was a working-class neighborhood, filled with plumbers, carpenters, secretaries, city workers. Not many stay-home parents. The only people around most weekdays were the retirees, and they stayed indoors during the winter. Would anyone have noticed someone back here?

Something in the snow caught his eye. He bent down for a closer look. There were three or four of them, and they glinted in the spotlight like diamonds in the snow. The largest was about the size of a dime. He flicked two or three of them into his palm and held them closer to his face. Tinfoil. Tiny bits of tinfoil. Squatting there, he noticed the deep and irregular furrow that scored the snow for about fifteen feet to his left. It ran along the fence, and seemed much too irregular for the smooth path of Rodney's drag-ging stomach. He looked closer. At one spot, the dog had fallen onto his side, leaving a perfect profile. At another, he seemed to have fallen and convulsed, sweeping snow with his runty legs, digging almost to the dead grass underneath.

Just beyond that, another profile. He'd died there on his side, with enough body heat left to melt the impression of a basset hound clear through to the grass.

Jesus, it was cold. He'd come out without a jacket. Downing put the bits of tinfoil into his shirt pocket and retraced his path, stepping carefully into the footprints he'd already left. He climbed the back-porch steps and pushed into the warmth of his kitchen. Trix hadn't moved. Neither had Rodney.

"Hard to tell what happened," he said.

She didn't turn around. She just watched the flames, listening to the pop and hiss of the burning logs. Rodney was her dog, always around, more dependable than her husband and much more affectionate. She'd told Downing as much, several times.

He sat on the hearth, closer to the white-hot coals. "I'm sorry, Trix."

"Will you bury him tomorrow?" Her eyes stayed on the fire. "Somewhere in Highland Park, maybe? I know the ground is hard, but I don't want to turn him over to some disposal service."

"I'll take him tonight," he said. "We'd better do it in the dark."

Finally she looked at him. "You really couldn't tell what happened?"

He shrugged. "He might have had a seizure. You been giving him his phenobarbs?"

"Every morning."

"It was so cold today. Maybe he had one of his spells and didn't come around in time." He hated lying to his wife. Against all odds, she still seemed to trust him. Which made it worse.

"That's probably what happened," she said, wiping a tear from her cheek. Big sigh. "Well, shit."

He wrapped the dog in a comforter, the ratty one they used to use for picnics when their daughter was young. She'd just left home again after a visit—better she wasn't here. Downing carried the bundle out the front door and

back down to the driveway. The Ford's engine was still
ticking.

He laid Rodney into the well, moving his Kevlar vest and
spare shotgun to make room, and slammed the trunk. Trix,
who was watching from the window, opened the front door.

"Won't you need something to dig with?" she shouted.

"Right." Downing retrieved a shovel and a pick from the
garage at the side of the house, if only to maintain the
illusion that he was going to the woods to bury her dog.

The delivery entrance to the Allegheny County morgue was
in the basement, just off Third Avenue. Downing hit the
opener that was clipped to the Ford's visor. The garage door
in front of him yawned slowly open and he drove into the
century-old building, which was tucked behind the jail and
county office buildings like a Gothic three-story mausoleum. There was no reason his gut should tighten like it did.
He came here a lot, whenever he thought he might find God
in the details of an autopsy. He'd watched a hundred
procedures, maybe more. So why did he feel like jamming
the car into reverse and slipping out before the garage door
closed behind him?

He parked beside Pungpreechawatn's black Crown Vic-
toria. He wasn't surprised to see it. Coroners kept odd hours.
But he was glad, since he'd hesitate to ask a favor of one of
Preech's creepy deputies. The top guy at least made big
money. But what's with deputy coroners? Who'd want to
spend all day hauling floaters out of the Mon River or
sacking road meat when you're making $20,000 a year?

He unlocked the trunk, lifted Rodney out, and closed the
trunk lid with his elbow. The garage was lit only by a small
ceiling fixture, so he picked his way carefully past the
floater freezer, stepping around the stacked boxes of alcohol, xylene, and formalin to the battered green freight
elevator to his right. The place reeked of formaldehyde.
Preech swore the cheery spider plants he hung all over the
building completely eliminated the odor. Preech needed to
get out more, obviously, but the plants did seem to thrive
here.

Downing stepped onto the corrugated steel surface of the elevator's scale, startled as it registered 310 pounds. As it lurched to the second floor, he calculated. He weighed 185, plus the dog's 60. Then he remembered to add the 65 preset pounds—the weight of an empty gurney. That was the 310.

The morgue was an architectural gem that had stood since 1897. Downing had watched the county struggle to upgrade the building in recent years, as if a granite masterpiece with walls twenty-eight inches thick could be improved by cheap wood paneling. The publicly accessible areas were a 1970s-era hell, complete with molded plastic chairs the color of a pumpkin and dropped ceilings that hid not only computer wiring, but the building's original gaslight fixtures. Scrape away the morgue's tarty makeup, Downing mused, and there'd still be a beauty underneath. The floors in the third-floor courtroom, now overlaid with durable nylon carpet, were solid marble, just as the embalming tables had been until the 1972 remodeling. No matter what ghastly surprise awaited him inside the cooler, Downing always paused before stepping into its 42-degree chill to marvel at the original foot-thick oak door.

The elevator opened into a nightmare of fluorescent light, linoleum, and bad wood paneling. The plastic pumpkin chairs lined a wall to his left. Preech sat behind his desk, eating curry out of a Tupperware bowl.

"Mr. Grady Downing," he said as Downing pushed through the door. He spoke with a heavy accent, but always in the proper English he learned as a child in India. "How do you do?"

Downing sat in the office chair facing the coroner, letting the dog's weight rest on the chair's arms. "Need a favor, Preech."

"We're very, very busy tonight, you know. The holidays. Much work to be done. We have four different crews out right now and they should return any moment. Any moment."

Downing lifted his bundle slightly. "I think Ron Corbett may have poisoned our dog."

The coroner stopped chewing, studied the comforter. "The same Ronald Corbett?"

Downing nodded. "I've been nosing around about those Greene County cases. They were practically in Corbett's backyard. So I'm sure it's got back to him by now that I'm talking to people again. Then tonight, our dog turns up dead. Looks like somebody fed him something through our back fence."

Preech forked another load of curry into his mouth and chewed it slowly. "What sort of favor do you need from us?"

Downing smiled. "I'm guessing the dog was dosed with the same stuff they found in Greene County. Can you check?"

"You believe cyanide to be involved in your dog's death as well?"

"Maybe. Hydrogen cyanide, I'd bet."

Preech shook his head. "It would be a very difficult problem, working here on a dog. The taxpayers of Allegheny County might not be pleased about my authorization of staff time and county resources to—"

"Please, Preech. For old times' sake. Just check him for chemicals."

The coroner looked at his watch. Downing looked at his as well. 9:30 P.M.

"I will not be able to do it until much later. The crews should be back anytime, and I will wait until they finish their work. There may be a break toward morning. I will do it myself between shifts."

Downing was already thinking about the nearby crime lab, and who there might do him a favor. Traces of whatever killed Rodney were probably all over the bits of tinfoil.

"You're a prince, Preech. Can I call you tomorrow?"

"Late. After dinnertime."

Downing stood up, unsure about what to do next. The dog was getting heavy.

The coroner sighed, deeply and obviously. "Put it here behind my desk," he said. "I believe it best that no one sees."

20

Sonny stood barefoot at the pool's rim, his toes curled over the edge. "Don't forget your rainbow arms!" he shouted. "Try it." Annie listened, as attentive as Christensen had ever seen her.

From his plastic chair near the coach's office, Christensen worried again about bringing Sonny along. As productive as their recent sessions had been, conversations in his office offered a limited view. He occasionally liked to see clients in less artificial situations, which gave him a more three-dimensional understanding. Annie's weekly swimming lesson seemed a perfect chance to get Sonny out of the office, to build another level of trust. They'd probably need that in the weeks ahead. But the fact remained: The chain between Sonny Corbett and his father was a short one. How much of himself should he share with someone so close to a killer?

"Let's see those rainbows!"

Annie pushed off the submerged platform, what she called the tower, and dog-paddled furiously to the edge of the pool fifteen feet away. After three months of lessons, she'd never even attempted that distance. She hated their Saturday ritual in the Highland Park Natatorium, hated that he hadn't given in to her protests to quit. The only reason she'd agreed to stay after her regular lesson was that, in the ninety minutes since he'd introduced her to Sonny Corbett, she'd developed a devastating crush. She would do anything he asked, and her father, for all intents and purposes, had ceased to exist.

"That was great!" Sonny said. "Try it again, back to the tower."

"Did you see me? I swam!" she shouted, asking Sonny, of course, not her father. Her tiny voice echoed off the empty building's high ceiling. The other kids and parents had left. Annie's swim teacher, Wendy, was finding reasons to hang around—picking up towels, straightening kickboards, lining up the lane dividers just so. She was nineteen, pretty, with legs up to her shoulders, and she blushed crimson when Sonny shook her hand and politely asked if he could work with her student for a few minutes after the lesson. Wendy and Annie were eyeing Sonny in much the same way, although Sonny didn't seem to notice. He just bent down and slapped Annie five.

"Ten more times. Just back and forth. Don't forget: rainbow arms. And breathe!" He stood and demonstrated the Australian crawl, his head turning mechanically for breath on every second stroke. He was sweating heavily in the humid, 80-degree heat, and a dark patch dampened the T-shirt stretched tight across his back. In his dreams, Christensen had shoulders like that.

Annie dog-paddled back to the tower. No form whatsoever, but no hesitation either.

"She'll do fine once she stops being so afraid," Sonny said, easing into a nearby chair. He wiped his feet with a towel and pulled on his white socks and off-brand running shoes.

"You've got a real fan club going here." Christensen nodded first to his thrashing daughter, then to Wendy, who was arranging pool chairs in a precise line along the natatorium wall. Sonny looked up but continued his shoe-tying.

"The skills will come," he said. "Most instructors try to move too fast. Right now, she just needs to build up her confidence. They never make any progress until they let go of the edge."

"That goes for any of us, Sonny" he said. "Don't you think?"

No reaction. Annie was doing as she'd been told, splashing back and forth between the tower and the pool rim.

Wendy lightly touched Sonny's shoulder, her shyness lost to astonishment at Annie's sudden progress. "How'd you get her to do that?" She'd pulled on a baggy sweatshirt, but those legs were still bare. "She's been a total Cling-on since we started. Now she's, like, Little Miss Fearless."

Sonny shrugged. "Kids are funny. Sometimes they just have to hear the same thing from a different person and all of a sudden they listen. All I did was ask her to do it, and she did."

"She's got a plan, I'm sure," Christensen said. "Machiavelli in pigtails." Again, no one seemed to hear. Why did he feel invisible?

"Does poop float?" Annie shouted. She'd stopped at the tower and was looking toward the south end of the pool. "Gross. I think there's poop and it's coming toward me."

Wendy confirmed the sighting and sulked off to get a net and some disinfectant chemicals.

"I'm staying on the tower," Annie shouted.

"One of the hazards of teaching toddlers," Sonny said. "I used to teach that age group sometimes, but only when I really needed money."

Christensen gathered up Annie's towel, sweat suit, and sneakers. He'd finally remembered to bring a hair dryer so she wouldn't have to cross the parking lot with a wet head, but now he wondered where to plug it in.

"Can I ask you something, Sonny?" He didn't wait for an answer. "We've been at this a few weeks now. How do you feel about it?"

Sonny finished tying his shoes, then sat back, avoiding eye contact. "Wanted to talk to you about that," he said. "I'm not sure I'm ready to go on with all this."

"No?" Hardly the answer Christensen had anticipated.

Sonny held out his hands and flexed them, palms down. "Started talking to you because of my hands, but now we're getting into all this other stuff. And some of it's pretty weird. I'm not sleeping. My training's way off. And nothing's changed with my hands. They still short out on me pretty regular."

"So you're wondering, What's the point? Right?"

Sonny nodded.

"A legitimate question, I guess."

They watched Wendy corral the turd with a long-handled net. Annie watched her, too, shivering on the tower in her frilly pink suit.

"Like the dreams. They're getting stranger. Scary sometimes. Like, I woke up the other night yelling and coughing and crying about how I couldn't breathe. My roommates think I'm nuts. Wonder myself sometimes."

Christensen untied the double knots in Annie's shoelaces, getting them ready. "And it was scary to you?"

"What do you think?" Sonny said.

"Painful?"

"You try not breathing and let me know."

In his office, Christensen might have pushed. Not here. But he didn't want to just walk away from it. "That's all started happening since we met, hasn't it?"

Sonny nodded.

"Do you think that might be significant in some way? That talking about growing up, your family, all that, seems to trigger these disturbing dreams? We know a lot of them are just dreams. A few we've pegged as memories that just felt like dreams. But either way, I'm wondering, if we keep talking, maybe we'll find the reason your hands started going numb in the first place. That's still what we're after, right?"

Sonny flexed his hands again. "Not sure."

"About what?"

"About going on. About talking to you. I feel like I followed you into this long tunnel. Can't see what's ahead, and didn't like what I saw on the way in. I just want to turn and run back out."

Christensen touched Sonny's knee. "I'm still with you, though. I wouldn't just leave you there."

"But you don't have a flashlight, either."

Christensen laughed. "Got me there. But I think you know you can't just run back out."

"Why not?"

"Listen to what you're saying, Sonny. Do you really think you can stop the dreams by not seeing me anymore, by not talking about it?"

They stopped while Wendy began the rescue operation. Annie was refusing to get back in the water. "Hang on to the edge of the tower," Wendy said, hooking the platform's leg with a long aluminum rescue bar. "I'm going to drag it to the side."

"I'd like to try," Sonny said. "Nothing personal, but I need a break."

Christensen was used to clients walking away from therapy when it got too painful. Chances were, Sonny would be back. But Downing wasn't going to take it well.

"Your choice, Sonny. But you call me anytime if you need to talk. And if you ever feel the need to start getting together again, don't hesitate." Christensen opened his wallet, pulled out a business card, and scribbled on the back. "Here's my home number."

Sonny studied the card. "No address?"

Christensen studied Sonny, wondering why he wanted to know it. Annie suddenly bounded up, soaking wet, wearing her towel like a cape. "Pooping in the pool's not okay," she said.

"No, it's not," he said. "It puts bad germs in the water."

She leaned an elbow on Sonny's knee and nodded disapprovingly toward the pool. Sonny didn't seem to notice. "Probably just some kid," she said. "Where's my treat?"

21

Annie was asleep against her door, as usual, before the Explorer got out of the natatorium parking lot. By the time Christensen dropped Sonny at his apartment, she was an exhausted heap in the backseat, a half-eaten bag of potato chips somewhere underneath her. She'd probably sleep until dinner.

Sonny'll probably be fine, Christensen thought as he carried Annie up his front steps. He was strong and resilient. Downing was another matter. He wasn't looking forward to that call, to telling Downing his best shot at resolving the Primenyl case might have failed. But Sonny's decision made Christensen realize how much stress their relationship had added to his life. The time commitment was one thing. The constant in-the-headlights feeling was something he'd never imagined.

"Call Brenna," Melissa said. She brushed by with her coat on, headed out the front door as he was headed in. "Mail's on the kitchen counter. I'm going out."

He stood there, holding Annie, struggling to keep the storm door from slamming shut. "Where are you going?"

"Where does a fire go when it goes out?"

"A straight answer, please, Lissa."

"Sarah's," she called over her shoulder. She was moving

down the sidewalk at a good clip to discourage further conversation.

"Be back for dinner, please," he called, but she walked on.

He laid Annie on the couch and covered her with the plush goose-down comforter Molly had bought years ago in California. He was a grad student then, living off practically nothing, and they'd fought about the extravagance of it, about her refusal to compromise on quality. She only bought things that lasted, and the house was still full of her.

The kitchen was reasonably intact, although Melissa's lunch dishes were in the sink, unrinsed. He flipped absently through the pile of utility bills, credit-card solicitations, and university newsletters on the counter, then picked up a paper-wrapped package a little bigger than a paperback book. The mailing label was typed. The postmark was from the Highland Park station, about a mile away. It was lightweight but solid. A videocassette maybe?

He slid his thumb underneath the tape on the back and tore away the wrapping paper. A video. Unlabeled. Unboxed. It wasn't even in a sleeve. He checked the torn wrapping paper. No note. No return address. If it was direct-mail, it was intriguing enough to be effective. Sheer ambiguity saved it from the trash, where he always put the real-estate previews, merchandise catalogs, and other direct-mail videotapes that showed up from time to time. This one he laid on the counter while he made himself a sandwich from a leftover roasted chicken. He dumped the carcass and the rest of the pickings into two quarts of water. A couple diced onions, celery, some dried noodles and thyme, a bouillon cube or two, and voila! An all-natural eat-when-you're-ready dinner for himself and the girls, one made almost entirely without anything packaged.

Annie was stretched out like a warm cat under the comforter. After pushing the videotape into the VCR, he moved her feet to make room to sit, set his plate on the coffee table, opened an Iron City Dark, and picked up the remote control. The Penn State football game on ESPN was a rout, with Michigan State down 24 in the fourth. He didn't care about the Ohio State game on CBS. He clicked the remote to VCR and aimed. The screen turned black.

The first scene, a crowded street, appeared suddenly in a jostled blur. Definitely not a slick promotional video. The date in the lower right corner said November 28. He boosted the volume but there was no narration, only the uneven thrum of passing traffic. The camera lurched along the crowded sidewalk. Christensen recognized a building across the street as the Pitt law library. The light meter adjusted as the camera passed beneath a dark awning. A polished oak facade came into view on the left. The front entrance of Primanti Brothers. He could almost smell the fish sand-wiches.

If it was a promotional video, somebody was ripping off the Primantis. Christensen took a bite of his sandwich and a long pull on his beer. It tasted like a carbonated Fudgsicle. He wished he could get it year-round instead of just in the fall.

The camera burst back into daylight, then zoomed. The bustle of the sidewalks filtered away, and the frame filled, ultimately, with the backs of two men walking away from the camera. As they rounded a right corner, the lower floors of the Cathedral of Learning loomed into view. They walked at a leisurely pace, talking. Puffs of vapor occasion-ally curled around their heads and trailed away. One wore a tan trenchcoat. His hair thinned at the crown, but only slightly. The other wore some sort of black-and-gold ath-letic jacket. All four hands were in jacket pockets.

Christensen swallowed another mouthful of sandwich and savored the frothy bite of the beer at the back of his throat, then checked his watch. He'd better call Brenna, he thought. He was reaching for the remote when the man in the trenchcoat turned toward the other.

Grady Downing?

He looked closer, but the man had turned his face away. The profile was gone. Christensen rewound the tape. Down-ing, definitely. The mustache gave it away. And all the pieces fit. The bald spot. The broad back. The trenchcoat. Why would Downing send him a videotape of himself?

No, wait. Downing obviously hadn't shot this tape. Someone else had.

The two men turn another corner, into the side parking-lot entrance of the student union. Christensen stopped, the sandwich suspended inches from his mouth, finally recognizing the second man as himself. The jacket had thrown him off, but now he remembered Downing pulling a Steelers jacket out of his car and offering it to him that day they'd walked around Oakland talking about the Primenyl case, the day Downing had asked him to evaluate Sonny Corbett. They were on their way back to his office in the student union, where Brenna was waiting with a sack of groceries.

The screen went blank, then sparked to life again. Christensen put his sandwich down, his appetite gone. This was creepy.

A panning shot of a street, his street. His house, shot from where? Some distance away. He did the triangulation. Probably from the corner of Kent Drive, a block away and across the street. He checked the volume. Nothing still. The camera continued its slow pan, stopping finally at Mrs. Taubman's house. A zoom. Her front yard, green. No snow. The date in the lower right corner of the frame disappeared before he thought to look at it, so he rewound. December 5. It blinked off again. Zooming again. Mrs. Taubman's house. Tighter. Her front yard, littered with day-care toys. Tighter. Her front steps. Tighter still. Someone sitting on the steps in an oversized parka, a Barbie in each mittened hand.

Annie.

A car passed across the screen, briefly blocking the view. Its engine noise faded, and the screen blanked again. The whole segment lasted maybe thirty seconds, but Christensen's heart was pounding. What until then had been confusion and vague discomfort suddenly focused: Someone was watching from the moment Downing had first approached him about the Primenyl case, and that person apparently knew where he lived.

Another scene. Sidewalks again, but indoors. A fountain. An escalator. The East Hills Mall. A group of teenagers slouched on a bench outside the Mrs. Fields cookie shop. They talked, but he couldn't make out the words. He recognized Melissa's friend Sarah first, even though her back was toward the camera. She had hair to her waist. And Melissa. She was smoking a long, thin cigarette. Another zoom. His daughter filled the screen, practicing her French inhale.

Son of a bitch. *Who's following my kids?*

Black again. Or was it? Pinpoints of light crept across the screen. Was it night? The lights weren't moving, the camera was. Then it stopped. Still December 5. His backyard. In the glow of the spotlight on the rear of his house, a steady rain fell. Camera lens flecked with droplets. His garbage cans lined the front wall of the garage. His toolshed in the background. A panning shot of the house. The upstairs lights were dark, the kitchen light on.

Black again, then the shot resumed from a slightly different angle, this time focused on the garage. Whoever shot it must have been in McAllister's backyard. Christensen moved from the couch to the coffee table to be closer to the screen. The door to the garage loft was open. He looked closer. Someone in the shadows. The figure leaned out into the rain, then leaned back in. He was wearing his faded Pitt sweatshirt. He knew right away he wasn't alone. He never went into Molly's loft alone. When he finally ducked into full view and headed through the rain toward the house, Brenna was close behind, laughing, holding his hand and wearing one of his blue oxford shirts with the sleeves rolled up. The camera followed them in the back door, then went black again.

He looked around the room, feeling invaded and vulnerable. Annie stirred, then burrowed deeper beneath the comforter. His sandwich lay on the floor between the couch and the coffee table in mayo-smeared piles of bread and roast chicken. He didn't even realize he'd dropped it.

The videotape continued, crushing his illusions of security with each innocuous scene. Another yard, this one unfamiliar. Daylight. Snow. The camera panned a row of houses stretching side by side into the distance. He didn't recognize the scene; it could have been any one of a number of city neighborhoods. In the foreground, a chain-link fence backed up to an alley. The camera returned slowly until it was pointed almost straight down.

A dog, a sloe-eyed basset, stared up into the lens, tail wagging, snuffling. Slobber streamed from his lower jaw, barely visible against the snow. The camera wavered, then something fell into the frame. Something silver, or red, landed near the dog and disappeared beneath the snow, and the dog set right to the search with his short front paws.

Christensen was numb. He didn't know the relevance of the scene, but he knew something was wrong. Something was about to happen. He knew it as surely as the time he'd watched two speeding cars collide at the base of Negley hill. Nothing he or anyone else could do until the sickening hulks of twisted metal spun to a stop. And even then, nothing could be done.

The dog delicately pulled the foil from the snow by an unfolded corner. The contents looked like hamburger, and after a cursory sniff, the dog ate it in a series of almost dainty bites. He stood licking the streamers from his chops. Ran his snout over the foil again, then snaked his tongue inside for the remaining morsels. Tail whirling like a propeller. The dog held one corner of the foil down, tore off a piece with his teeth, chewed, and swallowed. It seemed to be reconsidering this when suddenly its legs collapsed.

Lying belly down in the snow, the dog shuddered. Its neck seemed suddenly weak, like it was trying to lift its head but couldn't. Its chin was buried, plowing snow as the head moved from side to side. Its rear end rose, then collapsed again. The tail went limp.

Christensen instinctively looked away, then forced his eyes back to the screen. The dog was up, trying to walk away from the camera, making guttural sounds, almost like a cow, as it moved along the fence. It turned back, lips curled off the teeth in a half-snarl. The eyes were wide, confused, desperate. It gagged and fell again. It struggled to its feet, lurched a few more steps, fell again. This time, it didn't get up. Its body heaved, the buck and thrash digging a grisly dog-angel in the snow. Then, finally, it was still.

Black again. Christensen buried his face in hands as cold as ice. The screen was still black when he looked up. Please let it be over, he thought. But he let the videotape roll, ten, twenty, thirty seconds. He was about to shut it off when the screen filled with a still shot of hand-painted numbers on decorative tiles. Tiles Molly bought in a craft store in New Hope three years before she died. Tiles he spent an entire Saturday mounting on the wall beside the front door. Tiles that in sequence read 3545 Bryant—his address.

Then it was gone, a blip of a scene. Fast forward. Blank. Rewind. He released the button when the final scene flashed past. His address tiles blinked on again, maybe three seconds, then off. Rewind again. No sound. No movement. Just a primal-fear moment chiseled forever into his psyche by someone with a video camera standing on his front porch.

One more time. This time he noticed the date, stark and white against the dark green trim around his front door. December 19. The day before yesterday.

22

Downing coughed twice, sounding as pathetic as he could, while the councilman's niece read off his messages. One was from Christensen, logged an hour earlier. "He wants you to call him right away," she said. "Sounded pretty upset."

It could wait. First things first. He hung up and dialed the phone, and the morgue receptionist put him straight through.

"Ah, Detective Downing," Preech said. "I am very, very sorry for the delay. We have been quite busy. The Christmas holidays, you know. But I have been trying most diligently to reach you since this morning."

"Had some errands, Preech. What's up?"

"Let me find my notes." Shuffling papers. "It was quite difficult to find a time to work on your doggie in private. Things are quite hectic here, quite hectic. But it is done, mostly, although we are still awaiting the toxicology results, the blood work and so forth. The physical symptoms most definitely were suggestive of poisoning, quite possibly cyanide. Not a very cheery picture, I'm afraid."

"He was bloody when you opened him up?" Downing wasn't surprised at all, but there was a weakness to his voice he hadn't anticipated.

"Doggie's organs were full of blood. That is how the body reacts to the presence of the toxin, as you know. And a definite odor of bitter almonds. We have seen all this before, have we not?"

"Thanks, Preech. You're keeping this between us, right?"

"As I have promised."

An afterthought. "What did you do with him?"

"An excellent question, Grady Downing, because I will need your help to please remove doggie from the premises. I put him back together, of course, but right now he is in my freezer. That must by necessity be a temporary arrangement."

Downing imagined a black plastic garbage bag secured by a twist-tie at one end, a standout among the refrigerated cadavers in the morgue's icebox. Someone was sure to ask questions. "Can't you just handle it, Preech? Send him out with the garbage so no one will know. I don't think we should leave him in your cooler too long, either."

"You misunderstand, my friend. I could not risk putting him with the others. Doggie is in my office refrigerator, in the freezer, and for that I had to move my frozen entrees to the refrigerator. I can eat one this evening, but the rest need to go back in."

Downing's stomach lurched. "Beyond the call, Preech. Thanks. I'm headed out. I'll stop by in a bit, but if anybody asks I'm home sick today, okay?"

"Please be prompt. My prepared meals are beginning to thaw."

23

Downing checked the alley in both directions, then heaved the garbage bag over the side of the Dumpster. DiOrio's Pizzeria would never know. Even if some greaseball trash diver did open the bag, Rodney's choke chain and tags were in a white coroner's office envelope in his car. There'd be no tracing it back to him. He checked the alley again as he limped around to shut the trunk. All clear. So long, old buddy.

Interstate 79 ran due south from Little Washington to Waynesburg, a relatively straight shot considering the Appalachian foothills that rolled along through coal country. Downing got back on at the same exit he got off, dug his fingernail into the skin of a Texas Ruby Red, and steered the Ford into the fast lane with his knees.

Traffic was light. Could have followed 79 straight south, to Morgantown, Charleston, Beckley, Bluefield. Then where? Where could he go that he wouldn't see Ron Corbett's grizzled face every time he closed his eyes?

He fanned the stack of phone messages clipped to the dashboard. Should have returned Christensen's calls before he left. Something could be up with Sonny. But even if it was, it could keep until the end of the day. Too much to do. Between sloppy bites of grapefruit, he worked the radio dial. The scanner was off. So was the two-way. So was his beeper. Those were for official police work. Today, he'd told DeLillo, he was too sick to come in. Nasty flu, he'd said, offering just enough detail to make the bastard believe.

KDKA had the strongest signal, even if the music sucked. Just find something and drive. He checked his watch. 8:30. He'd be there by 9:15. That gave him a full day. He turned up the volume for the half-hourly news, taking it as a good sign when the lead story was about the JoAnn Cuddy product-tampering case. Family of the dead woman was suing the Ranch Bounty supermarket chain, trying to ease their pain with a few million cash in actual and punitive damages "to focus attention on the lack of security." Bless their grieving little hearts.

He ordered the day in his head. Ranch Bounty was the first stop. The manager's asshole was probably pretty puckered because of the lawsuit, so he'd have to convince him he wasn't the family's PI. The yogurt shipment had arrived mid-afternoon two days before the woman bought it, so the locals had narrowed the killer's window of opportunity to the forty-eight hours before she was in the store. They'd already checked the store's security camera tapes and declared them worthless when no one turned up on tape poking a big fucking hypo through the yogurt lid. Like Corbett would do it right there in the store. He'd wanted to smack Ramsey when he said it, ask him if maybe it was possible the killer injected it somewhere else and brought it back to the shelf, so as not to be too obvious. But he'd held his tongue. Less said, the better.

He'd go over the tape himself if he could, then start nosing around. See if any of the checkers or stock boys recognized Corbett's picture. Do the same at the two licensed cyanide distributors in the area, see if anybody knew the face or wanted to share purchase records. He wanted to be in Outcrop once the sun went down to check out the view again from behind Corbett's house, look for a faster way out of that strip-mine hollow just in case he ever needed it.

And he'd been thinking he might. All options were still open, even the extralegal one. He'd be retired in a couple months. He'd have the rest of his life to sort out the morality questions. There'd be a lot, but he could live with them. Lot of other people might live, too.

The manager fancied himself quite the stud. Late twenties. Knowing smile. TV anchorman hair. A John Davidson look-alike in a red Ranch Bounty blazer, eyes locked onto the baby blues of an idle checker with a seventeen-year-old's ass. Downing guessed the manager's career would peak right here, in this godforsaken chain supermarket in Waynesburg, Pennsylvania, the future filled with aisle cleanups and a succession of fresh-meat hires and lonely housewives seduced by a man in uniform.

"You the store manager?" Downing interrupted.

John Davidson turned, annoyed as hell. Name tag said Richard. He forced a smile as the girl walked back to her checkout register and flipped the "Closed" sign to "Open." A customer immediately raced from another line, unloaded half a dozen items onto the conveyor, and swiped what looked like a credit card through a magnetic reader.

"What can I do for you?" the manager said.

Downing fished his badge from inside his coat. "Grady Downing, Pittsburgh Police Department. Got a minute to talk, Dick?"

The manager led him to a sweltering office at the rear of the store, behind the refrigerated dairy case that blew hot air into the back rooms. He closed the door behind them and sat down.

"You're a little late," he said, propping his feet on the grim metal desk. "Cops and TV people stopped coming around weeks ago."

Downing faked astonishment. Guys like Dick could turn ten seconds on the local news into a lifetime of pickup lines in a town like this. "TV people? You were on the TV?"

"Channels 2, 4, and 11. Radio, too. That was right after. But now you have to go through corporate."

Patient smile. "And I'd do just that if I was a reporter. But I'm not. Besides, corporate wasn't here that day. I'm guessing you were, along with some of your employees. No big deal, Dick. I just want to talk. No pressure."

"It's Richard."

"Richard, then."

"They see me on TV again I'll get fired. Especially with the lawsuit."

Downing gestured grandly around the office. "See, no camera crew. No microphones. Just curious little old me."

The manager produced a piece of paper on Ranch Bounty letterhead. "They gave me this statement to read," he said. "Basically says we're sure the tampering took place some-where else since nothing turned up on the security camera tapes. Cops already went through all that."

"Tell me about that."

"You'd have to talk to them. They wouldn't let me in. But they spent, like, nineteen hours going through tapes of the two days before Mrs. Cuddy bought the yogurt. All I know is they said they weren't any help."

Downing leaned against the door. "Still got the tapes?"

"Cops took 'em."

Shit. He could have bullied them out of Dick here, but trying to get them from the locals would raise a lot of questions. Like what the hell was he doing? Like why was he second-guessing their investigation?

"I'll talk to them about it, then. Detective Ramsey's an old friend."

"He's my cousin."

"No kidding!" Downing said, thinking, *Fuck*. He should have known better in a place as inbred as Greene County.

"Where'd you say you were from?"

"Pittsburgh. Say, is it me, or have supermarkets changed a lot? My wife does all our shopping, I have to confess, but I didn't even know you could pay for groceries with credit cards nowadays."

"Pittsburgh? Down here?"

"Noticed it when I came in," Downing said, forcing the conversation in a different direction. "Your checkout stands have those electronic credit-card reader things. Must make it easier for you guys, not handling all that cash."

"That's for Bounty Club cards. We do take the majors, though. And ATM cards."

"Whoa, whoa, whoa. Bounty Club? What's that?"

"Discounts," Dick said. "What planet did you say you were from?"

Downing faked a ridiculously hearty laugh. "Maybe I should get out once in a while, huh? So how's it work?"

"You join the club, you get automatic discounts on stuff. Just swipe the card through before you check out, and the register gives you credit for anything that's discounted on the inventory computer. Customers feel like they get something for nothing, and we get a record of how often people shop, what stores they shop at, what they buy. Then we can send them coupons for the things they buy most. Keeps 'em coming back here, see?"

"I'll be damned," Downing said. "Very smart."

The manager puffed up. "I'm the pilot store in Greene County. Only one. You probably got a lot of stores with it in Pittsburgh. Been around for years, just not here."

"And it keeps a record of everybody that buys something?"

"As long as they're in the Bounty Club. Doesn't cost nothing to sign up."

"What'll they think of next?" Downing said. "I suppose the police went through all that when they were here."

"Not really," the manager said, then stopped. "But you'll have to go through corporate."

"Is the computer in the store here?"

"Big mainframe up in Little Washington," he said. "So I couldn't let you see it even if I wanted, which I don't."

Downing grinned. "You get printed records, though, don't you? So you'll know who your customers are. So you'll know what stuff to put in end displays or at eye level. You probably handle all the direct-mail stuff here, right?"

"Nope. All that's done from Little Washington."

"You get a list, though, I'll bet. I'm imagining a big alphabetical list, or maybe one arranged by date. Which is it?"

"Really can't say."

Downing had come prepared. He reached into his pants pocket, peeled a bill from the outside of his small wad, and laid it on the desk. Dick stared.

"I can't," he said.

Downing produced another fifty. "Sure you can."

"I'll get in trouble."

"Who'll know?"

"You can run it either way, by name or by date. If I run it, they'll know. Computer keeps a record."

Another fifty. "When was the last list run?"

"Week before last. For the big Christmas mailing. But we keep them for six months."

"Alphabetical?"

The manager nodded. His eyes went back and forth several times between Downing and the money.

"Perfect. And I'll bet you wouldn't mind giving me five minutes alone with that list. That's all I need."

Come on, Dickie. Think of all the rubbers a hundred and fifty bucks would buy. The manager stood up, folded the money into his pants pocket, then stooped down behind the desk. From a bottom drawer, he pulled two inch-thick computer printouts.

"September and October," he said. "I've got to run up front to check on a produce delivery. Be back in five minutes."

Downing moved to the desk chair as soon as the door shut. Maybe Corbett was a regular Ranch Bounty shopper. At the least, he'd have been in the store once or twice in the weeks before making the drop to check the layout and develop a plan. He'd probably have bought something, if only to seem less suspicious. Was he the type to use a Bounty Club card? Probably not, but it was a shot.

He unfolded the September printout and ran his finger down the list to the names beginning with C. Cakula. Cernan. Ciecelski. Cochran. Connelly. Connor. Corcoran. Corbett, Carla. Corbett, Peter. Corbett, Rose Ann. Corbett, Thomas P. He felt a chill as his finger reached Cuddy, JoAnn. But no Corbett, Ron.

Shit. He traced one of the listings to the far right edge of the page. Adrian Ciecelski, whoever she was, visited four times in September, showing a fondness for Weight Watchers entrees, Vlasic kosher dills, and diet Coke. Last visit that month was on the 29th. Bounty Club member since the previous April. Downing scanned other "Member since" listings. Most were since April, nearly all issued by this store. April must have been when they started the pilot project. He marveled at the abbreviated paragraphs of purchase records. James and Kim Corcoran cleaned their toilets with Sani-Flush, ate too many salty snacks, and bought Frankenberry cereal. Must have kids. Kim apparently preferred Lightdays sanitary napkins. Rose Ann Corbett and her family ate Great Grains cereal at a two-box-a-week clip, and they liked Bounty-Brand Garden Style Spaghetti Sauce over the name brands. She also used K-Y jelly.

Up and down the pages, the computer matched names with products, little snapshots of lifestyles and personalities. Good old American marketing. Why hadn't he heard of this before? Why hadn't some shrewd defense attorney subpoenaed this kind of stuff for a rape trial and used the victim's contraceptive foam purchase history to show what a fuckbunny she was, show how it was all her fault. Just a matter of time.

He set September aside and opened the October printout, running his finger along the left edge, looking for Corbetts. He ran his finger past Corbett, Sandra and Ronald, then came back to it. He traced the dotted line across the page to their Ranch Bounty biography. Member since 1985. Downing drew a sharp breath: The card came from a Ranch Bounty store in Pittsburgh's East End, where the Corbetts lived at the time. The manager was right—advanced supermarket technology had arrived late in Greene County.

He steadied himself against the edge of the desk. Someone had used the Corbett family's card in this store just prior to the latest poisoning. What were the chances the basket case in Ridgeville would drive an hour south to Waynesburg to buy groceries? Sonny did most of her shopping anyway, and there's no way he'd come down here to do it. Had to be

Ron Corbett using an old card issued jointly to him and his wife.

Downing checked when the card was used that month. One visit: October 26. A week before JoAnn Cuddy died. The list of purchases was short: a box of Tide laundry detergent, Pearl Drops tooth polish, a pint of whole milk, a package of Squeezie Pops. Hardly the comprehensive grocery list of a regular shopper at this store; definitely not enough stuff for someone who only came in once that month. No, this was the shopping list of someone trying to justify his presence, someone planning his next move.

Downing jumped as the office door swung open.

"Time," Dick said.

Downing checked his watch. "That was five minutes?"

"To the second. Anything interesting?"

Downing nodded to the copy machine in the corner. "Not a thing. Mind if I copy a page, though?"

"Not a chance."

He wanted to crush the little prick's skull. He couldn't leave without a computer record that apparently placed Ron Corbett in the store the same week of the latest killing. Downing stared Dickie down, then fished another fifty from his pocket. The manager didn't hesitate this time. He took it and gestured grandly to the copier.

"One page," he said. "And you got no idea where it came from."

24

"Just roll the dice and get on with it."

The voice woke Sonny from a dream about Lake Erie. He was swimming hard and steady, on course and making good time. It was dark, after midnight, and the shore lights were disappearing into the gloom. Suddenly, something was behind him, moving like it was after him. Then his navigator was gone, leaving him alone. He swam harder, hoping to make it to the lake's northwest shore. Sixty strokes a minute became seventy. Then seventy-five. Eighty. He kicked with his legs instead of using them for balance. Working those large muscles would drain him, but it didn't matter. In the blackness behind him, something was closing in.

Again, Hawk's voice cut through his sleep like a foghorn.

"Science and nature, for the game. And as always, Mr. Doyle, good luck."

Sonny sat up, untangled himself from his sweat-soaked sheets, and rose. He was naked and unsteady. Trivial Pursuit at . . . what? He glanced at his clock radio. One-thirty in the afternoon. Of course. His roommates were matching wits for dish duty. At twenty-two, he was the same age as both Hawk and Doyle. Why did he feel so much older?

Sonny pulled on his Western Pennsylvania Swimming Federation sweatshirt and a baggy pair of Quiksilver shorts. He entered the living room just as Doyle was draining a half-finished bottle of Rolling Rock, closing his eyes, and readying himself for the next question. Their Christmas tree had fallen over. No one else seemed to notice.

"Ah, I see Mr. Corbett has joined us," Hawk said, waving an iron fireplace poker at Sonny like a sword. "Pleasant sleep after your morning swim? To bring you up to speed, Mr. Doyle needs only to answer this question correctly to avoid that diseased stack of dinnerware in the kitchen. A correct answer will end the game and doom me to an afternoon of drudgery. Do you have any questions?"

Sonny rubbed his fingertips across his eyes. "What's wrong with the kitchen-duty schedule we set up last month?"

Hawk smiled, shook his head. "Nothing, nothing at all. But you must understand, Doyle and I are men of danger. A three-day duty rotation is functional, but—how shall we say it?—it's not exactly living on the edge. This," Hawk said, sweeping an arm toward the game board between him and Doyle, "introduces an element of risk."

Doyle finally spoke: "Hit me, assface."

Hawk fished into the box and withdrew a card from the center of the stack, then turned it faceup on the wooden cable spool they used as a coffee table. With his free hand, he twirled their fireplace poker like a baton.

"Hell-o bee-utiful. Ready? 'What does a hippophobe fear?' And, as always, good luck, Mr. Doyle." Hawk was cocky, humming the *Jeopardy!* theme.

Doyle took another long drink. Seconds passed. He was taking too long.

"Tick. Tick. Tick," Hawk prodded.

"I think it's a trick. Hippos."

Hawk emitted a loud, buzzerlike sound. "We're so sorry, Mr. Doyle. That's incorrect. You'll get neither the washer-dryer combination nor Carol Merrill, our lovely hostess. May I recommend Ivory liquid? So gentle on your hands. Care to venture a guess, Mr. Corbett?"

"Horses."

Both roommates looked up, Hawk at Sonny, Doyle at Hawk.

"He right?" Doyle asked.

"Unfuckingbelievable," Hawk said. "Of course Flipper's right."

Sonny never lost. His mind was a rich storehouse of useless knowledge, one of the benefits of having lived and worked so close to Carnegie Library since he'd turned eighteen. Trivial Pursuit was the perfect channel for it, but lately the dish-duty challenge bored him as much as his inventory and ordering job in the university's chemistry department.

"All right then, Mr. Corbett, let's see how you are at history, shall we? Double or nothing for the dishes." Hawk pulled another card from the box. "What war ended with an armistice signed at the eleventh hour of the eleventh day of the eleventh month? And, as always——"

Sonny picked up his breakfast dishes from the dining room table and walked them toward the kitchen. "World War I," he said over his shoulder. He dropped the dishes onto the crusty mound of silverware in the sink, obliterating his roommate's reply. "I'm going out for a walk."

Hawk was on his feet, waggling the poker at him. "Wait a minute, wiseass. At least help us put this stuff away, or I'll be forced to beat you to within an inch of your life. What's the big hurry, anyway?"

"It's almost two o'clock. Life goes on"—Sonny gestured toward the kitchen window—"*out there*. I may stop by Rec Hall to lift. Need more shoulders for the Lake Erie swim. February's not that far off."

"The mighty musclehead." Hawk feigned awe. "Dollar to squeeze your bicep?"

"Supposed to exercise my hands, too."

"They still going numb?" Doyle asked. He stood, lost his balance for a moment, and sat back down. The Rolling Rock he was holding was obviously not his first of the day.

"Once in a while. Nothing seems to help."

Hawk seemed to consider that, stroking his chin, at first, then grabbing his crotch. "I know a great exercise for lower-arm strength. Three times a day. You'll notice the difference."

"Strength's not the problem," Sonny said, folding the game board. He picked up the box of trivia cards and searched the floor for its top. "They just tingle sometimes. It's weird. They say there's nothing really wrong. You seen the lid to this thing?"

From the apartment's entryway came the clank of the mail slot and the rustle of falling paper. "I'll get it," Hawk said. He pretended to sheathe his poker by thrusting it down through a belt loop of his jeans, then swaggered off toward the sound. Sonny scanned the floor under the couch for the missing box lid. Hawk was back by the time Sonny stood up, still without the box top.

Hawk flipped through the stack of what looked like credit-card offers and thrift-store flyers, then pulled out a plain white envelope. He held it out to Sonny without looking up.

The only thing on the envelope was Sonny's typewritten name, no postmark or address. Must have been in the box before the mail arrived, Sonny figured. He juggled the box of trivia cards in one hand and slid the thumb of his other under the flap. It opened clean and Sonny somehow got the envelope's contents out without dropping them.

Hawk was still sorting mail when the box of cards suddenly fell onto the floor and scattered trivia like brightly colored confetti. The plain white envelope and the single page it contained fluttered down in its wake. Sonny returned his roommates' startled glances, then all three looked hard at the hands Sonny suddenly couldn't feel.

"What's the matter?" Hawk asked.

"I don't know. My hands."

"What about them?"

"They feel really weird."

"They finally match the rest of you!" Hawk was trying hard to keep things light, but stopped after seeing Sonny's face. "No, really, what do you think it is?"

Hawk stooped and picked up the envelope and the letter, which had landed faceup. All that was on the page was a single typewritten paragraph, and his roommate read it to himself.

"This a Bible verse, or what?" He held the letter out to Sonny, who tried to grasp it but couldn't. Sonny pressed his limp hands together with a corner of the page between them, then brought it closer to his face. He stared without speaking.

Hawk prodded again: "From somebody you know?"

25

Downing eased the Ford to the curb and checked the mailbox. Ruff Creek Lane, number 29. Not a mansion, but definitely upper crust in a college town like Waynesburg. He jammed the gearshift into park and turned off the engine, still buzzed by what he'd found at Ranch Bounty.

Late afternoon. Sun would be down in an hour, and he'd lose its warmth to the cold and dark of rural western Pennsylvania. Which was fine. After this, he was heading for Outcrop again, and this time he was ready. Thermal underwear. Heavy boots. Ski gloves. Wool watchcap. He wanted to watch Corbett long enough to establish his rhythms, to predict his movements. He'd brought his deer rifle, too, a Remington 30.06 with a long scope. He liked to be ready for anything.

The walkway was icy, almost like someone had hosed it down. Downing stepped off into the grass and limped toward the front door of the Cuddy house, hoping the day's luck would hold. One more score like this morning's and he might be able to make a circumstantial case against Corbett even if Christensen struck out with Sonny.

A young man answered his knock. Downing recognized the kid's voice from the recording of the 9-1-1 call.

"You must be Mark," he said.

A man appeared behind the boy, opening the front door wide but keeping the storm door locked. He looked like a man who'd recently lost a lot of weight.

Downing flashed his shield. "Sorry to intrude, Mr. Cuddy. May I come in?"

A Waynesburg College professor, Downing remembered as he followed Cuddy down a hall lined with overfilled bookshelves and into the kitchen at the rear of the house. The kid disappeared up the carpeted stairs without a word, six weeks into a lifetime of rage. He'll be a death penalty supporter someday, Downing said to himself, one of the people cheering outside the prison when the state finally seats Ron Corbett in Old Sparky. Maybe the gods will be kind and let them both watch Corbett broil in that decrepit chair from behind the witness window. Maybe then the kid could move on, maybe then he could go to his own grave in peace.

The kitchen. Downing suddenly realized where he was. He tried to absorb the details, to imagine the scene. The telephone was on the wall near the refrigerator, its long cord tangled into loops and snarls. A cupboard door beneath the sink was missing. The wooden frame where its hinges attached was splintered and cracked, like the door had been torn away. His head echoed with the recorded sound of splitting wood and the solid thump of flesh on floor. Downing tried not to stare too long.

By all accounts, Charles Cuddy had been lecturing in front of seventy-five Waynesburg College undergrads at the moment his wife died. Took only three days for Ramsey and the local posse to rule him out, the geniuses. They noted in a follow-up report that Cuddy took his wife's death particularly hard, and that he probably wouldn't be much help with the investigation.

"You're probably sick of answering questions," Downing said, settling into one of the breakfast table chairs. Cuddy had not spoken since answering the door. "Sure would appreciate you answering a few more."

Cuddy arched his eyebrows toward the ceiling. "That's

our son. My son. He was with her, but you probably knew that."

"I heard the tape," Downing said. "He did everything right."

"He thinks he could have saved her."

"He's wrong," Downing said. Cyanide is unforgiving. The dying starts the second you swallow. He thought of Carole, of their last hours together, of her last minutes alive, alone. He'd needed to get home to Trix that night. If he'd stayed, would he have snatched the Primenyl bottle from her hand when she got it out of the car's glove compartment? Would she still be alive?

"Is he talking to anybody?"

Cuddy nodded. "Good people. But it'll be years——"

After an uncomfortable silence, Downing cleared his throat. "I won't take any more of your time than I need, Mr. Cuddy, but I do have one question. And I trust it'll stay between us, because I'm treading on fairly thin ice here, being that the Pittsburgh PD has no official role in this investigation."

The professor leaned against the counter, apparently confused.

"See, I have a lot of experience in cases like this, and I'm following up on the local investigation, just making sure they've covered all the bases. You remember the similar cases in Pittsburgh in 1986, I'm sure."

No reaction.

"Maybe there's no connection, like Detective Ramsey says. The cyanide wasn't a chemical twin of the stuff used in Pittsburgh. The methods are different. But with something like this, it pays to be sure. And you can appreciate the delicateness of that situation. I'm just backstopping, but if they know I'm nosing around it'll come off as second-guessing. You follow?"

Long silence. Finally: "I'm not particularly pleased with their follow-up."

Yes. "Really?"

"I've called twice since the funeral with information. Just random thoughts. My wife——"

Cuddy peeled the wire-rimmed eyeglasses from his face. A strange smile, less happy than pained. Downing waited.

"There was a man, several years ago." Cuddy's eyes strayed to the family portrait on the wall: father, mother, only son. " It was a difficult time in our marriage. It's probably irrelevant."

Downing kept his eyes fixed on the husband's. An old investigator's credo: Nothing is irrelevant until the investigator says so.

"I don't know his name, but I know enough about him that somebody with access to records probably could have tracked him down. It was a long shot, but I at least wanted him questioned."

Downing knitted his fingers together so he wouldn't fidget. "Why do you think it isn't relevant?"

Cuddy crossed the room and opened a drawer near the stove. He removed an envelope and laid it on the counter, but didn't offer it to Downing.

"It ended years ago, apparently. Just one of those things, something I should have seen coming but didn't. I had no idea. But I found one of the letters he wrote to JoAnn after the funeral. She had it tucked in a book."

Downing winced, imagining him discovering her betrayal so soon after her death. He stifled his urge to reach for the letter.

"I thought it should be followed up," Cuddy said. "There's no return address, but I know he lives in Colorado. I know he worked a while at the college, so the administrative office may know where he is. Detective Ramsey took the information, but he never came to get the letter. I don't think he even tried to check it out."

This was good. The victim's husband wasn't happy with the local investigation.

"I'd be happy to make some calls on it," Downing said, reaching for the letter. "In their defense, sometimes investigators working a case like this get so bogged down in the day-to-day they have trouble stepping back, seeing the big picture. But someone should follow up, even if it's nothing."

A Boulder, Colorado, postmark. Downing tucked it into the inside pocket of his sports coat. He would make a call or two, eventually, but at this point he didn't intend to spend a lot of time chasing down old boyfriends with no grudges who lived two thousand miles away. "Anything else you think we need to know about Mrs. Cuddy's death?"

Six-thirty. Pitch black outside. The only downstairs light in the house was from the television screen's glow as the videotape of JoAnn Cuddy's funeral service dragged into its twentieth minute. The priest droned on. Candles flickered. A somber group of five men and the woman's only child lifted the bronze casket into a waiting hearse. Downing had seen most of this on the local news, only with better camera work.

Downing checked his watch again. No way he'd get out to Outcrop tonight. "Who'd you say shot this?"

"Truman, her brother. Thinks he's Cecil B. Demille. Set up a tripod and videotaped his own angioplasty two years ago."

Cuddy obviously needed to talk. Sometimes it paid off when grieving relatives mind-dumped on willing strangers. Sometimes it was just a pain in the ass. And so far Downing hadn't seen or heard anything that struck him as useful. Cuddy had relived their courtship, their wedding, the birth of their son. Their vacation to western Canada two years ago. Her fondness for artichokes and Rice Krispies squares.

The cemetery. Truman was relentless. He zoomed on the red burst of roses on top of the casket, on the priest, on Mark's blank face as a spray of holy water hit him square. Truman pulled back to show the shuffling assembly, its breath turning to vapor in the chilly mid-November air. Dark suits. Black dresses. Red eyes.

"That's JoAnn's father there, in the wheelchair," Cuddy said, pointing at the screen. "Her mom died in '83. Breast cancer. JoAnn was religious about mammograms."

Downing nodded, checked his watch again. He wanted to get to Outcrop before Corbett went to bed.

The priest committed JoAnn Cuddy to the earth and sketched a cross in the air over the open grave. A few people stepped forward to kiss the casket, but most walked toward their cars. Truman pulled back, but kept rolling straight into a panning shot of the cemetery. Three hundred and sixty degrees, starting with the line of mourners' cars parked along the curb. A distant mausoleum. A grove of flame-red maples. A utility building. The gravedigger's backhoe. A sturdy oak. Neat rows of headstones stretching up and over a hill.

"Go back," Downing said.

Cuddy stopped describing his wife's collection of Hummel figurines. "What?"

"Rewind it a little, but just a little."

Cuddy aimed the remote. The tape skittered back to the mausoleum. "Like that?"

"Let it run again."

Downing got up from the couch and crawled toward the screen. "Now stop," he said. "Right there. Wait, back up again. There."

The videotape paused. The oak tree filled the screen. Downing focused on the base.

"What?" Cuddy said. "Is that somebody?"

Somebody, shit. Downing leaned closer, then turned around. "Can you stop it from jiggling like that?"

"It's an old VCR."

Downing looked again. The image wasn't good, but no fucking question. It was Corbett's hairline. "Any idea who that might be?"

"Who?"

"Behind that tree, the guy leaning out in the flannel shirt."

Cuddy squinted. "Nobody I know, but it's hard to tell. Don't remember him at the funeral."

"That's the thing. Doesn't look like he was at the funeral. Looks like he was watching it, but not part of it, know what I mean? How far away was that tree?"

"Never even noticed the tree," Cuddy said. "I was kind of a mess that day. Looks like a hundred feet or so, maybe."

"And you don't recognize the guy at all?"

Cuddy looked again, then turned on a table lamp beside the couch. "No. Why?"

"Does he turn up in any other footage of the funeral?"

"Not that I remember. Maybe it's one of the people who work at the cemetery."

Downing wanted to kiss the screen. Unfuckingbelievable. Videotape of Ron Corbett as an uninvited guest at JoAnn Cuddy's funeral. The dumbest goddamned jury in the world would recognize Corbett's hairline. What had he done right to deserve this?

"Could be," Downing said. "Probably is. Tell you what, though. I'd like to borrow this tape, maybe have our lab guys clean it up a little and get a better look, just to be sure. This the original?"

Cuddy hesitated. "I can ask Truman. Probably first generation. But I don't know. It may mean something to Mark one of these days and I'd hate to lose it."

Downing gritted his teeth. Patience. Patience. The VCR had two tape bays. Downing patted it gently. "You could copy it and give me the original, see. That way our guys would have the best possible version to work with."

Cuddy squirmed. "You really think it's that important?"

"Won't know until we look at it closer. Sure hate to overlook something, though," Downing said. He summoned his best trust-me smile. "Assuming it turns out to be nothing, Mr. Cuddy, I'll get the original right back to you. You have my word."

26

Downing closed his notebook. He was taking the new information directly to Kiger—fuck DeLillo—and his list of things to do first was fairly short. Double-check the Irondale Ranch Bounty supermarket for the pedigree of Corbett's Bounty Club card. Get the videotape to Randy to see if he could pull a clearer frame of Corbett from the funeral footage. If he had time, check on that name, the one Sandra Corbett mentioned.

He opened the notebook to the first few pages, held it up to the light from the Waynesburger Restaurant sign. Peebo Balkin, or Balken, or something. He tried to make sense of the scrawlings he made after their strange discussion: "S. C. sez R. quit sending checks after Peebo Balkin???? nearly drowned." Probably another blind alley, but he'd try to scan incident reports for the name. Maybe something would turn up.

God, he was tired. His leg ached. Even the buzz from the day's progress was wearing off, and he wanted to sleep more than anything else. He started the car, then turned it off again when he noticed the pay phone on the outside restaurant wall. It was nine already, at least an hour from home. He dialed his number, then punched in his calling-card number.

"Where the fuck have you been?" No hello. No who's this. He expected sarcasm, but this was serious attitude.

"Hey, baby. On my way home."

"That's just fine. I've been trying to find you since eight-thirty this morning. Your office said you called in sick. Jim Christensen's called here four times since noon looking for you, and he sounds more like Chicken Little every time."

"Trix, I said I'm on way home. I'm down in Greene County."

"I don't care if you're with the goddamned Pope, Grady. I'm done. I stuck around all day to make sure you weren't dead, but I spent the time packing. I stayed in 1986 because I loved you and didn't understand what the hell was going on. Now, I don't even care. So I'm done. I don't need this."

"Trix—"

"You haven't learned a thing, Grady, in ten years not a goddamned thing. Have a nice life." The receiver banged down, hard.

Downing faked a pleasant "See you in a bit, then" and hung up, checking to see if anyone was watching. She'd done this before. She'd be back. She was pushing fifty-three. Where would she go?

What had he told her when he left that morning? Or had they even talked? He got up, made a couple calls, and was gone before she woke up. She must have called him at work, then gone berserk when they said he wasn't in. Shit. He should have told her what was up. DeLillo thought he was home sick, and she may have blown it.

She'd be back.

Downing dialed Christensen's home. His hand shook. Maybe he should have called Christensen before he left. It wasn't like him to call the house. He tested his voice to make sure it betrayed nothing. Hello? Hello? Deep breath. The answering machine picked up. Downing waited for the beep.

"Grady Downing, Jim. Got your messages. Sorry I've been out of touch all—"

Christensen picked up after a screech of feedback. "Where the hell have you been?"

"Having a great day until about five minutes ago. What's up?"

"How soon can you get here?"

"I'm at least an hour away. What's that noise?" It sounded like running water and breaking glass.

"I'm throwing out every goddamn open container in my house. I've sent the girls over to Brenna's. I'm halfway out of my fucking mind." A soggy thud, more breaking glass. "Shit. We've got to talk. Now."

"I'll come straight there."

"You do that."

"Can you give me a hint?"

"Something's way off here, Grady, and either you're not playing straight with me or the FBI profilers are way off guessing your Primenyl guy is a random killer."

"Nonspecific multiple murderer."

"I think that's wrong. I think we're dealing with somebody here who's got a very *specific* agenda, and at this point I'm pretty sure I'm part of it. I got this videotape in the mail that scared the bejeezus out of me."

Downing felt a jolt. He tried to talk but couldn't. He shut his eyes, tight, trying to blink away the scene that was replaying in his mind, an ordinary scene of him with Carole in his car outside her apartment, kissing, saying good night, a scene videotaped just days before she died. It had also arrived by mail.

"Videotape?" he managed.

"Somebody's been following me, Grady. Me and the girls. And I think it started that first day when you came to my Pitt office and told me about Sonny. So whoever it is apparently is following you, too. Followed you straight to me."

Downing felt dizzy. He put his head against the cold metal of the pay phone, felt its bite between his eyes. What could he say?

"It'll be okay, Jim. Don't panic."

"Oh, shut up. Right now I'm not inclined to give you the benefit of the doubt."

"I can be there in forty minutes," Downing said. As soon as he hung up, he wished he'd added, *Destroy everything in the refrigerator and medicine cabinets. Take no chances.*

The dog stopped thrashing. It happened exactly as Downing had imagined it. A foil-wrapped packet of meat tossed over the fence. Rodney devouring it without hesitation. The sudden collapse. The struggle. The last shuddering gasps in the drifted snow.

"Jesus," he said.

Christensen let the tape play on. "It looks like it was poisoned, doesn't it?"

"Uh, maybe," Downing said.

"What else could it be? The whole goddamned thing's an implied threat, Grady. I was almost ready to write off the sample-products thing as a coincidence, but not now. It all started when you cranked up this investigation again."

Downing held up his hands, then put them down when he realized how defensive it looked. He needed time to think. "How much longer does it go?"

The address tiles blinked onto the screen, then off. "That's it," Christensen said. "I fast-forwarded to the end. The rest is blank."

Downing laced his fingers together and squeezed. His heart was pounding. He took an evidence bag from his coat pocket, and when his hand stopped shaking, he wrote the date on it in black Sharpie. He ejected the video, used the pen to pull it out of the VCR, and dropped it into the bag. After sealing it, he put it on one of the end tables.

"Did you save the wrapping?"

Downing pulled on a latex glove that was in his other coat pocket and folded the wrapping paper into another evidence bag. He laid it beside the videotape.

"Mind if I use the head?" Downing asked.

He locked the bathroom door, but didn't turn on the light. He wasn't sure he could handle a mirror right now. In the darkness, he felt like someone had him from behind and was crushing the air from his chest. The pace of his breathing picked up, shallow and forced, and he knew what was coming. He couldn't stop it. He groped around, found a damp bath towel on a rack, and crumpled it into his face just as he started to hyperventilate. He held it there until the carbon dioxide did its work.

Think, Downing told himself. Christensen didn't know Rodney was his dog. Did he need to know? Of course he did. Just like he needed to know about the video Corbett mailed him ten years earlier and the 9-1-1 recording he mailed him right after the Primenyl anniversary. Like he needed to know about Carole. But what could he tell him? That the last time Corbett sent one of his innocuous little video threats, he followed through within days? That when the threat didn't back Downing off the 1986 investigation, Corbett slipped a bad capsule into the Primenyl bottle in Carole's unlocked car and destroyed the only woman Downing ever really loved? That the FBI's behavioral science team was wrong?

In the end, it would come down to the question of why he hadn't told Christensen all this before. He imagined Christensen's rage if he told him the truth now: Ron Corbett isn't just capable of random killings. He'll find a way to the soul of anyone who gets too close.

He flipped the light switch, avoiding the mirror. When his eyes adjusted, they fell immediately to the two toothbrushes beside a small toilet kit on the counter. One was an unremarkable blue; the handle of the other was covered with Power Rangers. Christensen must be taking this stuff to his daughters over at Brenna's, thinking they'll be safe there. He forced his eyes to the mirror, startled less by the sickly face and raccoon eyes than by the question that popped into his head. If something happened to Christensen's girls, could he ever look in the mirror again?

The knock made him jump.

"I'm fine," he said, then flushed the toilet. "Be right out."

He turned on the faucet, letting the cold water run into his cupped palms. He lifted handfuls of it to his face until his head cleared, then dried himself with the towel and smoothed his hair. He was close, maybe closer than he'd ever been. The new evidence might be solid enough to make the Greene County case stick. *Might* be. But say Sonny did remember something significant, maybe not enough to charge Corbett in the 1986 killings, but enough to show a pattern. Then you've got a fifty-fifty shot with a jury. Without Sonny, Kiger might not even take the Greene County evidence to Dagnolo. And even if he did, would the DA file charges in a high-profile case without a slam-dunk guarantee? Especially a case where he didn't trust the cop?

He hung the towel on the rack. Settled. He needed Christensen, because he still needed Sonny. The less Christensen knew, the more likely he was to continue. Downing took two deep breaths, practiced his trust-me smile, and turned the doorknob, ready to lie some more.

27

Christensen was scanning the nearly empty refrigerator shelves when the bathroom door finally opened. Downing's color was back, but he still looked like hell.

"Sorry," Downing said. "Long drive."

Christensen closed the refrigerator door. He'd thrown out everything that could be opened, pricked, or otherwise penetrated. "Spare me the bullshit, Grady. I feel like you suckered me into getting involved with Sonny."

Downing pulled a chair out from under the breakfast table and sat down. Big smile. "You want out now? Just when things are getting good?"

Christensen glared. He was sick of the attitude, the shoulder-shrugging indifference to what he was going through. "That's it. I'm done."

"Jim, what does that accomplish?"

Christensen knew he was pacing, knew he looked agitated as he moved back and forth across the kitchen floor between the sink to the far cupboard. But he didn't care.

"It at least gets us out of harm's way, Grady. I'm not a cop, remember? I'm a psychologist. I see clients in air-conditioned comfort. We talk about things that make them sad and how to make their spouses appreciate their feelings. I do a little research, write a paper about the brain and memory now and then. And I spend a lot of time trying to raise two daughters by myself. Throw in a full-time job as a homicide investigator and you can imagine my schedule!"

Christensen hated that kind of sarcasm, knew it made him sound like a man trying to rein in his rage. But he couldn't stop himself, just like that time outside Tataglia's house when he and Downing were crouched in the bushes with shotgun blasts whizzing overhead, waiting for the SWAT team. It felt good to lose control.

"So you can see, detective, there's damned little time left in the day to deal with mass murderers who decide to stalk my family. Did I mention I'm the only parent my kids have?"

"Jim—"

"Oh, I suppose there are orphanages that would take them in. But it's not a great option, really. Hey! How would you feel about adopting? Just a thought. Talk it over with the wife."

Downing returned the glare. "Don't lay this on me. You knew we weren't dealing with a scout leader here. You read the file. You knew the situation when you agreed to work with Sonny."

"Did I?"

Downing didn't hold his gaze. His eyes moved quickly to the floor, a body-language red flag. Christensen bore in.

"You told me everything I needed to know to make an informed decision?"

"You know what I know, goddamnit. Probably more, since Sonny's been talking to you, not me. All I've got is your promise to tell me if he says anything relevant to Primenyl."

"I keep my promises."

"Meaning what? What promises did I make? I know you're rattled, and I'm sorry. This is scary. But we're on the same side here, working two different angles. I came up with some good stuff in Greene County today. Corbett's fingerprints are all over that killing. And if you've made any progress at all with Sonny, any progress, we've got a shot. We're close."

Christensen gripped the edge of the counter, anchoring

himself to stop the pacing. "You don't get it, Grady. What's wrong with this picture? We're supposedly after a nonspecific multiple murderer, or at least that's what you're telling me. I'm no genius, but I know that whoever sent that video doesn't fit that profile. It's *very* specific."

Downing stood up too fast. The wooden chair fell over backwards. "Listen to yourself, then. It's too late. You're in the deep end whether you like it or not, so we either sink or swim. What do you accomplish by bailing out?"

"The girls and I live long and happy lives."

"No, you let a goddamned killer get away."

"I heard that's *your* specialty."

Christensen could tell he'd gone too far. The words seemed to hit Downing with the force of a bullet. The detective opened his mouth, but nothing came out. Then he stood, clenching and unclenching his fists. His body shook, like a man going into shock. He turned suddenly and walked out of the room. Christensen caught him as he was halfway out the front door.

"Wait."

He touched Downing's shoulder, and the detective wheeled. They were face-to-face, inches apart, both breathing hard. They stood like that a long time, eyes locked. Christensen blinked first.

"That was uncalled for. I'm sorry I said it."

"You don't know what happened in 1986. Nobody does but me. And my conscience is clear."

Downing followed him back into the living room, knocking over a floor lamp as he passed. The detective didn't seem to notice.

Christensen retreated into a corner on the other side of the couch, hoping Downing would keep his distance. "Don't you see where I'm coming from, Grady? I'm so goddamned scared. Not for me so much. For the girls. Melissa kind of knows what's up. We talked after she got burned. But Annie has no idea. How do you explain something like this to a five-year-old?"

"You drop it now, Jim, how you gonna explain it to yourself?" Less a question than an accusation.

"I'll manage."

"What about the parents of that eleven-year-old kid down in Greene County who may never wake up? How would you explain it to them? How'll you feel the next time Corbett kills? Or the time after that?"

Christensen felt like a treed fox. He picked up the evidence bags with the video and the wrapping paper in them. "What about this?"

"How you gonna explain it to Sonny, Jim? 'Sorry, kid. Hope things work out.'"

Christensen waved the evidence bags, trying to look defiant, then tossed them one at a time across the room. Downing caught them and put them into his trenchcoat pocket.

Christensen folded his arms across his chest. "I have a right to protect myself and the people I love."

Downing turned again toward the door, which was still open. The room was cold, and a spray of snow was melting on the oak floor. Downing stared at it a long time, then threw a rug over the puddle with his toe. The detective muttered something, then realized when he turned back that he hadn't been heard.

"I said I thought you understood the stakes," he said.

"My kids are at stake, that's what."

"A lot of other people's kids, too, Jim. You know who we're dealing with here. You know more people may die if we can't pull this together. Do you have any idea how far out on a limb I am on this thing? I'm putting twenty-eight goddamned years on the line. I'm up against a city full of people who think I blew it last time. I fail again, it's not just another bang to the ego. People die. Nasty, horrible deaths. And you know what else? They'll fire my ass in a minute. I'll spend the next ten years trying to get my retirement money. So if you want to preach to me about your fucking rights, you go ahead. But you should know you sound just like every other jellyfish who could have helped me get Corbett but didn't."

Downing's words hung between them.

"Look, I've got no choice on this, Jim. God, I wish I did,"

he said finally. Downing studied the damp floor, then stepped into the front doorway and turned around. "But you're right. You do."

He pulled the door shut behind him, leaving Christensen alone, shivering, still cornered behind the couch.

28

Christensen found Sonny's car dusted with fresh snow in the parking lot Downing described. He still wasn't sure he believed this, though. He'd made a lot of assumptions about Sonny's swimming——that he was unusually dedicated to his training; that he enjoyed the solitude of it; that his interest bordered on compulsion. But the notion of self-torture hadn't even come to mind until Downing had told him *where* Sonny trained.

He tucked his scarf into his jacket and zipped up the front. The thermometer at the parking attendant's booth said 40 degrees, but it was in the sun. The morning air felt 15 degrees colder with the wind whipping off the river and moving like a jet stream down the Boulevard of the Allies. He walked straight into it, headed for the Point, leaving behind the street roar for the strange, hollow silence of the city's sprawling urban park.

Why had he just assumed Sonny trained at one of the local indoor pools? Hell, what reasonable person would assume otherwise? In almost any other context, swimming daily in the frigid Ohio River would have seemed unthinkable. The more he mulled it, though, the more it almost made sense with Sonny. For every action there's an equal and opposite reaction. Extreme trauma can lead to extreme behavior.

What he didn't understand was the physiology of it. The human body isn't designed for prolonged exposure to cold water, which leaches heat many times faster than cold air. To survive more than a few minutes, the body's core organs would either have to be evenly insulated by a considerable amount of fat, or the body would have to generate heat as quickly as the water leached it away. The swimmer would have to keep a furious pace, or die.

He passed underneath the Fort Pitt Bridge overpass, his footsteps echoing off the once-white walls that arched over his head like a gray cavern. Except for a few tourists, the park was nearly empty. The fountain had been drained for the winter. The symphony stage was shuttered until spring. On Mount Washington, the electronic aluminum clock read 10:32 A.M. Downing said Sonny usually finished between 10:30 and 11. He walked faster, even though Sonny couldn't get out of the park without passing him. He needed to see to believe.

Sonny's towel, backpack, and thermal blanket were where Downing said they would be, stowed in a hedge to the right of the fountain. But there was no sign of Sonny. Christensen pulled on his ski gloves and waited, watching downriver, looking for proof. He took the glove off his right hand and lay down on the cold concrete rim of the Point, reaching, trying to touch the water. The Ohio was high enough that his fingertips grazed the eddying surface. The river was all but ice.

He stood up and looked again toward the arch of the West End Bridge. As impossible as it seemed, a solitary swimmer was moving upriver, maybe twenty yards off the north bank. Christensen squinted, guessing the swimmer was about three-quarters of a mile away.

"My God," he said.

He felt helpless, found himself retrieving Sonny's things from the hedge. At least he could have the towel and blanket ready. He stood there, still not believing, imagining the pain, watching the swimmer moving arm over arm over arm, closing the distance in a surprisingly short time. The pace was frenzied but still graceful, a hypnotic rhythm, as though the swimmer were pulling the entire city toward him. Even with the swim cap and goggles, who else could it be?

Sonny didn't slow even as he neared the Point. His shoulders were neither in nor out of the water, but skimming the surface, as though he'd achieved perfect zero buoyancy, was at one with the water. In a single motion—a final, powerful dolphin kick—he thrust himself up to the concrete rim and pulled himself out of the river about fifteen feet away. He stood there, bent at the waist, hanging his arms straight down and shaking his hands, like he was trying to restore circulation. River water pooled at his bare feet. His skin was bone white.

Christensen walked to Sonny, holding the towel and blanket out for him to choose. Sonny pried the goggles and cap from his head and noticed him for the first time. With a weak smile, Sonny took the towel and managed a "Thanks."

Christensen fought for words. A queasy feeling crept over him, like the time he'd glimpsed the wrist scar from a client's recent suicide attempt.

"Blanket," Sonny said. He was breathing hard, but not nearly as hard as Christensen had expected considering the exertion of a miles-long swim. With the goggles and cap still in one hand, Sonny wrapped the blanket around himself, an Indian chief in reflective silver.

"Jog with me," he said, setting off toward the city skyline.

"Jog?"

"To the car," Sonny shouted over his shoulder. "Before I get cold."

Christensen grabbed the backpack and towel and took off on a dead run, trying to catch up. This was Sonny's idea of jogging? Sonny was still barefoot, moving away fast.

Christensen pulled alongside him as they neared the underpass. "You get cold *after* you get out of that water?" he said.

Sonny nodded. "Body temperature starts to drop."

"Explain that to me sometime," he said.

They passed through the dim underpass, then crossed into daylight on the other side. He knew the sensation. The city's annual Great Race 10K finished here every year. But instead of reliving his steadily improving finishes of the past two years, Christensen found himself imagining the damage its rough pavement might do to Sonny's numb feet. They caught the traffic light at Commonwealth Place and crossed in front of the State Office Building and the squat brown *Press* plant.

The parking-lot attendant looked up from his comic book as Sonny approached. "Hey," he said, pressing a set of keys into Sonny's free hand.

"Thanks." Sonny dropped the keys as he tried to guide one into his car's door lock. Then he dropped them again.

"Let me," Christensen said.

When the door was open, Sonny folded himself into the driver's seat and slammed the door. Then he reached over and pulled up the lock on the passenger's door. Christensen circled the Toyota and got in. Sonny was starting to shiver underneath the thermal blanket. His face was still pale, but not nearly as pale as it was when he'd climbed out of the river. Blood was slowly circulating back into his skin. Sonny closed his eyes as the shivering got more violent.

Christensen watched, helpless. "Want me to start the car and turn on the heat?"

"No." Eyes still closed. Body quaking.

"Call an ambulance?" He was serious, but Sonny laughed, an awkward, sharp thing Christensen found reassuring.

"It'll stop in about ten minutes. It's normal."

Christensen thought back to his impression of Sonny that day they first met in his office. How normal he seemed, considering what he'd been through. How apparently unaffected he was by the train wreck of his childhood. He'd suspected after that first meeting that Sonny had an outlet for his rage, some way to deal with the pain, but he couldn't imagine then what it was. Now he knew. But why this? If you wanted to punish yourself, why not just drive nails into your hands? He answered his own question: If you survived, cold-water swimming did no visible damage. Like electro-convulsion therapy.

Sonny flexed his hands, then draped them over the steering wheel like wet socks. The car rocked with his shivering. The windows fogged over, erasing the city, leaving them alone in a slate-gray mist. Christensen watched, horrified, fascinated, as Sonny's body struggled back from the brink, doing everything it could to survive.

When the shivering finally stopped, Christensen waved his hand in front of Sonny's face, thinking he was asleep. He'd read a lot of Jack London stories as a kid, and seemed to remember hypothermia victims just drifting off to sleep. The seat back was fully reclined, and Sonny hadn't opened his eyes for at least five minutes. Then his body had become very still.

"I'm okay," Sonny said without opening his eyes.

Christensen exhaled. "Sorry."

"The shivering's part of it. No way around it. Thing is, there's not usually anyone around to watch."

"They make these things called wet suits, you know."

Sonny finally blinked. "Sort of defeats the purpose."

"Which is?"

Sonny, eyes open now, stared straight ahead. Christensen rushed to fill the silence.

"Can you explain it to me? The thing about your body temperature dropping."

Sonny pulled the seat back upright and flexed his hands. "As long as I'm swimming, I'm generating enough heat to maintain temperature. As soon as I stop, the temperature starts to fall."

"So your problems don't really start until you're out of the water?"

Sonny turned the key, wiggled something under the dash, and the Toyota coughed to life. He set the heater on low. "Basically. The other thing is, capillaries in my skin start to open up once I get out of the water. But since my skin is so cold, it cools down the blood that starts flowing back into them, like a car radiator. So it drops a few more degrees. But physiologists tell me they're important degrees. That's why I needed to keep moving."

Christensen took off his gloves and reached to the floor, thawing his fingers at the heater vent. Sonny threw the blanket off his shoulders, apparently comfortable now in only his dark blue Speedo. Christensen figured the temperature inside the car was probably 45 degrees.

"You do this how often?"

"Four days a week. Sometimes less. But there's a crossing I want to try in late February, early March. And I need to stay acclimated. So I try to swim whenever I can get down here."

"A crossing?"

Sonny hesitated. "Lake Erie."

"In winter?"

"Nobody's done it."

Christensen shook his head. "With good reason. Can't you pretty much walk across at that time of year?"

"In parts. This place I want to cross, near Buffalo, should be okay."

"How far?"

Sonny hesitated again, then said something under his breath.

"Come again?"

Sonny cleared his throat. "Fifteen miles."

On the one hand, it was a goal. Goals are good. Goals are forward-thinking and positive. On the other hand, it was suicide—not a goal most psychologists consider healthy.

"Nobody's done it," Sonny repeated.

Nobody's ever climbed into a vat of molten steel either, Christensen was tempted to say, at least nobody who expected to climb out again. But he knew that confronting Sonny would complicate things, that it was best just to leave it for now.

"I came down for a reason," he said. "I think we should keep talking."

Sonny turned the heater down, then reached into the backseat for a pair of sweats. He opened his door, stepped out and pulled them on, then got back in. "Okay," he said.

"That's it? I figured you'd put up a fight."

Sonny held his hands up, palms facing the windshield. "It's getting worse."

"The numbness?"

"All the time now. And I don't sleep much. When I do, it's really weird."

"Still having the dreams?"

"Whatever they are."

Christensen waited, seeing which direction Sonny wanted to take this, gauging his need to talk. Sonny closed his eyes again.

"My father shoved my aunt Rachel down the stairs once."

"This was a dream?"

"I'm not sure. But I can see it. She's lying at the bottom of the stairs in our house on Jancey Street, holding her head. He's standing over her. Ever see that picture of what's his name, Muhammad Ali, standing over some bleary black guy flat on his back?"

"Clay Defeats Liston." Christensen remembered the headline.

"Whatever. Like that. He's screaming 'Bitch' over and over. And she's screaming back at him."

Sonny's hands suddenly curled into tight fists, like they were cramping. His eyes were still closed, but he clearly was in pain. He shoved both fists under his knees as they started to shake.

"What provoked it?"

"She wouldn't take his shit like my mother did. Just the usual."

"What happened then?"

"I don't know. It's like I see these things so clear, but just parts of them. Just scenes. As soon as I try to figure it out, it's gone."

Christensen took a chance. "Maybe you don't want to see the rest."

Sonny didn't seem to hear. "There was one dream about a book. He went off on my mom when he found it."

"On your mother? What kind of book?"

"Ore? Gold ore? Just some book."

"And it made him angry?"

"He beat her with a broom handle and left. David and I cleaned her up." The image seemed to trigger something in Sonny. He shuddered.

"There's something else," he said. He reached across the car, his hands still curled, and opened the glove compartment with one extended finger. "See that envelope?"

Christensen peered into the jumble of maps and repair receipts. "The one on top?"

"Came in the mail a couple days ago. Scared the shit out of me, but I don't know why."

The letter inside was a single typewritten paragraph, centered on the page:

I am baptizing you in the water, but there is one to come who is mightier than I. His winnowing-fan is in his hand to clear his threshing floor and gather the wheat into his barn; but the chaff he will burn in unquenchable fire.

It was attributed to John the Baptist. Christensen read it again. "This mean anything to you?" he said.

"Not really."

"No idea who sent it?"

"No."

"And you don't know why?"

"No."

But it scares him, Christensen thought. Maybe it was meant to. Like an innocuous videotape. Like a threat.

"Can I take this? I think Grady Downing should see it."

Sonny turned toward him. "Why?"

He ignored the question and didn't wait for Sonny's permission, figuring he'd just slip it casually into his jacket. Remembering the care Downing used in handling the video, he became suddenly worried about destroying evidence with his fingerprints. He pulled his ski gloves back on and tried to fold the paper back into the envelope. It looked about as casual as open-heart surgery. Sonny watched, saying nothing.

Christensen tried to divert Sonny's attention from the note. "How do you feel about all this stuff?"

Sonny stared into the misted windshield. "Like I'm standing on the edge of a cliff."

"But how does it feel?"

"I don't like heights."

"Scary? Dangerous?"

Sonny nodded.

"Can you still come in the evenings?"

Sonny nodded again.

"Tomorrow, then. Six-thirty. You'll be there?"

"I'm scared."

"But you'll come?"

Sonny nodded. Christensen opened the car door. Cold air rushed in. As he shut the door again, he saw Sonny pull the thermal blanket a little tighter around his shoulders.

29

Christensen shoved a toothpick into the tiny hole. The butter churn was looking good. Annie's whole "Long Ago Days" diorama project was looking good, if he did say so himself. They'd put most of it together at Brenna's a couple hours earlier. Annie cut a picture of a stone fireplace from one of Brenna's *Architectural Digest* magazines and pasted it to the back wall of the shoe box, then stapled some chintz curtains over the hand-drawn windows. They'd made a writing desk from heavy cardboard and created a tiny journal to sit on top. The coup de grace was a pillow feather scissored into the shape of a quill pen and stuck into a reasonable facsimile of an inkwell.

The butter churn was his idea, hatched during the drive home after the girls were safely in Brenna's foldout sofa bed. After he double-checked the house, as was becoming his habit, he made a tiny churn out of shirt cardboard and glued it to the floor of the shoe box, figuring he'd explain what it was when he picked Annie up the next morning. He lost himself in the project until someone rapped sharply on the front door. The wall clock said 11:20.

The rest of the house was dark, as was the front porch. He looked around the kitchen, his fingers still crusted with Elmer's glue. Did he have the stomach to grab a knife? He pulled a meat mallet from the utensil drawer and held it behind his back, then circled into the front hall through the dark living room so he wouldn't be silhouetted against the light from the kitchen. Through the living room window, he could see a solitary figure waiting at the front door, a pinpoint of orange at the face. The cigarette's glow was the only significant light, and it wasn't enough. Staying out of sight, he reached around the hall wall and found the porch light switch, counting one, two, three before snapping it on.

Downing waggled his fingers through the glass. The grinning bastard.

"Figured you'd be up," he said when Christensen opened the door. He crushed out his smoke on the porch deck, leaving the smoldering butt beside two others. How long had he been standing there?

Against his better instincts, Christensen let Downing in. "I'm totally puckered here, Grady. You scared the hell out of me."

"Thought you'd want the print results from the videotape as soon as we got them back," he said. "But it can wait until tomorrow."

The detective rubbed his bare hands together as he wandered into the living room. He picked up knickknacks, flipped the pages of Molly's Renaissance art coffee-table book, arranged sofa pillows. Something was wrong. Downing's toxic personal charm was intact, but he seemed nervous.

"Cut to the chase, Grady."

Downing stopped, like he'd suddenly remembered why he came. "Got nothing. Only prints on it were yours. Nothing on the wrapper, either. Local postmark, though. Highland Park."

Christensen stared. "Damned good detective work on that postmark, Grady. I can read, too. Some reason you couldn't have waited until tomorrow to give me that enlightening information?"

"Yeah, well." Downing wiped dust from an end table, rearranged a stack of unread *New Yorker*s.

"Something else on your mind, Grady?"

Downing walked to the picture window and closed the miniblind.

"Grady, what's going on?" A terrifying thought. "Are the girls okay?"

"What do you mean?"

"You're acting like something's wrong."

"It's not the girls, at least as far as I know. They still staying at Brenna's?"

Christensen's heart was pounding. He wanted to shove Downing out the door. "It's late, Grady. If you want to chitchat, I'd appreciate—"

"I need to tell you about something. Somebody, really. I haven't been as honest with you as I probably should've." Downing settled onto the couch, waiting. "You should sit," he said.

"I'll stand."

Downing fidgeted with a button on his trenchcoat. But he left it buttoned. He stared at it, moved to another button, stared at it, too. If Christensen had to guess the underlying emotion, he'd pick remorse. And that made him really, really nervous.

"There was this woman," Downing said. "Carole Carver. Nobody you know, I'm sure."

Christensen nodded and sat down in the wing chair across from the detective, purely by instinct. Downing was about to share something difficult and personal for the first time he could remember, and Christensen was trained to listen to people in pain.

"It's funny," Downing said. "You go through life thinking you're happy. Love your work. Love your wife. Love your kid. Things are great, all in all. Then you see someone who makes you wonder. They don't do anything outright. They just are. And you suddenly realize that person is your missing piece."

Could be a late night, Christensen thought. "You fell in love," he said.

"Wham! I realized I'd lived most of my life as a half, and this person, Carole, was the half that was missing. Two halves of a whole, you know? Deep down, I knew that everything up to that point had just been holding her place until I found her again."

"Again?"

"Long story. We knew each other for four years in college."

Christensen realized Downing was staring at the meat mallet. He tucked it into the chair cushion. "When did it start up again?"

"Ran into her in February 1984. She was standing under the Kaufmann's clock, one of the only times in my life I'd ever walked along that sidewalk. Pure chance, fate, you know. Hadn't seen her in thirty-four fucking years. That's when it started again. I knew right away. We were like two railroad cars coupled, headed down a track that only goes one place."

Christensen turned on a lamp beside his chair, suddenly aware that the living room was very dark. "Every guy runs into old girlfriends from time to time, Grady. You share a few memories, a knowing glance or two, then get on with real life. Sounds like you were ready to turn your life upside down. Maybe she just happened along at the right time."

Downing smiled. "It's hard to explain. The physical attraction was as strong as ever."

Christensen glanced at his watch.

"She died in late '86," Downing said suddenly.

"I'm sorry."

"Not your fault."

"So you were, what, when the relationship started again? Fifty? Fifty-one? Kind of late for a midlife thing."

"Go to hell."

"Sorry. The symptoms just sound familiar."

"This was different," Downing said. "Trix and I had been through that, anyway, back in our mid-thirties. Even separated for a while to work it out. I was just stupid back then, thinking with my dick. Trix knew that and took me back, eventually. But Carole, something else was happening there."

"So you took the chance."

"You figure it out," Downing said. "Career going great

guns. Our daughter ready to go off to college. But I'd put a part of myself away all those years of raising her and being a decent husband, the spontaneous part that liked to skinny-dip in daylight and fuck in the backyard, the part that likes to go for a dog and fries at Dirty O's at three A.M., then go watch the produce trucks unload in the Strip until dawn. That's not Trix. Never was. So I just sort of, you know."

"Put it away for a few years? So that's the half that was missing?"

Downing nodded. "Trix and me were plowing along just fine. Maybe a little bored, but comfortable as ever. She's great, you know. My best friend. She's—"

"Dull?" Christensen wasn't going to waste these late hours mincing words. He wasn't sure where Downing was taking this, but he wanted him to get to the point.

"I've never been more comfortable with anybody in my life."

"Interesting word choice, Grady. 'Comfortable.' Like this chair. Like the pants you wear both days on weekends."

"It's true, though. Trix and I had a great partnership."

"Had?"

Uncertain smile. "Another story. We'll work it out."

Long silence. Christensen looked over Downing's shoulder at the clock above the fireplace. "Grady, what's really on your mind?"

"It's a complicated story."

Christensen was losing his patience. "*What* story, though?"

"About Carole."

"Sorry. Lost track there."

"It wasn't just about sex." Downing sounded defensive. "Maybe in college it was. Christ. Fight like dogs, fuck like rabbits, we used to say. But later, it was more than that."

"You saw her as everything your wife isn't, right? Beautiful? Glamorous?"

"Trix looks great for her age and for having a kid."

"*There's* a qualified observation. Face it, Grady. 'Looks great for her age' wasn't working for you at that point in your life. Nothing to be ashamed of. You were rediscovering a part of yourself through this other woman."

"Carole. And the thing is, I'd reached a point in life where everything made sense. Us meeting again after all those years. Her being single again after her divorce. Life was gonna be what it was supposed to be all along."

"You'd decided to leave Trix?"

"Wasn't a decision. Had no choice. Tried to fake it with Trix as long as I could, but I was already gone, mentally. She knew that, even if I never told her I was leaving, or why."

Christensen was confused. "So you never told her, then?"

"Never told anybody. Not a soul. Didn't want Trix hearing it somewhere, because I knew it was gonna hurt her bad. Not kill her; she's stronger than that. But I kept imagining how her face would fall. Her bottom lip would tremble like it always does just before she cries, then she'd tell me to go jam a telephone pole up my butt and walk out. Worst part was, I knew she'd hate me. After everything we'd shared, she'd still hate me. Forever. I walked through the scene dozens of times, blocking it out the best I could to cushion the blow. And I was just about ready when Carole—"

Downing adjusted the arm cover on the couch.

"When she died?"

Downing's head snapped up. "She was murdered."

Christensen felt a chill at the sudden shift in the conversation's tone and direction. "What do you mean?"

"It was like, well, nothing you could ever imagine. Pain like I've never felt, and I've been shot three times. Actual physical pain. Like someone took a dull knife and carved out whatever it was that made me, you know, feel."

"Grady, I'm sorry. But I think right now I need to know what happened to her more than how you felt about it. I don't mean to be insensitive, but—"

"Ron Corbett."

Christensen swallowed hard, trying to make sense of it. "She was one of the six?"

Downing nodded, said something under his breath. "The only one—"

"Pardon?"

"I said the only one that wasn't random."

Christensen stood up, dizzy, then fell when his leg gave way. He pulled himself up on the arm of the wing chair and made it to the hall bathroom just before he vomited.

The bathroom coasted slowly to a stop. Christensen opened his eyes. He was sitting on the toilet, head in his hands, reviewing the elaborateness of Downing's deception. He'd lied from the start about Corbett, about the risk. If Corbett was capable of locating and killing Downing's secret lover in 1986, surely he was capable of finding out where he and Brenna went for privacy, or where Annie and Melissa spent their afternoons. And if he killed Downing's lover at the height of the Primenyl investigation, it was probably the act of a man who thought the detective was closing in. Christensen felt his stomach churn again. Nonspecific multiple murderer, my ass.

Downing knocked lightly. "Jim?"

He couldn't talk. He wanted to walk out of the house, pick up the girls, and drive straight to California. Start over as far away from this nightmare as he could manage.

"I'm sorry, Jim."

Christensen yanked the door open. Downing was leaning against the doorjamb. His red eyes immediately found the floor.

"You son of a bitch, Grady. You had no goddamned right."

Downing backed away. "I had my reasons for not telling you the whole story."

"Fuck your reasons. You don't sucker somebody into working on a case against their better judgment without telling them what they're in for."

"You know what we're dealing with. I told you that."

"You told me the Primenyl killings were random. You told me the FBI was looking for a nonspecific murderer, not somebody capable of what you just described. Big goddamn difference. You think I'd put my kids in that position if I knew?"

Downing smiled, a nervous, sad smile. "That's why I couldn't tell you. I need your help."

Christensen grabbed the nearest thing, a porcelain vase on the front-hall table, and threw it with all his might. Downing ducked and the vase shattered on the mantelpiece, spraying the living room with tiny shards. "You had no goddamned right!"

"I'm here to tell you the story, Jim. It's late, but I'm here. But I can leave now if you want."

"What? There's more?"

"Full-disclosure time, right?" Downing took out a pack of Winstons. "Mind?"

"Yes."

Downing put the cigarettes back in his coat pocket. The look was less hostile than pathetic. "*I* got a video, too."

"Oh, Christ." He wanted to run, rage. But he wanted to know the rest, needed to know.

"Same thing as yours," Downing said. "Nothing too hostile. Nothing outright threatening. Just a couple minutes long, a bunch of ordinary scenes that made it pretty clear he knew my routines, knew about Carole. He'd videotaped us one night sitting in my car outside her apartment building. Talking. Kissing. Totally vulnerable. Then Carole got out of the car and went inside. That was it."

"And that was in the middle of Primenyl?"

"Eight weeks after the killings started. About a week after my last interview with Corbett. That was probably the only time since the first wave of killings that I'd seen Carole, that night he taped us. I didn't even tell anybody about it, because I wasn't sure there was a connection between the tape and my role in the investigation, at least not till three days later. That's when she died."

Downing scissored open the miniblind with his fingers and peeked out the front window. Then he twirled the control bar and opened the blind into the midnight darkness and turned back toward Christensen. "She kept a bottle of Primenyl in her car, in the glove compartment, already opened. Somehow he got some bad capsules into it. She couldn't find any Primenyl in her apartment, and I know she had a headache that night. I was there."

The detective's face contorted. He rocked back and forth as he pressed his eyelids shut tight, fighting tears. "We made love an hour before," he said.

Christensen was transfixed, forgetting his rage in the presence of raw emotion. "My God, Grady. She died that night?"

"In the parking lot, maybe ten feet from her car. Car door still open, the lid still off the bottle from the glove box. Capsules everywhere. Couldn't have been more than thirty minutes after I left. Got the call at home an hour later, sitting at the kitchen table with Trix, eating leftover salmon loaf. Looks like another killing, the watch commander said. Female Caucasian, tentative identification from the license plate number. But I knew the address, knew the car."

Christensen imagined the scene. The wife knowing something terrible had happened, something worse than she could have dreamed. Downing, probably paler than he was now, bluffing his way through a hurried good-bye, maybe conceding that the latest victim was an old friend.

"So everybody assumed it was random," Christensen said.

"Might as well have been. Only way anyone could have known was the unmatched lot numbers. But at that point, we weren't splitting hairs."

"And you were the lead investigator."

Downing shrugged. "Look, it was obviously Primenyl. It looked random. I hadn't told anybody about the video. So Carole became the sixth victim. Couldn't tell the truth, and not just because of Trix. I was there half an hour before Carole died, the last person to see her. Hell, I was still inside her. They'd have pulled me off the case in a second. I might even go from cop to suspect."

Christensen didn't react. Couldn't. Couldn't even absorb it all. He remembered Brenna's early warnings about Downing, her inability to comprehend the botched investigation, how a seasoned investigator could screw up so badly. If only she knew. He was probably half out of his mind by then.

"Try to understand, Jim. I needed more than ever to stay on that investigation. And I needed to keep what I knew a secret. I know I didn't kill her. You know I didn't kill her. But can you imagine how some defense attorney might twist that information? So I had to stoneface it. Nobody knew about Carole and me. I knew that much. So they had no way of making the connection."

"To you?"

"I was the only one who really understood what was happening. Corbett knew I was getting close, too close. He'd tried to intimidate me with the video, but I wasn't backing off."

The two men settled into uncomfortable silence. Everything made sense now—Downing's blunders in 1986, the relentless pursuit of Ron Corbett, his unwillingness to retire, his lying to get him involved with Sonny. This wasn't just some professional obsession. It was personal.

"You've carried that around all these years" he said.

Downing's face crumpled again, and the tears came. Christensen went into the bathroom to get him a Kleenex. Downing's face was oddly blank when he returned, and he didn't seem to notice the tissue Christensen tucked into his left hand. Clear mucus ran from Downing's nose onto his mustache, but he didn't try to stop it or brush it away. His tears still ran, but from eyes gone suddenly dead.

"I watched them bring her into the morgue," he said. His lips were the only thing moving. His gaze was fixed.

"Jesus, Grady." Christensen reached over and touched Downing's forearm.

"Nothing I could do. Had to pretend she was just another body while we waited for her dad to come down and identify her. He's eighty-one fucking years old, Jim; she was his only child. There's a little cubicle in the lobby with a TV screen. It's all done with a remote control, so the family doesn't have to go in. Heard him wailing, and I was up on the third floor. Same guy that used to ream me for bringing her home late when we were kids."

Christensen needed to do something. Anything. "I'm going to make some coffee."

"She was so beautiful. Hair down to her knees."

"Grady, I'm sorry."

"Ever seen an autopsy?"

Christensen closed his eyes. He'd seen a dissection, imagined the horror of watching the clinical dismemberment of the woman you loved, watching a pathologist's scalpel do its work on the body you'd held just hours before.

"Know how right before they take off the top of the skull with the head saw, they have to loosen the skin? So they cut around the hairline with a scalpel."

"Grady, I—"

"Then they peel the scalp away, then push the face down and tuck it under the chin. Simple, really. It slides right off the bone and muscle. That way they can do their three-notch cut and pop the top."

Christensen flirted with the idea of slipping upstairs to call 9-1-1. Downing was starting to sound seriously disturbed.

"Know what I remember most, Jim, what I can't, God help me, get out of my mind? What comes back to me at the oddest times, like whenever Ron Corbett's name comes up? I think about Carole's hair. Her head was propped on a V-block at the end of the table, and when the lab tech peeled her scalp back, her hair reached all the way to the floor. Ever seen the floor at the morgue?"

Christensen shook his head. He couldn't speak.

"And the lab tech, he's got these sneakers on, all crusted with gore, and he's standing at her head. He plugs the Stryker saw into one of the overhead sockets and gives it a whir, just to test it. While he's doing this, I notice he's standing on Carole's hair. Every time he moves his feet it pulls down on her scalp, and the skin behind her ears is tearing. And he's testing his saw and bitching about how the county doesn't get them the funding they need, and he's wiping her blood on his apron."

Christensen wanted more than anything to get away, to walk out of the room and find a place to breathe.

"He's just doing his job, getting ready to carve out Carole's brain, and he's standing on her hair."

"Grady, stop."

"I can't. I watched it, start to finish, and nobody ever knew."

"But why, Grady? You already knew it was Primenyl. Why watch the whole thing if you didn't have to?" Christensen considered the possible answers and wished he hadn't asked, but the detective didn't respond.

Christensen turned off the lamp, afraid Downing might see the horror he knew was registering on his face. And he couldn't watch Downing's blank stare any longer. At least in darkness the man could have some privacy. As they sat in silence, Christensen's dilemma settled over him like a shroud. It was too late to back down. Too late to run. Corbett already knew everything he needed to know to play his terror games. And Downing was losing control. The three of them were locked together in mortal combat, and someone had to lose.

Downing stood up, finally noticing the tissue in his hand. He wiped his nose in the pale light from the kitchen. "I just wanted you to know."

The man had just turned himself inside out. What to say? The son of a bitch should be down on his knees begging forgiveness. He should offer to post a twenty-four-hour guard, hire a food taster, make amends for suckering some blissful academic into the same whirlpool of a case that was apparently taking him down. Christensen opened his mouth, but all that came out was, "What now?"

Downing moved toward the door. "Plan B," he said.

"Which is?"

A sad smile. "You don't want to know. Look, Jim, I understand if you think I'm an asshole. What I did was wrong. But you wouldn't have helped if you knew. And I needed your help. So I made a choice. Still got no idea how Corbett found out about you. He must have been following me since right after the Greene County killing, knowing I'd try to get involved. We know he was following me that day out at Pitt, followed me right to you."

Christensen found his voice. "I was just a face on a video, Grady. He still wouldn't have known who I was."

"Unless Sonny said something to him later. I didn't think they still talked, but who knows? His mother, Jesus, she could say anything to anybody. Maybe Sonny told her and she told him. Corbett wouldn't need much to put it together. He's smart. And he likes to play. Hell, I'm wondering now if the whole Greene County thing was just a way to get me to play with him again. For all he knew, I'd lost interest. But Jim, I never would have lied if I thought there was a chance he'd turn on you, too."

Sonny. Christensen suddenly remembered their appointment. "I'm supposed to see Sonny again tomorrow. What should I do?"

Downing shrugged. "I should get going," he said, opening the front door.

"Wait a goddamn minute, Grady. I'm not the only one you suckered here. It took a lot of guts on Sonny's part to go after the memories he's retrieved so far. Christ, I think he's been on the verge of complete regression a couple times."

"Meaning?"

"He didn't just remember something—he started to relive it. That's where this stuff gets dangerous. If he crosses into psychosis, he could hurt himself, other people, anything. We've got him out on a very shaky limb, and I won't just leave him there."

"Your choice," Downing said over his shoulder. "Doesn't matter."

Christensen followed Downing down the front steps toward his car, shivering in the frigid midnight air. "It does, goddamnit. It matters to Sonny!"

Downing turned around, one hand on the car door. "Then help him, Jim. Do what you can. If dredging up those memories helps him get on with his life, fine. But they won't do me any good now."

"What do you mean?"

Downing opened the door. A cardboard box the size of a brick was on the driver's side. Christensen recognized a

distinctive Pegasus logo on the box above the words
"Webber Industries."

Downing noticed him staring and shoved the box under
the seat. Then he closed the door and started the car.
Through the frosted window, he mouthed the words "Plan
B."

30

Christensen wasn't easily spooked, but Downing's midnight confessional was too much. He locked his house tight and fled his wide-open city neighborhood for Brenna's house in Mount Lebanon, a secluded South Hills enclave of suburban tranquillity. They wouldn't be expecting him at 1:30 A.M., but he felt safer there. Nothing so far suggested Corbett knew Brenna's name or where she lived.

Christensen knew he wasn't followed. He'd passed two police cruisers as he steered through the dark and quiet streets, one of which executed a U-turn and followed him into her driveway. The cop just wanted to check his ID, bless his overzealous, civil-rights-be-damned heart.

Brenna's front door opened silently with an easy turn of the knob. He hadn't told her specifically why he wanted the girls to stay there, but he'd been very specific about her keeping the door locked, reporting anyone loitering in her neighborhood, and thoroughly checking packaged products. Brenna accused him of overreacting. She had no idea.

Voices in the kitchen. A low murmur, but still odd. Who'd be up this late on a weeknight? And unless Annie was awake, who could possibly be talking? Melissa hardly ever spoke to Brenna. He checked the living room. Annie was curled into a tight ball on the sofa bed, the tattered remains of Molly's silk nightgown clutched to her chest. Taylor,

Brenna's four-year-old, was snug against her. Spoons in a drawer, even at their ages, he thought. He moved the copy of "Love You Forever" from under Annie's leg and laid it on the coffee table, then covered them both with Brenna's thick goose-down comforter.

Christensen froze. Melissa's voice. And a phrase: ". . . Kevorked my mom." She'd used the term once before—a sneering adaptation of the name Kevorkian as a verb—and it rose above the murmur like it was wired directly to his ear. It pulled him into the dark dining room adjacent to the kitchen. Curiosity outweighed his fear of detection as he leaned close to the swinging door, unabashedly eavesdropping. His daughter and his lover were talking about Molly.

". . . could have been talking about getting new tires. He wasn't upset or anything, just sort of, you know, 'I made the decision and I think it's best.' That was it."

"He didn't tell you the whole story?" Brenna said.

"Once, the morning the police let him go. This little speech I could tell he'd been rehearsing all night. Then he wanted to take us out to breakfast, like a Grand Slam at Denny's would make everything okay. She's dead twenty-four hours and he's saying, 'I think we can get this behind us and move on.' I'm like, 'Well, sorry, Dad. It doesn't work that way.'"

Christensen peeked through the crack in the door. He could see Brenna, who was in her blue flannel pajamas, sipping from a coffee mug at the kitchen table, nodding her head. At the moment, Melissa was somewhere outside his narrow field of vision.

"I probably heard the same speech the night before, when I first met him in the holding cell," Brenna said. "And I know what you're saying. No emotion. It took me about four hours to get him talking about what happened. About your mom."

Brenna sipped her coffee. "Can I tell you something?"

"That's when you first met him?"

"That night. Why?"

"Nothing."

"He needed a lawyer and somebody gave him my name. He called me cold from the police station."

"And you'd never met him before?"

"No. Why?"

"I just thought you knew each other from before my mom died, that's all. That's what somebody from school said." Long pause. "What did you want to tell me?"

"We're being honest here, right?"

"I am."

Brenna leaned forward. Christensen closed his eyes to hear better. "That night changed my life," she said.

"Yeah, well, mine too."

Brenna ignored the bait, as he hoped she would. She ran a hand through her hair, twisted it into a ponytail and let it fall.

"Maybe my change wasn't as profound as yours. I know it wasn't easy for you and your sister, losing your mom."

"It gets a little hairier when your dad actually does the killing. When your friends all read the newspaper stories about what he did. When everybody at school knows your dad couldn't be bothered with a wife on a Veg-O-Matic."

Christensen knew he should leave, but he couldn't.

"That's a pretty superficial way to look at it, Melissa, don't you think?"

"I guess I'm just a superficial person."

No one was better than Melissa at turning communication into confrontation. Hang in there, Brenna, he thought. Fight the urge to reach across the table and smack her. Don't give up on the conversation. Recognize the child in pain and her elaborate machinery for emotional defense.

"Spare me the horseshit, okay, Melissa?"

Uh-oh.

"I mean, if you want to talk about things that matter, let's talk. But you need to get around your attitude. It's poisoned every conversation we've ever had."

Christensen shrunk into a corner, expecting his daughter to burst through the dining room door. He imagined how betrayed she'd feel when she found him there, spying in the dark. The one time he'd tried the no-horseshit-tough-love approach, it backfired so badly Melissa had stayed at her friend Jerilyn's house for a week.

But instead, she apologized to Brenna in a voice he hadn't heard in years. Then she asked, "What did you mean, it changed your life?"

Christensen reached the door crack just as Brenna ran a fingertip around the rim of her cup. "I was never very good at love. It just happens for most people, but it never did for me."

"Even when you were married?"

Brenna smiled. "People get married for all kinds of reasons. If they're like my parents, they get married for all the wrong reasons and end up splitting after a year or two. Some people, ta-da, get married because that's just what people their age do at a certain point in life. I just went along. He seemed like a nice guy."

"You make it sound like puberty."

Brenna laughed. "Fair enough. That's probably how I approached it. Scared, confused. I didn't have a good role model like you do. Your parents loved each other. A lot."

"My dad talks to you about that?"

"Not in so many words. But it's pretty obvious the way he talks about life with your mom before the accident. I know you don't agree, but it's obvious in the way he handled things afterward, too. Every once in a while, I see the hell he went through before he decided to end her life. He loved her so much, Melissa."

Christensen listened to the slow drip of the kitchen faucet. "They were nuts for each other," Melissa said finally. "Always holding hands. I used to catch them necking in the kitchen." Melissa's voice trailed off. "Does talking about that bug you?"

"Not at all. I mean, we've never talked about their relationship in those terms. But we never had to. I can tell just the way he talks about her. I know she had a crooked smile and was self-conscious about her overbite. I know she wouldn't let him kiss her in public, and how irresistible he found that. Every once in a while, he'll quote something— part of a poem, a descriptive phrase—and I'll just know it's something she wrote. He's got a lot of her stories and poems memorized, like Scripture."

"Did he ever show you *Carrie's Dirty Shoe*? It was one of the kid books she wrote." Melissa laughed. "My mom was so deranged. It's about a kid who steps in dog doo."

"I like it," Brenna said.

"She's wearing these shoes with tread and she tries and tries to get it all off, but she can't. And everybody at kindergarten treats her differently even though it wasn't her fault. I loved that story. The last line is, 'What would *you* do with doo on your shoe?' "

Carrie's Dirty Shoe was one of Christensen's favorites, too. Molly only wrote a few children's stories, but he considered each one a gem. *Dead-Eye Daryl* was about a boy who couldn't hit the toilet.

"She had a sense of humor, huh?"

"Totally demented," Melissa said. "Listen, can I ask you something? About when you met my dad."

"You seemed confused about that before."

"It's just, see, somebody at school said you and him were . . . that he was seeing you before my mom got hurt. That you guys were having an affair or something."

Christensen braced himself on the doorjamb. In an instant, his daughter's words had made sense of two years of hostility. My God, he thought, if that's what she assumed about his relationship with Brenna, what must she think about why he ended Molly's life? No wonder she hated him.

Brenna seemed just as stunned. Finally, she said, "You and your dad don't talk much, do you?"

"He tries."

"You never asked him that question?"

"I couldn't."

Christensen peeked through the crack. Brenna was holding her head in her hands, her fingers laced through strands of fallen hair above her forehead. "You really should. He's so confused about you."

"Yeah, well, the feeling's mutual," Melissa said. "So?"

Brenna sipped her coffee. "What did he tell you?"

"Nothing. For the longest time he said you were just his

lawyer. Then I asked him what was going on one night after you dropped him off out front and you guys kissed good-bye. He got all nervous and told me you were seeing each other, but that was it."

"Nothing else?"

"He asked if it bothered me once. Like, what am I supposed to say?"

"No offense, but sometimes your father can be a real asshole."

Christensen thought Brenna looked right at him when she said it.

"No offense taken," Melissa said.

"You need to talk to him about this, Melissa. But for the record, we weren't having an affair. The day your mom died, he was just another guy in trouble who needed a lawyer. We'd never met before then, but we had mutual friends. He never told you how the whole thing unfolded with your mom?"

"Swear to God."

"It's an amazing story. A love story." Brenna stood up, and Christensen tensed. She went to the coffeemaker on the kitchen counter and refilled her cup, then sat back down. Smelled like Starbucks Gold Coast.

"What I remember most vividly was the way he talked about your mother's face."

"Her face?"

"That night he called me, when the police were questioning him downtown—they were still talking about murder charges then. We talked a lot about your mom. Not at first. Like you said, at first he gave this little robot speech, no emotion at all, about what he'd done and why he'd done it. But then, all of a sudden he broke through to something deeper, something raw. I still don't know why. But he started talking about her face."

Christensen closed his eyes. Tight. He remembered the conversation like it was yesterday, one of the few times his professional detachment had failed. He didn't know why he'd opened up to Brenna, either, but that night she was the sympathetic stranger, and more than any other time in his life he'd needed to talk.

"He said when your mom smiled, the outside corners of her eyes dipped as the corners of her mouth went up. The lines of her face rearranged themselves so smoothly, he said it was like watching good animation, the way it changed her whole character. And he talked about how the years had changed those lines as they got older, made her face more and more interesting. He said he imagined holding that face in his hands when they were eighty, feeling the loose skin, the softness, kissing her, talking about you and Annie and how good life had been. That's how he expected things to go."

Melissa's hand snaked into view, picked up a paper napkin and disappeared.

"God, it was so painful to hear, to watch him struggle with that," Brenna said. "I've never heard his voice the same way since, so damaged. Never seen him cry again, either. I could tell it was something he'd never talked about before. And all I could think of was how much courage it must have taken him to end the life of someone he loved so much."

"It was so unbelievable, seeing her in the coma," Melissa said. She blew her nose. "No expression at all. Face like wax."

"He talked about that, too. As soon as he accepted what the doctors were telling him, that she wasn't coming back, that she could never smile again, or write stories, or hold her daughters, he made his choice. I don't think he ever had a second thought about the moral rightness of what he was going to do—he wouldn't let God do that to her was what he told me—but I think it took him months to screw up the courage."

"We used to go to church," Melissa said. "We don't anymore."

"He had to blame somebody. The drunk who hit her died in the crash."

Christensen counted a dozen faucet drips before anyone spoke again. He brushed a tear from his cheek. How could he have been so stupid, to share with a then-stranger what his child had most needed to hear? He wanted to push open the door, embrace Melissa, beg her forgiveness. But he couldn't.

"That conversation changed me," Brenna said. "I'd never understood love before, never had someone look me in the eye and explain it so clearly."

"You fell in love with my dad that night?"

Brenna let the steam rising from her cup wash over her face. "I don't know. I'm not sure people with as many scars as me *fall* in love. But sometimes we stumble onto it in the strangest places, at the strangest times. It's not something I would have predicted, and I know for sure your dad wasn't ready. Isn't ready. So I've just let him know how I feel and tried to give him space to grieve. We're both single parents. Right now it's more of a convenient partnership."

"But, I mean, you guys sleep together. Right?"

Brenna walked to the sink and poured out the rest of her coffee. "Life's complicated," she said. "He'd die if he thought you knew."

"He knows I know. I've been pretty rough."

"I'm meeting a client in seven hours," Brenna said. "Not that the conversation wasn't nice, but I'm going to bed." She paused. "Look, I know I came into your dad's life at an awkward time. We spent so much time sorting out the legal stuff after your mom died, then we started seeing each other, it probably seemed like I was trying to take her place. I can't do that. I wouldn't even try."

Melissa was up as well. She was still in the clothes she wore to school, carrying her backpack. He'd asked her to come straight here from school, but she'd obviously come in late. Brenna must have been waiting up for her. Christensen stepped to the hinged side of the swinging door, hoping they'd leave the kitchen through the front-hall door instead. He held his breath. The kitchen light went out and Melissa headed up the stairs to the spare bedroom. Brenna followed her into the hall, but stopped in the living room, at the sofa bed. She started to tuck in the kids, then stopped. She picked up "Love You Forever" from the coffee table, looked around the room, and set it back down. She checked the front door, then disappeared down the hall toward her workroom.

Christensen's head pounded. His blunder hit home. He'd moved the book. He'd covered the kids. She must be wondering. An eternity passed. Down the hall, the distant sound of a door opening, then closing. What was she doing?

The front-hall light clicked on. Footsteps. The sliding door to the hall closet opened and closed. The hall bathroom light, with its rattling fan, clicked on. The overhead kitchen light. Christensen suddenly realized she was searching the downstairs, room by room. Nowhere to run, nowhere to hide. He waited for the blaze of light from the dining room chandelier, shielded his eyes when it finally came. Brenna was standing in the broad dining room entryway holding a cordless phone to her ear with one hand, a gun in the other. His hands went up, spaghetti-Western style, purely by instinct.

"You shit," she said, lowering both hands.

Christensen started breathing again. "A gun?"

"I figured it was you. Burglars don't tuck little kids into bed. But why take chances?"

Christensen dropped his hands. They were shaking. His voice was unsteady. "I'm sorry."

"How long were you there?"

"I don't know."

"Why'd you come?"

How to explain? "I'm pretty sure Ron Corbett knows where I live, and he apparently pulled some stuff with Downing in 1986 that's got me worried."

"You talking to somebody down there?" Melissa called from the top of the stairs.

"Just checking CNN," Brenna said. "Good night."

They waited until the spare-bedroom door closed.

"I'll leave," he said.

Brenna clicked on the gun's safety. Defense attorneys keep rough company, but he still couldn't reconcile the image. She kept a gun?

"We could tell her you came in later," she said. "Or you could tell her the truth. Your choice."

"I'll just leave. She doesn't have to know I was eavesdropping."

"How brave of you."

He cleared his throat. "She hates me enough as it is. What about you?"

"I should have shot first."

They stared across the room. He had no defense. Excuses would seem pathetic. "I'm sorry," he repeated.

He swallowed hard and fought back tears. She moved away as he passed into the living room, heading for the front door. Thank God Annie was still asleep, he thought.

"It's not over," he said, turning back.

"No," Brenna said, "but I have a lot to think about. This kind of stinks, snooping on a private conversation. I'm not sure how I feel about it."

Christensen nodded. "I meant the Primenyl stuff. I still need your help. Can the girls stay here a while?"

Brenna nodded. "You, I should throw to the wolves. But if it's getting that weird, I guess you can stay, too."

31

"The Aquazoo or something?"

Sonny held the photograph closer to his eyes. It was the first of ten in the folder Christensen had shoved across the desk moments before, the folder he'd assembled that morning with countless reservations. Before handing it over, he'd memorized the order. The first picture was of a man seated on a plastic chair, staring through a thick window at a passing fish. He'd found it, like half of the others, in a box of Molly's old black-and-white prints. The rest he culled from magazines and books, all but one.

"There's no right answer, Sonny. Just tell me what comes to mind with each one." Christensen turned on his desk lamp for more light, angled it toward the pictures in Sonny's hands.

"The Aquazoo. We went there on a school field trip once. Pretty funny picture, though."

Sonny had arrived on time, apparently eager to resume, unaware that the stakes had changed. Christensen needed a breakthrough, and he couldn't let Sonny explore his mind's dark caverns any longer without helping him focus the search.

The second picture was of an immense woman handmaking pierogies. Molly had met her after photographing a High Mass in Polish Hill. The finished pierogies were stacked like bricks beside her, and her fingers were crimping the edges of yet another little dough bomb. A smiling priest stood behind her.

"The fat lady's cooking something. Not sure what. And there's a preacher."

"Good," Christensen said. Sonny was being too literal. "Again, you don't have to stop with just describing what's in the picture, Sonny. The point of the exercise is to let you explore a lot of different feelings. Anything else come to mind?"

Sonny studied the print. "My grandfather was a preacher. That what you mean?"

"Really?"

"He died when I was four. Mom never talks about him, but I know that much, that he was a preacher. And he was a real son of a bitch, strict and everything. Smoked cigars and spit little bits of tobacco all the time."

"Funny the things you remember when you're that young."

Sonny flipped up the third picture. The dancer. One of Molly's strangest. They'd gone to see Les Ballets Trockadero at Heinz Hall. One of the male dancers, dressed as a ballerina in a parody of *Swan Lake*, had struck a regal pose. Head up. Smile fixed. Left arm raised gracefully above his head, exposing a full thatch of armpit hair. Sonny laughed out loud. Christensen laughed, too, thinking about the picture, one of the most sexually confusing images he had ever seen.

"Twisted," Sonny said. "I'm not a fudge-pounder, by the way. You could have just asked."

The kid was bright, no question. "What? And waste all this expensive psychological training?"

Even as they joked, Christensen could hear the edge creeping into his voice. Four more pictures and Sonny would find the one image that was there for a reason. Could he tell? Could he sense the anticipation, the purpose? Did Sonny know how uncomfortable this ambush made him, how contrary it felt to everything Christensen believed about the safest and most reliable ways to recover repressed memories?

Sonny flipped to the fourth photograph. A tenement family—two girls, two boys—sleeping on a fire escape on a hot summer night in the Hill District. That one he got from a back copy of *Pittsburgh Magazine,* the one with the story on "Unseen Pittsburgh."

"They're not dead?"

"You tell me. What's happening in the picture?"

"They're just sleeping, I think. Looks like outside. You can see parked cars underneath them. Not sure where they are, but they look like they're sleeping."

"What else?"

"They don't have much money. They're black."

"Do you think their race is significant?"

"No. They're just black."

"Fair enough."

Picture five. A Pulitzer Prize–winning image of police taking an abusive father into custody as his bruised wife and ten-year-old daughter cower in a corner of the family's small living room.

"Home sweet home," Sonny said. A pained smile. "You know about my dad."

"Knew that one might be painful for you, but I thought it might be a basis for discussion. What did you think when you first saw it?"

Sonny stared at the picture. "How little the kid looks."

"Little?"

"And how sad the mom looks. He must have been hitting her, but somebody called the cops."

"Do you think they could have handled the situation differently? The mom and daughter, I mean."

Sonny grinned. "Name Lorena Bobbitt ring a bell?"

Christensen marveled at Sonny's grasp of his own emotions. He was bitter, had every right to be, but somehow maintained an objective distance. It was like he'd watched his entire life on TV rather than experienced it firsthand. Christensen swallowed hard, knowing he was about to put that objectivity to a severe test.

The sixth picture was a cipher. A color weather service photograph of a tornado bearing down on a small town as two residents in the foreground calmly record the scene on their camcorder.

"Dumb shits," was Sonny's only comment.

The seventh picture. Christensen steeled himself.

"A gun," Sonny said. "Looks like a .38."

Christensen studied Sonny's face for a reaction. He seemed to absorb the details of the black-and-white glossy. At first glance, it could have been a gun manufacturer's promotional close-up. The gun was propped neatly at an angle that highlighted its details against a distinctive diamond-pattern backdrop. Nothing in the frame would have suggested the grisly context to anyone except Sonny Corbett, who, Christensen hoped, might recognize the background as the shirt his brother was wearing when Sonny found his body a decade earlier. The gun had come to rest, improbably, on David's shoulder, the backspray of gore invisible against the dark shirt. The coroner's photographer had underexposed it, and Christensen thought its ambiguity was a plus when he found it among the more graphic suicide-scene shots in Sonny's file.

Sonny flipped to the next photograph.

"This one—" He smiled as he held up the eighth picture, one of Molly's shots, the one she called "Coitus Interruptus." A fat man had been forced to evacuate a Liberty Avenue massage parlor after a water main break. He was wrapped in a small towel, dancing beneath the parlor's "Magic Fingers" neon sign. Before Sonny could finish, the picture slipped from his hand and fell to the floor. He tried to pick it up, and when he finally did, it fell again.

"Shit," he said.

It fell again, then the whole stack of pictures fell from Sonny's lap onto the floor when he bent to get it. Something was wrong. Christensen circled his desk to help and found Sonny on his knees, sitting back on his heels and staring at the photograph that had landed faceup on top. The gun. Sonny was suddenly pale, his hands limp and apparently useless.

Christensen touched his shoulder. "What is it?"

"Nothing. My hands. It comes and goes." He pressed them between his knees, palms together.

"I'll get these," Christensen said, sweeping the pictures into a pile. "Can I get you some water? You need a break?"

"I'm fine," Sonny said. "You know what, though. I just remembered I'm supposed to work tonight. What time is it?"

Christensen checked the clock on the bookshelf behind Sonny. "Quarter after seven. I thought you were working days."

"I am, or was," Sonny said. He stood up and started pacing. "Oh shit. Dumb me. There's this new department head who screwed around with the chem-department work schedules, and I was supposed to fill in for someone. Can we finish this next time?"

No eye contact whatsoever. Flexing his fingers as he talked. Sonny was upset, but probably didn't know why. If he did, he wasn't letting on.

"You'll still be able to come at least two nights a week?"

"I'll check the schedule and let you know," Sonny said, hooking one arm through the strap on his backpack and moving toward the door. "Sorry about this."

The office door was slightly ajar, and Sonny pried it open with his foot as he wriggled the pack up to his shoulder. "Later. I'll call."

He disappeared through the outer door and his footsteps faded down the carpeted corridor. Took the stairs instead of the elevator. Christensen started to panic. Should he follow? If Sonny had recognized the picture from the suicide scene, even subconsciously, Christensen had forced the young man to confront what probably was one of his most painful memories, one he had repressed for ten years. What a clumsy, ham-fisted thing to have done. He should have paid more attention to his reservations.

From the window, he watched Sonny jog across a parking lot covered by an inch of fresh snow. Distance was comforting. If Sonny hadn't been wearing only a cotton shirt, Christensen might have pretended he was just another student headed for a night class instead of an emotional time bomb. Maybe he really was late for work. Maybe his hands hadn't gone numb when he saw the coroner's picture. Maybe Christensen hadn't just crushed Sonny's only defense and shoved him one step closer to the edge.

He picked up the pile of photographs and laid them on his desk, the coroner's picture still on top. He turned it facedown, then sat. For better or worse, Sonny was getting closer now, an arm's length from whatever demons he'd locked away. Experience told him Sonny was either going to open the door and confront them, or they were going to burst through and devour him. For Sonny, now, there was no turning back. Was he ready?

Christensen dialed his answering service. All he could do was make sure Sonny had somewhere to turn if—when— the time release began. He left Sonny's name and made sure the operator understood it was a priority. He hesitated, then approved the release of his home number and address if Sonny asked for. He hung up the phone, shrugged into his overcoat, and turned out the lights, then sat down in the chair beside the door feeling helpless, waiting, knowing that neither he nor Sonny would ever be more vulnerable.

32

The car's dome light was pale, but bright enough. Downing laid everything out on a towel spread across the front seat, making sure he was ready for anything. He opened a small envelope and let the seven capsules spill into his palm, one of each major brand of pain reliever on the market, including Primenyl. No matter what Corbett kept in his medicine cabinet—and everybody got headaches now and then—he'd find a match. He poured them back into the envelope and picked up his fail-safe, testing the needle guard on the syringe he'd loaded an hour earlier.

A single headlight rounded the corner ahead, bumping toward him along the rutted road. He'd expected to wait hours, maybe overnight. Could he be this lucky? Downing rolled everything back into the towel and shoved it into the satchel. In his various visits to Outcrop, he'd only seen three working cars parked among the rusted junkers and rickety houses. One was usually on blocks, an orange-colored Dodge. Another, an old Beetle, was dark blue. He could tell by the engine noise it wasn't the VW. The third was Corbett's. It wasn't registered, so he'd never been able to nail down the make and model. But it was light-colored and it rolled, making it easy to identify even at night. He'd know soon enough.

The car turned left, its light sweeping the grove of spruce, hemlock, and pines where Downing was parked. He squinted into the country darkness. It was Corbett's car. Had to be. The cone of its headlight beam moved down the access road, away from the strip mine toward civilization. The son of a bitch would be gone at least thirty minutes, because there was nowhere to go between here and the main road, and the main road was at least fifteen minutes down the goat path that wound its way to Outcrop. "Bye-bye, Chickie," Downing said.

He planned to work fast anyway, to be safe. He pushed the small silver button on his wristwatch. When the watch beeped in twenty minutes, he'd know it was time to clear out.

He locked the car out of habit and crossed the road at the curve. Something skittered into the underbrush to his right, making him jump, but the sound of his breathing and the crunch of his footsteps on the night-crusted snow calmed him again. The open pit to his left stretched forever, like a black ocean.

The path that wound through the woods to the back of Corbett's house angled steeply up from the road. Downing climbed the bank to the flat path, breathing a little harder now, his nose tingling from the sulfury smoke from the houses. Would anyone wonder about the fresh footprints? Since this could take weeks or months to work, would the footprints even be there by the time Corbett died? And even if they were, would the Greene County investigators think to look for them? He'd get rid of the boots on the way back, just in case.

Downing was close enough now to see the faint glow of lights in every house but Corbett's. Had to have been Corbett in that car. He stopped in the pine grove behind the houses to map his path to the back door. No chance of being seen. And unless Corbett had changed the back-door lock since his last visit, getting in would be a piece of cake. This might be easier than he'd imagined.

Or would it? He'd killed twice, but both times had been pure instinct. There's no decision when it's a simple question of survival, when a gun's pointed at your chest.

Those killings hadn't involved painstaking preparation. Or premeditation. The world didn't call them murder.

This was different—but no less moral, he reminded himself. He closed his eyes, looking for an image to give him courage. He found himself again at the Allegheny County morgue, thinking about lopping shears. Lab techs call them rib-cutters. How easily the tech had scissored open Carole's torso. How unforgettable the sound, like someone pruning wet branches from a tree.

He shoved his ski gloves into the satchel and pulled on a pair of latex surgical gloves, then started down.

His leg tingled as he climbed the back steps. Funny. Hadn't bothered him in days, but suddenly it came back as he stood there working the tool into the keyhole. He was in Ron Corbett's kitchen in less than a minute, groping into his satchel for the flashlight. He left his boots on the back steps. He intended to ditch the boots, so he wasn't worried about being identified. He just wanted to make sure Corbett didn't suspect someone had been in his house. If this was going to work, everything had to seem normal.

The kitchen smelled of cigarettes, grease, and mildew; the floor was sticky beneath his stocking feet. Downing set the satchel down beside the battered Frigidaire and opened its door. *Shit.* Practically empty. Three cans left from a Bud six-pack on the top shelf. A jar of baby kosher dills. Yellow mustard. A squeeze bottle of ketchup. He opened the carton of eggs, wondering if Corbett would notice a needle prick in one of the two that were left. Too risky. He lifted the lid from a saucepan to find what looked like a pork chop in tomato sauce. Slipping it into the red mess would be easy enough, but that would be all wrong. He needed something that would go straight from a store-bought container into Corbett's mouth.

An orange in the vegetable drawer. If nothing else turned up, that was a possibility. But that would be risky, too. If it sat too long, it might get discolored. Corbett had probably experimented on everything, and even a slight imperfection might tip him off. Downing closed the refrigerator. Maybe he'd have better luck in the bathroom.

The flashlight beam cut through the gloom, and Downing followed it from the kitchen into the tiny living room at the front of the house. Corbett didn't spend a lot of time decorating. An old recliner was anchored in front of a small TV, which sat on an upturned wooden fruit crate. The only light source was a fixtureless overhead bulb in the center of the ceiling. Downing kept the flashlight trained on the floor so he wouldn't attract attention from outside.

He passed a narrow stairway leading to the second floor, but he didn't go up. It was clear from the night he'd watched Corbett double-team the neighbor lady that the bedroom was on the ground floor. After checking the bed, just to make sure he was right about it having been Corbett in the car, he moved to the door he thought led to the bathroom. Even before he opened it, revealing a closet jammed with boxes, he remembered the outhouse. Goddamn. If Corbett didn't have a bathroom, he didn't have a medicine cabinet. And if he didn't have a medicine cabinet, where would he keep his medicine? Downing checked his watch. Five minutes already gone.

He opened every kitchen cupboard, sweeping his light across the mostly empty shelves. Did the same under the sink. He rifled the contents of a cardboard box on the counter: A half-empty bag of sugar. Salt and pepper. A few canned vegetables. Christ. Think. Where would the guy brush his teeth or shave? He played the beam on the kitchen sink, then on the windowsill just above it. He moved closer. On the left corner of the sill sat an old leather travel kit. The zipper was broken, and it yawned open wide when Downing lifted one rigid edge. Bingo. Buried under a half-empty Aqua Velvet bottle, down among a nest of crumpled Band-Aids and rubbers, was a beautiful white plastic bottle. He set the flashlight on the counter and poked a finger in, rotating the bottle so the label faced up. Could the gods of fate have a sense of humor?

Primenyl capsules.

Downing carefully unloaded the kit, laying each item on the counter in the order he removed it. He wanted to put everything back just the way he found it. The bottle was open, about half full. Perfect. The Primenyl killer *should* die this way, in an apparently random death that seems like the work of . . . the Primenyl killer. The symmetry of it! He pulled the towel from the satchel and unrolled it on the counter. Only a childproof cap stood between him and the end of this nightmare.

Downing poured the capsules from his envelope into a tiny mound on the towel and brought the flashlight beam in close. He separated the green-and-white Primenyl capsule from the rest, then poured a few capsules from the bottle into his hand just to make sure they matched. The moment he dropped the loaded capsule among the others in his hand, it was lost; no way he could tell them apart even if he wanted to back out. He poured them all back into the bottle, replaced the cap, and gave the bottle a quick shake, just to make things interesting. As he reassembled the contents of the travel kit, he thought how sickeningly easy it had been.

He held the flashlight close to his wristwatch, then set it back on the counter. Seven and a half minutes left of the twenty he'd given himself—a comfortable cushion to get back to the car. But he planned on staying in the car until Corbett got back. He didn't want to take the chance of passing him along the goat path. He'd wait all night if he had to. If Corbett wasn't back before dawn, he'd have to chance it. No way he'd get out unnoticed in daylight.

The kitchen suddenly got bright. Downing froze. He counted, one-one thousand, two-one thousand, three-one thousand, then slowly turned his head to the left. The generous neighbor lady was in her kitchen, maybe twenty feet away, in a loose burgundy robe. Same peroxide-nuked hair, which was bound up in pink curlers. She'd looked younger with her clothes off. A sullen, pan-faced boy with a crew cut, maybe twelve or thirteen, trailed behind her. Straight out of *Deliverance*. No curtains filtered the light pouring through their window into Corbett's kitchen, but then, none of these people seemed too worried about privacy.

The boy turned and left the kitchen, and she disappeared for a few seconds from the window that framed her. She was

working on a slice of white bread when she reappeared, then
stopped at what must have been a kitchen table. From there,
she could see straight into Corbett's kitchen. Downing tried
to follow her eyes. Was she looking down at the table, or at
him? Reading something? Downing noticed his flashlight
on the counter. Still on. *Fuck*. What would she notice more
easily, light or motion? He decided to stay still, leaning as
best he could into the shadow of Corbett's refrigerator. What
was she doing?

She turned a garish, colored page. One of the tabloids.
Christ. The kid wandered through the window frame again.
Then an older guy, talking at the kid's back loud enough that
Downing could make out a few words. Had to be his father.
The kid passed again, and for a moment all three were
framed in the small window. Downing stole another look at
his watch.

At least he was ready to go. In the unexpected light, he
double-checked the floor for any sign of his passage. He'd
touched nothing in the kitchen except the refrigerator handle
and the travel kit, and that was back on the windowsill
where he'd found it. Nothing he'd brought had left the
towel, which was rolled back into the satchel at his feet. His
boots were on the back steps, and he could pick them up and
disappear into the woods in a few seconds. All he needed
was darkness.

She was alone again, absently flipping pages, tuning out
the rumble, which had moved into another room. She
opened her robe, exposing one bulbous breast, then cinched
the belt tight again. Downing felt himself get hard. Trix was
right: Men are pigs. He knew it. He should have been
repulsed watching Corbett's three-way circus through the
window that summer night. What he was, though, was
jealous. For one lost moment, he was Ron Corbett. Tasting
the whiskey, watching the action from bedside, savoring the
chance for seconds, fucking a woman while her husband
watched from a chair. On an average day, how different was
he, really, from that hateful bastard?

A tinny electronic beep. In the tense silence, his watch
alarm seemed like a factory whistle. Did she see him recoil?

See his right arm move to shut it off? Could she have heard? Blondie flipped another page, oblivious. Then, as suddenly as she arrived, she turned out the kitchen light and was gone. Darkness returned. Downing breathed.

He pulled the back door shut behind him, making sure it locked, then grabbed his boots and ran through the snow toward the trees behind the house and onto the trail leading back to the car. His heavy wool socks were soaked by the time he stopped, but he wanted to get away from the houses, away from possible witnesses. He peeled off the socks and pulled the boots over his bare feet, then took off running again. Out here, he was exposed. Corbett was probably just making a cigarette run, and that Stop-N-Go store wasn't far off the goat path. He could be back any minute, and Downing wanted to be safe inside his car when Corbett got home.

And he was, but barely. The pinpoint of Corbett's single headlight appeared somewhere down the hill just as Downing was opening his car door. Downing was still panting from his run, watching through the gray fog on his windshield, when Corbett's car swept around the right curve toward the houses.

"Sleep tight, Chickie," he said, watching the car bounce over the rise and out of sight.

Corbett's engine noise would cover the sound of his car starting, assuming the Ford didn't stutter too long in this cold. Downing turned the key, thinking, *Start, you bastard*, saying, *Thank you, Jesus* when it did. He backed up to clear the trees, then started down the goat path in the winking moonlight, waiting until he was halfway to the main road before turning on his headlights.

Downing was forty miles away, somewhere along Hartwell Creek, when he pulled off I-79 to find a place to get rid of the boots. That's when he wondered, for the first time, where he'd left his socks.

33

"Who's the guy on Mom's porch swing?"

Christensen interrupted his parallel parking. Annie was pointing through the Explorer's windshield at their porch, at the antique wooden swing Molly had stenciled by hand. Melissa had her headphones on in the backseat, oblivious.

"I can't see around the big bush, honey. Who does it look like? Somebody we know?"

"He looks cold is all. Wait. It's that guy that came to swimming lessons."

"Sonny?"

Christensen strained to see. He still couldn't make him out, so he finished wedging the Explorer into the too-small space between the Koslowskis' Caddy and a mound of plowed snow. He never parked in the garage during these occasional visits home, when they picked up fresh clothes to take back to Brenna's. He wouldn't have been surprised if it *was* Sonny. Ever since he'd shown him the coroner's photograph, Sonny had been walking a knife edge of emotion and didn't know why, which confused and frustrated him. But Christensen knew they were close to a breakthrough, for better or worse. It was like watching a pot come to full boil.

He didn't expect this, though, even if he had authorized

the release of his home address and phone number to Sonny. He wasn't entirely comfortable, either, now that the killer's son was sitting on his family's front porch. The closer Sonny got to a breakthrough, the more desperate his father was likely to get. Christensen thought of 1986, of Ron Corbett's cruel assault on the detective who was tormenting him. Threatened, he'd simply killed the thing Downing loved most.

"Wait here, ladies," he said, turning off the engine. He was halfway across the street when the passenger-side doors slammed one after the other.

"We're just going inside," Melissa said.

"Yeah, it's cold," Annie said.

Sonny was sitting at the exact center of the swing, his legs tightly crossed and extending to the floor, balancing on a single toe, a daypack slung over his right shoulder. The swing seemed suspended halfway through a downward arc. No jacket, only a flannel shirt. His arms were wrapped all the way around his upper body. He seemed cold, damaged. When he looked up, his face was the color of oatmeal and his eyes had the suspicious look of a feral dog.

"Hey," he said. His lips were almost blue. His teeth chattered.

"Hey," Annie said. She climbed onto the swing beside him.

Christensen felt Melissa prying the house keys from his hand, so he gave them up.

"You look half frozen," he said to Sonny. "Been here long?"

Sonny shrugged, then lifted his foot, letting the swing continue its arc. He stopped the backswing with an awkward stomp. He looked past Christensen and waved at Melissa, who was struggling with the front-door key. Sonny was what she and her friends might call an SLS—a Suitable Love Slave—and she seemed flustered by the proximity.

"That's right, you two haven't met," he said. "Melissa, this is Sonny Corbett. Sonny, my daughter Melissa."

"Hi," she said. She was working the lock furiously now, a living portrait of hormone-fueled anxiety.

"And I think you know Annie"—who was staring up at Sonny with the same reverence she used to save for the mall Santa, the one who this year she accused, loudly and publicly, of fakery.

"Sorry to just show up," Sonny said. "Tried to call, but I kept getting your machine. Nobody's ever home."

"Long story. Come inside." Annie climbed down from the swing and followed her sister through the front door. Sonny didn't get up when Christensen put his hand on his shoulder. He seemed anchored, determined. He whispered something Christensen didn't understand.

"I want to go to the house," he repeated.

"Which house?"

"The one where David died."

Christensen froze, trying hard not to react. This was significant. Sonny had maintained as recently as last week that his brother died in a car accident; now he was admitting he'd died at the Jancey Street house. The oblique photograph must have had some impact, but what?

"That's a big step," Christensen said. Should he acknowledge Sonny's reconstructed memory? "I'm not sure I'd recommend it just now."

For the first time, Christensen noticed the bandage on the top of Sonny's head. A white, gauzy thing mostly covered by his hair.

"It's vacant, but my dad still owns it. I have a key. We can get in."

"That's not the point, Sonny. We just need to take these things slowly. What happened to your head?"

"That's part of it, I think." Sonny touched his scalp. Lightly. "Had an accident this morning, in the river."

Christensen tried again to guide Sonny into his house, but he wouldn't budge. "You hit your head?"

"A plank or something, real heavy. Swam right into it. Knocked me out for I don't know how long. But man, things got hairy."

"Stitches?"

"Seven. No biggie. Almost drowned, though. And that's when it started happening. I'm going down, right? I can feel the cold water in my lungs, and it's like I've felt it all before. What do they call that? Something that happens that feels like it happened a long time ago? And all of a sudden I'm remembering that same sensation, clear as can be."

Repressed memories, Christensen knew, could be triggered by anything—a color, the sound of a car horn, the scent of a menthol cigarette, a soft brush of wind against a cheek. It didn't have to be a sensation as powerful as water in the lungs. But a recovered memory also could be a case of brain-chemical trickery, like déjà vu.

"Remember that dream I told you about?" Sonny said. "The drowning one where I was underwater and couldn't pull my head up?"

Christensen nodded. He also looked around to see if anyone was watching. He desperately wanted to get Sonny inside. "You were on your back or something."

"Lying on something hard and looking up at this square kind of light, but my head was underwater. I was twelve or thirteen. I couldn't breathe."

Christensen sat beside Sonny on the swing. Annie was pressing her face against the picture window just a few feet from them, puffing out her cheeks, trying to get Sonny to notice. He didn't, and she seemed to understand from her father's disapproving look that now wasn't the time. She retreated into the house. "We talked about that dream a few weeks back," Christensen said.

Sonny walked stiffly to the far end of the porch. "It wasn't a dream. Something about that sensation, I don't know why, but I know it really happened. Down in the basement of the Jancey Street house. There's a laundry sink with a window above it. A font. That's what the voice calls it."

"The voice?"

Sonny was pacing now. "I don't know. I don't know. It's the same one I hear underwater, all burbly: 'I am baptizing you in the water, but there is one to come who is mightier than I.' Remember that?"

"That note you got," Christensen said. "The one that wasn't signed."

Sonny stalked back and forth across the porch. "'His winnowing-fan is in his hand to clear his threshing floor and gather the wheat into his barn; but the chaff he will burn in unquenchable fire.' I can hear the voice."

"Who?"

"I don't know. I'm underwater, so it sounds, you know, all garbled. I can feel the water in my lungs, and the adrenaline. The need to breathe. Next thing I know I'm in the ER at Allegheny General and they're stitching up my head. As I'm lying there, I flashed on some other things. And I know *they're* not dreams either. One was this guy, Peebo. He and his old man still live next door to my mom's apartment. When he was little, I think I—"

Sonny shut his eyes. "He was like three or four. I was fifteen, maybe sixteen. He'd do anything I said. So one time I, uh, I—"

"Tried to hurt him?"

"No! No. I don't know why I did it. But I held him underwater once, you know, to see what would happen. I can feel him fighting me, pushing me away, kicking. I remember feeling so strong, holding his life in my hands like that."

"But he was okay?"

"My mother stopped me."

"Do you think you would have stopped anyway?"

Sonny hesitated. "I don't know."

"What else, Sonny?"

"My brother," he said. "The house on Jancey. David died there, didn't he?"

Christensen tensed. "From what I understand, yes."

"I know he did. He died in our room. I remember it now."

If Sonny linked the memory to the photograph, or if he remembered anything more specific about David's death, he didn't let on. For now, the gamble seemed to have paid off. "You seem pretty sure about all this," Christensen said.

"It's weird. Like this stuff suddenly came into focus."

Melissa pushed through the front door with an armload of clothes. She walked between the two men without a word, headed for the car. Sonny didn't seem to notice her.

"How could I have been so wrong about my brother?"

Careful now, Christensen told himself. He cleared his throat. "Sometimes we tailor our memories so we can deal with them better. Losing a brother is a pretty tough thing. Maybe your mind just did what it had to do to deal with the loss."

"But you knew. You didn't say anything."

"I knew you'd remember it when you were ready."

Sonny stopped and leaned against the porch rail.

"I'm going to the house. You don't have to come if you don't want, but I'm going."

He couldn't let Sonny go alone. "You've worked hard to get this far. It's a big step, Sonny, but you're the best judge of whether you're ready."

"Can we go now?"

Annie appeared at the picture window in a wedding dress. A flower-girl dress, really. She'd worn it in a cousin's wedding last year, and at the moment was a vision in white lace and pink satin ribbons, topped by a frothy veil, hands folded as if in prayer. Very pious. Very subtle.

"You're pretty popular around here," Christensen said.

Sonny wasn't diverted. His face was as intent as Christensen had ever seen it. When Sonny leaned forward and repeated, "Can we go now?" Christensen knew he had no choice. Sonny was going to the house. His demons had an address.

"I want to go with you, but I need to make one stop first, to drop off the girls," Christensen said, his stomach churning at the thought. Brenna's house was still safe, separate, away from this madness. Did he really want Sonny to know where the girls were staying? He swallowed hard. "You can ride with us."

Without another word, Sonny hoisted the daypack and started down the steps toward the Explorer.

Brenna wasn't home. They'd resumed a relationship of sorts, but not a healthy one. His deceit seemed always just beneath the surface of every strained conversation. They still weren't sleeping together.

"Where is everybody?" Annie asked, laying her fresh

clothes on the living room couch. "Taylor!" Her voice echoed through the house.

"Brenna probably took him across town to see his dad, honey. They should be back this afternoon. Will you be okay here if Dad goes out?"

"Is Sonny staying? We could play Candy Land."

Sonny wouldn't even get out of the car. He'd had a death grip on the front-passenger seat armrest all the way to Brenna's, and Christensen had wondered again if this visit to Jancey Street was somehow avoidable.

"Sonny and I need to go out, honey. It's important. I'm sorry I'll miss a Saturday with you, but maybe we'll take a day off this week and do something, okay?"

Annie's bottom lip quivered. Melissa stomped into the room, dropping her clothes onto the couch. "That guy's got a serious attitude problem," she said. "I said good-bye twice and the stuck-up jerk didn't even answer."

"I'll explain later," Christensen said. "Right now I need you to promise me you'll stay here with Annie until Brenna and Taylor get back. I have to go out, and I'm not sure how long I'll be."

"Guys like that always think they're God's gift. So excuse me if he's twenty-two. Big friggin' deal."

He put both hands on his older daughter's shoulders. She was agitated and he expected her to pull away, but instead she returned his gaze. "Melissa, remember after you got burned by the shampoo, I told you about the Primenyl case? How I've been working on something that had to do with it?"

She nodded. He couldn't remember the last time he had her undivided attention.

"Sonny may know something about the killer. He may have seen something when he was a kid that the police think could be really important in finding the person who killed those people, the one they think is killing again."

"Cool," Annie said.

He'd forgotten his younger daughter was in the room. He kept one hand on Melissa's arm and stooped to Annie's

level. "This has to be our secret. Please. It's very important."

"Not even Brenna?" Melissa said.

"She knows," he said, then immediately knew he'd
blundered. Both girls looked hurt. Betrayed.

"Look, I can't tell you the whole story now, but Brenna
knows a lot about the case and has been helping me. But she
doesn't know anything I haven't told you."

"Bullshit," Melissa said. "She just knew it long before we
did, that's all. You don't trust us."

"Yeah, bullshit," Annie echoed.

"Come on, guys. I need your help here."

"Just go, okay?" Melissa said.

"I wish I had a choice."

They stood together for a long moment, close enough to
feel one another's warmth. Annie was still mad, her body as
rigid as an ironing board when he tried to pull her into a hug.
Melissa, though, threw her arms around his neck when he
stood up. She seemed as startled as he was when she stepped
back.

"No big deal," she said, turning away. "Just be careful."

His wink forced a tear onto his cheek, but he brushed it
away before she saw. "No big deal."

He repeated it irrationally as he strode down the hall and
shut the door to Brenna's study. "No big deal," he said as he
opened and closed the drawers of her desk, wondering
where she kept her gun.

34

Irondale was one of those classic Pittsburgh neighborhoods where the houses and people were sturdy and unchanging. It sat on a bluff overlooking the Allegheny River, with three main streets that ran perpendicular from Braxton Avenue at one end to Allegheny River Boulevard at the other. It was hidden, in a way, between the upscale Highland Park and downscale Braxton Heights, and as Christensen steered down Chislett Street, he noted its remarkable whiteness. Not the snow. The residents. Working-class Eastern Europeans were notoriously suspicious of people they found racially or ethnically mysterious, including anyone who didn't share their broad, flat faces or heavy legs. Neighborhoods like Irondale resisted integration like a granite outcropping resists erosion.

"Turn here?" Christensen asked.

Sonny nodded. His agitation level had been creeping up since they'd passed Shadyside. By the time they turned onto Chislett, Sonny was wired. He opened and closed the Explorer's electric door locks twice. He rocked back and forth. He tightened his right-hand death grip on the armrest, leaving fingernail marks Christensen figured would be there forever.

They passed a Catholic church on the left. "St. Bingo's," Sonny said. "That's what my dad called it."

A "Bingo Every Friday" banner hung across the church facade, twice as large as the sign identifying it as St. Thomas More. The notion of Ron Corbett having a sense of humor struck Christensen as odd, almost unimaginable. They passed the drugstore where Molly used to drop off the girls' prescriptions on her way to work, one of three Pharmco stores made famous by the Primenyl killer. The one where Downing said Ron Corbett worked as a pharmacist and store manager in the autumn of 1986. Christensen felt like he was walking onto the set of a movie he'd seen many years ago.

"Left at the next street," Sonny said. He opened the glove compartment, then closed it. He opened it again, closed it.

Time to get him talking, Christensen told himself, or at least to try to. "What are you feeling right now?" Christensen asked.

"It's weird. Tense."

"Do you know why?"

"No." Sonny swallowed hard. His breathing was getting shallow. Faster. "Been a long time. Haven't been here since I went into foster care."

"Never? No friends here you kept in touch with?"

"Left again on Jancey." This time Sonny gasped as he spoke. He inhaled two times, quickly, let the air out slowly. Twice more, out slowly again. The door locks kept a disturbing cadence.

"Were you happy here?"

Sonny shook his head from side to side like a halfback trying to clear cobwebs after a vicious tackle. He pretty much had his breathing under control.

Christensen repeated the question.

"Don't remember," Sonny snapped. "It wasn't yest—"

Sonny's body went rigid, and what little color was left in his face drained away. He was staring at a house on the opposite side of the street, a three-story brick Victorian that, except for its obvious disrepair, looked a lot like every other house along the south side of Jancey.

Christensen pulled the Explorer to the curb. The house

had no obvious house number, but clearly they'd arrived. "You okay?" he asked.

No reaction. Christensen studied the house's redbrick face. The trim paint was a dull brown, cracked and peeling off in strips the size of yardsticks. The broad front porch was littered with junk. Fitted plywood filled the large ground-floor picture window, and it was well-scarred by taggers. The only decipherable symbol among the graffiti was an artful pentagram. Vandals had stolen all of the removable outdoor hardware, including the porch light fixture and, judging by their faint outline, the address numbers identifying it as 154. Christensen wondered briefly if squatters might be living inside.

His eyes settled finally on the single third-story window. In a sickening rush, he remembered one of Sonny's stories, the one about the top-floor window seat where he and his brother watched their father make their mother bark for the neighbors. He turned back toward Sonny, who was wide-eyed and unblinking. The motor was still running.

"We can keep going," he said.

"No."

"If you're at all uncertain, Sonny, we should wait."

Sonny closed his eyes. "Give me a minute."

Christensen turned off the engine. A Port Authority bus roared past, accelerating from the stop sign at the end of the block. As it disappeared out of sight, Christensen realized they were being watched. Up and down the street, huffing snow-shovelers and bundled stoop-sitters paused and stared at the unfamiliar vehicle now parked on their street. Christensen stared back. Did any of them remember the Corbetts? What Corbett family cataclysms had they witnessed? How many had they excused as none of their business?

"Think any of these neighbors remember you?"

Sonny forced his gaze from the house. Nothing seemed to register as he scanned the faces up one sidewalk and down the other. He looked back at the house, then did a double take. An old woman, dressed in the telltale black of an Italian widow, trundled toward them and turned up the steep steps to a house on the high side of Jancey, directly across from the Corbett family home.

"I don't know her name," he said.

"You remember her, though?"

"My dad called her 'the Inspector.' Always on her front porch, sweeping, saying rosaries, taking everything in, never saying a word anybody could understand. Knows everything that goes on around here."

Sonny closed his eyes tight, as if in pain. Then he shuddered. "She was watching when they brought David out of the house. I remember her shaking her head at all the cop cars and stuff."

"She's got a pretty good view of your old house," Christensen said. "What else do you think she saw?"

Sonny opened the Explorer's door, got out, and steadied himself against its frame for a few seconds before slamming it shut. Christensen unbuckled his seat belt and climbed out, worried what Sonny might do next. Sonny still had one hand on the car when he reached the passenger side, and his eyes were closed. His expression was bewildering, a look of part-wonder, part-terror, as if watching a frightening scene unfold on the backs of his eyelids.

"David killed himself." Sonny's eyes shot open, and he pointed directly at the solitary third-floor window. "In our room. He shot himself in the head."

"Sonny—"

"Oh, Jesus Christ. I thought it was the TV."

"You thought what was the TV?"

"The gunshot. I was downstairs, and I heard it, and I didn't go up."

"Who else was in the house?"

"I don't know."

"Your dad had moved out the week before."

"I know."

"Were you and David alone?"

"No. My mom, my aunt, I don't know. Somebody else was downstairs."

"They didn't hear it either?"

"I don't know. They didn't go up."

"Who went up, Sonny?"

The young man winced and kept his eyes shut tight. "I found him. Izzy came down, real nervous, tracking something all over the kitchen floor. It was dark by then, and I went up. David was sitting in the big chair when I turned on the light. Oh Christ. For a second I thought he was asleep." Sonny slammed a fist down hard on the Explorer's hood. Its report echoed down the snowy street, drawing even more stares.

Christensen looked again at the house. It was full of demons, all right. They hadn't even waited for Sonny to open the door. They'd sensed his presence somehow, and had swarmed to the curb to greet the boy who'd ignored them for ten years. "I think we should come back later," he said, putting a hand on Sonny's shoulder. "Maybe take this a little at a time. To be safe."

"No!" Sonny was trembling. Christensen tried to imagine the emotional toll of confronting for the first time an only brother's suicide. He'd helped guide others into their minds' scary places, but he'd always built in time for decompression, time to pull back and think about the confrontation and what it meant. He was well aware that anyone opened up to a sudden onslaught of emotion was in danger. If those wounds weren't stitched up as they occurred, things could get out of hand fast.

It was Christensen's experience that most people could handle it. For someone like Sonny, though, who might never be more open and vulnerable than now, psychosis was a short step away. Some therapists called it the Great Escape, when the cognitive structure collapses completely and reality becomes irrelevant. He *had* to coax Sonny back toward reality.

"How about we get a cup of coffee first?" he said. "Must be some place around here."

"I don't want coffee."

"You take yours with cream?"

"No."

"Sugar?"

"No!"

"Never been able to drink it black myself. Somewhere we can get donuts here?"

"Look," Sonny said. "I want to go in. If you're not coming, just go."

"I don't think it's a good idea. Not now. We could even come back tomorrow. The house isn't going anywhere."

Sonny started across the street, shifting his daypack to the opposite shoulder as he walked. Christensen's first impulse was to retrieve Brenna's gun from under the driver's seat, but he dismissed his irrational fear that Ron Corbett could be inside. His second impulse, pure habit, was to pull the keys from the Explorer's ignition. He ignored that, too, and followed Sonny, staying close.

On the porch, Sonny dropped to one knee and unzipped his pack. He rummaged among what looked like the remains of a lunch and pulled out two sturdy keys held together by a paper clip. Had he carried them all these years? He held the keys in his open right palm for a few seconds, then closed his fingers and raised the fist to his forehead. Suddenly he was up, reeling toward the porch rail along the far side of the house. The guttural roar of his vomiting filled the narrow walkway between his house and the one next door.

"Leave me alone," Sonny said, waving him off. "I'm okay."

"You're not okay. We need to slow down, take this slower."

Sonny emptied the rest of his stomach onto the concrete below. Christensen watched his shoulders roll with the effort. "Sonny, please," he said.

Sonny gripped the railing fiercely, for a long time. When he turned around, a glistening strand hung between the corner of his mouth and his shirt pocket.

Christensen found the image terrifying. "Tomorrow," he pleaded.

Sonny wiped his mouth on his sleeve. "You coming in or not?"

35

The front door opened unwillingly into a small tiled vestibule just large enough for visitors to leave wet shoes or umbrellas. It had been a craftsman's house once. The inner-door window was leaded glass, intact against all odds after years of neglect and vandalism. That door opened easily into a foyer behind which rose a two-level switchback staircase. Halfway up, a narrow wedge of sun shone through a milky stained-glass window, a picture of a white-sailed boat against a yellowing sky.

"I'm okay," Sonny said.

He was halfway inside, standing with the toes of his sneakers on the dusty hardwood floor, his heels still on the blue-and-white tiles of the vestibule. Christensen, standing behind him, closed the outer door and waited. They were uncomfortably close, but maybe this way he could get a look at the emotions registering on Sonny's face. Sonny blocked the doorway, moving at his own pace.

"Don't rush it," Christensen said. "You've got options every step you take. Remember that."

Sonny moved forward, a single step. The oak floorboard creaked with his weight, flushing something small, furry, and frightening from beneath the front-hall radiator. It scampered along the baseboard and disappeared into a dark-wood gap at the base of the stairs. If Sonny noticed, he didn't react.

Christensen fought the impulse to run back outside. "Why'd your father never sell this place?" he asked.

"Don't know."

"But no one's lived here since 1986?"

"Don't think so. Looks the same. This is all our stuff."

Christensen peeked around the doorjamb, noticing for the first time the furniture in the living room to the right. The vandals had stayed outside, for reasons he couldn't begin to understand. The house had a history, with its frightening record of Corbett family violence, suicide, and madness. But how could an abandoned house full of furnishings apparently remain untouched for more than ten years?

As Sonny moved slowly into the foyer, Christensen was overwhelmed by instinct. They shouldn't be here. The risk to Sonny was too great. A visit to one's childhood home is bound to generate strong emotions, in anyone. A home like this, frozen in time during Sonny's most difficult years, probably would generate a whirlpool of feelings. The place was full of memory triggers.

"You hear something?" Sonny asked. He was staring straight ahead, into the kitchen.

"No."

"That scratching."

The house was as silent as a tomb. "Sonny, I don't think this is a good idea," he said, but Sonny paid no attention to his words or to the hand Christensen placed gently on his forearm. Christensen brushed past, finally getting a look at his face. Sonny's eyes were wide, like open lenses, as dilated as his pupils. The house was dim, but not that dim. Sonny was taking everything in, letting the light into the corners he'd kept dark for so long.

A white plaster wall rose directly across the narrow passage at the bottom of the stairs, straight ahead. Sonny ran his flat palm across it at chest level, then down toward the floor. He bent to an indentation about two feet off the ground. Christensen looked closer. The thick plaster was dented smoothly inward, as if something round and heavy had fallen down the stairs and struck the wall. Sonny massaged his fingertips into the bowl like a potter, then looked up the stairs to the landing.

"Bitch!"

Christensen jumped. Sonny's voice, edgy and hard, echoed through the house.

"What do you see, Sonny?"

Sonny closed his hand into a tight ball, raised his right arm across his chest, and slammed the fist into the wall, hard. Christensen heard the unmistakable crack of bone, thinking, oh Jesus. He grabbed Sonny by the elbow and stood him up, then pinned his shoulders against the wall. They stood eye to eye, but Christensen felt like he was staring into a void. "We need to leave, Sonny. Now. Come with me."

It would have been better if Sonny had shoved him away, called him an asshole, asked to be left alone. Instead, he simply pushed away from the wall, ignoring Christensen's determined effort to prevent him from doing so. Sonny was young, powerful. It was one of the few times in his life Christensen had ever felt physically overmatched.

He backed off, unwilling to force a confrontation. Sonny started up, toward the bedroom he and David shared, then stopped on the second step and retreated. He started up again, one step, then stepped back down and walked into the kitchen.

Christensen followed, onto the same checkerboard linoleum-tile floor he remembered from the coroner's photographs. He half-expected to see the bloody paw prints that had once stitched its surface, but they had been cleaned up and the floor was covered by a thick layer of dust.

Sonny ran his broken hand along the edge of the yellow-tile counter, looked up at the pressed-tin ceiling. His indifference to what surely was intense pain made Christensen uneasy. Could he be watching a mind and body operate simultaneously on two different planes?

Someone had emptied the kitchen of its furnishings, but it had been orderly, not the work of thieves. A few cupboard doors hung open enough that Christensen could see the bare shelves. Four small dents in the linoleum suggested where the kitchen table might have been. At the sink, Sonny, without wincing, turned the ancient faucet with his right hand. Something groaned in the wall behind the basin, but nothing came out. The pipes couldn't have survived all these winters unless Corbett had shut off the water, Christensen thought.

A small window above the sink overlooked a rotting wooden porch, and Sonny's eyes fixed somewhere on the other side. Christensen peeked through the back-door window at the same scene. The porch's battleship-gray paint was cracked and flaking, and what had once been a handrail leading down the steps to the small backyard had collapsed. Beyond that, the bare branches of an apple tree rose from an otherwise empty patch of fenced ground.

"David! Trooper's sick!"

Sonny was on his tiptoes, pointing through the window at the porch floor. His eyes were open, but he was watching something Christensen couldn't see. Sonny lurched for the back door, shoving Christensen aside, and tugged at the knob. He stopped, twisted the dead bolt, then tried the knob again. The door opened with a dried-paint crack and a rush of cold air. By the time Christensen followed, Sonny was on his knees at the center of the porch. He looked up, helpless and panicked.

"What's wrong with him?" he pleaded.

"With who, Sonny?"

"Trooper! He was just eating, then he fell down."

Trooper. One of the Corbetts' dogs. "Tell me what's happening, Sonny."

"Convulsions or something. I don't know. Why are his legs doing that?"

Christensen flashed on a scene: a dying basset in the snow.

"What's wrong, David? Help him!"

With a chill, Christensen realized Sonny wasn't talking to *him,* but to his older brother. Sonny had fully regressed to a moment long ago; beyond simply remembering an event from his childhood, he was reliving it. And Christensen knew Sonny wasn't ready to handle that level of emotion.

"I can't, Sonny," he said, testing the theory. "I don't know what's wrong either."

"He's gonna die!" Sonny screamed. Crying now, head down, watching something awful, apparently hearing sounds Christensen could only imagine. "Get Dad!"

"Where is he?"

Sonny saw someone come out through the back door, waved whoever it was over with his broken hand. With his other hand, he seemed to be cradling something. The pose reminded Christensen of the famous photograph of an Ambassador Hotel busboy kneeling over a fallen Robert Kennedy.

"What's wrong with him? Do something!" Sonny's head snapped to one side, like he'd been struck across the face. "Please!" he screamed through his tears. "Just try! Rachel? Somebody help him!"

"Is Aunt Rachel here, Sonny? Dad, too. Who else?"

"Stop smiling!" Sonny screamed. "He's dying!"

"Everything okay over there?" A voice from the alley, across the backyard. A heavily bundled man was watching them, a look of genuine concern on his face.

"My dog's dying!" Sonny sobbed, gesturing to the empty porch floor. Christensen waved the man away with confidence, hoping the stranger would perceive him as someone perfectly in control of the situation. Without the illusion, the man might call the police. It worked, or at least seemed to. The man kept walking.

Christensen focused again on Sonny. "Why is Trooper dying?" he said.

"Why is this happening?" Sonny screeched. In grim pantomime, he gently laid the dog's head back on the porch. He stroked it again and again as a tear tumbled from his cheek and became a tiny wet circle on the painted floorboards. He looked up, as if listening to someone on the porch, and suddenly covered his ears with his hands. Emotion swept across his face like a prairie storm—despair, disbelief, and, finally, rage. "But Trooper didn't do anything to you! He's a fucking dog!"

Sonny turned, addressing someone else on the porch. "You never do anything!"

"Maybe they can't," Christensen said vaguely.

"Who *can*?" Sonny demanded.

"Your mother?"

"For shit. If she was ever fucking here when it happened. She's so goddamned worthless, what could she do?"

"What do you mean, worthless?"

"Like trying to get a turtle out of its shell."

"So your mother can't help you?"

"She's never here!" Sonny protested.

"Your father? David?"

"She's got the spirit! She's stronger!"

Christensen tried to make sense of it. Things were moving too fast, and nothing fit. He imagined the people on the porch, taking a head count.

"Your aunt?"

Sonny stood, hands still over his ears, and reeled back into the house, swept away by his own emotional dam-burst. Christensen followed, stopping abruptly when he collided with the young man standing motionless at the center of the empty kitchen. Sonny didn't flinch as Christensen's full weight crushed against his swelling right hand.

"Don't," Sonny said, his voice almost a whisper. "Please don't."

He seemed transformed in an instant from manic to morose. His shoulders slumped, and as Christensen squeezed past he thought he heard a low whimper like that of a frightened puppy. Sonny's wide eyes were fixed on the opposite wall, on a white door that seemed too large for that of a cupboard.

"What is it, Sonny?"

"Not down there."

The basement. The water dreams. "Someone wants you to go down there?"

Sonny collapsed to his knees on the checkerboard floor. "I don't want to pray!"

"Who wants you to pray, Sonny?"

"Rachel!"

"Aunt Rachel wants you to pray?"

"But I didn't do anything!"

Sonny's head hit the floor with a sickening thud. He kept it there, submitting to some greater, malicious power. He looked like someone had a foot on his neck.

Christensen fought the impulse to turn away. Who the hell was Rachel? Her name threaded in and out of Sonny's stories, but she remained, to Christensen, little more than a bit player. As far as he could tell, she didn't even exist, since no one on either side of Sonny's family knew who she was.

"Forgive me, Father"—Sonny choked off the words as he struggled for breath—"for I have sinned." He rose to all fours, head bowed, then stood and walked unsteadily to the basement door.

When he turned around, his face was vacant, accepting, without fear. He twisted the knob with his broken hand. The door opened silently into darkness, and Sonny started down. "Lord have mercy."

36

In the pale light of a side-door window, Christensen looked for a wall switch. He groped into the collection of winter coats in children's sizes that hung on pegs just inside the basement door, but it wasn't there. He reached again into the dark wool mass, and again found nothing. "Where's the light, Sonny?" he said, thinking about rats.

Sonny was moving down the stairs slowly, like he was walking underwater. If he heard, he didn't answer. Christensen creaked halfway down and squinted into the cellar room, his head numbed by the coarse smell of mildew. It wasn't pitch black, as he'd imagined, but dimly lit by daylight filtering into a basement window-well and through a grimy pane just above the laundry sink.

The center of the room was a tangle of garden tools, hoses, clotheslines, overturned bikes. In the far corner, a table saw and lathe, someone's small wood shop. A Ping-Pong table, folded for storage, leaned against the back wall. Christensen listened hard for the skittering rush of rodent feet, but heard only Sonny's labored breathing.

Sonny was at the sink now, running his ruined hand along the empty countertop that stretched five feet in both directions from the basin. The hand cut an irregular trail through the collected dust, which swirled up into the shaft of light like an apparition.

"Why are we here, Sonny?"

Sonny's hand continued its methodic passage across the countertop. "To be closer to God." His voice flattened into recitation: "I am baptizing you in water, but there is one to come who is mightier than I. His winnowing-fan is in his hand to clear his threshing floor and gather the wheat into his barn; but the chaff he will burn in unquenchable fire."

"Who told you that?"

"Rachel."

Rachel again. "Wait. She brought you down here to be closer to God?"

"To wash our sin away. Make us pure. We were conceived in sin."

"Who's we? David, too?"

"You. Me. We have the stain."

"Who else has the stain? Our mother?"

Sonny nodded. A knowing smile. "He used her as his vessel. Rachel says she'll be forgiven."

"Who, Sonny? Who used her? Dad?"

"Papa Richard, too. Rachel told me. Mom was their vessel. The dark angel's vessel." He paused. "Wasn't her fault."

Papa Richard. Sonny's grandfather, Sandra Corbett's father. Like Rachel, he was little more than a caricature in Christensen's mind: The stern and possibly abusive minister. Died in the late 1970s. Christensen tried to fit Sonny's words into a puzzle that now seemed even more complicated than the day he first sifted the Corbett family history from the juvenile court file. Incest might explain why Sandra's mind unraveled, her submissiveness to years of abuse from her husband, but there was so much else he didn't understand.

"Rachel was Mom's sister, right? Older or younger?"

"She knew everything."

"So Papa Richard used Rachel, too?"

Sonny shook his head, his eyes never straying from the sink. His broken hand seemed twice its normal size. "Papa never touched her. Dad couldn't touch her, either. Rachel's smart, David, not like Mom. She knows who they are. She couldn't save Mom, but she wants to save us. She told me. Down here."

Sonny reached for the cold-water faucet, turned it on full. The pipes moaned again. "She'll take me to God while you're gone to the store, then take you when you get back."

Water. Baptism. Salvation. Had Rachel tried to drown the boys in this sink? Christensen wished he could dismiss the whole thing as a typical repressed-memory aberration. But this was different. Sonny's recall of specifics—the Bible verse, the relationships between the characters, his grasp of chronology—gave his words gruesome plausibility.

"Tell me how she's going to save us."

Sonny turned suddenly. He was smiling, a peaceful smile, uncomfortably close, conspiratorial. Christensen stepped back. "The water," Sonny whispered.

Would a woman be physically capable of drowning a struggling adolescent boy? Not unless she coaxed him into a vulnerable position. Christensen looked at the sink, the counter, remembered Sonny's memory of being helpless underwater, on his back but not swimming, struggling toward a rectangular light above. He looked up at the window. Maybe he'd submitted, convinced that baptism would take him to a better place.

"She stopped Papa Richard from hurting Mom, you know," Sonny said. "She told me."

Christensen shivered, not knowing why. "Rachel? I don't understand."

"She said nobody ever knew. He was old. They thought he choked on something and died."

The weakness in his legs forced Christensen to the counter. He held on tight. Steady, he told himself. *Holy shit.* "Sonny, you're saying Rachel killed your grandfather?"

"Nobody ever knew. Served it to him herself in a bowl of bean soup. She had a plan for Dad, too. A different plan. A better plan. Show the world what he was. Show the world the evil."

"Tell me."

"The potion."

The words hung in the musty air, a twist Christensen

could not have imagined. Could Downing have worked all these years on the Primenyl case, and still have been this wrong?

"The potion," Christensen repeated. "I don't remember the potion."

"Don't lie."

"I don't remember, Sonny. I don't."

"The potion that made the world see. The potion that made Dad go away because everybody thought he was the one that put it in the stores. She made you keep it in your hidey-hole, and nobody ever found it. You remember, David. Don't lie."

Christensen couldn't argue about what Sonny's older brother did or didn't do ten years ago, and pleading ignorance was pissing Sonny off. He tried a new tack.

"Show me the hidey-hole," he said.

Sonny's eyes went straight to the floor. "She made us swear. On the Bible, remember?"

"It's my hidey-hole, so I already know, don't I? I just forgot where it is. Show me, Sonny."

Christensen could hear his own heartbeat as they stood still and quiet, face-to-face, only feet apart. He wanted to run from this place. Downing should be here facing down the beast, not him. This was a cop's work.

Sonny moved across the room, picking his way through the clutter, and into a shadow at the far end of the basement. Christensen squinted at first, reluctant to follow. But curiosity overtook him. He crossed the room, following Sonny's path, until he stood beside him at the irregular stone wall that was the house's original foundation. It rose maybe six feet from the floor, and the thick floor joists above ran in parallel lines across the basement ceiling, each one anchored to the top of the stone wall. The third joist from the left was supported by a mine jack, a quick fix for a subsidence problem.

Sonny studied the joists, his body swaying slightly but otherwise still. "Gimme a boost," he said.

Christensen swallowed hard. "I'd almost forgotten."

"They looked everywhere but. Boost me."

Christensen cupped his hands and Sonny stepped in. Above him, he saw Sonny reach into the space between the joist and the mine jack, all the way up to his shoulder. How willing would a cop be to blindly reach that deep into a place already showing signs of collapse? Downing wouldn't have hesitated if he'd noticed the space, but he also could have overlooked such a small, dark void.

A rustle of pages. Christensen looked up as Sonny pulled a handful of something from the hole. He was using his left hand now, probably because the swelling limited movement of his right fingers. "You had *Playboy*s?" Sonny said, and dropped them to the floor. They whistled past Christensen's ear and landed with a solid thump.

What would an older brother say? "You were too young." "Down."

Sonny stepped back onto the basement floor holding a tear-shaped bundle, a soft white blob that seemed to glow in the darkness. It looked like a small pouch, about the size of a softball, made from cheesecloth and knotted at the top. Christensen felt as if he'd swallowed bees. Downing should be here. He took the bundle when Sonny held it out to him, cupping his hands beneath it for support. Something inside the pouch pricked the base of his left thumb.

Christensen threaded his way back across the room toward the sink, where the light was better. He laid the bundle on the counter in the square patch of sunlight beneath the window-well. Should he open it, or wait and call Downing? He studied it for a long time.

"The potion?" Christensen asked.

Sonny stayed in the shadows, saying nothing.

The knot was loose. Christensen picked at it, and it loosened even more. He pulled its ends apart and laid the filmy corners away from what was inside. What he found seemed too familiar to be scary. Two of the three items he recognized: a tube of instant glue and a thin, dull-metal X-Acto knife, its triangular blade exposed and thrust through the cheesecloth. The third item was a small brown glass bottle with a black screw cap. He'd watched enough crime shows to know he should keep his fingerprints off potential evidence, so he lifted the corners of the cheesecloth and rolled the bottle from side to side. No label. He bent down, wishing he could pick it up, wondering if he could see its contents by raising the bottle to the window. His head suddenly filled with a familiar odor. What was it? He closed his eyes, but didn't need to inhale again.

Bitter almonds.

Anyone who lived in Pittsburgh in 1986 knew what that meant. Christensen backed away, not realizing he was doing so until he bumped into a support beam. "Sonny, we need to go." Struggling to control the tremor in his voice. "Now."

Still no answer. He looked into the shadow where he'd last seen Sonny, squinted until a human form emerged from the darkness. Sonny was on his knees. He was holding the frame of an ancient bicycle, its tires flat but otherwise intact. What little light there was played off the spokes and the accumulated cobwebs. "Your bike?" Christensen asked, moving toward him.

Sonny looked up. "No, yours," he said.

"Mine?"

"Rachel said we could help, remember?"

"Tell me."

"Deliveries," Sonny said. "She asked us to take it back to Dad's store."

"Take what, Sonny?"

"Just take the box in and put it on the shelf with the other headache pills, she said. Don't worry about the receipt. Don't let him see you. Don't talk to anybody. Come straight back."

"Did you want to help her, Sonny?"

"No. Did you?"

"No."

Sonny stood up, dropping the bike. It fell onto its side with a crash.

"Paper, scissors, rock," Sonny said. "Remember?" He put both hands behind his back, starting a game Christensen had taught Annie only a few weeks ago. "Come on. That's fair. One, two, three."

Sonny pulled his left hand from behind his back. Scissors. "Come on," he said. "Do it."

Christensen put his hands behind his back. Another hunch. If Sonny was scissors, he'd be paper. Scissors cut paper.

"One, two, three," Sonny said. Scissors again. He stared at Christensen's upturned palm, and suddenly all expression left his face.

"You win," Christensen said. "I lose." He played out the scene in his mind. Sonny the victor, relieved of his aunt's strange and incomprehensible chore, gloating as his brother pedaled off with a box of Primenyl. They couldn't have known then what was inside. When did they realize?

"You lose," Sonny said, bringing both hands up to within a foot of his face. He tried to flex the left, but it seemed suddenly lifeless. He appraised the bloated right, as if seeing the damage for the first time.

"What happens next, Sonny?"

"My hands. I can't feel them."

"Should I take the pills to the store?"

"You did. You took them back because you lost. I had scissors, you had paper."

"I lost. How do you feel about that?"

Sonny trembled. His face seemed to collapse. Tears. Hands held out like dead birds. "I'm sorry, David. I was scissors, but I'd have gone. I would have."

Something clicked. Paper, scissors, rock. The numbness in Sonny's hands. "Guilty? You felt guilty because David had to take the pills back?" Christensen realized too late that he'd spoken out loud.

"Then we saw on the news about all those people—"

"You realized something was wrong with the pills, didn't you, Sonny? Something Rachel did."

"—and the police started coming around—"

"David figured it out, too."

"—and the city canceled Halloween and we saw Dad on TV and you went upstairs. David, you didn't know! I didn't. She tricked us!"

Christensen's head swam with questions. Had awareness

crept up on the two boys, then ages twelve and fifteen, or
had it struck them like a thunderbolt? How long after that
did David commit suicide? When did Ron Corbett realize
Rachel had set him up? Christensen recalled the chronology
from Sonny's file. Corbett abandoned his family two weeks
after the last Primenyl death. David shot himself a week
after that. Two weeks later, their mother was involuntarily
committed to Borman and Sonny entered foster care. The
family exploded, scattering damaged souls like ghastly
debris. And at ground zero stood some cipher named
Rachel, a lit match in her hand.

He groped for words. "You didn't know, Sonny. It wasn't
David's fault. Or yours."

"Oh God!" Sonny's face changed. His eyes, which had
seemed to see nothing until now, shifted to his hands. Pain
shot across his face as he took a closer look at the obviously
broken right. He looked around the basement, apparently
disoriented, like someone stepping from a long tunnel into
bright daylight. A full half-minute of silence.

"I know this place," he said finally.

"You're safe, Sonny. No one can hurt you."

Sonny cradled the broken hand. "We're alone?"

Christensen nodded. "Let's go upstairs."

"Wait."

Christensen tensed. He wasn't sure how conscious Sonny
was of the memories he'd just relived. No two reconcilia-
tions were the same. Sonny's eyes had settled on the laundry
sink. He moved slowly out of the deep shadows and into the
sepia light beneath the basement window, stopping in front
of the basin but staring now at a small shelf above it.
Laundry supplies. A measuring cup, a dusty box of Tide, a
wad of dryer lint. Sonny picked up something from the shelf
that looked like a pencil. He laid it carefully in the patch of
sunlight beside the sink. Christensen saw it now, an ornate,
black-lacquered chopstick.

"She always wore them in her hair," he said, his voice
toneless. "She was wearing them the day she sent David to
the store, the day he came back and caught her holding my
head underwater. Oh, Christ—"

Sonny crumbled. His wail rattled the window, the cry of an animal in pain. He swept the chopstick from the counter and it disappeared into a snarl of garden tools against a far wall. "Damn her to hell!" he screamed. Kicking hard at the base of the cupboard, rousting the demon, prodding it from his subconscious into his conscious mind. It finally had a name, a face, Christensen thought. Confronting it hadn't been easy, but at least now Sonny could see it, wrestle it down as best he could.

"I'm here, Sonny. Let it out."

A baseboard splintered. Sonny kicked some more, crushing a cupboard door. Cursing her. Hating her. Kicking until his white shoe showed a deep red stain at the toe. Christensen watched, helpless and scared but unwilling to intervene. When Sonny's rage slowed, he fell to his knees and sobbed. His shoulders, once so imposing, sunk beneath some unseen weight and rolled with each ragged breath. His right hand was cradled in his lap, his face buried in his left even as he spoke.

"She could have taken me to God. I wish she had."

Christensen bent down. "Wouldn't have changed a thing. All those people still would have died. You couldn't have saved your brother or stopped your father from leaving. Couldn't have kept your mother out of Borman. What happened then was bigger than everybody. Thing is, you're the one who survived. You."

Sonny's hand roved up through his hair, revealing a face still haunted. He shook his head. "I wish she had."

"I'm glad she didn't." Christensen cleared his throat and offered an awkward hug. He let pass what he thought was an appropriate time. "Sonny, there have been other killings, or attempts, very similar. A few months ago, down in Greene County, down near where your father's living. Some others around here. Your aunt Rachel may be at it again, and I think the police need to know about this. Understand what I'm saying?"

A single nod. Nothing more.

"So, where is she now?"

Another nod, an indecipherable smile. "You don't get it, do you?"

"Not everything, no. You and I have a lot more talking to do."

"No, I mean—"

"But Sonny, she's still a threat, and right now I think we need to let someone know where to find her."

Sonny hooked his good hand around the back of his neck and put his chin on his chest, then muttered a single word: "Ridgeville."

37

Late afternoon. Winter dusk. The flurry that had started just before they arrived on Jancey Street had become one of those early February storms that in two hours left four inches of snow on top of the front-porch railing. Christensen checked his watch in the fading daylight. He wanted more than anything to call Downing, but knew better than to rush Sonny through the aftermath of something so traumatic.

Sonny was sitting on the Jancey Street living room's low hearth, his broken hand packed in melting snow and wrapped in an old towel they'd found in a downstairs bathroom. His left arm held both knees tight to his chest, an almost fetal posture, but his eyes were alive again, questioning, comprehending.

"What's your first memory of Rachel?" Christensen asked.

Sonny studied his shoes. "Hard to say. My mom's been sick for so long," he said. "At first she'd have these spells where she just acted different. But that was it. Just different. Rachel came later."

"But at some point you knew she'd dissociated?"

Sonny looked confused.

"When someone creates an alternate personality. You're sure that happened?"

Sonny nodded. "She didn't have a name, at first. But my mom would talk different. Carried herself different. It's funny, my dad wouldn't cross her when she was like that. David and I kind of liked that at first. She stood up for herself, and he backed off. But I knew something was really wrong because of the cigarettes. One night she just lit up during dinner."

"She doesn't smoke?"

Sonny shook his head. "Hated it. Rachel's a neat freak, too, not like my mom."

Christensen flicked a dead fly from the windowsill. "So eventually you knew her as Rachel?"

"She just one day asked us to call her that, is all."

"And you always knew who was who?"

"They were so different," Sonny said.

Christensen shook his head. "Dissociation isn't always that extreme. And without knowing more about her, without knowing more about her perp, I can't—"

"Her what?"

"Your grandfather. I can only guess why she needs an alternate personality like Rachel."

"Guess, then," Sonny said.

"Think about it. Rachel is strong, independent, aggressive—everything your mom isn't. Most people can integrate the parts of their personality that aren't consistent and become fully functioning. For people who can't, sometimes it's easier just to take the inconsistent parts and create another identity, or identities. That's why alters, typically, are so different from the person who created them."

Sonny perked up. "So there can be more than one?"

"I've read about cases with more than a hundred alters. That's the exception, but it happens."

Sonny's sudden deep breath was hard to interpret. Frustration? Relief? "She went out sometimes, to bars, the nights my father was away. She'd leave my brother and me with Mrs. Sadowski down the street and go off for a few hours to party. Sometimes she'd bring guys back to the house. Never inside, but right to the doorstep. In summer, when the windows were open, we'd hear them fucking on the porch from three houses away. Everybody knew."

Christensen imagined the commotion that would make along a street as tightly packed and nosy as Jancey. "Maybe it was another alter," he said. "The part of your mom that wanted to humiliate your dad the way he humiliated her. What did he do when he found out?"

Sonny smiled. "Nobody ever told him. He wasn't the most popular guy around here. Everybody knew he would have killed her."

A thought passed quickly, and Christensen kept it to himself: If one of Sandra Corbett's alters couldn't humiliate Ron Corbett by boffing strangers on their front porch, if the neighbors didn't play the tattletale role she wanted them to play, maybe she created Rachel to take it to the next level. Another thought: "Do you think the name is significant?"

"Rachel?"

"Why Rachel?"

Sonny rewrapped his hand, slowly, methodically. "It's from the Bible, which makes sense, because of my grandfather. He died when I was five, but I know my mom hated him, hated everything he preached. Only thing I ever saw her get passionate about."

"Rachel sure knew her Scripture."

Sonny was silent and intense, like he was replaying some long-ago conversation. "All I remember about the Bible Rachel was she was married to the same guy as her sister."

Love those Bible stories, Christensen thought. "An aunt to her sister's children," he said. "Interesting. See, all that stuff was in your mom's head, probably drilled into her as a kid, but she apparently had no use for it. So she gave it to Rachel, who I'm guessing interpreted it pretty broadly."

Sonny nodded. "Talked a lot about Revelations."

"The Apocalypse," Christensen said.

"About the angel Michael, too. That's who I'm named after."

Against all odds, Christensen dredged a biblical biography from somewhere deep in his parochial-school past. Michael, leader of the righteous angels in the battle for

Heaven; Michael, star of the Renaissance painting where he's casting Satan into the pit. Rachel probably kept the picture in her wallet.

"How you feeling, Sonny?"

"Like shit. Wrung out."

"The hand?"

"Hurts like hell."

"There's safer ways to have done this, you know. That's why I didn't want you to come back here. You'd probably have remembered everything eventually, but a little at a time, not in a flood. Would that have been so bad?"

Sonny ran his good hand through his hair and closed his eyes. "If I'd lived that long."

"Meaning?"

Sonny's eyes drifted around the room, eventually settling on the steel ribs of an ancient radiator. "I had a dream I never told you about. A water dream. Must have had it a dozen times in the last couple years."

"Tell me now."

"It's different than the drowning ones at the sink. Not something that ever really happened, I'm sure. Just a dream."

Christensen moved across the room and sat cross-legged on the floor beside Sonny on the hardwood floor. "What happens?"

"I'm swimming in open water, a channel or something. It's night. I'm alone, swimming hard. But there's something behind me, something fast, much faster than me. I swim harder, but it's still coming. I can't get away from it, and it's scary. Really scary. I don't know what it is, but I'm sure I can't outswim it."

"It's chasing you?"

"It's going to kill me."

Christensen put a hand on Sonny's knee. "But it doesn't, does it?"

"I always wake up. But it was getting closer each time."

Across the room, a dark shape the size of a golf ball moved along the baseboard beneath the stairs. A mouse.

"We should go, Sonny. I still think we need to call Grady Downing."

"Another minute." Sonny fished into his daypack and rooted around, pulling out a dripping navel orange that had apparently been crushed when Sonny stumbled over the pack a few minutes earlier. "Wondered why my pack was soaked."

The room was almost dark. The smell of ripe citrus filled Christensen's head, cutting through the mildew and dust of the abandoned house. It smelled good, familiar, comforting. But there was something else, another smell. He took the smashed orange from Sonny and split it, sniffing again more analytically.

"What?" Sonny said when the two halves fell.

"Something's not right. Where'd you get this?"

The wavering halves stopped on the floor between them. Sonny's face became a mask in the fading light, vacant and emotionless. Christensen answered his own question: "From your mother."

Sonny flinched, staring at the orange. "She loaded me up with food the last time I was out," he said.

Christensen picked up both halves and shoved them into the daypack. Sandra Corbett may have given Sonny the fruit, but Rachel worked on it first. Still trying to take Sonny to God. He grabbed Sonny by both shoulders, forcing him to look into his eyes. "Let's go. I need to call Downing. Now."

"In a minute."

"We need to go."

Sonny looked away. "I'll wait here."

"I think you should come with me."

"I'm okay. Really."

Christensen checked his watch. Maybe he could borrow somebody's phone. "Five minutes," he said, and bolted out the front door. He'd tell Downing what happened—about Sandra Corbett's dissociation into Rachel, about the cyanide in the basement and Sonny's breakthrough that finally brought the Primenyl killer's face into focus, about Rachel's willingness to kill even Sonny as he closed in on the truth. He'd turn the whole hellish nightmare over to people who knew what to do now. He wanted Sandra Corbett in custody, but mostly he wanted out.

He was standing in a suspicious neighbor's foyer, snow melting off his shoes, when, from the corner of his eye, he saw it through the front-door window. A flash of forest green accelerating down Jancey Street toward Braxton Avenue.

The Explorer.

"Oh Jesus," he said just as Downing's phone clicked into voice mail.

38

Christensen flailed his arms at the Yellow Cab rounding the corner onto Jancey. The neighbor, a suspicious crone, watched his anxious dance from her front window and shook her head again. She'd remembered the Corbetts, all right. Hadn't seemed surprised that someone who knew them would appear at her door close to panic ten years later and ask to use her phone. Hadn't been particularly startled when he dropped the handset and charged into the street, chasing a fleeing sport-utility. She'd watched him rush back in and furiously dial Downing's office number, then Downing's home and beeper, then a cab, never saying a word.

The wait had been torture. All his efforts to reach Downing had ended in voice mail, and there was no telling when he'd return the page. The cab company was deluged by calls as the snow piled up. Nothing for at least half an hour, the dispatcher had said. So he'd made small talk with the crone, Mrs. Torisky, suppressing his desperation, waiting in the swirling butter-onion smell of frying pierogies for her ancient black telephone to ring.

When Downing had finally called from West Virginia, Mrs. Torisky hadn't even pretended to give him privacy. She'd listened as he spun the story at full volume: Sonny's sudden urge to visit the house; the dangerous flood of

tormented memories; the cyanide they found deep in a
basement wall; Aunt Rachel as a figment of Sandra Corbett's tortured psyche. "She's the one, Grady, not Ron!"
he'd blurted. "She made her goddamned kids drop the
Primenyl!"

All Mrs. Torisky ever said, in her heavy Slovak accent,
was, "Crazy people." She was holding a rosary as he
climbed into the taxi and waved.

"Ridgeville," Christensen barked, checking his watch. He
was at least forty minutes behind Sonny, but he had no
doubt where the young man was headed. He repeated the
apartment name Downing gave him. "Lakeview Pointe
Estates."

The driver turned around. "In this shit?" Serious kielbasa
breath.

"How fast can you get there?"

Big laugh, yellow teeth. Mr. Kielbasa adjusted his pork-
pie hat. "Where youn's been, Skip? Parkway's a fuckin'
mess. Take us a fuckin' hour just to get through the Fort Pitt
Tunnel. I'll get you there if you gotta go, but you better have
plenty of cash."

Christensen pulled his wallet from an inside jacket pocket
and fanned four twenties, a ten, and two ones, every cent he
had with him. He dropped his bills over the back of the front
seat.

"That'll spend," the driver said. Big wink. Then he began
to whistle "Winter Wonderland" as a back tire whirred and
the cab started to move. Please God, don't let this guy be a
talker, Christensen prayed. There was too much to think
about.

The puzzle was coming together, but the picture was no
less baffling. Had Sandra's dissociation revealed itself
during her years of therapy? Were her doctors aware she'd
developed an alter aggressive enough to kill? She should
never have left Borman. Probably one of the Reagan era's
deinstitutionalized mentally ill, he reasoned.

Christensen thought about Sonny's grandfather. If her
original perp was dead, maybe Sandra had focused her
alter's rage on the tormentor she married, the only one upon

whom she could inflict revenge. Maybe that single focus intensified the rage, made it combustible. But why wasn't it enough just to kill him? Why this elaborate and deadly plan to show the world his evil?

As improbable as it seemed, the Primenyl case had taken on an even more sinister meaning: Killing didn't simply fill some sociopath's twisted need. The random poisoning and their attendant agony were nothing more than a means to an end, one necessary strand in a spider's intricate web. He imagined Sandra at its center, surrounded by the sons she'd inadvertently snared. David's body spun into a silken sarcophagus; Sonny fighting for his life; the intended prey, her husband, lucky enough to have avoided capture and smart enough to have removed himself from her life.

Christensen recounted the circumstantial evidence Downing was sure pointed to Ron Corbett: the abusive past, the pharmacy training, the typewritten list of licensed cyanide distributors found inside Corbett's home. How flimsy it all seemed now, and how neatly it meshed with Sonny's retrieved memories. Corbett's sudden flight in 1986 and lack of contact since—what Downing interpreted as callous belligerence—probably was the frantic response of a man who knew what his wife had done but felt he couldn't come forward. If he had, who would have believed him? Downing?

The cab crept through Oakland's slushy streets, then onto the Parkway East high above a gentle curve in the Mon River. He could see the water clearly now that the old J&L steel plant was gone. Ice clung to the riverbanks, and he found himself trying to make sense of Sonny's swimming. Why did he force himself into a river's excruciating winter embrace four times a week? Was it self-destructive, a victim's subconscious punishment? That's what he'd first thought, but now he wondered if maybe it was something far different—an extreme expression of self-preservation by someone who couldn't forget a near-drowning in a basement laundry sink.

Traffic slowed as they neared the Fort Pitt Bridge, but the snarl wasn't as bad as he'd feared. Five lanes of cars knitted themselves into two strands that snaked across and disappeared into the tunnel on the other side. Green Tree Hill beyond the tunnel was bound to be a slip-and-slide, but for some reason traffic was moving.

"Youn's must be praying back there or something." Two laughing eyes in the rearview mirror. "This is light even for a Saturday. The snow's keeping people home."

Christensen leaned forward. "How much longer do you figure?"

"Don't get all bunched up. Another twenty minutes, Skip, at least." The driver tossed a crumpled paper lunch bag into the backseat. It bounced off Christensen's knee. "Pickle?"

39

Sonny paced at the base of the stairs, turning the snow into gray slush. He hesitated again at the apartment door and stared at the window and its tightly drawn curtains, dreading the moment when she'd peek out, avoiding the woman he pitied more than loved.

That she tried to kill him—in a basement laundry sink then, and now with a poisoned orange—left him mostly numb. He knew by Jim Christensen's reaction what was in that orange. When it had really sunk in, he was alone in the house on Jancey, alone with remembered horrors in the place where he'd lived them. He shouldn't have ditched Christensen, just like he shouldn't have jammed the Explorer into four-wheel drive with his good hand and roared across town, past the snow-stranded drivers on Green Tree Hill. He shouldn't have bumped down an unpaved hillside and into a vacant lot when a semi skidded sideways and blocked the Ridgeville exit. But he needed to get off.

Having done all that, why was he here?

The Explorer's engine was still ticking, the driver's door open, as he started up the steps. The truck's interior was a bubble of pale yellow in the dark parking lot. All the way here, he'd imagined this scene. Moving up the stairs. Knocking. Waiting for her to scissor open the curtains and start unlocking the door. But then it stopped. He couldn't imagine the scene beyond that point, just as he couldn't avoid confronting the woman on the other side, whoever she was. Everything in his past was drawing him to his mother's doorstep, to this moment. That much he knew.

"It's me," he said to the dark eyes inside. He held his breath as she worked the locks.

The door chain caught and she peeked out the gap. A puff of warm, stale air. "Saturday already? Oh goodness, Sonny. It's nighttime. I'm a mess. My hair. My teeth aren't brushed. I'm not dressed. Can you come back?"

"Just open up."

"It's just that I'm—"

"Open the goddamned thing." He backed away two steps, then rushed forward and buried his shoulder into the door. It sprung open with a sharp wooden crack as pain shot through his fractured hand. While what was left of the chain lock swung like an off-balance pendulum, he stepped inside. All he saw was the hem of her flannel nightgown as she rounded the corner and disappeared from view. Somewhere in the warren of small rooms, a door closed. The apartment was still and dark except for the endless chatter and ghostly blue glow from her TV. On top of the TV, the silhouette of a video camera he'd never seen before.

Sonny crossed the living room in three steps. A short hallway to his left led to the bedroom. The breakfast area was straight ahead, and a wide arch to the right opened into the kitchen. "I came to talk," he said, turning right. He'd been sure she went that way, but the kitchen was empty. Where could she be?

"Bad day, Sonny." From the bedroom. Sonny whipped around, disoriented by his miscalculation.

"I'm not leaving," he said, "not until I say what I came to say." What had he come to say?

"Please come back. I can't. Not right now."

Sonny turned on a light and surveyed the kitchen. It was spotless. The small table was bare, the floor gleamed, the sink was emptied of the dirty dishes that usually collected there. The only disorder was a section of the counter between the sink and the refrigerator where she'd neatly

stacked the remnants of some indefinable project—
transparent red cellophane like that used in gift baskets, pale
straw, scissors, tape, ribbon. A bag of oranges and two
grapefruit sat on the windowsill nearby.

He felt like puking. As careless as his mother was about
cleaning, there were times when she was practically obsessive about neatness. Why hadn't he noticed it before? In the
room's weird tidiness, he felt another presence.

"I'm not going anywhere," he called. "There's a story I
want to hear, and I want to hear it from you. You owe me
that."

She didn't answer, so he went to her bedroom door. The
hallway was narrow and dark, its walls bare. The overhead
light fixture was missing. Its wires dangled from a ragged
hole in the ceiling. He tried the doorknob.

Her voice, soft but panicked: "Please go."

"Unlock the door."

"You're scaring me, Sonny. What do you want?"

Then it came clear, as sharp and sudden as a needle prick.
He knew why he'd come: "I want to talk to Rachel." Sonny
waited, closing his eyes and laying his forehead against the
door.

"She's gone," his mother said.

"She's here!" Sonny screamed. "She wants me dead!
Open the fucking door!" He crashed against it with his
shoulder, screaming from the pain, but it held. He tried
again, and lightning exploded behind his eyes. When the
pain subsided, he leaned back and kicked again and again
with his bloody shoe until he lost his balance, then tried to
kick the knob loose as he fell onto his broken hand. He felt
himself plunge into a prickly fog, but struggled to stay
conscious.

Had he? He wasn't sure. He'd somehow ended up with
his knees gathered to his chest, slumped against the wall
opposite his mother's bedroom door. Why was he crying?
Then it drifted back to him.

"Who the fuck are you?" Sonny said.

Nothing.

He said it again, but his voice was starting to fade. Rage

was draining from him in spurts, like blood from a neat arterial wound.

"Damn you," Sonny whispered. Even as he said it his voice dissolved into a sad whimper. He didn't care anymore. He'd seen everything, knew everything; the secrets of his past were laid bare. Now he felt empty. Even the white-hot burning in his right hand began to fade. He thought of the poisoned orange, wishing he had eaten it. Better, he wished he had died years before, thrashing against cold water and cold metal and merciless hands in a rusting basement tub.

"I remember," he said, every scar alive now. But he also remembered how he'd survived. How he'd retreat down his throat, to the warm and safe place inside. The storms outside could rage and batter him, but it didn't matter. Sonny drew his knees tighter, protecting himself. Ride it out, he thought. Obey. Submit.

The door popped open, an inch at first, then two more. The bedroom was darker than the hall, and from it came the rasp of a pack-a-day smoker: "Hello, Sonny."

His whimpers became sobs. He closed his eyes again. "Bitch," he rallied.

"Let it out, Sonny boy," it croaked. "Everybody's got a breaking point."

He pressed himself against the wall. It was hard, unmoving, offering no escape. Then, in an instant, Sonny was swimming, surfacing from a dive into the icy Ohio, still safe inside the hard shell of his bloodless skin. He focused on his stroke, on the seamless arm-over-arm rhythm that carried him away. He felt better, strong, but not strong enough. Whatever was behind him, the presence he'd felt in a hundred water dreams, had finally closed the gap. It was too powerful, too fast, close enough to touch and speak to him in its sandpapery voice.

"There, there," it soothed. "We're almost done."

"Yes." The word came in a sob, his voice distant.

"Yes, Sonny boy," it said. "We'll go where they can't find us, just like we planned. David's there. He stopped us last time, delayed our destiny. No one can stop us now."

His brother. Sonny saw David standing at the base of the

cellar stairs, his father's pistol in one wavering hand, ordering her to let him go. He gasped, the taste of death suddenly at the back of his throat. "He came back from the pharmacy too soon," Sonny said, choking. "We were almost there. Almost to God."

A husky sigh from behind the door. "That policeman, that therapist, they never understood. I worked so hard to keep your daddy alive, dangling him between life and death. Purgatory on earth! Alive, Sonny, but tortured. Despised! I created that for him, sentenced him to it. Those who interfere must be winnowed from the floor."

"Winnowed," Sonny repeated.

"You tried to help them, didn't you, Sonny boy? They asked you to help, and you did. You'll have to be purified before we go. It has to be done. You remember our prayer, don't you? Sonny boy?"

"John the Baptist," he said. " 'There is one to come who is mightier than I. His winnowing-fan is in his hand to clear his threshing floor and gather the wheat into his barn; but the chaff he will burn in unquenchable fire.' "

"Good. Very good. I've winnowed the chaff, Sonny. Your friends won't bother us again. We can go now. We can. It's right. It's beautiful. Your daddy will burn in the lake of fire for the rest of his days, and we'll go, the rest of us, where no one will follow. My will be done."

"Your will be done," Sonny said.

The door creaked. Sonny opened his eyes. Looming above him, naked except for a white bedsheet around her shoulders, was a woman who seemed much taller than his mother. She stood like royalty, not stooped or manic or desperately sad, but still and regal, the sheet clasped to her breast like a risen saint. Her feet, too, were bare, and Sonny slowly lifted his head to meet her eyes. They were alive, penetrating. He felt them boring into his soul.

"Rachel." He curled even deeper into himself, fetal now, moving inside a body that no longer seemed to matter.

"It's time," she rasped. "Come with me to the font."

*   *   *

The cab's headlights swept across the peeling plywood sign for Lakeview Pointe Estates. The driver stopped and studied the steep driveway. A single set of tracks, straight and steady, scarred the foot-deep blanket of snow leading to the apartment building at the top of the rise.

"No fucking way, chief," the driver said. "Somebody made it, but you can bet your hairy left nut they had four-wheel drive. Youn's're on your own from here."

"You're sure this is the place?" Christensen said.

"You wanna debate it? I'll set the meter."

Christensen stepped out and slammed the door. His loafers weren't suited to a climb like this, but what choice did he have? He started up, sidestepping, digging the edges of his soles into a hard-packed tread track he recognized from a familiar set of Firestones.

The Explorer was sitting sideways in the middle of the parking lot, like it had been left where it skidded to a sudden stop. The driver's door was open, the interior light on. He scanned the apartment building, looking for the second-floor door that said 2B. When he saw it, nearly dark and lifeless, he started toward the concrete stairs. Then he stopped, went back to the Explorer, and reached under the driver's seat. Brenna's gun was icy cold. He held it up to the ashen light, wondering if it had a safety. He found a tiny, gnarled button and slid it to the left, breathing easier when the gun didn't go off. His hand was shaking. Could he pull the trigger if he had to?

Across the dark plain toward Ridgeville, he'd seen no sign of approaching headlights. The roads were as uninhabited as they were unplowed. Even I-79, which he could see in the distance, was a vast desolate ribbon lit orange by PennDOT's towering lights. Not a single driver dared brave it. Do cop cars carry chains, he wondered, and would Downing have the sense to use them? Even if he did, how long might a crosstown trip take on a night like this?

At the top of the stairs, Christensen heard a voice, low and coarse, the words indistinguishable and monotonous. A woman's voice, but one engaged in memorized lines, like the rote prayers of a congregant at High Mass. The gun in his right hand weighed a thousand pounds.

The door to 2B was wide open, its frame splintered. Through the opening, the voice droned on. Christensen leaned close, snatching a word here and there from the toneless stream. ". . . baptize . . . right hand . . . forever and ever."

Christensen leaned close to the door again, listening. The voice had stopped. He started to knock, but held back. Instead, he pushed the door open wide enough to see into the apartment. It opened without a sound into what seemed like a sparsely furnished living room, stuffy and dry, lit only by the soundless glow of a small television set atop an upturned milk crate. At least two people were in the apartment, he figured, but where? In a place this small, the silence was even more unsettling than the low murmur of an unfamiliar voice.

A passage to his left was brightly lit, and it led into a small breakfast area. Christensen moved to it, and as he did he heard the sound of trickling water. The room around the corner had to be the kitchen. Slowly, watching his feet, he moved tighter against the wall and listened. The sound was oddly comforting, reminding him of the times he and Molly bathed one or another of the girls in the kitchen sink, sponging warm water onto a squirming, kicking baby.

He edged closer to the corner, committed now, compelled to see what was happening but scared half blind. Slowly, he leaned his head around. The room swept into view, until finally he saw the scene. Sonny was on his back, stretched across the kitchen counter with his head tilted back into the sink. He seemed relaxed. A woman draped in a white bedsheet—who else could it be?—was supporting the back of his head with her left hand and running tap water in a gentle stream over his forehead. With her right, she stroked Sonny's temples and smoothed the long dark hair that floated like kelp in the pooled water just below his head. The sink was nearly full.

"There, there," came the throaty voice Christensen had heard from outside. "Almost home now."

Now what? Christensen felt awkward, standing uninvited in a stranger's apartment with someone else's gun, a gun he wasn't even sure was loaded, watching a scene that to an outsider might speak of nothing so much as the gentle trust between a parent and child. Suddenly, the woman yanked down on Sonny's hair. Sonny's head snapped back, and he reacted with a kick that rocked the cupboard above him, opening one of its doors. The second kick jarred a stack of plates into motion. Several spilled through the open cupboard door and into the void, splintering against the edge of the counter as they fell. Shards scattered across the floor, a few traveling as far as Christensen's feet. He realized only then that he'd stepped fully into the room.

"Almost home!" she thundered. Using Sonny's hair as a handle, she held his head under the water and anchored her right across his throat by grabbing the base of the spigot. Sonny's head was gone, fully submerged. He couldn't possibly lift it, and his body was thrashing helplessly in the constricted space between the counter and the overhanging cupboards. Sonny remained powerless even as his thrashing grew more violent.

Christensen lifted the gun on instinct and leveled it at the woman's back. "Leave him alone!" he bellowed.

She turned slowly, seemingly unconcerned by the ferocity of his demand. The sheet fell from her shoulders and gathered in a heap at her ankles, leaving her naked. A strained and ghastly smile split her face as she fought Sonny, giving no quarter to the intruder with the gun. She turned away, recommitting herself to her grim work.

"Rachel!" Christensen roared. "I said leave him alone!" He gripped the gun's handle tighter.

Her sinewy back muscles moved like serpents beneath her pale skin as she leveraged herself against her son. She had position. Strength didn't matter. "You . . . don't . . . know . . . me," she said without turning around.

Christensen bolted across the room and shoved her with his free hand, hoping to break her grip. "Let him up, I said. Now!"

He backed off four steps, his panic rising. It was as if

she'd simply ignored him. Sonny's body suddenly went limp. His legs twitched, but they had no power. All that seemed left were reflexes.

"Move away from him, goddamnit," Christensen said. "Get away now! Don't make me kill you."

The woman eased her grip on Sonny's hair and let go of the spigot. Sonny's head remained, sickeningly, beneath the water.

"I said move away."

She turned fully toward him, unashamed, panting from the struggle, and took one small step toward the refrigerator to her right, then another. Even as her chest rose and fell, she leaned almost casually against the counter. Her right hand disappeared behind her back.

"Kill me," she said.

"Across the room," Christensen ordered. He wanted her away from the sink when he tried to revive Sonny. "Move across the fucking room, I said."

He heard the scream, an almost feral sound, before he realized she was charging. She was ten feet away when he recognized a pair of silvery sewing scissors in the hand high above her head. In that instant, Christensen felt the gun become weightless, independent, an extension of a hand driven by adrenaline and fear and a powerful will to live.

It popped once and jumped, and the woman spun, a single off-balance pirouette. She faced him again, still clutching the scissors, and touched the dark nickel-sized star below her left shoulder. Christensen steadied the gun with both hands, keeping her in sight. He wanted to vomit as a tiny red stream curled from the wound and traced the outer curve of her breast.

"Holy Jesus," he said.

She smiled. A sad, unknowable smile. Her legs wobbled beneath her. She opened her mouth, and for a moment Christensen thought she might speak, might forgive his intrusion, might simply declare the moment impossible and ask Sonny to rise and start the scene again. What came out, though, was a thick red bubble. It burst, and was followed by a low rumble from somewhere deep within. The sound built slowly, like the basso profundo of an approaching locomotive. When it reached a guttural howl, she raised the scissors again.

This time, Christensen aimed. Her head snapped back as the bullet crashed into her forehead, then immediately jerked forward again, propelled by the red-gray jet from the exit wound. She crumpled at his feet, and he spun away, letting the gun fall. The scream continued, but it was his own.

Christensen grabbed the collar of Sonny's shirt and in a single motion heaved him off the counter and onto the floor. Sonny's face was as gray as fog, his eyes closed. No pulse. Christensen laid his ear against his chest. The heart was faint, but beating. He rolled Sonny onto his stomach. Christensen hadn't had a lifesaving class since the Boy Scouts, had never actually used what he learned, but he knew the drill.

He kneaded his hands into that muscular back, pumping the water from Sonny's lungs. After thirty seconds, Sonny coughed and vomited. Water poured from his mouth onto the kitchen floor, diluting the deep red pool beside him to a garish pink. Sonny struggled onto his elbows, choking, gasping, drawing quick, shallow breaths. He vomited again.

"That's it, Sonny," he said. "Get it all out."

As Sonny struggled, Christensen tried to stand. He fell back against the low cupboards and sat down on the floor, covering his eyes with the heels of his hands, pressing hard, blotting out a scene he could never have imagined. How had he been drawn into someone else's nightmare? When he opened his eyes, Sonny was sitting back on his heels, staring without apparent emotion at the vacant face of his mother. She'd died on her back, eyes wide, mouth open as if stopped in mid-sentence.

"Sonny?"

Sonny tried to talk, but coughed up another mouthful of water. Without taking his eyes off his mother, he steadied himself and tried again, this time choking out the words.

"Are they dead?"

40

Sonny struggled to his feet, bracing himself on the refrigerator handle. Elbows on the counter, he sobbed and laid his head in his right hand, recoiling from obvious pain.

Christensen got up, unable to take his eyes off the horror on the floor. Sandra Corbett lay faceup in a widening crimson pool. The back of her head where the bullet emerged was a soggy clump of hair, clearly the source of the blood. Her pale breasts slumped toward her armpits, and one leg, the right, was bent beneath her. She'd probably died before hitting the ground. The scissors were still in her hand.

He put a hand on Sonny's shoulder, only to have it batted away. The second time he tried, Sonny didn't resist.

"We'll get through this," Christensen said. "Really, we will." He wanted to believe it. Had to.

Sonny ignored him. Or his mind may simply have shut down, unable to process what he'd just seen. The accumulated brutalities of his life could not have been more traumatic than what he'd been through today, Christensen thought. He knew Sonny might never recover from it, might not even survive it.

The sink was still full. Sonny dipped his hands in and splashed his still-wet face. Then he yanked the silvery bead chain attached to the rubber plug with his good hand. He seemed transfixed as the water swirled away.

The bag of oranges and two grapefruit on the windowsill reminded Christensen of what had set this disaster in motion. This must have been where she'd prepared the orange they found in Sonny's backpack. A man's toilet kit, black leather, sat on the sill beside the fruit. He unzipped it and looked inside at a dozen or more safety syringes, each individually wrapped.

"She was diabetic," Sonny said. The last of the water gurgled away.

He imagined her at this spot surrounded by her tools. A syringe. A yogurt container. An orange. Somewhere in the apartment, he was sure, was a brown bottle of cyanide similar to the one they'd found in the Jancey Street basement. Had she worked here, too, with the Squeezie Pops and breakfast cereal and the shampoo that burned Melissa? They'd probably bury the answers with her.

She moaned. Christensen spun around, his heart pounding. Sonny's mother was still twisted in the same pallid heap. She couldn't be alive.

"Air from her lungs," he said, but Sonny didn't seem concerned.

Christensen inspected the neat pile to his left on the counter, wondered about the roll of red cellophane, the pale straw, the ribbon. She'd been gift-wrapping something, which explained why the scissors were within easy reach.

Outside, a car door thumped shut. Sonny laid his head on the counter, his right hand hanging limply at his side.

"Wait here," Christensen said. He eased past the body and bumped his way into the living room, still lit blue by the soundless TV. He fumbled with a lamp, looking for a switch, but only managed to knock it to the floor with a ceramic crash. When he opened the apartment's front door, he found Downing crouched in the snow against the balcony railing, his gun steady and extended with both hands, aiming at his chest.

"Jesusfucking Christ," Downing said. He lowered the gun and shook his head. "That could have been bad."

"It's already bad," Christensen said.

Downing pushed past him into the apartment. Christensen found him in the kitchen stooped over Sonny's mother, searching with two fingers for a pulse in her neck. "Who did this?" he said.

"She was trying to kill Sonny. She came after me when I tried to stop her, Grady. I had Brenna's gun."

Christensen started into the kitchen again. "Stay back," Downing said. "Don't track the place up any more than it is."

Sonny hadn't moved, his head still buried beneath his arms on the kitchen counter. He looked as if he was folding into himself, awkwardly, like some damaged origami. Downing laid a hand on his back. "Just leave me alone," Sonny said, his voice muffled.

"How about you, Jim?" Downing said, turning back toward the arched doorway where Christensen stood.

"Been better."

Downing checked the other rooms, opening every door, his gun still drawn. His face was a grim mask, missing the studied nonchalance that Christensen had always found so reassuring during a crisis. Unable to look at the crumpled body any longer, Christensen retreated to the living room and sat down on the floor. He slouched against the wall.

Downing finished his search, holstered his gun, and stooped down, his face betraying nothing. He leaned close. "Nice fucking shot, Kojak," he whispered.

Christensen noticed Downing's trembling hands, his forced attempt to seem casual. "I'm scared, Grady. I know you are, too."

Downing offered a weak smile. "I, uh, I . . . Scared? Christ. I'm still not sure I . . . It's just I, he . . . Look, I'm not gonna bullshit you. Any chance you're wrong about this?"

It wasn't what Christensen needed to hear. But what could Downing or anyone else have said at that moment that he'd have found reassuring?

"She's the one," Christensen said. "She set Ron up. Wanted everyone to hate him the way she did."

Downing lit a cigarette and fumbled with his lighter, then paced back and forth across his smoke trail.

"Oh God, Grady," Christensen blurted. "What'll happen now?"

Downing peeked through a gap in the front curtains, then went to the open front door and looked out, to the right and left. Satisfied that none of the neighbors had heard the commotion, or that at least they were pretending not to have, he came back in.

"Think anybody heard?" he asked.

"I don't know."

"Because if nobody heard, we've got options."

They waited. Two minutes. Five? Hard to say.

"Okay," Downing said finally, glancing at his watch, "here's what'll happen." The cigarette dangled from his lips, and he squinted through the white ribbon that rose past his nose. "You stay here. If nobody comes around, wait another thirty minutes and call 9-1-1 and report the shooting. The local cops will take you in, but then they'll take you and Sonny to the Public Safety Building downtown to answer questions."

"You'll be with us, right?" Christensen said.

Downing looked away. He flicked his ash into the palm of his still-shaking hand. "I'll be there as soon as I can to corroborate the story."

"But you'll go downtown with us, to tell them? They know I was working with you, right?"

Downing shrugged, still avoiding Christensen's eyes. "A lot'll depend on who handles the questioning."

"I want you there, Grady."

"Jim, it'll be fine. Just tell them the story. The truth. Ask for Chief Kiger if they give you problems. He and I talked a while back. He may not admit it, but at least he knows. Tell him the truth."

"Goddamnit, Grady, I want you there. Where do I start a story like this, where I wind up shooting"—he swallowed hard—"killing a woman I've never met in front of her only son, my client?"

"Start it at the beginning, when you and I first talked

about Primenyl. Lay it off on me. The facts will bear us out."

"The facts," he repeated.

"What you found at the house. What Sonny remembers."

"I need you there, Grady. I'm not sure how much help Sonny'll be in telling the story. What's so goddamned important that you can't just go with us?"

Downing stood and turned his back, looking at his watch again. "Just something I need to take care of. Look, by the time they get you downtown, I'll be back. Just don't say anything until I get there, okay? Call Brenna, too. You'll want an attorney there."

"Grady—"

"Trust me."

They stared across a widening gulf. Trusting Downing had gotten him into this. He put his head between his knees and sobbed. When he looked up, Downing was gone. He wasn't in the kitchen with Sonny, either. The sound of a starting car drew him back to the front door. From the balcony, he heard the chink-chink-chink of tire chains and watched Downing's Ford slide down the steep drive of Lakeview Pointe Estates. It skidded onto the dark and deserted road, its headlights illuminating the gauzy-white snow as the car moved off through a tunnel of trees toward town.

Christensen watched it coast through a red traffic signal, past Ridgeville's only gas station and onto the entrance ramp of I-79. Downing was headed south in a snowstorm on the main road to Greene County.

41

Maybe all police interrogation rooms were the same, Christensen thought. Maybe they all had the claustrophobic feel of a bunker, without windows or ventilation. Maybe they all had a badly disguised two-way mirror and a thermostat set at "broil" and reeked of tobacco and sweat and certain doom. But they couldn't all have the same vertical gouge in the edge of the same sticky oak table, the one that looked like the work of some nervous detainee's fingernails.

Christensen marveled at the spent energy that had created the gouge, the fidgety panic of someone under intense scrutiny, his nail tracing and retracing the same path for hours, marking his passage through this sad portal. Yes, he'd been in this room before. Two years before.

"Something I don't quite follow, Jimmy," the detective said. "Mind if we go over the Primenyl part again? Kind of a special interest of mine."

Brenna stood up. She was wearing jeans and a cashmere sweater, what she'd been wearing, apparently, when he called. This whole thing must seem like déjà vu to her, too, Christensen figured, though they'd only acknowledged it with their eyes.

"Look, Detective Pawlowski," she said. "We've said everything we're going to say for now. If you guys are talking to Sonny, we assume he's corroborating everything up until the point where he blacked out. And it sounds to me like almost everything else in the story can be backed up with supporting evidence."

"Really?"

"At the Jancey Street house," she said, "and at the apartment in Ridgeville."

The man eased one massive thigh onto the table and sat down, a hippopotamus trying to look casual. The seams of his pants were performing heroically. "Sorry, counselor," he said. "We don't know that."

"I guess you gentlemen have some fieldwork to do, then. We'll wait."

The detective laughed. "Like you've got a choice?"

The door opened. Cool air swept in as the second detective, the polite one with the rheumy eyes and damp yellow crescents at his armpits, returned with the promised drinks. "Hope Orange Crush is okay for everybody," Pit Stains said, a bit too deliberately, a bit too close to the running tape recorder. "They only restock the darned machine once a year."

"Anything from Grady?" Christensen said.

Brenna shot him a look. She'd asked him not to open his mouth again.

"Hasn't returned his page," Pit Stains said. "Shame."

"Funny thing," Pawlowski said. "You'd think if Grady Downing was working on the Primenyl investigation again, he'd at least mention it to somebody." He smiled. Teeth the color of wheat. "Like me, for instance. Not that he'd have to, of course. You'd just think he might, being as it's been my case since the feds bowed out. See, the thing about Prim—"

The ringing phone punctured the moment. Pawlowski glared at Pit Stains, who snatched the handset off the wall beside the door.

Christensen felt sick. He was piecing together an image of Downing as a rogue cop, a man driven less by pure investigative zeal than by an obsession to avenge a lover's death. He'd suspected as much since the night Downing told him about Carole. But even with his tunnel vision about Ron Corbett, even with his motives clouded, Downing's instincts were right. The Jancey Street house *was* the staging area for the 1986 killings. Sonny *did* know the truth.

"We've said all we're going to say right now, gentlemen," Brenna said, popping open her soda can. Both detectives watched her drink. Then Pit Stains said, "Oh, Christ. Don't fuck with me, Wally."

The detective's eyes fixed on the far wall as he listened. Something was happening, or had happened. You could tell from Pit Stain's posture, his manner, the way he avoided looking directly at anyone in the room, including his partner. And they were all looking at him. He listened for another minute without a word.

"Jesus," he said under his breath. "Trix know yet?"

Christensen's brain fired. Trix. Downing's wife. "What's going on?" he asked. He needed to know, imagined the worst.

"Like I fucking know," Pawlowski said. "Just shut up."

Christensen pulled Brenna closer and whispered into her ear, "Something's wrong."

Pit Stains curled away from them, hiding his face as he listened, aware he was being watched. Christensen's eye twitched, the coppery taste of insurgent fear suddenly at the back of his throat. No one spoke until they heard a muttered "Okay" and the sound of a telephone handset being gently returned to its cradle. "Excuse me, if you would," the detective said, and led Pawlowski out the door.

Christensen and Brenna strained to hear the muffled voices outside. The tape machine recorded the room's stifling silence, unless it picked up the bee-sound of the voices or the soft caress of Brenna's lips on Christensen's forehead. She rubbed his hands, too, looking for pressure points.

The door opened again, and Brenna backed off. The two detectives came in, their faces drained of even the pretense of goodwill.

"What is it?" Christensen asked.

"I want the tape recorder off," Brenna said. "And if this is some bullshit ploy—"

"Grady Downing's dead," Pawlowski said.

The words washed over Christensen like an anesthetic. It simply wasn't possible. Where would that leave me? he asked himself. He imagined the predicament, remembered the collision of circumstances that had brought him here. He laughed. He couldn't help it.

"Strange sense of humor," Pawlowski said. "Not the reaction I'd expect from somebody who just lost his alibi."

Christensen laughed again. It was just too impossible. Brenna dug her fingernails deep into his shoulder.

"If you guys are jamming us here—," she began.

"Car accident, about two hours ago," Pit Stains said. "Skidded off 79 down around the Greene County line. Hit a bridge abutment."

Pawlowski shook his head. It looked choreographed. Everything he did seemed calculated. "God strike me dead," he said, "but what kind of asshole tries to eat a grapefruit at seventy miles an hour in weather like this? That's just fucking nuts."

"No," Pit Stains said, "even weirder than that. PennDOT had just cleared the road, and he had chains on the tires. No skid marks, so he never lost control. Drove straight into it."

Brenna squeezed harder as the implication settled: suicide. Pawlowski leaned over the table, checking the tape recorder but trying hard not to look like he was doing so. Christensen buried his head in his hands, overwhelmed by the room's weighty calm.

"Let's go over something again," Pawlowski said. "Detective Downing showed up at the apartment, saw Mrs. Corbett there all shot up and dead, then left?"

Brenna eased her grip. Christensen nodded.

"Interesting." Pawlowski turned to his partner. "Hey, Al, does that seem like something a homicide detective would do? Walk into a murder scene, have a look around, then decide to go for a drive out in the country in a snowstorm?"

Christensen looked up. "He seemed pretty agitated," he said. "And he told me he had something he needed to take care of. Those were his words, I swear. Then he just took off. Said he'd meet us down here."

"What else did he say?" Pit Stains said.

"He told me to tell you the whole story, from the beginning. And to call Brenna. And, oh Christ—" Christensen buckled. " 'Trust me,' he said."

"Did you?" Pawlowski said.

The room started to move. "I don't know," Christensen said.

" 'Cause he's really left you way out on a limb here. Left us all with a big mess to clean up. Anything else he said that seems relevant?"

Christensen shook his head. "No, wait. He said to ask for the chief if there were problems."

"The chief?" Pawlowski and Pit Stains traded looks, then snickered. "Kiger? I doubt they'd even met."

Brenna's hand was back on his shoulder, like a vise, stopping him from answering. "Look," she said, addressing the detectives. "You asked him what Downing said. He's trying to tell you. So back off or I'll shut this little tea party down right now. We're trying to cooperate."

"Are you?" Pawlowski sneered. "Like we're gonna buy that fantasy about him and Grady Downing playing Hardy Boys with *my* investigation?"

The interrogation room door opened so quietly that neither cop noticed. Both stood over Christensen, glowering, but behind them, a third man stepped into the room. He was short and thick, a walking cannonball in a tailored brown suit. It took a second, but Christensen recognized him from news clips as the city's new chief of police. Kiger. The man nodded a greeting as he entered, and Christensen nodded back.

Both cops whipped around. Pit Stains's hand went reflexively to his shoulder holster.

"Sorry for the intrusion," the chief said. He cocked his head toward the mirror. "Hope ya'll don't mind me bird-dogging you here."

Pit Stains tried to remove his hand from his gun without anyone noticing. Everyone noticed. Kiger stepped deeper into the room, between the two detectives, and stabbed the tape recorder's stop button with a stubby index finger.

"I wonder if I might interrupt your discussion here for a few minutes to speak with Detectives Pawlowski and Joyce?" He crossed the room again and twisted the doorknob. "In my office."

The two detectives reacted like schoolboys in trouble. They looked at each other as Kiger held the door open. It felt like a pivotal moment, but Christensen couldn't say why. He wished he knew what it meant. The three were almost out the door when his brain suddenly engaged.

"Wait," he said.

The door slowly opened again and the chief peeked around its edge. "Something the matter?" he said.

Christensen wasn't thinking; it was more of a delayed reaction. "Something he said, about grapefruit."

"Jim, let's let them talk first," Brenna said.

"No, no," Christensen said. He needed to know. "The one detective said something about Grady peeling a grapefruit. What was that?"

The three cops shuffled back in. Kiger looked at Pawlowski, who knocked the wall phone off the hook as he squeezed past his partner and into the room.

"Just something the Staties told Al about the accident," Pawlowski said. "But it's still under investigation, so I'm not sure if it's appropriate—"

"It's all right," Kiger said, turning to Pit Stains. "Tell us what they told you."

"I don't even think it's relevant," the thinner detective said.

Kiger crossed his arms. His smile could have melted steel. "Please answer the gentleman's question, detective."

Pit Stains looked like he'd been slapped. "But—," he began, then stopped. "State cops still aren't sure what happened. Just from the patrol officer's report, it looks like Grady never touched the brakes and drove straight into the concrete abutment. Nobody saw it—no other cars on the road because of the storm—but the plow had been by just

a few minutes before. If he'd skidded, they'd know. He
didn't skid. Died from the blunt force of the impact."

"But the grapefruit," Christensen said. "What about
that?"

The detective shrugged. "Just something they said. They
found some kind of fruit basket on the floor of the front
seat." Pit Stains turned toward the chief. "See, Downing had
this thing about grapefruit. Ate 'em all the time, these bright
red ones. Carried 'em in his pants pocket sometimes, stuck
way out to here. His coat pocket. Had a drawerful of them
in his desk. Hardly ever saw him without one."

"But there was a basket?" Christensen said. "With red
cellophane?"

"No idea. It was like a gift basket or something. He was
getting ready to retire."

"But it had grapefruit in it?"

"From the records-room girls," the detective said. "The
Staties told me that's what the card on the basket handle
said."

"It was open, though? He'd eaten one of them?"

"That's what they think. There were rinds on the floor."
The detective stopped himself, trying to reconcile something. "But if he'd been peeling one and lost control,
wouldn't he have hit the brakes at some point?"

Christensen clasped his hands at the back of his neck and
brought his elbows together beneath his chin, looking at the
floor. He knew what happened. He closed his eyes and
watched the scene play out. "Unless he was unconscious,"
he said. "Or already dead."

He looked up into four confused faces. Kiger shifted his
weight from one foot to the other. "What are you saying,
sir?"

"At the apartment," he said. "She'd been doing something in the kitchen. I saw grapefruit and oranges, and stuff
for making a gift basket. Red cellophane. Straw. And
syringes. All that stuff was together on the counter. Sonny
said that's where he got his orange. I'm guessing you guys'll
find cyanide there somewhere."

Kiger leaned against the grimy wall. "Anybody know where he got the basket? Or when?"

The two detectives shook their heads. "The card said—"

"Let's find out," Kiger said. "Crime-scene people back from the apartment?"

"Not sure. We can check," Pawlowski said.

"Do that. I want to know if they found any chemicals there." The chief waved dismissively, then turned to Pit Stains as Pawlowski lumbered out. "You call the state cops back. We'll need that basket and everything in it for tests. I want it treated like evidence, at least for now. If the same chemicals turn up in the grapefruit and that orange, we got us an explanation."

Christensen felt Brenna's hand on his shoulder again. He looked up, surprised to see her crying. The second detective followed Pawlowski out the door, leaving them alone with the chief of police.

"Thank you," Christensen said when the door closed.

Kiger scratched his nose, never taking his eyes from Christensen's. "Sir?"

"For believing me."

The police chief studied him, saying nothing. Saying everything. "Don't leave town," Kiger said. He nodded to Brenna, said, "Ma'am." Then he stepped out of the room and closed the door behind him, leaving them alone.

42

Melissa sipped her tea, which must have cooled considerably since she'd last lifted the mug to her lips. Her face crinkled and she got up to put it in the microwave. It was five-thirty, nearly dawn.

She'd cornered him as soon as Annie was asleep, set a kettle to boil and gently shoved him down in a kitchen chair. "Start at the beginning," she'd said. So Christensen did, recounting for her Downing's approaching him about Sonny, his initial skepticism and reluctance to get involved, and the gradual recovery of Sonny's memories. Then he told her about going to the house on Jancey Street, about what happened there ten years ago, about finding the bottle in the basement.

He'd expected to stumble, but didn't, at the part about Sandra Corbett, about the patterns of abuse that helped create an untraceable killer named Rachel and about his own role in her death, still less than twenty-four hours old. Sonny was being kept in the hospital for observation. His mother, or Rachel—the Primenyl killer—was dead, an unsettling smear of her blood still on his left shoe. He distilled the whole affair to a chronological accounting, pleased to have presented it without judging the people involved. "Then Detective Downing apparently made the mistake we didn't," he said, nodding toward the gift basket of oranges on the counter.

He and Brenna had left the Public Safety Building about two-thirty in the morning and got to her house thirty minutes later. The sitter and Taylor were asleep, but both of his kids were awake. Between Brenna's hurried explanation as she'd left and the eleven o'clock news, they'd figured out something was wrong. They were up and wanted to go home. He'd wanted to go home, too, to walk into their house again without fear. He'd wanted to wrap himself in its groaning pipes and creaking floorboards knowing that at last they were safe. Brenna dropped them off about four.

The gift basket, sitting on the doorstep of the empty house since who-knows-when, hadn't rattled him. He was almost expecting it, and he carried it inside using rubber scrub gloves from the downstairs bathroom. Once in the kitchen's warm light, he read the greeting attached to the handle—one of Downing's business cards with "Thanks for everything" scribbled on the back in a woman's handwriting. It dominated the room, at once horrifying and reassuring. He'd been right about what happened to Downing.

Melissa said nothing during the twenty seconds it took to warm her tea. She pulled out the mug and sat down. "So when are you going to call?"

Soon, he thought. "I'm so tired of dealing with the police, but I guess it can't wait much longer."

"I'll call," she said.

"No, I will. I just didn't want another scene while Annie was awake."

"She'll be pissed if a bunch of cops show up and she misses it," Melissa said.

He smiled. She was right, but he knew the less Annie was exposed to all this, the better. Melissa sipped from her steaming mug, staring at him over its rim.

"What?" he said.

"Nothing."

"No, what's bothering you?"

His daughter set the tea on the counter. "It bothered me when you told me about Mom, but it doesn't bother me now," she said.

"Honey, what?"

"The way you just talked. Brenna called it your robot speech. All this stuff happened, but it's like you were telling me about a dentist appointment or something. 'Then this happened, then that happened.' You never say how you feel."

She'd listened to his counsel more closely than he'd thought all these years. "I guess I sort of shut down," he said. "It's just the way I deal with things."

"Or *don't* deal with them. I thought you were so cold about Mom, like snuffing her was on that day's to-do list. I mean, you help people deal with their emotions every day, but you really suck when it comes to dealing with your own."

"Aren't you precocious?" he said. "Now you'll want your own couch?"

"It's true."

Christensen didn't need this, not right now. Not after all that had happened. He stood up. "Well, I guess I should call back downtown about the basket."

Melissa shook her head. "See what I mean?"

He moved toward the telephone, but she blocked his way. "Look—," he started to say, but his daughter wrapped her arms around him. She held him tight, then put her hand on the back of his neck, pulled his head down, and whispered in his ear: "I love you anyway." He stopped resisting and held his daughter in the middle of the kitchen, the two of them swaying in silence, her cheek wet with his tears.

Pawlowski had gone home, and Christensen couldn't remember Pit Stains's name. Kiger was gone. Since it wasn't an emergency, and the crime-lab crews changed shifts at 6 A.M., the watch commander said it'd be at least an hour before someone could pick up the basket and take his statement. Christensen thanked him, then donned the scrub gloves and carried the basket carefully into his office. Even though he wasn't going to let it out of his sight, he put it on his highest bookshelf, well out of Annie's reach, just in case.

With Melissa in bed, he leaned back in his desk chair. She'd told him she loved him once more before she went upstairs. It felt like a first gasp of cool air after being too long underwater.

The house was unusually quiet, settled for the moment rather than settling. Closing his eyes was risky. He didn't want the police pounding on the door and waking the girls when they arrived. And he didn't want to torture himself by replaying the unforgettable scene at the apartment. His mind fixed on Downing and the questions that wouldn't go away.

Why had he left the apartment so suddenly? To go where? He rewound the scene in his mind, scanning for clues. Ron Corbett lived in Greene County. But confronted with the truth about the Primenyl killer, why would Downing go there?

Why?

Christensen remembered the late night a couple weeks earlier when Downing had made his confession about Carole. He'd seen a change in him that night that he'd never understood. His smarmy, wisecracking manner replaced by . . . what? Resolve? No. More like resignation. "Doesn't matter," he'd said when Christensen asked how to proceed with Sonny. "His memories won't do me any good now."

Christensen had followed the detective out to his car that night. "What now?" he'd demanded. Downing had repeated his answer, "Plan B," the second time mouthing the words through the car-door window just before he drove away.

Another memory bobbed to the surface: Downing's flustered reaction that night as he shoved a brick-sized box under his car's front seat. Christensen strained for a detail and, like something from a Polaroid photograph, an image slowly appeared: Pegasus. The box's logo. He'd seen it again, just hours ago, it seemed.

The sun was coming up, graying windows that had been black when Christensen first shut his eyes. He closed them again, trying to read the words beside the logo on the box. God, he was tired. But he had the uneasy feeling he had fixed on something important, a key for unlocking Downing's last secret.

Opening his bottom desk drawer, he hoisted the Greater Pittsburgh White Pages to the center of his desk. He fanned

to the P's and ran his finger down the page headed
Peeler-Pegman. Two listings for Pegasus. Neither seemed
relevant. Pegasus Roofing & Paving. Pegasus, Demitri. He
reached again into the bottom drawer and pulled out the
Yellow Pages, then put them back. Those listings were by
subject, not by name. Where would he start when all he had
was a logo?

He did have something else, thought. A hunch. He lifted
the Yellow Pages again, fanning to the C's. It was worth a
shot. Chemical cleaning—Industrial. Chemical plant equip-
ment & sales. Chemicals—Retail. Chemicals—Whsle &
Mfrs. The company names meant nothing, but he felt a chill
as he turned the page. The winged-horse logo stared up at
him, big as a silver dollar, from a quarter-page ad in the
lower left corner. Webber Industries, "Complete Line of Lab
Chemicals Blended to Your Order."

The name on the box in Downing's car.

The name on the hulking plant along I-79 in Ridgeville,
the one he'd noticed from the police car as he was being
driven away from Sandra Corbett's apartment.

He didn't believe in fate. Or God. But he believed there
was a strange natural logic that sometimes guides the human
mind to specific and inescapable conclusions. And here, at
this time and place, his mind had linked a seemingly
inconsequential memory with a peculiar image, and linked
both of those with an unexplainable hunch. And somehow,
they'd all connected. It meant something.

Christensen tried to think it through, adding up the day's
events, weighing what he knew, piecing together a theory.
Maybe the Webber plant in Ridgeville was the source of the
cyanide used in the poisonings. Sandra Corbett grew up
nearby, probably knew people who worked there, maybe
knew how to get in and out unnoticed. But why would
Downing have had something in his car from Webber? Why
did he head for Greene County as soon as the real killer's
identity was revealed?

Plan B.

Christensen bolted upright in his chair. He ran through the
facts again, testing the theory. Everything fit. Downing's

obsessive pursuit of the Primenyl killer. His apparent
resignation when it seemed Sonny's memories wouldn't be
enough.

Plan B. Killing Ron Corbett with a fatal dose of cyanide
would have had the twisted symmetry that Downing would
have enjoyed. Plant the poison somewhere in Corbett's
home, disappear, and wait. To Downing, justice would be
served when the coroner declared Corbett a victim of
cyanide poisoning, perhaps even the latest victim of the
dreaded Primenyl killer. The perfect crime in every way—
except that Downing would have killed an innocent man.

Christensen remembered Downing's rushed departure
from the shooting scene. That, too, suddenly made sense.
For all his faults, Downing was not without a conscience.
Having sown the seeds of Ron Corbett's death, and having
realized his mistake, he would have acted. Christensen was
sure of it. Corbett was scum, but he wasn't a killer. The
detective was headed for Greene County to undo whatever
he'd done, to save the life of a man he'd despised and
pursued for a decade. He never made it, and a new thought
perched like a crow in Christensen's mind:

If he was right, Ron Corbett was still going to die.

Christensen ran through the theory again. It was seamless. He checked his watch, sure that a great burden had
fallen to him. Somewhere in Greene County, an unsuspect-
ing man was living with a chemical time bomb. No one else
knew; no one else could save him. On the grand karmic
scorecard, Christensen felt like he owed a life.

His White Pages only included listings in Allegheny
County. He dialed directory assistance and got three numbers. The first, R. J. Corbett of Waynesburg, was a woman,
Raylene. He apologized and hung up fast. The second
number, for Ronald Corbett of Enterprise, was no longer in
service. Christensen wiped the sweat from his hand before
dialing the third number, also listed as Ronald Corbett. A
woman answered, hoarse; she'd obviously been asleep
when the phone rang.

"Ronnie moved out," she said. "Ain't seen him in four
months."

"It's important," Christensen said, figuring her next move would be to hang up. "I have information about his wife and son."

He waited through the long silence. "My Ronnie's wife and son? Who is this?"

"I know it's early. I'm sorry. It's very important. The Ron Corbett I'm looking for was married to a woman named Sandra and has a boy, about twenty-two, named Sonny."

"Wrong Ronnie."

"You're sure?"

"If he'd fathered a son when he was six, mister, I'd know it."

Christensen did the math. "Ronnie's twenty-eight."

"Bingo," she said. "So fuck off."

The sun was up now. Christensen's watch read 6:20 as he drummed his fingers on the handset of his sturdy desktop telephone. He had to follow his hunch as far as he could, or live with the consequences. What to do? His eyes eventually fell on Sonny's juvenile records file, which still dominated one corner of the desk. He pulled it toward him and flipped it open, searching for information about Ron Corbett. An address, at least. If he was lucky, a phone number.

He found one on a 1987 foster-care report. No address, but with western Pennsylvania's 412 area code and an unfamiliar exchange. Steadying his trembling hand on the edges of his phone and praying out loud for the first time since Molly died, Christensen punched in the number, checking his watch as he listened to the distinctive ring of a rural phone. 6:15 A.M. What was he going to say?

"Speak." The voice sounded like a building collapse, surly and sleep-stupid.

"Mr. Corbett?"

A grunt. "It's the middle of the fucking night."

"Sorry, but I—"

"Who is this?"

"I can't give you my name, but I need to talk to you—"

The line went dead. Christensen dialed again, hoping Corbett hadn't left the phone off the hook.

"Go to hell," Corbett answered.

"Your wife's dead," Christensen blurted. "It's over."

The only sound was Corbett's deep-bass breathing. Christensen used the silence to reassure himself. "This *is* Ron Corbett, right?"

"Who's this?"

"Somebody who knows what happened," Christensen said. "Somebody who knows Sonny. I know about the killings in 1986, about Rachel."

Christensen waited through the long silence, letting the groggy man react. Why had Corbett kept the truth to himself all those years?

"This that cop?" he rasped.

"He's dead, too." Christensen unhooked his wire-rims' cable stems from his ears and laid the glasses on the desk. "Poisoned."

"Sonny okay?" the man said.

"He's fine."

"She said she'd kill him if I ever—"

"He remembered what happened. He remembered his mother, or Rachel, loading the capsules and sending him and his brother back to your store. She thought he was about to tell the police, and she tried to kill him. That's how she died."

"Oh, Christ." The pain was obvious even in Corbett's improbable voice. "Sonny killed her?"

"No."

"What then?"

"Look, there's something you need to know." Christensen stopped, thinking about Downing. How much did he want to tell Corbett? He needed to know there was poison in his house, but did it matter who put it there? The gift basket gave him an idea.

"In the last few days, I think your wife was trying to poison anybody who knew anything about what happened back then. I think she got Grady Downing, the detective. Sonny was luckier. So was I. Get what I'm saying?"

No answer.

"Throw everything away, Mr. Corbett. Go through your refrigerator, your pantry, your bathroom. Everything. Get rid of anything that could be tampered with, anything you'd put in your mouth, especially oranges, grapefruit, yogurt, capsules. Anything. Don't take any chances."

"Crazy goddamned woman," Corbett said. "You don't know what it is or where she put it?"

"Something, somewhere. I'm almost sure. Please just do it. That'll end it. It'll be over."

Christensen wanted to talk more, to ask a thousand questions, but he'd said enough. His index finger, steadier now, hovered above the phone's disconnect button. Something held him back, something instinctive. A therapist's need to heal. "You still have a son, you know," he said, then brought his finger down.

Epilogue

Spring, even a false one, brought an overpowering sense of renewal to Highland Park. Up and down Bryant Street in front of Christensen's house, kids reappeared, the sidewalks dried, and neighbors said hello again, even those who'd been reading about him in the *Press* and watching TV news in recent weeks. He could almost feel the promise in the skeletal branches of the neighborhood's great overhanging oaks. All Sunday mornings should be like this, he thought.

"Let me at least warm your coffee if I can't persuade you to come in," Brenna said.

She was at the front door with the coffee carafe, dressed now, still a vision in jeans and an oversized sweatshirt. Annie pushed past her—through her legs, actually—followed by Taylor. Both were wearing hooded sweatshirts, and each held a half-eaten banana. Annie stopped in front of him and looked him square in the eye. She grinned broadly, and without warning banana mush began oozing from the spaces between her teeth.

"Gross," he said.

Without a word, she led Taylor off the porch and on to her next project. He waited until they were around the corner of the house before he turned to face Brenna, who was restraining a laugh.

"Where does she learn that stuff?" he said.

"It'll all come out when she's about fifteen," Brenna said. "At her sentencing hearing."

She sat down on the top step and put her arm around him as she poured. "It's not even fifty degrees out here," she said. "Not exactly stoop-sitting weather."

"Joe DiNardo said it'll be the warmest day of the year," he said. "He's a weather professional. I trust him."

His thick wool socks rested purposefully on the front page of the Sunday paper. Brenna reached down and tugged at it, frowned when he resisted. He wanted to put it all behind him, wanted no more of the strange celebrity that had accrued to everyone involved in the final resolution of the case that, three weeks later, KDKA-TV was still calling "Primenyl: The Final Conflict."

"Just more fallout, what the crime lab people told us Friday," he said.

Brenna tugged again, then gave up. "The chemicals in the oranges and grapefruits?"

"All cyanide," he said. "Mine, Sonny's, and Downing's."

"Nothing else new?"

"All three samples matched either the poison Rachel put in the yogurt five months ago and in the Popsicle things, or the stuff she put in the cereal. That was powder."

"Like we figured," Brenna said. "How big was the bottle of liquid they found in her refrigerator?"

Christensen shrugged. "Little goes a long way. Did I tell you what Annie's teacher said? She's had three time-outs since all this happened. Walks around pointing her finger like a pistol, greasing the kids she doesn't like. Pa-chew! Pa-chew!"

"She's a kid, Jim. Just talk to her about it."

An uncertain drone preceded a small car, an old Toyota, up the street. It stopped at the curb two houses away.

"I *did* talk to her, after the first time. She knows it's inappropriate, but she did it two more times." Christensen hated when Brenna rolled her eyes. "Look, don't say it."

"You're such a weenie," she said. "Just roast her rump once or twice. You'll have her attention forever. Don't think of it as a spanking. Think of it as a valuable little life lesson."

Months earlier, they'd agreed to disagree on the subject. Brenna had argued that most of the ne'er-do-wells she represented would have benefited by a few well-timed parental strokes earlier in life, long before the first bust. He'd argued against any form of corporal punishment, demonstrating with study results from the American Psychiatric Association, the American Academy of Pediatrics, and the American Psychological Association that violence teaches mostly that violence is okay, and little else. He stood firmly on the issue's high moral ground, he felt. Brenna had called him a weenie then, too.

"Decided what to tell Downing's wife?" she asked.

Tricia Downing's letter had arrived two days earlier, and he'd given himself until Monday to decide what to do about it. She correctly suspected her husband hadn't told her the whole truth about his obsession with the Primenyl case. She suspected, too, that he'd confided in Christensen. Widow Downing wanted answers.

"It seems just as wrong to cover for him as it would be to tell," he said. "What do you think?"

"Hey."

Christensen looked up, startled that they weren't alone. Sonny stood at the end of the front walk, maybe ten feet away. His hair was shorter, well above his collar, and he was reasonably dressed in a wool sweater and light jacket. His left hand was in one of the jacket's pockets, the right in a plain white cast held stiffly at his side. For a fleeting, panicked moment, until Sonny smiled, Christensen wondered if maybe he had a gun.

"Hey," Christensen said, suddenly flushed with guilt. Forget the circumstances—he'd killed Sonny's mother. In the note he wrote Sonny three days after the shooting, he'd said what he could, but didn't say what he felt. Melissa was right: He was going to have to work on that. But the note was sincere, and he was disappointed Sonny hadn't answered or accepted his invitation to call.

"Sorry to crash," Sonny said. "I just wanted to see you."

Brenna put out her right hand, and Sonny seemed to notice her for the first time. He stepped up and shook it awkwardly with his left. "You must be Sonny Corbett," she said. "I'm Brenna Kennedy."

Christensen stood, too, reaching for Sonny's left hand. The young man's grip was firm and warm. Without thinking, without any reason at all, he pulled Sonny into an embrace that caught them both by surprise. When they stepped apart, there was a clumsy silence.

"So how're you doing?" Christensen said finally. "When you didn't call or write, I figured—"

"Thanks for the note," Sonny said.

"I just—"

"No, really. Thanks for everything."

Christensen remembered Sonny's gray face floating just beneath the surface of the water in his mother's sink. He remembered Sonny's expression, almost peaceful. Christensen had in his darkest hours after the shooting weighed his impulse to save a life that night against the years of painful recovery he knew stretched in front of Sonny. Which was the better fate?

"For everything?" Christensen repeated.

Their eyes met, but only for an instant; then they both looked away.

"Listen, I'm going to go check on the kids," Brenna said. "I think it's great you came, Sonny. Nice meeting you." She picked up the empty coffee carafe and went inside, closing the door behind her.

"I *am* glad you came," Christensen said. "A little nervous, maybe, but glad to see you. I've wanted to talk to you ever since, but so much happened, and so fast. I wanted to give you some space."

"Appreciate it."

"Sonny, what I've really wanted to say is—" Christensen stumbled. "If there'd been any other way, you know, any way at all to resolve it that night . . . but there wasn't. I didn't think. There wasn't time. I made a judgment—"

Sonny reached out, touching Christensen's arm. "You saved my life."

"But I killed her."

"She would have killed me, and probably you, from what I heard. That wasn't my mother, never was. Not her."

"Your mother died with her, though."

Sonny looked directly into Christensen's eyes. "She died a long time ago, I think."

Christensen stood up and walked onto the porch, settling against the heavy rail overlooking the front yard and Bryant Street. He felt lighter.

Sonny followed and leaned his left elbow on the rail as well. "Know what else I think? I think the only reason my mother still existed at all was because Rachel needed her, you know, so nobody would suspect. As a cover. What was left of my mom was just—"

Sonny never finished the thought. After a minute or so, he said, "Why didn't she just try to kill my father? Do you think she ever talked to anybody about it, like Dr. Root or somebody? I want to know."

"Hard to say, Sonny. There's so much about her I don't understand."

"All those people who died, back then and now. That kid who's, what, eleven? And my dad. I mean, he knew. He's known all along. Know what he said?"

"You've talked?"

Sonny kicked the front-porch railing with the rust-colored toe of his running shoe. "Sort of. He called. Said he was sick, still drinking, but that he'd call in a couple months once he got cleaned up." He brushed a tear from his cheek. "Said he wants to see me."

"You believe him?"

"No."

Fair enough, Christensen thought. "What else did he say?" he asked.

"That he was afraid she'd kill me if he ever told. He said she told him she would." Sonny's tears were coming too fast to hide now. "Maybe that's why he moved off to wherever he is and just kept his mouth shut. It doesn't make him any less of an asshole, does it?"

Christensen wasn't about to answer that one.

"All these feelings, Sonny, they're normal. And you're right for asking the questions. But the questions may not have answers. And if they do, you may never find them. Whether you do or don't, though, at some point you're going to need to put them behind you."

The young man squinted into the distance.

"Because they'll eat you alive, Sonny. As sure as we're standing here, they'll eat at you and you'll lose sight of what's really important."

"Like?"

"You. You're here. You're clear. You came out the other end of a tunnel that caves in on a lot of people. It's not over. You've got wounds you won't even feel until you're thirty-five or forty years old. But Sonny, you're the strongest person I know. You'll handle it—now, later, whenever."

Sonny scanned the length of Bryant Street. It was dry, one of the few times since last fall. "Can I still call you?" he said.

"You've got the phone number," Christensen said. "And the address. Anytime."

Sonny toed the porch rail again, but now he was smiling. "Lost my job at Pitt," he said. "Didn't show up for a week after all this happened. I should have called in."

"Anything I can do?"

"You sound like Grady Downing," Sonny said. "He was always trying to help me out." Sonny shook his head. "Thanks. Got something else lined up, I think, not far from here. Highland Park Natatorium."

"On Highland Avenue? Doing what?"

"Teaching tadpole classes, lifeguarding. A coach I know has a junior team, too, five- and six-year-olds. Said he could use some help through the end of summer. Just five and a quarter an hour, but it'd be a steady nine to five. So I'll be fine."

Christensen watched his breath drift out over the shrubbery and vanish. He was getting cold, and the sensation triggered a memory of Sonny hoisting himself from the icy Ohio River.

"Nine to five wouldn't leave much time for your training, would it?"

"None." Sonny shrugged with an indifference that surprised Christensen.

"You're giving it up?"

"Maybe. Water's getting awfully warm, so what's the point? Anyway, coaching kids that age might be a kick." Sonny nodded to the front corner of the house, where Annie and Taylor emerged pulling a wagonload of charcoal briquets. They didn't seem to notice, or didn't care, that Christensen and Sonny were watching. They stacked a dozen or so briquets in an unsteady pyramid on the concrete walkway alongside the house, then disappeared again. Christensen held an index finger to his lips, curious about where this was headed.

The children came back a few seconds later with a can of charcoal lighter fluid and a box of wooden kitchen matches. Christensen tiptoed to the side of the porch overlooking the two children. A surprise attack.

"Do you think that's a safe thing to do?" he asked, straining to sound casual.

Annie looked up, but not intimidated. Annoyed. "We're barbecuing, Dad," she said, soaking the briquets with a blast of fuel. "Go get that long fork, okay?" She pulled a match from the box and got busy trying to strike it. Sonny snatched the match from her hand before she even knew he'd sneaked up behind her.

"Matches can hurt you," Sonny said. "Playing with them is a good way to get a spanking."

Christensen cringed.

Annie wheeled, ready for combat. But when she recognized Sonny, she all but swooned. Then she meekly handed him the box of matches. Sonny put them in his jacket pocket. "I remember you!" she said. "You came over that day. And from the pool. You taught me." She bent at the waist and pantomimed a perfect Australian crawl.

"Nice rainbow arms!" Sonny said. "You've been practicing. Who's your friend?"

Annie looked at Taylor, her faithful coconspirator, who

was waiting wide-eyed to be introduced. "Nobody," Annie said. "Just some kid."

"Annie!" Christensen said. "Sonny, this is Taylor. He's one of our most special friends. He stays with us sometimes."

"I'm four," Taylor said. "I need floaties or I sink."

Sonny's face brightened. "Bet you could learn to swim, just like Annie. Want to? I'm gonna teach at a pool not too far from here."

All three faces turned up to the porch, where Christensen was leaning out over the rail. Now that his daughter's self-immolation was canceled, he was actually enjoying the scene below.

"We'll talk about it," Christensen said. The thought made him uneasy, and the reason made him feel guilty. He'd allowed Sonny into his personal life in calculated professional increments. Now his patient wanted more, needed more. Was he willing, or able, to give it?

Sonny got more animated. "I have a late afternoon class with some openings," he said. "I could even pick them up and drop them off. It's a great plan. Come on."

"I don't know—"

"Please," Sonny said. "I want to do something. I owe you so much."

The words washed over Christensen like absolution. Sonny showed such courage, such trust, walking with a virtual stranger into the ghastly labyrinth of his past, not knowing where they were going, or why. What would it be like to trust like that again? To live without a paralyzing fear of pain? To feel, like he did before Molly's accident?

Christensen took a deep breath, knowing there were no easy answers. But he drew courage from those upturned faces—all three of them. Because if he read them correctly, Sonny's was every bit as hopeful as the others.